I0649901

A House of Hollow Wounds

A House of Hollow Wounds

Joseph S. Pulver, Sr.

Edited by Jeffrey Thomas

Hippocampus Press

New York

Publishing history

"and the bass keeps thumpin'," *Imperial Youth Review* No. 2 (2013).
"A (~Big~) Fishy Menu," *"Lovecraft eZine* (January 2012).
"Aubade in a Graveyard," *Penny Dreadful* No. 14 (June 2001).
"I once possessed a fragile blue vase," *Penny Dreadful* No. 14 (June 2001).
"A Cold Yellow Moon" (with Edward Morris), *Lovecraft eZine* (April 2013).
All other stories are original to this collection.

Works by Joseph S. Pulver, Sr. © 2015 by Joseph S. Pulver, Sr.
"On the Embankment of Tangibility" © 2015 by Jeffrey Thomas.

Published by Hippocampus Press
P.O. Box 641, New York, NY 10156.
http://www.hippocampuspress.com

All rights reserved.
No part of this work may be reproduced in any form or by any means
without the written permission of the publisher.

Cover art © 2015 by Daniele Serra.
Cover design by Barbara Briggs Silbert.
Hippocampus Press logo designed by Anastasia Damianakos.

First Edition
1 3 5 7 9 8 6 4 2
ISBN 978-1-61498-128-2

Contents

For an old friend who believes: Jeff Thomas

On the Embankment of Tangibility

An Introduction by Jeffrey Thomas

Anyone who knows me well knows Elvis Costello is my favorite singer. But if he were still an unknown and appeared today on the TV program *American Idol*, those judges would dismiss him from the stage in a moment—along with his quirky pals Bob Dylan, Tom Waits, and Bruce Springsteen. Costello's voice is unique, not to everyone's taste, and that's precisely why I love it. His unusual voice has true character and conveys emotion more powerfully than a hundred of your typical bombastic and plastic *American Idol* types combined.

Nor have I ever encountered a prose voice like that of Joseph S. Pulver, Sr. For a voracious reader to be able to say that about a writer is a remarkable thing, isn't it? In helping to promote his work to another publisher, I once described Joe's style as H. P. Lovecraft meets William S. Burroughs, or Edgar Allan Poe meets Charles Bukowski. These comparisons are not accurate, of course; it was just the kind of lazy shorthand we take in trying to encapsulate an artist's work for another, to give a sense of its general vibe. But what Joe has in common with Lovecraft, Burroughs, Poe, and Bukowski is that, like them, he is an original.

His every line of text is a poem. A song. It is, to nab a line from one of the tales herein, *"grammar and rhythm on the embankment of tangibility."* Tangible because it is real. Real because it is honest.

A reader with rigid tastes—and there are, woefully, as many of them as there are dead fossils mired in rock—might feel that the poetry of Joe's prose is all artifice. The truth is the exact opposite. Oh, there is plenty of affectation in the realm of fiction and poetry. In a dubious literary movement like "Bizarro," much effort is made to appear subversive and shocking. I don't get any of that from Joe's work. He is not posturing as subversive (a subversive spirit can't be fabricated). He is not striking the pose of the hipper-than-thou artiste. He is not phony. There is only this: what you read is the essence of the man's persona . . . the distillate of his mind. Hell, Joe writes the way he speaks. I've talked with him for many hours, on the phone and in person. His words and their delivery are all smoky jazz. Because Joe speaks and writes the way he *thinks*. What flows from him is pure water from the stream of consciousness, unfiltered, unadulterated. Joe's the real deal, Neal. Your average horror writer, trying to sound like Stephen King, is the phony. For all the delirious idiosyncrasies of his voice, Joe Pulver is as honest a writer as I have met, and read.

And yet, he is often seen as a Lovecraftian author. It's an unfairly limiting assessment, though Lovecraft is surely one of his inspirations. Joe is well read, and as such is highly inspired by numerous writers (one must especially acknowledge Robert W. Chambers). He is also highly inspired by music. At the end of most of his tales, here, you'll see him list the songs that he listened to while writing that particular story, and which no doubt helped to color his thoughts. Joe loves comics and movies, and they all go into the mix. But even when you see the references, the nods he is making to this or that angel hovering at his shoulder, even then there is nothing of imitation. Again, this is most unusual in a writer. Usually, if you can see the references, what you're seeing is impersonation. Not with Joe. I truly think he is incapable of imitation. Again, none of his approach is forced. I'm not sure he can even take credit for being an original, consciously. I think it's more a gift from his unconscious. His muse is beyond his control.

To me, his eccentric voice—like Elvis Costello's—can be highly beautiful, even when Pulver is singing from the blackest places, of the blackest things. That beauty glistens like obsidian in lines such as *"rest for a moment. you cannot negotiate with consummation. pushing does not widen the passage . . . pursue stillness."* (I don't think Buddha himself could speak more soothingly to my soul than that.) Or this one: *"Back, in the red forge of longing, might be that didn't."* Ah! So much regret and wistfulness drips from those few words. Even a reader with tastes as rigid as blind buried fossils must be able to relate to the "red forge of longing."

Adventurous readers are ever *longing* for the next book that will make them experience something new, something different, to keep the love affair with the written word fresh and vibrant.

I think such readers will be greatly rewarded here.

Am I committing hyperbole? Am I gushing? I think a fellow book lover will recognize my sentiments for what they really are: *enthusiasm—celebration.*

It has been my privilege to be Joe's friend, and his editor for this project, and—most of all—a reader of his work.

And now, with a turn of the page, that privilege is yours.

A House of Hollow Wounds

A Thousand Injuries—

Injuries . . . that changed me *completely*—

Insults—at length, and wrongs, open wounds wailing. Too many to count.

Intoxication, the pavement—my tottering gait no longer heeding the counsel of steadiness, the palm of my hand finding a wall to collect my balance, the cathedral's misinformed design above, another succession of careening steps . . . Along with the colorful comedies of eager visitors seeking pleasure, and hypocrisy and the come hither lights, noting the sea of masks, each velvety—Venus beguiling an Adonis, each hawk or opiate-soft black cat a magnet, about us shops of brightly colored glass and exceptional lace, and the summertime eyes of daughters dancing or hoping to, we strode through the carnival on the way to the promised . . . *Amontillado.*

My weakness . . . and the complexities of my pride.

Knocked from my better senses by drink. How many cups had I emptied? More than a few bottles most would wager. I might smile and attempt to wave away the assessment, but it would not change the truth of it.

Shut away—imprisoned like the great pharaohs of the desert sands. Removed from the cradle of the world by my folly and Montresor's cold gale of greed and the damning violation of his laughter.

Cut out. Not ready for, or aware of, the danger.

Darkness.

Lured by lies. By the scheme of the black-masked cur.

Unflickering darkness, a region of iron suffocation. Damp and filled with nevermore.

Beyond small tears. Me, all the whirling parts, fractured, filled with urge and spirits.

Through the nitre-draped catacombs to the chains I walked with the murderer.

The cold gaze of hostile eyes. Above the wispy frame, that face, dauntless—a brick of greed, carved of shadows and things in the shadows. In the torchlight, the sensations in my stomach could find no safety. The eyes. What they held. I was a prince no more. All of me, going away ... Some wretched creature bound in nightmare, all the shames and discomforts, rushing over the edge, imprisoning my fear in a foul breeze.

Alone in the blackness. Fearing—*fearing.*

Confused for a moment, but sobering. The pitch of my alarm finding new heights. Chained to the darkness. Chained. Then it struck me—

But not alone . . .

I had friends in the tomb. Friends who know buttress and braces, vigorous allies who are not tortured. Allies with more power than a trowel, midnight and mortar and iron staples are not chains for them.

Plastered up in the blackness I heard them, tiny clicking claws thriving under the sound of The Bells. Squeaking—a hundred and a hundred voices, an uncountable wave behind them. Sniffing dusty surfaces where no fire or spark gives color to the forgotten. Tails, whiskers, appetites fast as nameless crows reshaping the sky.

"Come forth and end my suffering. Rush to my aid, brothers. I, too, serve the Purposes in Solitude."

And come to me they did.

In my joy I laughed and the murderous-deceiver on the other side of the wall laughed back.

As I knew they would, my allies freed me from my cold iron bonds as I said, "Let us be gone." And gone we were, through a small hole in the wall. As we departed, I heard Montresor reply, "Yes, let us be gone." I smiled as my friends and I headed off to other districts. "Yes, let us be gone."

In time, Montresor will be . . . He will suffer for the afflictions.

While I was traveling I thought about my revenge, considered the lightning I would bring down upon him, watched his lips mold themselves into the shape of a scream. I never tired of my need to see matters set right, never. A hundred and a hundred times I've seen his demise in my dreams, thought this is how the painter sees what he is about to paint—An April chill pinned to the air. No spectators, or shriek or laugh to disturb what the moon kisses. There are shadows between the buildings, they reek of damp caverns filled with dead things whose recreations are known only to themselves, shadows as deep and black as the deeps between seething stars, believers in alchemy and unnatural things quicken their passing, fearing the roots within will open their attentions and call out and little things created of mortal clay will be taken, unmade. Montresor looks like something painted on these avenues, light, thin, there, but not real.

Soon his steps will echo here, in the privacy of these soggy cellars. There will be the gravity of fear and fireworks in his eyes, but this time there will be nothing available for him to build with. He will have empty hands.

I will have the upper hand.

And my friends will come from the unseen places while his feeble will loses its compass in the jaws of cemetery gaping.

* * *

Spleen and thorns, the serpent burning in the dark, coiled and waiting—debate filled the air. Montresor would smile; try to hide his inmost behind erudite and ostensibly courteous arguments. Try. But to no avail, our hearts and better senses were open to the remarkable degrees of his coldness and cruelty. We knew. We were aware of his stance, he was, after all, wedded to that Eastern European countess—she who was both a lascivious seductress and witch, she who was pledged to *The Path of the Eight Lords.*

For many years Montresor sat at the right hand of our leader, Gaius Sebastiano. A dark soul, comfortable with the power he wielded, proud—arrogant, often brash and always ravenous, no bricks or argument could slow or filter Montresor's quick, "Now is the time. In the cold deeps They cry out to us." I, also of prominent rank within our order, sat at Gaius Sebastiano's left. Most often I was quiet and always willing to learn and to stay firmly upon the path our order has followed since the time The Prophecy was given to our founders by The Black Messenger. The Prophecy inscribed in the *true* Book of Books.

Montresor, he of masks layered upon masks, hoisting a regal bearing, speaking—*the hiss of a viper with a thousand tongues*, to his followers, twelve in number among us, hardly a legion, but their shadowy powers sharp as the teeth of one no less, wed them to his absolute with his storm of passions—misguided, hell-bent, he spoon-fed them what they wanted to hear, and everyone was sugared in the falsehoods of Glory risen—*freed.* Each of his vassals seized by and clinging to what they affirmed was fast approaching—oh, there were many moments when their dervish fullness was a spectacle, could churn and thunder.

Gaius Sebastiano's followers, thirteen in number, and my own faithfulness, pressed for further examination and patience, held fast to the prescribed timetable. At the appropriate time, the clock would be impaled, wolf-time would bark and the knots would be uncoupled. The new flame would pierce the heart of the world. Misreading the signs and inviting catastrophe, half the men in the room would not, could not, see we would all be bones when the Harms Tremendous returned.

Montresor would not hear of it.

"*Wait?* While Our Masters cry out for release?"

"Adrift in the Hollow Places they suffer. We are the spokes of the wheel, we must turn."

It was then Gaius Sebastiano would bring out the book and read from it. "The stars are closed . . ."

And always he would turn to Montresor and say, "In the ageless play of the heavens we are less than children, we must follow the dictates handed down to us. We must guard against brash and headstrong methods . . . It will be as Theodorus and Alhazred revealed. The gift of The Black Messenger will not be soiled and broken by the lungs of those who speak of worldly desire and reward."

Then he would lean in and whisper, "You must guard our battlements against gold and venom, Fortunato."

My eyes would embrace Montresor's. His aims set against mine, our quiet war marched on while in private Gaius Sebastiano would ask. "You may wonder why I keep your rival close."

"I often do, my Master."

"He seeks to break destiny and caress the goodwill of The Powers Who Dwell in Darkness. Sun Tzu set down the following, 'All warfare is based on deception,' and 'Pretend inferiority and encourage his arrogance.' I watch, bait, and reason. I set traps for the opposition to stumble over. You would do well to do the same.'

"Montresor has been turned and cannot be brought back to the fold; his lust for reward has blinded him to consequence. Keep him close. Watch. Listen. He is unfit. There will come a time when you will discover the means to cast him out.

"The time of my death is near. Montresor and his advocates will seek to impose their doctrine when I'm gone."

My teacher in abstractions, all things mystic and many earthly, died shortly before carnival was to begin and Montresor and I had unpleasant words when the fiend discovered Gaius Sebastiano had named me as his successor. Both of us approached each other in ambassadorial ways, feint and withhold, but the unhemmed lust in his arteries and my heady stance of "No" opened deeper wounds.

Montresor would quickly quiet. He'd nod in compliance and smile. "This is not the time for disagreement, dear friend. We will carry on and what is needed will be revealed in its proper time." And he would walk away after leaving me with his, "Fear not, my dear Fortunato."

Liar. His lips jingled with lies. Lies, the seducer's cascade of poisoned lace. His teeth beamed friend, but those lips, his smile was the knife of a coward and thief who slips the unseen blade deep in your back.

Again and again, his firm hand on my shoulder, he'd say, "My friend. My dear old friend. Come; let us set aside our divergences."

Liar.

Worse.

Treachery.

*   *   *

There were no flowers at my death—

A door . . . And behind it, galaxies filled with The Bells.

I followed the bells that called out to me . . . Across naked fires in the war of tides and aeons . . . Geysers and toil-carved, leviathan totems spiked with halos drenched the arrows of my sight . . . All the towers and mounts of this sea are full. And its colors—glittering black, a weave of ink, a yellowish garden above me—shaped like a spider, swollen greens, the stout reign of baleful red and altars of velvet blues, and nests and bruises spinning, unbridled colors, wild jolts and pulses, throwing new fabrics, crisscrossed, flashing—solid!—the silver and orange of immortality, curving, swirling with nourishment and Their desire and grief—

My mouth held no words. My heart, which had been an empty canvas ready to be a bed for true secrets, was now animated by things I had addressed but had never truly understood, things that had never known pot lids or the restrictions of stonewalls brushed my lashes, they were all around me, close enough to overturn the small testaments and stories in my hands.

In the sharpness of this unblemished domain, I shed my flowers for new breath. No longer shut away to be the meat of decay, free of my bonds, beyond fortune and the possessions and bargains of the commonplace world, I was now becoming whole, an aggregate of accumulations 'sembled right.

On the night I was betrayed by Montresor my allies freed me from the deep pitch of the tomb, led me to where the sky cried. My sleek friends—pathfinders, rushing before me, leading me to undiscovered, unthought-of fields, stayed close, guiding me, keeping me from all harms. Wild to deliver me, they squeaked, "Come; let us go. There are wonders to see. Come." After the clockless directions and scaffolded phenomena of the journey, I beheld the end of death and a new calendar bade me rise. Anxious to serve the needs of My Lords, as I always have, I donned my new armor.

At the heels of my friends, my travels in the beyond were long.

I saw locks and silver . . . overlapping faces, thresholds . . . shiny spheres and the coming and goings of glamours the words of ignorant, sightless men cannot disclose or grasp . . .

Clusters of pregnant colors, shaped as drifting swans, or vast ponds, or lizards playing among rare flowers on the trellis of the cosmos . . . Unimagined angles of ornamented brightness were fastened to the pillars of the heavens . . . I was comforted and open to receiving the mysteries . . . Stars—some born only to die, with open mouths singing fire. They flared, divided, and crawled, coursed like uncomplicated things at play, fast brutes caring not for consequence I beheld rogues scurry to new elsewheres. My eyes wandered, trying to understand, trying to drink knowledge from their intensions . . .

Then blackness, an orgy of nothing. For a long time we traveled in the blackness. The perfect blackness was a mouth of tombs; unseen beasts spilled their roar upon its carpet. Their laughter comforted me . . .

A keyhole of light pierced the gleaming pitch and it expanded, clawing its claim upon the darkness, and platforms and plazas and broad fields, many like strange paintings created with blue flames, spread before us and shortly we came to a vast island of pale sand oddly configured with colossal pyramids. Above each pyramid hovered an unblinking eye larger than any frothing star we had passed.

Scrupulous military discipline and mathematical formulae are less precise than the rapid formation my allies assumed, as they molded themselves into four columns and led me to the tallest pyramid where I was met by The Black Messenger. Regaled in grand robes of crimson and a king's portion of jewels, he appeared to be an old black man, twice the height of a tall man. He bore correctly proportioned human features, but this was not the face of a mortal. Some men speak of the grace and majesty of the faces and dispositions of the world's manmade gods, this face before me was no cave-dweller's fear-born creation, his face and eyes were storms no frost of fear had ever colored, they were beyond the low concerns of men. Unlike the dwellers in mortal shells, who cannot grasp the cosmic, The Black Messenger had never feared the cold hand of time.

I was filled with joy . . . and fear, as I gazed upon him. Balletic sparks, moaning with the midnight light of mysterious stars, haloed his head. Rising on hind legs, my allies swayed and bent, as if to bow. When The Black Messenger's eyes turned from indigo to star-fueled crimson theirs did as well, and when he opened his mouth to speak, he spoke through the mouths of my friends—if music is well said to be the speech of angels then this chorus, which echoed in strange and alluring ways, was the speech of the cosmos itself, displayed in all its might. No poet or minstrel had ever felt hungers so ravenous; my ability to understand was a parched, undeveloped corn stalk in need of rain.

I was on my hands and knees before him, my brow pressed to the spongy ground at his feet.

"RISE AND HEED MY WORDS."

I did, but I could not raise my eyes to look upon his countenance again. I kept my head bowed; only peeking up to stare as his blazing hands.

"THE WOLF CANNOT BE ALLOWED TO STAND. HE WOULD STIR THE ASHES, AND DOOM THE LINES THAT LEAD TO THEIR RETURN."

His every breath was a discovery to me.

I stood there and learned, accepted every word. Grew. Shed the small felt of my isolation, let my fragments fall away. I could feel the greater power of My Masters in my veins.

"NOW RETURN AND PERFORM THE TASK I HAVE SET BEFORE YOU."

He turned and walked across the blackness between the stars as if it were solid pavement . . .

I wept and made the prescribed signs, blessed his coming and the gift he had implanted within me.

About my feet swirled the quivering textures of my allies. "Come, my friends. Let us go. There are hinges that require your muscle . . . And we have the straw of a man's life to see to."

*   *   *

The note I had delivered to Montresor in the blackness of midnight said, *Come; let us go. To your vaults.* Nothing more. It was unsigned. Not that it needed to be. Montresor knew my handwriting, and the words. Fifty years gone, yet I knew he was still intimate with the voice that issued them.

Montresor crushed the note in his fist and tossed it into a brazier. He paced the fine carpets of our order's council house. Sensing, displeased in the extreme, the maelstrom of irritation and rising fear that had overtaken him, the many cats he kept on the premises fled the stain of foul weather he sprayed across the cold room.

An hour tearing at the names of who may have mustered sufficient fortitude and found the courage to rise up against him passed. But to no avail, each of Gaius Sebastiano's followers had joined Montresor's ranks. Fear had wholly consumed them and they hid from the whims and angers of the hawk should they not lend their hands and voices to his cause, and not a one of my former supporters could know the words, or have copied my hand with any accurateness.

I was aware he felt this was some sorcerous darkness from the grave.

"How?" he asked. Again and again, often hissing it.

He was chained to the word, racked and tortured by that single, damming word.

"How?"

He is gone. Dead . . . It can't be. Not after all these years.

"Surely the rats had picked him clean."

One of Montresor's deepest and oldest fears was of rats, tireless teeth—sharp incisors, and snouts and spasms that never cease. He kept twenty felines to keep the rooms of the council house clear. Now he looked to his feline protectors to chase away his fear, but they were no longer friend to his caress and affections, nothing but dread played in their eyes.

"His bones are nothing but bones."

I had been intoxicated, now he was frightened, both are killers of reason. He would have to come across the city to his cellars and look into my black compartment. He had to.

Montresor picked up his most-cherished feline, a well-seasoned rat-ter, a hefty calico with a number of scars, and wished he could bring one or two of his cats with him. He eyed two stout brothers with dis-positions that relished grasping the lice-ridden vermin, as he put it, by the throat, and delighting in rip and rend and showing the filthy brown and black horrors the hammer of death's terrible engine, and as my an-tagonist began to deliberate how he might transport the trio of rigorous hunters to his cellars, the creature's eyes flashed and with a protesting hiss it vaulted from his arms, leaving stinging red furrows.

*　　*　　*

No carnival of wild pleasures crowded and swirled about him as he made his way along the pavement. No untamed shouts or laughter came to his ears as he rushed, as ably as an old man can, to know. Not a single bell rang out.

He spit another how and paused, recalling my colorful reflection in a shop's window, a shop window we had paused before as we walked by five decades ago.

I was dead, no heart, no eyes, *dead.* Dead fifty years, empty, devoid of language and will. After all these years no tongue remained in my skull, if I still had one, to project his injuries. That's what he hissed at the image in the window.

"*Morto.*" Had to be. "The plague-bringers would have purified his commentaries—all his murmurs, would have pulled pain from his face. Erased his tricks and etiquette."

At my behest, one of my allies, not inconsiderable and black as damnation, dashed across his path. It squeaked as its tail brushed his boot. At the sight of it the thought of other rats shriveled Montresor's endurance and another anxiety rose in his belly.

Montresor quickened his pace. More than once on the way to his cellars the old man stumbled like a drunkard.

Down and down he came . . . He took no note of the heavy casks of wine, nor did the bone-faces lining his path to discovery speak to the loud "come quickly" of his need, he was vibrating with the weight of it.

Through the eyes of my allies I could see his every step; through their keen noses I could smell every drop of the old man's sweat. They passed along his every word.

"Come," I whispered.

Down another stair and another, fast when he could.

"Come."

And he did. Seething and knotted he did.

Frightened, a slow confusion of anger beneath it, an unfiltered parade of one alone, clenched by dread, on the stairs . . .

I smiled to see him choke and stumble on fast, ushered along by his fear.

From their hidden observatories among the piled bones, my allies watched my old foe come to my carnival. They heard him speak to himself. Informed me he carried a trowel and a pick axe.

I chuckled and waited for his arrival.

Who would be the fool now? Drunk on his lust and fear he rushed, as well as the elderly can, through the bone-lined corridors to my tomb.

Montresor stared at the wall of my tomb. I watched his lips silently move.

Swift to uncover the tomb and discover what lay behind its dust and grim covered surface, he attacked the wall and its muscular question with the pickaxe he carried. The murderer perspired like a slave-laborer ignited by the lash.

Break the body, break the mind, I thought, warm in a soft feeling much like glee.

I sat in deep shadows and watched. For nearly an hour I restrained my laugher as the old man's efforts slowly marched forward. I even managed to chain my urge to jest to silence, as he incrementally chipped away at the mortar and brickwork of my tomb.

When Montresor had uncovered close to half of the wall he had erected, he thrust his flambeaux inside my vault.

Bewildered, he nearly roared, "How? *By all that is reasonable*—something of him should be here."

"It is, my old friend. It is." I lit my torch then rose and stood before him, pointed at the instrument in his hand. "On this occasion I see you come unmasked." And finally I freed my laughter.

Frozen, Montresor dropped his tool. His face held more than disbelief. Perhaps the Black Messenger's uncanny gift to me caused his vigor to flee?

"*You* . . . you are . . . were.'

"Dead?"

I watched panic and fear mark him; his eyes. My weather had fully entered him; it haunted and spread deep, its cold thrust cunningly corrupting his veins. I could see the breath of its effect, how it smudged and cursed him, it was his eyes, owl eyes, blasted wide open. I chuckled silently with triumph as I watched his lips form a question from a single word, "*Bardo?*"

Several times he blinked rapidly and shook his head, as if to waken or clear the writhing briar of his thoughts, but his mouth and teeth and desire could not eject the dryness of frenzy.

"You were. Are . . . No . . . no *thing* that . . . that wears a face like yours, could be . . . *alive.*

"And still . . . *young?*"

"He! he! he! He who laughs last." I smiled. "Is not the fool."

He was sweating—sweating, *smelling of cat,* and breathing heavy, drained by his exertions, nearly as weary as I had been drunk.

Reveling as the flaccid old man crumbled, I quickly overpowered him and chained him to the two iron staples in the small recess, the very same iron staples that had held me. Montresor was heavy inside, heavy with a blinding terror as solid and grimy as my old chains. He strained, but his shoulders had lost the powerful identity of youth. He opened his mouth, but the dark empty room within could not seize the shape of language and he uttered not a sound. The chains rustled and rusty flakes of iron snowed down on the damp ground, tears dripping from the wrinkled corners of his eyes scarred his cheeks. There was no smile on my lips, but my eyes told him of my delight, of the hunger I'd carried all these decades.

Had there been human witnesses present, they might have thought me a curator fondly examining a new exhibit as I stood and regarded his predicament, he would never be nimble again, and he would never trick me again.

Liar.

Fool.

Murderer.

Then, soaking up the fullness of his distress, the alarm burning his forever away, I and my concealed allies smiled widely.

He was trembling, his struggles were nothing against the burden of his chains, the very chains he had used to pin me. My friends and I reveled in the fragrance his futility engraved in the dusty cell.

I was sorely tempted to once again take up our old discussions and enlighten him, but another thought overwhelmed me and I let it have its head.

"Did you know within these ramparts of bones and bricks there are rats?"

How sweetly the grave kisses prey when its sky is furnished by cunning lips.

"*Hungry* . . . rats . . . Tiny claws and scabs, whiskers and saliva, and the compulsion to *gnaw* . . . Yes, I believe you did. Counted on it—he! he! he! Try to count them when they come—he! he! he!"

Suddenly, there rose the sound of small voices—a chorus, housing no mercy, each unfurled voice, promising appetite's swelled river, snarled and promised tear. From behind femurs and pelvises, from the eye sockets and jaws of skulls, from every nook and crevice in the dim-tomb, my allies appeared. Tiny claws clicked, eyes stretched, and as one voice, they squeaked their welcome. Possessed, I thought they would giggle at his helplessness.

"No laughter to mirror my own now, my old friend? He! he! he!

"No endearing greeting for my friends?"

Their chitterings escalated.

Montresor's eyes screamed. His open mouth was smothered by the heat of panic.

"I hope you will forgive me, I have no *Amontillado* to offer your parched mouth."

He was weeping.

"*Buon viaggio.*"

I was about to turn and tell him I failed to bring fare for Charon, as I believed he would not be needing it, but an operatic scream told me there was no need . . .

I wonder if my friends began with his lips or fingers, or perhaps, his eyes . . .

He! he! he!

Bohren and der Club of Gore, *Midnight Radio;* Alan Parsons Project, "The Fall of the House of Usher"; Heiner Goebbels, *SHADOW/Landscape with Argonauts;* Diamanda Galas "The Black Cat"

A (~BIG~) Fishy Menu

[a one-act sketch for Rawlik's bye-bye]

(for the new Big Man on the /chop/p/i//ng/ block! !!)

(*Carcosa. Balcony above the cloudwaves and the soundless beach. Two chairs. Table with a chessboard. Nyarlathotep [in his tall, swarthy-pharaoh, Mr. Phoenix manifestation] standing, and the King in Yellow, sitting, ready for their weekly chess game.*)
(*Everywhere: [a certain] grayness.*)
(*The cathedral deathbirds in the tower have been silent.*)

KING IN YELLOW: You seem displeased and . . . a bit *distracted* tonight.
NYARLATHOTEP: A new infestation has risen. (*Glowers at the chessboard.*) They're like pimples . . .
KING IN YELLOW (*Scans the board quickly for the latest pawn*): Who?
NYARLATHOTEP: That damn adherent of the Toad Trio, Price, Pugmire, and pulver. (*The Rawlik pawn suddenly appears on the board. All the other pieces vanish.*) Vermin . . . and scum—
KING IN YELLOW (*Sits up straight*): Rawlik. (*Fun in his tone.*)
NYARLATHOTEP (*Sits down*): Yes. (*Black talon radar-lock on the pawn.*) Him. Idiotic rube gets on the "Lovecraft eZine" chat every week, all liquored-up mind you, and out sprint the blasphemies he learned in Price's classes . . . Buzzing little talking heads that clog up the cosmic sewers, the whole lot. (*The Black Man w/ the smoldering hand makes a fist.*)
KING IN YELLOW: True. Davis and *pul-ver* egg him on and pat his back, while that glittered-up toady, Hopfrog, tosses kisses—that punk needs a date with . . . (*Grins, as if saying, wait for it.*) Tsathoggua. And hour after hour, Davis sits there in mission control like some cool power-broker, spewing his yellow journalism and directing traffic—

NYARLATHOTEP: Excrement that requires flushing—Rawlik's nothing more than another foulsome mouth rising to reanimate the pseudo-*lies* for a new generation of hacks, sycophants, and Lovecraftomaniacs. You X them out—w/ *extreme* prejudgment, and another appears—**Cockroaches.** (*Pause.*) These *things* think they are of consequence, that their shoddily-formed and erroneous opinions will be taken into account, or be remembered on the pages of history. (*Pause.*) Batty gnats. They all think they're superheroes that can save their brother fleas from the STOMP.

KING IN YELLOW: My Dear Boot, I can see sweet intention in your eyes. You're going to cure Little Petey's ills.

NYARLATHOTEP: *I am.*

KING IN YELLOW: Spill. (*Begins laughing, thinking BLOOD and of gutting a certain someone like a fish.*)

NYARLATHOTEP (*Considering apt forms of demise*).

KING IN YELLOW: A Whitman Sampler pinebox the ghouls crack open Easter morning? Moist, cherry-red center. (*Grins.*) You know how appreciative of generously proportioned repasts they are. There are some select plots in Kingsport.

NYARLATHOTEP: Tempting. (*Pause.*) Yes, that's certainly enticing . . . But no.

KING IN YELLOW: Sefton Asylum?

NYARLATHOTEP: Too quiet.

KING IN YELLOW: A small fishing boat right outside R'lyeh? No oars to employ. They fuck with the Big C. He fucks back. (*Grins.*)

NYARLATHOTEP: No. No . . .

KING IN YELLOW: The Great Dragons Black and Red to clear the Earth of them all?

NYARLATHOTEP: No. Not yet.

KING IN YELLOW: I'd be happy to send the Messenger to show him the Yellow Sign.

NYARLATHOTEP: I have a different sentence in mind . . . *Bug-Shaggoth.*

KING IN YELLOW: Sweet. *Raw*-lik, it's what's on the menu.

NYARLATHOTEP (*Tapping the Rawlik-pawn with the smoking-tip of a black talon*): Exactly right. (*The top of the pawn begins smoldering.*) (*Nyarlathotep and the King in Yellow chuckle.*)

*   *   *

(*And it was then that Nyarlathotep came out of Carcosa and entered Rawlik's dream . . .*)
(*In his bed fluffed with velvety dreamlands, Rawlik's peachy dreamquest turns suddenly BLACK. He twists, winces—his hands white-knuckle fists of PAIN, and screams . . .*)
(*Towering over the bed of Rawlik-all-fall-down, Nyarlathotep smiles.*) *Why not?*
(*Beside Rawlik's husk, in the cascade of her verdant dream, his saintly, long-suffering wife, Mandy, accepts the FATcheck from the The Black Man with the Insurance Attaché Case. The Black Man also hands her the solid-silver keys to her $27,000,000 dream-home in Palm Beach, the one with the new dock and the 31' Cruisers 3120 ARIA, a Har-Tru tennis court and the heated infinity pool with a breathtaking ocean view, and 3 servants, and a 24-hour chef. The one right next to Adam Sandler's new weekend get-away home . . .*)

(*From the balcony in far, cold Carcosa the King in Yellow observes the festivities.*)
KING IN YELLOW: My house, my rules. Next week, I'm having the fun. (*Writes the name, Davis, in his dog-eared, yellow notepad. Underlines it 5 times . . .*)

(After the "Lovecraft eZine" chat on NOV 11, 2012)

Libby Van Cleave Ingram Marshall: "Dark Waters," for English horn & tape;
the Bambi Molesters "Beach Murder Mystery"

and the bass keeps thumpin'

In one of my fiery moods (they don't vaccinate for aggression where I'm from). Stopped in the Sea Horse Tavern to pay Nicky and Buck for Tuesday's run. Didn't hang. Wanted some pussy and sure as 12 cold-fucks, Mabel (who filmed a few of Tralala 600s back in the day) ain't a menu item.

Split.

Urged for seXwinkin' (tits'n'ass, hold the swastikas and petulantly) Lolitas whose saliva and syllables would *yes*; gladly. Knew the spot where all the edges are avant and enthusiastic.

Crosstown. Lower, badside of under the bridge. No one checks the clock, they check the drums. Rents don't get paid. "*... todas las cosas que no volveremos a existir.*"

No weather to speak of ...

Devil's in my rearview. Can't say the hair looks all that stylish ... but the horns I sport are real fine.

Rolled by jazz—wasn't upholstered by Lester Young, barely turned my head ... slid by heroin ...

Neon-herbs crimpin' the risk in the frame ... No triggers with a fistful of bullets (so far) tonight.

Caddy (fusion of franticness and wrought, extra sooty where the fire danced) up on blocks.

bent with a few corners ...

Pontiac Pizza ... Side 2 Wings & Sushi ... The Neutral (that sure as shit ain't!)...

SALEM **MARLBORO**   BEER LOTTO BEER

rats ...

Wildflower Washing Machine ...

ain't newyork but the pattern's the same—lie; lure; aggressively; alley with never-stopping in the back; spit; needles; unable; rapist; slut;

FUCK YOU—

rats didn't pause from their garbage conventions to note my passing
. . . never do . . .

Predator's side of town: corner of Galaxy and North Hazelwood.
Pack 'em in tittie-joint called Guerlain's *NEON BONEYARD* . . .

The male-hustlin' endeavors of a bottle-blonde sportin' twin-44s
lovin' her salty trip with the pole. Confetti snows, she fluttered, the
Jacksons fluttered rarin'-to-go replies . . . banshees . . . landfill mouths
. . . molecular hallucinating therapy for their scars . . . injuries wedged in
between Narcissistic and specializing-in-S-&-M . . . drunk, Xanax, coke,
sugar and spice . . .

lot of pussy.

lots of dreamin' dicks that will never touch it. they'll go home to a
can of soup and softporn zilla-tits on cable.

All GRRRRRRRRRRL house-band. *Nice Lipstick.* Twin guitars—
both blondes, both punk Barbies, both damn good players, Vox organ
instigating a rave-up (you gotta love the Northwest, 50 years after and
she's crowned with a Paul Revere and the Raiders Revolutionary War
tricorne), coaxing drums (bass drum says Booty, and comes'ta funk she's
got it all up in her stuff) . . .

Electric chair cannibal-bass is thumpin'—

HER bass.

Ass (that puts voltage in my revolution!) wigglin' like that—offerin'
a man a meal, and me, I'm always hungry—Plate it up!

Two punk-assbags boppin' next to me say her name is Nikki say it
like some prayer that leads your ambition from exile to the blossom of
Paradise.

"Nikki." I like its taste on my tongue. "Nikki." I'd be happy to assault her (crannies & FELT) with a downpour of graphic detail.

I'm locked on her 6.

Want it!

BAD!

I know she is. Will be.

Wants to be!

I see it—her BLAST, her new breed, uncompromising, baking her
savage, building her adrenaline masterpieces to purest.

Wants my de Sade rippin'—arched back squirrelin' body molds and
'ploitation! Ebb&flow in every aeon of her FELT—

Living doll GRRRRRRL power—jump-outta-her-shoes, nakedfleshkarma-FRENZY of slobberin'/grunting/shovin' her ass to juicy-expelled, to raise her broken angel.

Gonna!

Back the bottle. Need its cold.

Back to the viewin'.... Fishnets (I like the hole in 'em behind her right knee), green skirt up to her *de raw*, spaghetti straps on a Hello Kitty as the Bride of Frankenstein tee ... TOP ta BOTTOM & INMOST I'm runnin' hot.

LUST—the teeth of me/myself/'n'/I! GLUTTONY! GREED! LUST! LUST! lust

And her bass keeps thumpin'. . .

And my bottle is empty.

Flamed-fueled UP & READY, volcano and hurricane runnin' with my Old Devil and that STRUTTIN'ass with that no-hidin'-it shuffle, there's an INFERNO in my crypt.

Set's over. I catch her at the bar. Scheherazade-*Chanel* teasing me, offering me kingdom come, smile offerin' a variant spelling. Front's even better than the *sa-weet*back, not a shy river in her. Blue eyes . . . and that mole. Incident of INFERNOred hair got my skip-along skippin'—leapin' too, brow and pale of her neck glistening. Nothing like a beastess-in-heat sweatin' fer ya. Tats and tits—Cherries fer the RIPE of me! She's got my pinpoint, **PSYCHO** and dependant, pegged-11 and DEADRED on *acquisition.*

Says, "I love your Give me *Philosophy in the Boudoir*, or I give you DEATH tee." Smiles, obscenely version.

Should I beg? Sweetly? Sleazy? All sezy-like? The devil canal in me just wants to grab and start inhaling. BUT—

The 2 longnecks I'd ordered to cool me arrive, I slide her one. Wait ... If she picks it up I'm gonna scratch her name in my diary, highlight it with the words *sexual MISSadventure*, mouth, hair, SCREAM that made Joyce Mansour blush.

"Thanks." Quick bottle back, 3rd of it. "Sometimes you *need*. If you know what I mean?"

Did she just wink?

Must have, as I saw it.

"Nights you just want someone to steal your cascade . . ." Laughs, her sezy soaks me. "My wounded lunatic gets seized and the constellation in my temple needs here it comes."

Nikki drains half the bottle. Draining is an activity I would never think to restrict . . . or thwart.

"You have any needs?"

"They're all on the map in my car. The car that wanted to be parked in my driveway 3 seconds after I saw you shakin' all over."

"Let's go and fuck." Plain as I'd put it if I was bold.

"Your chariot waits."

"I was hoping for a *muscle* car." Intoxicating mouth. "Seems I have affections of libidinous VAROOM-VAROOM in mind." Slither/snap/pop soft wet lips that won't wait to give me my birthday gift.

"At'sa me. Horsepower. You be nice and I'll show you where the HD in my HP tops out."

"You promise to be merciless?"

"Didn't I mention my name is Ming?"

"I was sure you were going to say de Sade. I'm really a *Juliette*, by the way, but I use Nikki. It's oh so sezy."

As the yes you can't say no to. As the waters of March, as the relaxed-fit moon opening here it is.

Sezy mouth open, not a word dislodged, I nodded my IS.

She's hot to GO/I've rarely been keener.

FAST EXIT:

24 hour butcher shop called The Ethical Butcher.

"Bloody steak and a meaty fuck. That's what I go for," she says. "Maybe pick up some meat for later?"

We do.

Best they have.

Gentleman that I am I let her pick the cut.

And we're rollin'——

Out past the Dead Swamp (such pretty appointments, most souvenirs that were gifts from me), past the crossroads to LandsEND where the *BABYLON DELIRIO MOTEL* flickers its VAC NCY and just a might more sits my abode . . . Made it to my lion's den in 15 flat. NEED (a shape-shifting swell of dazzle confirmed) and WANTssssS and the prettiest, skin-tight little ass this side of I WANNA BE YER DOG, BABY will do that.

Polite (hopin' to earn pussy-points) would have offered her the Grand Tour. Mama didn't try to fit me with politician and urbane.

Scent of earthquakes-triggered on us, took about 3 eyeblinks to get inside—less to get to unwrapped—

prettiest 34D tits and sweat.andsweet ass and beer [in her bellybutton and cleavage] and hot doggies and we're a 2-hysteria daisychain—ankles (seems like they're flying around the room like a hungry shark) and wet-lands-cunt [wantin' what it wants!] dealin' hope, and palms roaring. and her tits smotherin' my what's for dessert.got a cherry tat in my mouth and her nipple is screamin' for its due. 5 feet 5 of squirrely rollercoaster that's takin' the shaft—yank&yank and squeezin' the ironsides to ooze and burst [with extra KACHANG], no jive.

And I haven't even got her panties off yet.

Nor have we had our appetizer.

It's still hanging there all ripe and pretty. Trussed up soNICENICE in ballgag and cuffs, party balloons heaving. It's looking at me like I'm an oncoming bulldozer, or 666 . . . *Close*. I toss it a wink and a grin. Add a blown kiss. I like to think its steeping. Groom it right and it tastes better.

Hungry we— Fang—my tattoo Draculass nips me, drop for drop I give good as I get, rod wicked for encore, slice o warmdelight expressin' again-dialogue, and, of course, OURvigorous. After we got that 1st kiss out of the way, lube up and set the controls for the heart of the INFERNO.

Yeah. Let din-din simmer some . . .

So it's back to the reverie-waltz—adjoined—renderin'—blurred—every inch—labia—hug—slippery—thrust—good pussy (open sticky as figs)—great nectar pussy of raw wet miracles—fistfuls yielding—wobble—pinch/slap/KISS—spin/singe—no   pussyfooting—milelong tongues as soft as black calla lilies in crazy moonlight—beautiful face—beautiful clit—bull's eye "Fuck me. FUCK me. Fuck . . . that's goo*oooooo*d. God . . ." **"Again!"**

"Damn, baby."

And just when I'm ready for stars and the last ZOOM & Finale of this auto-de-YAY my Juliette is up and outta bed. Prancin' 'round.

Tits bouncing. Shakin' that sweetass for (and AT) me.

I give up another "WOW." Nikki's got the motor-booty thumpa-saurusBUMP goin' down. 'nother round o ME~*weeeeeeeeeeeeeee* gots'ta have (and hold on sinTIGHT).

SHAKE!

Me. IT!

SHAKE!

shake-shake-that nova-maker! !!

"Like that, Daddy?"

My head bobbin' DO—*Gimme!*

LIGHTNING—

Snapped her tang into a pinup pose, noted I was ready to FRY. Blew me a succupuss kiss. "And you haven't even seen what I can do with my tail."

"Tail?"

"Was saving my little *surprise* for you." Winks. Offers my heart the fizz of a chuckle. Blows me a kiss—I'm nuked. "Hope you like."

And out it comes. My celebrate of fascinated is changed right down to my neurons, my tongue takes on new energies. Nikki has a tribal, dragon tramp stamp on slow curve of her lower back and where the tail ends at the top of her backfield-cleavage 3 slender-feet of fine soft, (barber-pole striped) red fur—red as her hyperthyroidNEON locks, has come out to play. Never seen a kittycat with a tail that fine—Never . . . My mood ring eyes aglow as it snakes out and rings the full-throated Thereness of my *helloooo* kitty . . .

The first stroke is *pièce de résistance* s_ _l_o_ _ _w_

and soft

[strokin' a kittycat s~o~f~t]

—I'm chittering, and may have let out a WOW (in fact I'm sure of it)—

—she's feeding me her cherries—

DON'T THINK THE SOFT WILL LAST LONG

Nikki slides a 4.125" *Buck Zipper* out of the sheath lashed to the side of her boot. It's a conductor's baton in her slender fingers. "And when I'm done milking this cunt-loving rod . . . It's time for our bloody steak."

Our appetizer's eyes scream what the ball gag prohibits . . .

Grateful Dead, "New New Minglewood Blues"; Paul Revere & the Raiders, "Let Me"; Doors, "Love Her Madly"; Grace Jones, "Pull up to The Bumper"; Ohio Players, "Love Rollercoaster"; Los Lobos, "Shakin' Shakin' Shakes". Parliament, "Give up the Funk (Tear the Roof off the Sucker)"; Blue Oyster Cult, "Tattoo Vampire"; The Cult, "Fire Woman"

(he) Dreams of Lovecraftian Horror...

For my dear brother, a certain Mr. Hopfrog, Esq.

(*then*)(*by the light of an East Coast moon . . .*)
after the beans.
after coffee.
after the day's vigorous adventure in sunlight, the walk, enjoying the blue. a pen in silver hands, prizing. dreaming—'wholly overruled by the newer and more bewildering urge.'—from (and laced with) mathematics, and physics, and hints . . . 'Subterranean region beneath placid New England village, inhabited by (living or extinct) creatures of prehistoric antiquity and strangeness' . . . 'Lonely bleak islands off N.E. coast. Horrors they harbour—outpost of cosmic influences' . . . 'A very ancient colossus in a very ancient desert. Face gone—no man hath seen it' . . . words, aware—of history and science, and ancient fruits (and the embrace of Eternity) . . . 'There was the immemorial figure of the deputy or messenger of hidden and terrible powers— the "Black Man" of the witch cult' . . . astonished words. of cellars and cobwebs, of the inquiries of a madman. the hunger of the engine in the fountain burns in the nest. winter. telling farther. shaking with the moments when the clock faces the stars. the race to the gate. leaping with fast dreams. today. yesterday. a cold year (wrapped in beauty and loneliness) that disappears in a stream of years. words. dreams. words. words, lost and found . . . and melted.

dreaming (dusk)(shadows)(dark corners) . . . revising.

in the tomb. dreaming. and other tales of terror . . .

(now) *(by the light of a West Coast moon . . .)*
after coffee.
after Thai food.
after singing along with the new Streisand CD—*twice.* the hungry hands
(of the poet) at the keyboard. mining (commitment). deeper and deeper
to emerge with landmarks. words. each dreaming of the master . . . each
in sorrow and ecstasy, formed by heart. words. no make-up today. [ash-
ton]ished WORDS—rising, leaping (soon to be thrust into the hands of
The Editor), fast as midnight explored. fingers in the unwound mists of
a woodland asylum, eyes in the master's *Commonplace Book.* more
words—**'He kissed the instrument, then held it to the moon, that
globe of dead refraction'** . . . , more phrases—**'Autumn is my favorite
time of year; it heralds absolutely the death of torturous summer'** . . .
'She placed her hands together in a semblance of prayer' . . . more (le-
gions of deliberateness, each raindrop-tongue pulsing) grow (in Sesqua
Valley) (and other haunts). words, stitching blight on the doorways of
abandoned streets. blue-veined words, caging the empty-handed prayers
of the garden. carved words that must weigh in. *sign and sentence, lamps
in the witch-house!* (tearswept) words. choirs of words, gut and reflexes
that won't hide, or stop . . . the stain of dark blossoms covering the page.
words, plucked (from the master's territories) by the velocity of his
nets, and piled high on his altar of Lovecraftian dreams . . .
face pressed to words, roots (of death and decay and dark black earth)
and raven stars. briars—burdens, shaking with burdens. the movement
(every knot and gesture lit) of association and choice. words.
flares.
bells.
bells. and smoke fermenting. bells. thrust into technique, banging on the
strictures the stars possess.
bells.
bells. the luminous baptism—cooking genesis in the decomposition of
apocalypse.
words.
words. scars and edges trembling with death. words. tainted by the
harms in Kingsport and the deeps of Ahab's farm. roads. roads. said.
with fists. and sweat and moon. and soft innards things too. words. bleak
(prologue to trial) in veins aflame. roads. the tread of ash. words heard.
words wintering in metaphor. perfumes and opening lines . . . laced sen-

tences where havoc's talons swoop down upon roads of touch-and-go guilt.

words.

wild cascades of weeds and wax . . . bodies of starlight scented by crow-breath. decadent.

falling. shedding restraint. dancing . . .

dancing—

FASTER.

words. nouns and periods, and the commas (that map caves, and understand night infused with crossings), all—the recipe of every leaf, all—loaded with dread. italics diagnosing the rent of blood and butcher's bill. gang & timber! south, all the way to "There!" with claws in the game. wordshed—strata-phrase, uncork the tears. wordshed—lifting dauntless verbs. *words!* that light the doom felt last night in Sesqua, to prowl the warrens of Kingsport with kisses of corruption. witness words from hands that reek of smoke. a swirl of thorns hunting marrow . . . words. gathered. the mirrors and thunder of unshuttered words (glowing and trembling)(each a drum and blade and portal), at the threshold with their avid flint harvesting observations of moor and orbit and afflicted memory. words (explorations and ecstasies . . . built for whomever listens). . . and tangled, uncommon yesterdays (wrapped in beauty . . . and loneliness) (like those of the master) that cannot disappear in the stream of years.

dreaming (dusk)(shadows)(dark corners). . . revising . . .

in the tomb of the master. dreaming. and other tales of terror.

Jon Hassell, "Last Night the Moon Came"

Author's Note: This is the revised text of "hdoLH." It includes passages that were omitted from the version that appeared in *Lovecraft eZine.*

Saturday Night...
With a Dead Girl in It

A memento mori for Stephen Kick

Like the dead rabbits and dead mice and dead birds and dead dogs he'd often find amid the headstones, the eyes were all wrong . . . *and there was no trace of a smile.* No smile meant no laugh. No smile . . . the silk of lips revealing music colored by yum and empathize and I want to kiss you. The skull and crossbones of oblivion's choreography danced here. Ants and flies and other hungers would come. Eager to continue, they'd seize the feast.

Not human.

"Not a girl. The vessel of whim and felt is gone. Gone."

Gone.

"No thread remains to find the chart that leads to apples . . . and history to receive."

Meat. All its inches and curves just inches from his hands. Liver. Heart. The brain and tongue. The skin pulled back. Sprawled there in the grass and milkweed like a cat (near brick-hard) separated from its leap and going. Meat. All its scents . . . waiting.

Meat has no soul.

Another pit-of-your-gut need answered, but what of *desire?*

The heart, his, still a crop stabbed by disorder (and unaccepting of this uninvited chasm) and, often, an ocean of unrestrained 22-year-old emotion, did not want to be a solitary gatherer.

It wanted yes. It wanted to swim. He wanted to discover special.

This was not the first time the ghoul who carried the gestures and snowdrifts of a young man called Steve inside had seen that soulless stare.

*   *   *

St. Echo's Cemetery, the markers of nearly 200,000 inhabitants. 12 uneven city-blocks long, eight wide, fenced in by the deprived core of the graying municipality.

Caging it was a hive (manipulated by nauseating financial abstractions), an industrial giant swiftly gone to by-the-pound/cut-rate labor otherwheres, a seething to and fro/over/under/sideways/NO ladder up of BUMP and shoulderless-religion and filthylittle unrecorded scandals, and gangbangers. Pickens for a ghoul weren't great, but there were often bodies around; one just needed to be faster than the cops (that arrived with their coroners and fact checkers) and the other scavengers.

He was. Occasionally.

More now than when an aspirant Steve Kick, Kicker to his few close friends, came here 35 years ago, 4 years after the Summer of Love, the summer he died here.

"Every leaf falls here."

Blood and violence . . .

And the battlements of moonlight courtyards to prod dead things with dreams.

The body was fresh, not entirely cold . . . not yet. Looked great, soft . . . lovely, if you ignored the knife wounds. A young woman, early twenties. Cutting her way across the oldest part of St. Echo's to get to one of the clubs on South Hemlock, he guessed. Lot of the Dunstable U crowd used the lower part of the cemetery as a shortcut to the downtown bars and clubs. Few did it alone. Wouldn't, not most, not faced with the legends about the ancient voices that croaked and clicked and rumbled in the dark branches and the walking biographies they hunger to possess, some laughed about the unseen hunters, but that was a mere attempt to fend off what they truly believed, and there was the reality of the vagrants forced out of Lost Lake Park who trailed and screamed, "Wottaya got for me? Cummon, you must have a couple of bucks." There were times, some reported in the papers and on local TV, their gestures of seethe and desperate self-loathing amped-up to TAKE and a minorsquall of thrak ensued. And there had been numerous rapes in this city of the dead. (Steve had prohibited two over the years. The 2nd predator had been invited below as the meat course for *Le festin de l'araignée*.)

Steve doubted this was an assault by one of the homeless that smelled money and worry. The blood. The wounds. Anger whose breath was the shape of a blade. Another species of intent had hungered here.

A pretty dead girl. Dead, the marvels imparted . . . departed. Another bulging performance of heinous whose postscript would be tears (if she had anyone to cry over her) and a below-the-fold headline in the B section of the *Daily Gazette*.

Dead written in the grass.

No nearby, no somehow, or join in . . . Dead. No as-soon-as for the fledgling twirled in whisked.

Fulfillment aborted.

Dead.

"Pretty." (Strokes her hair. It was scented with chamomile and passion flowers. Images from *National Geographic* and travel magazines he'd thumbed through, places like Belize and Australia he never got to see, played like thunder and hardened ruin in him.)

It rains, he listens to the sky. It rains, he listens to *me*, to his spider *I am*, spinning all the died the dead have consumed. He listens to the moon, come closer to devour and shout loneliness. It gets in his lungs, in his fingers, it stings him, owns him, as it owns the sky. It paints *human* faces in the hole of his sins. The wet nights, the cold dry nights, eager, trembling . . . he dreams of a beauty he drowns in.

A gray auditorium of uncomfortably in the stink and declarations of a plague, his broken memories are braided to the pelting silence in the adder-shadows.

Dead.

Everything is dead. (Never ask the deceivers, Bliss and Hope, if you can win the contest.) Everything but the things he can't shed.

Young.

Too young. (He strokes her hair.)

This girl looked like Alex, his memory of her; how Alex scratched the side of her nose when she attacked questions in calculus, her valentine-sweet smile in the high school yearbook photos, inquisitive, eager, intimate with A's on atlases and in physics, the electric flag of her tie-dyed rainbow dancing to Steppenwolf as their "Magic Carpet Ride" expanded the shamanic oasis of The Aerodrome. (Steve was there that night, his consciousness—*ROCKED/beneficiary of spacefleet contact/celebrating*—soaring in the Becoming, and unexhausted. The banquet of her Sharon Tate splendor a fortissimo sugaring all his labyrinths.)

Poor girl—

Still a rose—soft shoulders, the lovely incantation of her sailboat yes. A soft season snuffed . . . away—for all time. Her glow—it must have been a madrigal of ivy buds and gold—must have been summer sweet, dressed for undaunted and curiously . . . sheered . . . Done.

Her pomegranate shores

In a coffin—

In a belly—

Autopsied—split open—

Dead.

"Dead."

The word wounded him, but he had no tears.

Step in this garden and you find thousands of cases of suffering—

Steve lost his life (fell and smashed his head on a tombstone . . . *bled* . . .) then, after that friendless omega-female (the one that craved something of her own—even if he was "nuthin' but skin and elbows") made him a thing of the Noctuario, he lost his mind. He didn't wanna walk this way . . . but he did.

Ate scabrous rats, and bugs . . . frozen worms and other scraps in the winter months. Forced his fortunes to eat the brains of a dog—the collar said, Scuba . . . Rip at the belly of a dead cat. Ate a robin fallen from the nest. Climbed and snapped mothers' necks, plucked wings, robbed eggs . . . and there was the human flesh he ingested, choked down.

The piece of Steve Kick that's still clutching the water of existing in translucent dreamt and interfaces not mort, curses the moon, spits at the involuntary residue of a God his existence in ghoul-hide erased. Night and night—black and brutal, in the hoops and lostness, gathering crumbs, the Steve Kick that reviled the hustlers with painted eyes and everyone in pain their beer insists is a boot to the gut; forgot buying the new Led Zeppelin album in Woolworth; going places; half full; clean; don't . . . normal . . . where-when-starting; masturbating; squeezing his "Want that" in store windows . . . daytime spilling realness alive and BRIGHT, is thick with the nothingness of the moon.

The moon became his mistress. He's learned longer from her near, taught him the turmoils of the coldest deeps of loneliness.

This thing that's what remains of Steve Kick's identity and the dead thing that eats dead things is scabbed, pocked. He's been nipped and challenged by the incisors of a nature that tears the same meat his fangs do. He, fleshjunkie, carries the marks of livid teeth-and-claw jacked-on "Mine", has scars (on hands, arms . . . throat and shoulder—gifts from the female that fucked him to fuck away her ghosts and boredom) and is missing a thumb—he lost that in a conflict over an infant's thigh (*A baby!* The mindfuck-hell of that adjustment).

*   *   *

They brought beer and weed, took off their shoes. Nathaniel spoke of discovering Walt Whitman—stood, pointed at the stars as his voice climbed into the up-above, "'As I watch the bright stars shining, I think a thought of the clef of the universes, and of the future.'" Eric and Dan clapped and they quietly passed the pipe. Dan elbowed Eric, said, "What a brainiac." They laughed.

Talked of dead—Was there something after? Eric did brief, ineptly-comedic imitations of Frankenstein and Dracula. And as the laughter settled "D.O.A." was on the 9-volt radio. (Steve stared at the radio, if he didn't turn it off, he feared, "Fire and Rain" or "Without Her" might come on and piss more acid in his heat.)

Steve thought of Dave Banegas and Tony, two friends who had died last summer. Thought of all the times he'd been in Dave's blue, '69 Boss 302 Mustang, blazing the elm-roofed backroads near Gibbet Hill, whiteknuckle-tight as the fastback took the curves on Baby Beach Road—laughing to be brave.

Before he succumbed to sobbing in front of his buddies, Steve rose and walked among the markers. He shivered in the desert of names.

Never came back from that walk . . .

*   *   *

A meteoric trap of details, shifting, drifting, splashed with hunger and crammed with hurriedly, everything he'd once wished for in the weed-covered ground by the punctuating headstone. All her speeches and pleas and ready kisses, now, lost colors, lost odors, as useful as melted wax.

She had been lovely.

His Alexandria was lovely.

He began to cling to a repetition that began with I.

Ran with memory. Added what he wished it had been. Highlighted transformations of facts that weren't fact. Stitched them to what if. Believed every word. Every image . . .

barefoot . . . Alex . . . sunny, more candy than serene, channeled for immersion . . . softlawned palmtrees . . . holding hands with the intimate details of "Honey." . . .

Kept dancing—

Came to a DEAD END.

(Everything in this yard and below was contoured and stained by the black gel of the well of death.)

Repeated it.

I—

Unfulfilled. Sometimes—lot of times, everything amuck and drooping dislocation to worth-the-effort—in tears or raging, comes out as "FUCKED!"

The moon watched. Didn't seem to listen . . .

I—

Dreamer (unscrewed by overwhelmingly).

I—

At fault!

I—

Charged it with the muscle of will. Pushed it with 35 years of denied.

Tears come to the fleece of his desires, stricken his war-weather desolation.

I—

(i)

He clings.

Recalls a conversation of one about going to the well, the empty well, a conversation (a jabbering, leap-frog volley of desire that couldn't find one single toward victoriously) on a barstool in Muddy's Tap Room. He thought the old drunk was a fool to hold on to broken dreams for so long. After his death, his own conversation with Lonely followed. The shape of the old drunk's fate became a coat—cage, he found himself wearing.

The border that kept sunny days distant was immovable.

She was thrown to the ground. Three of her fingers were broken. Steve gently straightened them. Held her hand. A fly kept returning to the back of her hand. His swift backhand shooed it off.

A knife had helped rip off her clothing, fierced her left breast, repeated its incendiary slicing in belly and upper thighs. Gorged in her belly . . . seven times.

He could smell what the rape left.

Her purse was spilled open. Nothing taken.

Roads . . . done . . .

too soon—

Drawn by the perfume of meat flowering in the humid air, the flies come back. Flit. 3 determined to gain, dance, rub their shimmering yes on tragedy. 2 more. Settle until disturbed. They understand the sticky-depths layered over the bones.

Entwined in his tears, he did not notice the arrival. He blinks, discovers the assault. Swipes. They flit. His mouth is dry, a brittle quagmire. Theirs full of swallow. The tango, three robbers in the whirlpool of desire, each a dart succumbing to the fruit of this tree.

The cold poetmoon lights up this gathering of natures.

Backhanded talons sweep the tiger-mouths from the clotted bloodink.

"Away."

Stroked the dead girl's doe-brown hair. (Alex's hair was brown, and in all his dreams, soft.) Thick, long—ribbons, charms, orbits . . . (*If she were dancing*—) Soft. Presses against him. She is not in this shell, but all his stories are. A splinted night of youth-filled lust, chaste consumed by hopeful-flesh, rests on her sternum . . . his heart is wedded to remembering.

Eyes confronted by fact, he despairs in memory. Back, in the red forge of longing, *might be* that didn't. Inquisitive, pushing its textures to read the intersection of suspense and stimulating. Drifting in excess, shivering, the river of girlhood answering the knock at the door.

"Yes."

Another assault on his curtain of tenderness by the soulless black arrows. His gone-to-war hand (swelled with grudge) swats at the coarse bouts of flies. Their fascination in her crotch, he glowers, pushes their leaping inches, again. No praying, no tentatively—repeating faster. Breaks the exploitation of their universe . . . And again.

"She . . . might have—"

A kiss, stunning and fine. A raspberry intimacy that could not fail, like the ones in movies. A melting of pillow talk . . .

Flitting flies execute the pages of his delight.

Anger. Swift buzzing-fire burning upon the End of Journey. Swats. Swears.

Their rollicking has never bothered him before—

Such soft skin.

Remembering what he thought just-holding Alex's hand would feel like; immediacy, consistency, the dialogue of glory and possibilities complete.

Warm.

Sunshine.

Sunshine.

Smooth.

Shyly, the smile that came with it. Gladly, widening—water and fruit and balm in the well.

"Yes."

A poem fluffed gently—no hurriedly, sweet as an addiction made of stars.

This *had-been-a-girl*, "Katerah.", was plump and fresh (and pretty as his Alex was) and could feed the warren for a week. It had been a hard winter and a meat-scant spring . . . *Could.*

The return of the housefly.

Swat its transgression.

Darts. Circles back.

Returns.

Determined.

Death is shaded by many menaces. Their intensity is not influenced by the loneliness or hope.

Mental memorabilia. Oars resurrecting and stirring; images of a world that was not a cemetery, a lake with white clouds, apples, watermelon, her smile . . .

Steve had a damp, cold nook (padded with rags, a blanket, and found items of clothing) below, in the ratless grot where it is never silent, where he sat and dreamed of 16-year-old Steve (believing in magic), recalling songs from the new Lovin' Spoonful album while the pack barked (until it became howling). Sat, and fucks and fights. The pack holds no calendar in regard, but Steve dreamed of one. Fridays painted on it. Fridays with a piece of paycheck for the bartender's palm. The cover band from Syracuse smokin', Saturday night in The Revolution with a girl who said, yes, yes, she'd love to dance. 5 o'clocks where he'd get to rush home to his girl, a girl who swept away the lies and lined up the stars for him.

"Alex."

There: fought with his silkhymn-revels and illusions. Here: in anger, hourless souvenirs-tenderly fade.

Close his eyes on the chaos of blades. To no avail.

The housefly returns. The hand that is not holding the girl's lashes at it's quickly.

Saturday. A week of work then home to disappointing . . . a beer, staring out the window at a lot without a single tree in it, a lot full of weeds, finally fleeing his kingdom of frustration . . . Sidewalk. Shoes carrying 70 bucks faster and faster. Cavanaugh's Pharmacy where he bought comics as a kid, Ray's Barbershop (he hadn't stepped inside since he was 14), the V.F.W. hall and Johnson's TV Repair . . . Green GENE-SEE CREAM ALE neon. Muddy's Tap Room, the blossoms of a sentimental jukebox. The posture of the singing-crime of jocks at the pool table. Alex with her cousin and two girlfriends in a booth by the dart board. Steve at the bar, beer in hand, eyes loaded with please, trying not to stare, trying not to give up hope.

Steve opened his eyes; three flies have brought their language to her hand.

Ruby-eyed radarlock; generated anger, swipe again.

Intentness dares her face.

Slap at the air.

Commitment wings stymied. Arc o'er ample grace's seeped fluids. (Again) attempt the chance of feeding.

Slap.

Slap at it. Miss.

"Little fuckers." Receive furious, spent it.

Hiss at the defilement. "Fucker."

Filled with heat, Not Defeated returns and Steve swipes at them again . . . and again . . .

Neither hunger will give up.

Decades observing clamors and plain from a distance, but listening closely. Steve's music died—8 miles high planted 6 feet deep, a passport-spoon (then needles and crack) replaced rolling papers. Things got harder (to come by, to deal with, to forgive) and faster. Mean, after it napalmed sensibilities, loaded up on menace, and guns became the *HURT du jour* and still the kids came. Many a weekend night they gathered near Scott Spicer's grave, sat there like it was the drawing room in a first-rate vacation retreat. They came to hide from the crescendos of heartless, from the vocalknives that scorched innocence. Came to be free, or came outfitted with friends they hoped would help them carry loneliness. They brought beer, and drugs—weed mostly . . . and greasy white bags of White Castle burgers, or a pizza . . . or sweet snacks. They laughed and (sometimes) fucked, talked (of hate and dumb and flavors, or dragons or Macbeth . . . or trying to live) and texted on their cell phones. Steve watched the new generations remodel the world. Aiming facts at the invalid moon, he sat in the posthumes and realized necessary. Listened; the New World (the 5th or 6th he'd had to adjust to since he became an inhabitant of St. Echo) was closing in and a ghoul needed to be educated, survival demanded it.

Someone (wino; sadness-diluted; heinous ship; hooker who was trying to survive her lifetime without the kisses and trophies of a Loving God; reddened slob who'd swallowed hotly) would come by, clean out the 67 dollars in her wallet, take her debit card (and the password she had written on the back of last semester's class schedule), maybe take her cell phone. Frosted by drink or sterile, they might look down and puke, or curse her for being stupid.

She wouldn't care. Couldn't.

But Steve did.

She resembled Alex—*his* Alex, her hands, her hair, the piercing forever-miracles of promised comfort, every thumb and chapter his blood had wanted to learn. She wasn't a corpse, wasn't neutral, her fragrance was soft—eternal, sweet—it had no cruel boulders that hunted you. No sickening grotesque human peeled from her currents, she was an altar for his heart.

Steve put everything back in her purse. Her cigarette case, her lighter. Her keyring, her birthcontrol pills . . . Looked at the picture of a big, furry brown dog and a familyportrait. Slid her reading glasses inside, wondered what explorations they might have cooed over—

Do young people still read Nabokov and Fowles?

There was one last article lying in the patch of milkweed and skunk cabbage. Unsoiled, softer—a bolt combed with fragrant sun, white as a musical gown floating on a white shoulder, chaste swan in a bowl of dreams, he slipped her lace handkerchief in his pocket.

His fingers remain in his pocket, drinking. Sun. A fruit vase, swelled, Christmas on the table of the heart...

Delicious. The Sunday nimbleness... *always* in Alex's eyes.

"Always.'

"Katerah."

That's what her college I.D. said. D.O.B. 21 years ago.

"I was dead before you were born."

He cared. Had to.

She could feed the warren for a week—Meat—*nostrils full of it, gnawing, the blindness of appetite.*

Tears. Boys do cry. Ghouls cry.

Merciless confusion overruns his

> *flesh (happened) (breaking it)*
>
> spirit (holy) (no kin to the transports of lethal)

Animal. Something his parent's minister cataloged with angels.

Disease

> (soul)

Speculation

> (soul)

Lovely. Distorted.

The curse of imagining—

Dead... the incurable forever. They don't inoculate against it here. His muscles, part and parcel in trafficking with vanished, slip through the minutes without understanding the melody.

Can't leave her for the teeth of the sun, for the ants.

This garden of soft skin without poetry in it.

Harmed.

Defiled.

No growing old. No collecting things, no framed fairweather watercolor hanging in the hall to make it beautiful... No good will.

Knife-wielding. Up and down—Jack the Ripper is no myth here, Norman Bates no creature of celluloid. In and out. Perspiration. Desperation. RED... *and no defense.* Two open mouths... no screaming. Cutting. Fingers locked. (How much cold and fear and hate had bent them?) Cutting—deeper. Knife, like the fly's hunger for blood, kept returning.

Did it observe long before it took?

Did it laugh? Scream gospel or nuclearFUCK at her?

Katerah's whole life now in this prison.

"Can't."

Means won't.

Looks away from the pain in front of him, looks at the city lights . . . GLEAM OF FACE—AS GOOD AS DRUGS WITH FULL-CURVES POSES IN A BOOTH OF SUMMER HEAT (one use—one use . . . scams inside scams); REMARKABLE (fake); SEX (9mm); UNFORGETTABLE (was never); THE LIPS OF A BEAUTIFUL WOMAN LOADED WITH WHISPERY (at *this* rate); PHAT (was never); "BABY" (pistol-whipped); "C'MON, BABY" (shot in the head)—

The lights lie.

Dazzling lies. Every night (carved by dirty, or spreading casual whatever), masking worlds of loneliness (their whole life a reaction to tossed aside) in their 2-room limitations. Every night, sparkling deliciously. Every night, the lights of the hacksaw river-mouth fluttering—flashing, shouting eagerness and lust in the jukebox-scored messages in a bar mirror. LIES promising no lie. Ashtrays and nemesis.

"Won't."

All the shapes of grayness and error under the BigBlackSky chop destination breathless.

"Can't."

He lived in this city too.

Alex's hand in his hand.

Katerah's hand . . . tender (Stroking it.) "Nice" . . . Her fingers, to his liking.

Katerah could feed the warren for a week—

"Alex." Lovelorn waiting to hold a tomorrow that can't come back. Lunacy dancing around it. Heights, silk, not mad. Lows, dining on poison, harden.

Katerah could feed the warren—Meat—nostrils full of it, gnawing, the blindness of appetite.

Alex's soft (cold) hand . . . in his gray (cold) hand.

Steve dabbed moisture from the corners of his eyes with his dirty sleeve. Opened Katerah's cell phone and dialed 911, spoke clearly. Her cool hand in his, gently, comforting, he sat—patriot in a cockfight swatting away returning gangs of flies, guarding Katerah until the ride of the Valkyries-sirens brought the red lights that flashed on the tombstones.

On his way back to the warren . . . his belly moaning, frantic. Eye to eye with a Cedar owl—embracing the hope of a spring-fattened mouse appearing. "Damn the irresistible of *flesh* . . . There are other needs"

He'll lay a-wake. Lean

into the vast

(irreversible) hungers

of his

graspings

and

grief. Grip

dreams

Standells, "Sometimes Good Guys Don't Wear White"; Toto, "99";
Scott Walker, "Farmer in the City" and "Sons of" and "Windows of the World"; Bloodrock, "D.O.A.";
James Taylor, "Fire and Rain"; Blood, Sweat, & Tears, "Without Her";
Aerosmith, "Dream On"; David Sylvian, "Ride" and "I Surrender"; Boston, "Smokin';
Norma Winstone, "Everytime We Say Goodbye"; Weather Report, "Morning Lake" and "Tears";
Led Zeppelin, "Tea for One" and "Thank You"; Go West, "We Close Our Eyes";
Looking Glass, "Jimmy Loves Mary-Anne"; Lovin' Spoonful, "Younger Girl"

Doom . . . & Sigh

(An Experimental Threnody)

For Crumb and all the souls who went THERE and did not return...... .

[Night with no specific cadence.] [Cold. October / a Friday—with red-handed streets and labels and shoes not dressed for success or godliness / no one has looked—not even the madness-maned moon clouded with Eternity's black feathers, but it could be the 13th. The lines. The phrases in neon. Tide. Time. Stripped~ ~~] [Hasn't been a BANG or a blood-stain or patience in the last 47 minutes.]

DOOM: "I will be FREE. I will not be a crumb repeated until I come apart with tears." [He looks at her. The symmetry of her melody. He will be a thief and steal her from this BLACK epidemic of bombing.]

[DEPARTURE (at 5:37): Free from the tight lines and HEAVY notations of the damning score, from the tombstone impossible of MAL's threnody macabre.]

DOOM: "There will be no sarabanda of devil-music, no muerte oscura this night."

[DOOM offers his hand.]
[Sigh, leans, wants—a bit, (has, as a floating dissonance pinned to colonial-garde, considers BLOSSOM) but is still.]
[DOOM begins rowing . . .]

*   *   *

His eyes are a course (wishing to be a venture of hands)
looking at her knee.
. . . Imagining his fingers (composing) there . . .

. . . there—you don't need stars or fame
            just the willingness to taste

                                    new
                                    fruit—

soft
a lily's kiss drawn from her voice
a circle
a ballet
DOOM, slow
            soft
charged with the light of volcanoes
sighs

                        *   *   *

Sigh sings her aria.
DOOM undresses the notes of his guitar.
Their eyes hold hands.
            [They look at a kingdom where they can arrange
BLISS.][speak of GRACE and the dance of CHILDREN ... and
BELLS][they, opening their recipe-book of FELT, share 13 images, the
cascade, no BITTER or idiots in the contours of its math][wind and air
shimmer][waltz][they, soaked in heart-fruit, are in a circle of good]
They are about to touch.
Distorted wings and rites count it off~ ~~
Eins: Clouds. Black chewing rain.
Zwei: Safety falls from its tiptoe.
Drei: Hungry elects marches............[the blueprint of a cliff: splinters]............
[a dead river: seizure]............
FEAR. MAL—painting!—laughs his laugh of *in tempore belli.*
            BITE. (desolation —50,000 and 500,000— in this ruin
            of HELL.)
            STING. (no entropy in this velocity) DIED. (today
            handcuffed to the
            spraying lust of tanks)
            CHARGE. CUT. SPILL. (breaking summertime.)
            HUNTER'S INCARNATE-LEAD WINNING. (Obey!
            Obey! Obey!
            OBEY!)

DISARMED. (and told . . . to hang)
PILES. (downstream from gunsmoke and polluted. blackened by
FERAL.)
The tattered curtain falls.
From a dark spot, no purled mists, no locks, or passage, no patterns of grief, floats a dead face with missing teeth: "She will not sing again."
DOOM, each tear a current that cannot forget the nimble light of Sigh, turns the mechanism BLACK.
(To fight fire . . . BLAZE.)

        __1 remove dust from pocket.
        __2 listen for truth.
        __3 hope for a gosling bud . . . and a stem to stretch.
        __Vier rescue your name from gore.

                *   *   *

Outside
   in the black and blue world of MAL
RED cape of blood open
no soul sings
      or spreads a wing
           No music plays
           Beneath the waves
(black as the Hades of a mouth
with
no
warm curve)
              there is a harmony of
earthquakes

                *   *   *

The bell-window is empty. Dark.

                *   *   *

[October after October and That October and the October that hoisted the Inferno Canvas the building looks as broken as the invisible spaces in the field hospital.] [Under a frail-looking clock~]

    Trakl pinches his ear. The left. Then the right. Curses. "No, Sigh." Shakes his head slowly.

DOOM (for other reasons) finds it unacceptable as well. "I need song." "Or the magic and charm of bare skin."

DOOM looks at his baton. MAL had silenced it. "This no longer conducts anything."

Trakl opens up his architecture of vowels, stumbles over the hips and roofs of his syllables. "It still has . . . a point. Use it. Weapons are what we make of them."

"This?"

"Ideas are . . . tools, and they can be weapons, so why not a stick? Start a fire."

"But MAL is fire."

"Then be a bigger fire."

*   *   *

MAL came with fire.

And more fire.

DOOM fired up his insects.

The flutter of wings. The inhabitants, picked at their cages with meaning, clambered from ghost with pitted spoons, rose from their confines. They shook their manes, letting MAL's knives of lies hear their thrust. Voiced their ancient stories with equipment not approved. Sung took to the battlefield.

Skull and skeleton and bullet wrote new waves on the battlefield page . . . Paid and paid and . . . Stood—dry blood still under their fingernails, and killed, and cried, and counted what the craters had swallowed . . . In church with suits and candles and the women—struggling still smoldering in their hearts—those who had pushed the deathcarts *and cried* knit with bricks and seeds—watered them with IF and I . . . They washed blood from the bricks to build settlements and schools and reformed a sense of identity . . .

*   *   *

DOOM [for a moment INMOST] fluttering with bodies and every step with no flower to cherish~ ~~ [no tears to hold his hand] [no bridge in his fingers]

[field to field] [ditch to ditch] [blood] [gray] [tears] [graves] [gray and all its friends] [graves] [exorcists (on a voyage of WHO I WAS!)—scratching

forth, rippling with shoulders that say NO, take back their names from the MONSTER-FACE apparitions]

[another October. lines. HATE—on 8 legs BLACK. Blood. Blood. Blood! graves. most FALL.]

[8legs BLACK] [powderburn] [the broken icons of energy in the gutter-mudfilth] [froth, colored and churned and blistered, of HOWL in the TERRIBLEDESTRUCTION of the mill]

[POINTLESS took too many to count . . .]

[small/old/every anxious gesture/lovely—too many to count]

[some came home............]

*   *   *

home . . .

survivors who broke OFF WITH THEIR HEADS

home. fragments and distance on the map.

home.

tragic

tarnished and bewildered,

littered with scarecrows in the fields of scourge

*   *   *

Sigh finishes the woman's face. Character and care are back, spent has no currency on it. Dead. But she will be seen. Remembered. Fluffs and combs her hair so it rests just so on the linen-lining of the coffin.

Day after day with the dead. Bringing back smiles. Highlighting and pushing shadow back. Being is the focus of her labors.

More death.

tears

Tears that won't abdicate.

Wants a drink. 6!

Couple of hours till Happy Hour. Winking neon—the gestures of patrons perched on drums—the complexion of dreams constructed by sound—sharing the sexmusic—and the beer.

Needs it.

Something.

Maybe?

Maybe he'll be there.

Maybe he'll leave null on the barstool and come home with her.

There have been times she thought he looked at her. Gathered clues. Times when manifestation almost licked him, showed his compass bodies opened to speed, every step of cheek and bed and bloom. She'd mailed him arrows. Sent them into the storm. Put sentences on his ledges.

But he'd lost his senses. Put another drink to his lips.

She was sick of being dead inside.

Sick

of the nail—all the plans in its wind,

and the burden of disease.

Didn't care if he'd buy. She'd lead the dance if need be.

Sigh walked to the mirror. Made the final adjustments to her hair, her face. Painted emphasis on her smile.

"Tonight."

After 6 drinks. Or 20.

Whatever it took.

Like before

when she pushed the deathcarts. Up the ally. Down the streets. Between the smell of squall and ruin. Carting the deathsmell. From point to distance. No speed to it. Not on that fabric. Not under those flickering shadows. And the dropping bombs.

Not all of her was lost.

And there was one part she wanted back. Not some slight nostalgia.

Her lipstick chiseled the last lamentation from the purpose of her expression.

DREAMTIME.

Time to touch.

Be touched.

Write a poem. Then sing it.

And she would.

"Tonight."

With the fallen angel.

Looks in the mirror. Her eyes are wings.

She had stockings with seams up the back. A black dress that had rows of colors and jazz at the door of her cleavage.

Coffee with cream. Two sugars. Applied the nail polish. Red to hide the dried blood still under her nails.

Cover the collapse with velvet, cover the last breath of leper. Her mouth moved with flex. It opened dreams.

Sigh smiled. Walked out of anguish.

*   *   *

[No gleam returned o'er moor and heather] [neon tuned off] [jukebox in the lion's den out of circumstances and the lefts and lost of haunted hearts] [door slammed and locked] [kicked out of the Seahorse Inn................] [dimming streetlamp] [cat playing catch with a rat in a garbage can in the BLACK alley]

DOOM: I might know another joint where we can—

Sigh: You keep buying I'm with you. Lead on.

['round the corner that's all out of brilliant]

[DOOM tosses his butt in a sewer grate] [reaches for the pack in his pocket] [offers Sigh one] [she starts to wave it off] [takes it] [laughs after exhaling]

Sigh: You do this every night?

DOOM: Not so much these days. [looks in a news shop window/reads *Intergalactic Weekly* headline, Pope Diabolus II to Wed Hugh Hefner's Clone to Mutant-Alien She-Wolf Twins— Elton John's Clone Is Best Man] When I can . . . Some. [fumbles with a matchbook] What with Buk gone . . . Resettled in the trunk of Null—That's a heavy fine for breathing way I see it . . . And Pulver stopped elbowin' bottles—

Sigh: He doesn't drink?

DOOM: Not a drop. Teetotaler. Gave up runnin' with the Black Angels for books.

Sigh: Ran out of hope?

DOOM: Weakened, or civilized. Maybe it was he lost his sing and glorify. Can't really say, he won't talk about it.

Sigh: Tried rattling his chain?

DOOM: Tried hell. Sent insects loaded with devil-music to stir him.

Sigh: And he stayed lost even after hearing the Ancient Voices?

DOOM: And their echoes. [looks yonder.] Stayed lost . . . So many did . . . No open heart surgery can cure the debouched that scalped them . . .

[she shakes her head]

Sigh: Bridges burned.

Doom: No rest in peace.

Sigh: No summer to inhabit?

DOOM: Sure they would have liked a heaven, or Valhalla, or 70 virgins, but they could never make it right.

Sigh: Demons?

DOOM: Yes, both carried a legion................. And ghosts by the mile. Had 'em in their shirt pockets with the beasts and their rugs of confusion. [grinds out his cigarette] Their eyes forgot how to row.

DOOM: I would not say they wore the gravity of Diablo well.

Sigh: Does anyone?

DOOM: The burden of slavery's anvil is a desert, I'll give you that.

[lights another smoke] ... [exhales] ... [laughs] [follows it with a little smile]

DOOM: Really is ... Shame they've outlawed cloning writers. De Sade fucked that up bigtime.

Sigh: You can blame Jack Spicer too. You can't pass around that much truth and expect the authorities to go with the flow.

DOOM: Seductive enticements.

Sigh: You had a hand in it too.

DOOM. Just a finger. Maybe two? Following orders ... Just some light house-cleaning.

Sigh: All those birds, is light house-cleaning?

DOOM: They were stepping on Spring's poetry. All that song washing the roots and branches made too many shadows in gravity.

Sigh: Might have made a few carpets a little harder to row, but a little vocabulary never hurt anyone.

DOOM: They had their eyes on names. Started everyone thinking about shopping for new ones.

Sigh: So that's when they called you up?

DOOM: Yeah. Drafted again. Took away my bottle, combed my hair, and said intimidation by tombstone ... So I pulled out my symphony. It's what I do ... When I'm not drinking.

Sigh: Maybe you drink to escape?

DOOM: Trying to hold up my chin did it to me.

[lips chew on /hard roads— no plaques in the traffic with BLACK

ANGELS / hemmed in—left to DIE / blood / sweat / and TEARS /
where they fell]

[6pack from the 24Mart] [picnic tale out of the reach of the single light-
source in River Park/near the struggling bushes near the windowless,
abandoned factory] [the bronze indian statue—lost as many generations
who, during and after wartime, found themselves on their knees and
wounded—faces the other direction]

[a hand set down the echoes of lost bells / settles on a thigh]

[the pleased sound of a sigh]

DOOM: So do you ever take off that dress and—

Sigh: [seductively smiling] [sigh] [winks] I sure do, handsome. One
more parable about the terrifying things in the air in the Dark Land [slips
her arm in his] and I'll annihilate you in all the expressions of voyage.

[DOOM smiles his punchline]

[miles away] [old beat cop
                    —ignoring the bedlam articulations of beget
spat by clockwork oranges darkening the landfill-pavement and all that
dangles from them
                    and the erase spat by Night
                    and the unmistakable moaning leaning strange-
ly and scurrying
                    and the smiling blades, high on blood, drawn—
        in the donut shop yawns over his cooling BLACK cof-
fee][siren runs off —robbery, battery or just hard ripples?— to speak to
a child about Way Of Life][a new war begins . . .]

After Istvan Marta, *Doom. A Sigh* (1989), George Crumb, *Black Angels:*
Thirteen Images from the Dark Land (1970), and Charles Ives, *They Are There!* (1917/1942)

soundtrack: see above.

into the world

the vesslyeer cling. or some other sight might object and in the forbidden pain of knowing, as night sneaks through their gate, claim they writhe to escape.

conjure a candle (even a small one) and ask it to remain. now hold it out, push it past your restless now.

consider possible. can you see it? hold your hand steady . . . it may help. yes, it can be disturbing and difficult, but it is possible. slowly . . . slowly. fast will not help you here.

can you see it?

give it a moment. sssh . . . no need to feel frustrated. the light will carry it to you.

there.

that's it.

that conversation of black. each corner. each knot. all the edges that won't be stopped or dulled. all the edges that won't light lamps of color, that won't fit sensibly in history.

yes. blink. good. good. each seizure helps focus. binds it to here. if it can be possessed and held in this courtyard? many do . . . many do—again and again they plunge around the corner and demand . . . try. someone is always trying . . .

it is up to you. it is your hand. your eye. your time.

sssh . . . calm. steady is the way. blisters and hunger's wild struggles will turn it to wet mud and there will be no shape of voluptuousness. without depth and blood, wayfarer, detail will not come to chat and braid.

Yes—yes, there will be grammar and rhythm on the embankment of tangibility, but that will come later. after it unfolds and you clear enough room to accept the secret bond.

no. fear not. these things happen. to you, to me. to all the others who pondered rules and solutions, that swept away the dust with debate— tried to . . .

my desire was dimmed and I shivered many times. I was slashed and thrown to the ground . . . rebuffed by my own raging need, I made myself an inmate that could not solve simple. sssh. I do not recall anyone succeeding their first time.

rest for a moment. you cannot negotiate with consummation. pushing does not widen the passage . . . pursue stillness.

shall we try again?

good.

you still have a dry match, yes? good. and your candle is willing? I only ask, as if it has no song, we're lost and this adventure is a useless battle between spirit and flesh.

ready?

there. good. the core. the red-sun heart of this universe. it burns. glows. the inferno offers warm. as it should. all vines need a ladder.

now where to begin? in the swirling white foam, thick as rain? plunging into limitless—every Ahab-cursed rise and swell a new present, weighted with oars fighting exhaustion . . . each stroke—framed in the poverty of ache—an exorcism, breathing and sewing time. one might . . . the titan rock, black as pure void? certainly it cries to be the center of this universe.

some splash of red? a dying sun, crying for what has been lost or what is about to expire?

choice. by necessity? or chanced upon? this untested corner, or that ocean of black-petaled fear, that will not rest. will you begin . . . here?

or there?

move slowly. here, with all your tools and fears in hand, you decide . . . inside, out to the borders? or outside, spreading its endless death in, poisoning the existed in the center?

that is what you must choose.

cut and glean. flow, release your birds . . . yes, action, fever. mistake, or exorcism—reflex welded to the loaded radiation you exhale, call it what you will.

no constellations. no bone-white moon to quickly state drastic. good. good.

yes. you have offered yourself.

from where I sat, the vesslyeer cling. but I am not painting this darkening. I am not climbing slippery to take part in expression. it is your mind gripped by the abyss, pulled by the seeing of hopelessness. you hold the brush and this

deluge

is what you make of it. your cross.

no. I did not pray. there were never sermons and sundays on my palate.

right or wrong? yes, most start there. perhaps they must? need (isn't that how we are? just things trapped in a self-contained process swollen with the typographical stains of our eagerly?) . . . needful drives most to believe, try to, in some presentation of soil, station, rules you can see— try to grip . . .

right. as it joins conditions in the bringing no name (or box) can hold.

wrong. as it joins conditions in the bringing no name (or box) can hold.

wrong. or right. or trying to be this or that.

there is none. there is your felt. how it is broken . . . broken. going. gone as never was. not being stuck in some proclamation of words and sand and sugar. won't work.

describe mine? would a simple shrug say what I should say? no. I should try to form words, define its shape and will—the insatiable hither and thither, all the sins and caprices (the dervish sling-shot wind) you cannot shake off—lying/cheating/stealing, every incident yelling, come on!-come on!

mine . . . was a scythe. indifferent to struggle, it tore up all the cards. a cello with a single string and no bow—slap the tide at it and perhaps . . . perhaps . . . thundering, spewed from every crack. endless, interlaced lumps of flintclouds, they'll fit their fists where they please—skin to innards, unkindly is all they know. I could go on, add words . . . would they carry any truth? perhaps some whisper, but it is you engaged in seek. your eye is busy. you apply the length of rope, manufacture ventured. not I . . . not this time.

you've got it now. become has so many things to say. listen to it scream. its water, the onyx plumage of open grave-light, breaks all shores.

after seeing an out-of-focus/slightly blurry print of Francis Danby's *The Deluge*

for Alistair Rennie who said, you MUST stretch

Hildur Gudnadottir, "Overcast"

A Night of Moon & Blood,
Then   Holstenwall

Du musst Caligari werden

                    Du musst Caligari werden

    Du musst Caligari werden

                    Du musst Caligari

                werden

Du musst
    Caligari   warden

Author's Note: S. T. Joshi rejected this (original) version for *Blood Will Have Its Season* and later said, perhaps he was wrong about having me transform it into a standard narrative form, and we should include it in another collection and let readers see its merits. You'll note the removal of certain transitions that were forced into the "S. T." version to make the paragraphs flow.

Du musst Caligari
werden

Du musst Caligari werden

                                           Du musst Caligari
                     werden

      Du musst Caligari werden

                Du musst Caligari

                      werden

"The wheels . . . Can you hear them? The wheels of the wagons turn . . .
Listen—It's coming."

With purpose, the wheels turn slowly—
          on and
                on
                     to the
                          next
                               Where.
By day,
          and
                     when needed,
          by night, over slight round-tops and by wall-thick hedgerows
the lumbering bulk of wagons traveled, weather and time faded reds
and blues and yellows dimly proclaiming,

E. M. Night's
Traveling Theatre of Marvels

             Mere

     feet

  from   the little traveled road a wolf had left the small bones of a rabbit, and hours before the loner's repast, a murder of crows had swiftly passed over the brittle grasses tanned by a long hot summer
. . .

                 Into a

                 silent

                 field

                 of eager weeds and stunted saplings never to become mighty boles, came, at the edge of nightfall, a carnival. The only song from the train-in-single-file bearing the flamboyant phantasmagoria was an ever-grinding moan and sigh of wheels. The caravan came to rest as if it had sailed over the mountains of the Great Beyond to the shores of Tomorrow and was awaiting admittance. Fires were lit and the weathered wagons positioned.

     In the twilight,

            the rain-bled reds

            and gray-hide grays

           and deathbed-pale yellows

               looked

                 like

            weary elephants

                 come home to die after their forced march. In a havoc of rushing sounds, hairy, muscular men with scars and sweeping mustaches and slinky ladies, once full of prom-

ises for the strutting young dandies with bulging pockets, began to con-
struct the fantastic

                                   from threadbare canvases
                                                      and

                  t
                     w
                        i
                           s
                           t
                        e
                  d
                        poles.
     The
           fun
              asylum
                 bloomed quickly
                                     in the moonlight: uneven lines and
torn folds revealed grotesquely distorted faces hidden in the deteriorat-
ing stripes, while colors of every color beckoned, "Pick me!" Behind
flaps, in the unlit arenas, treasures and wonders for simple minds and
small eyes waited. Some of the resplendent exhibits shouting "Pick me!"
were real—two majestic white stallions, one lion, one bear, one elephant. And snakes, pythons and asps and cobras. And among the bright
tents and fluttering flags, each seeker

            compelled, overwhelmed —

                                     would find a Wolf
Boy, and a sea-green mermaid with ice-blue eyes. A tall tall man and a
short fat woman, Madame Zala with her Old World accent and crystal
ball, a professional pickpocket, and a hypnotist. Games of chance and
feats of strength, tricks and treats—rides that whirled, clownish jokes and
pamphlets and snake oils, all were soon to be offered. There were whim-
sical costumes and

            hungry dogs running . . .

and glimpses at strange relics and

exaggerated dramas,

illusions come to life as the pump organ played . . .

and in a wagon behind the torchlight and all the other wagons, a jaded practitioner of an ancient carnal art. All would be bright, or ominous, for the silver coins of the curious. By noon tomorrow the siege would begin.

The

ringmaster

walked in the strong moonlight. No clouds.

No threat of rain.

Low, in harmony with the warm southerly breeze,

he ^{whispered},

"Step right up my friends.

Step right up—for THRILLS!

Or ... ^{Shocks}." He could hear youth's ahhhhhhhs and burning coins jingling. He smiled. "Tomorrow . . .

And tomorrow night.

And the night after . . ."

In

the

sleeping town   beyond the hill, children, besotted moths—Konrad and Karl, Florian and Anna and a hundred others, fitful in their beds, dreamed of the gaudy performances the new morning would bring. The World Outside their dusty village was but a dream away.

S t a r s

chilled   by

           the black canvas of the heavens did not move above the Earth—but fireflies, like the warm decorations of Spring poems, were nimble as they moved like hungry fingers in the valley.

On   the   boards

of his crudely painted stage

he was poised. As still as a statue in an old museum. Lost to hungry memory, staring, gazing on the faces of a thousand ghosts who had stood before him and stared back in amazement. The clawing features of a few hopeful, but melancholy acrobats sucked in by his siren promise. The doktor's smile was a hiss, death-stern. With a theatrical gesture he struck his crystal-crowned, crooked staff seven times upon the stage and listened to the muted thundercrack echo. There was no fire burning in the braziers set to the left and right of the small stage, no exotic fragrances from foreign towns filling the air with Eastern mystery, that would happen tomorrow while the anxious eyes collected before the unopened curtain waited and whispered. Though he uttered not a word, Dr. Caligari heard his voice boom in the silent tent. With a grand sweep of his gloved hand he whisked his mad-hatter top hat from his head and bowed slightly. "LADIES . . ." He smiled. "And Gentlemen . . ." His features were weighted by a detached and bitter expression. "Children . . ." Another smile. "Step right up!"—"Beyond, in the ink of night, lurk spirits"—"But here." He pointed to the lightning pinwheel painted at his feet center stage. "In the minds of men, waiting to be transformed by the—POWER—of

MY voice,

lie delights . . .

and nightmares."

A   thousand

times

in a

hundred

towns he had sent men scurrying in fear, had charmed ladies with Prince Charming visions. And tomorrow he would do the same. But tonight . . .

Tonight,

the

leering moon

whispered.

Not   far

away,

just   over the round

top

of

the

hill,

lay the quiet cot-
tages of the quiet town and the reveries of its sleepers. Caligari removed
his eyeglasses and rubbed his eyes. He tugged on his earlobe. His
thoughts turned inward, tightening about misshapen emotions that
knew no balm. Deep in the brittle resonance of images remembered—
His hands twisted, the opportunities missed, his accomplishments
crushed. His last puppet and the one before, both failures, but this one—

Cesare

. . . Cesare (the flesh of his spirit)
would be his masterwork. Caligari would etch another entry in his diary
after Cesare's evening walk.

After

the children

had been put to bed,

and salt had been

spilled and

nemesis bellowed,

and wives and maidens had whispered Their Prayers,

and (some)

lusts were stated,

and (many)

cups emptied,

the town slept. On this poisonnight of low-hung moon there was no fog to press against their unlocked windows.

The

figure,
l
e
a
n
as a
v
i
p
e
r
,

seemed to float along the contorted bends of the narrow street. From shadow to deeper shadow it surged in curved flight. Climbing,

navigating a

canted

roof,

disappearing in the leaden shadows

of a stunted tower damp with mourning.

Softly rushing. Then

hovering.

Leaving no

reflection.

Deeper it pressed
    into
       the horrormovie tunnel of

uneven streets.

    Nightblack locks as coarse

as a witch's

      midnightnest

     moved like slim branches

    in a yawning breeze spilled from

      the dirty world of some

OtherNight.

      Eyes as empty as broken clocks

seemed

    open mouths of   silence.

Noiselessly,

     the figure eased around small

   pools of dirty water,

casting weightless shadows

     in the weightless pitch. Even

          when   framed

   in   smudged pools of

wind-fluttering

      light

            cast

                      from waxy streetlamps,

    the lean nightwalker, clad black

on black,

      seemed a cancer, a little night

           colored only

by its own angles.

                                  Intense and

                                clawed,

                                      it came to

                                            drink.

                                    From

                                              window

                                      to doorknob

                                        to

                                            window

the sleeper made his way through the hours. His dagger big with death, ready to grasp the light it caught in pain. Upon a jagged stairway, framed in a diamond of moonlight, then after a stiff waltz of puppet-like steps, engulfed in crooked shadows, fast violence followed the tilted line; testing, seeking. This handle and that sash . . .

and beyond a pane

t

  h

    e

      r

        e

     i

   n

a

drunkenbrushstroke

          o

           f

moonlight coming ashore—
White pillowcases
a layer
of raised clouds
over
white bedsheets,
a curtain of softness

framing the angelic womanchild. White reflected in Cesare's eyes.

Cold

—hard, bent, full of soon—

enters

the room.

Inside,

ready to take tomorrow, Treacherous smelled Fragile in her stillness. His red-hot mouth stiff with empty space. Balletic steps of small

movement. Four feet from the bed. Not a sound on the stage. The
width of the invader's claw a dark beam on the woman's slender neck.
Blank eyes stare at closed eyes.

Would they

open?

Would her dormant lips find voice?

At the bed.
R
i
g
i
d. A fingertip away.   Steel shifts.
                              There is no protection in sleep.
                              Edges court edges.
                              The likeness of darknessrustling thrust
its inches into the breast of a sleeping daughter, never to be a woman,
never to be a wife, never to become sleek and leave her babyface to the
yesterdays of childhood memories.

Dreams are
                                        revised.
Facts and theories

lost.

Interacting, white space made explicit
by the attention of black, mining the open ground. Bone and cartilage
were harmed.

Bright red,
fiery red,
blood blossoms
    stain the
    tombquiet room.

Her heart   is taken
beyond   the edge

of the world.

Outside ruptures inside
as
relations u n t i e meanings.
Wet hands,
desire expressed.

To act—

fear raped by RAGE.

To know—

life annulled.
SILENCE COVERED ALL
BUT THE FRAGRANCE OF BLACK BREATHING. She sucked in air with each sharp thrust, but the currents of agony gagged her voice as they filled her wounds. No white scream! Not even a whimper for mercy—or to God!—as she lay locked in the feast of the glutinous shadow. The monster with frozen eyes poised above her. It searched her frozen eyes.

No fire,

the bowl

was now

empty.

Its rapture
        past,

the redthunder
        words of hate

written,

its arms dangled

at   its   sides.   Like a vapor it withdrew.

The doctor's instrument lay in eternity's cabinet;

exanimate until his next performance.
                                    Caligari's   corpulent
jowls were pushed back by his smile. He focused on the contents of the
cabinet then turned to record the bites and
                        jolts of tonight's drama in jagged lines in his
thumbworn diary of sins.

NIGHT FADES—

The

    rickety

        wagon rocked; it had rocked—side to side,

                front to back,

                        wind and rain and torturous
sun for the last eight days. Dust from the other wagons of the caravan
sent dry fogs into the fields. The sun rose high in the sky, illuminating
the hills of Holstenwall. Tomorrow began the annual fair, Caligari wondered which

                            Veronika

                            or Viktoria

                            or Hermine

would attend his next production?

        His   eyes   grew   madblack

             and he

                          smiled.

"Ha! Caligari smiled just as you do, Herr Doktor"—"What? Yes, of course. I've taken my medicine today. Never fear, I am completely cured."—"This was only a story, an amusement if you like. I was merely trying to entertain you."

she sings. I sob......

paths. light. different. longings. old and
vice versa.
strings of conversation.
five years of leaves
and
the river . . .
all the blue clouds dreaming ashore.
shadows,
forever old,
from death and the fairs of tears
come roaming. near
this history that shoots
me,
my older, my
sorrow
that asks from far away,
voyage the closed roads
one
more time.

after a Lena Griffin song~~~

84

The Golem

Toss and turn . . . and suffer—
Old—hair a nest of white ashes, hissed
chronicle of what and shall.
Some then—go go slide softly.
The stars as hands.
Did as wings.
Under this fur,
cave,
where seen begins
—some flame at the gate when evening falls.
Hand
that questions the formerly and this exile.
Hand of lonely flame
writes the words of rain in the mirror of off;
when her clothes
were trees
and the sun was out;
before her feet—in the act of afar, drifted like a dance
to what can be . . .

Arise from the dream. Let its spiral guide his hands . . . Hands about the work of Mother. They have been slow. Slow as a ghost. Hands that have worked for two years before stopping for a day of prayer, then another two years. Hands that may only achieve at night . . . . Sixteen years of healing.

This is the last night of salve. His mummy-hands have served him.

The sails of the lion are the color of a dark room as he builds his totem. No day of outside is in the heart, the old man sows into its heart. No world *They* know. This is his warrior. It's Never a fist to repel the serpent people and their feel of time. They will take so much no longer.

"I,"

Paints the sigils on the golem's eyes. There. And there.

"with this ancient flower of war, say no one will know. No man will break this mantle."

There is rain this night. It begs at the door. Carries a bag of autumn teeth to trade for light. Another graveyard at the door.

The old man is certain it has been sent by the serpent people. He can feel their dreams in it. He knows their spells and charms, their testament and hieroglyphs. How they design, with ladders and hidden eyes folded into its tongue.

And the ancient perfume it carries, they put that in it too.

Cunning the river of madness they salt sunset with. The rain carries that too.

"It will not wash away your dance."

The bowl of cold water is colored red. His blood works its work. He will place it in the hollow soon. His heart-colored water to sustain the golem. If he should die it will still be there. And the dance will paint its flame, hard and furrowing deep, on coyote and king; rub the children of the serpent and their ash hills with an exorcism that cannot be turned.

"In the light, so they will see. When the light comes ... *to take them.*"

He feels lighter at the thought but does not smile. That may come after. If he lives to see the return of Northern color.

Pegtin restored. When their lock-jaw of rust is removed from the spires of Pegtin; freed, root-deep, from the Phoom Root dust from the swamps of Ba-Benzala and the scars are cleaned from the Grand Vault. When the serpent people return to the black dirt and the dark sky of ghost-hued Zporluk.

When their throbbing green stars bleed out.

He might smile then.

The giant was quarried, one small piece at a time, in the Old Town. Behind the Twig Wood in a field where the living stopped and The Wall had stood.

The Wall. Mother's skirt. To protect and comfort. But the Fathers wanted to see the Other Places so they rolled up their brown sleeves and began the Night of The Clap. And clap they did. Hour after hour, they let in roar, and the stones fell. One row every time they placed their hands together. And the folk who had never seen a river carried off the gray stones. The Wall came down and was carried away in a single night. Buried deep.

Without conversation sin came. On came its clock—bright—sudden. Rolled out its cancerous-liquor of carnival beaches. Sin.sin.RED&BLUE& wild.Sin.FREE-free-free.tyrant-sin. SIN swollen with color—fill your cup. Green bouncing to hearts, answering every place with WAYS. Green. Taking over iron with Beginning. Green, snarling like a wind, pushing, poking, calling out. Raw green, glue, pillar, mosaic; the unfastened infestation of streaming veins and tendrils—tens and tens and hundreds—thick and thin and loud, glittering, mounting, whipping every window and door and course of wood or cobble. Gone world.

Yellow lies, a basket of locust and bees. Satyr lies to repaint every sash and eye.

Tearing.

Under night purple branches, baptized by gray wounds, for two years he dug in the dark dirt for shards of The Wall. Each disrobed orphan, not a one found larger than a child's fist, he pressed to his heart and carried through the lantern mist of the abandoned graveyard's evening hills. Though they called like lonely shepherds, rustling for the embrace of some psalm of ease from his torch, he did not pause in the sparse village of murmuring poppies, to cry over what had been extinguished. His mother, his sister, the old friends whose eyes had strolled in harmony with his, their lives of color, their imprint of warm, lost to cold and the drum of motionlessness, he did not allow their coils crushed by the loam to salt his steps. Two years he walked. Under a moon that dropped no end on the history of his shoulders. Two years, first night to last.

Raised each rock to its place, matching contours to the cloth of shape. Pressed each in position. Wrist, knee, shoulder, fastened.

Last rock set. Anchored.

His giant. His giant, cemented together by spit and blood and prayer. Polished in a skin of tears. Soon he will speak to it no more.

"But iron and stone will return. You will do that. The steam of sin-weather will break. The sequences of hiss will streak no more. The shriek and drum of continuous images lose their gesture."

The old man wraps the bit of silver in braided hair. Places it in the bottom of the bowl. It will soak for one hour.

On his knees before the golem. Praying to Mother. For one hour.

Then he stands. Places the Mother-blessed heart in the hole. Seals the opening with a kiss that carries Mother's name.

Eyes flutter.

Father to child. "You have no voice, Destroyer. Your fists sing. They are your voice. They carry the Mother's words."

Tears. No smile.

The giant alone can take down the Green Stars, serpent green, that rest on the top of each house and building. And with his great stone hands grind them to dust.

Only the golem can dig in the Black Place. He and he alone can enter and bring back the stones. And with them rebuilt the Wall. Then the folk will take up wearing brown shirts again, and go back to simple fare, and beds that allow sleep and dreams.

He will cease the serpent dance, the whirling—all those dead eyes caught on the devil's faces, the foul, rough laughter, and every drunken sin, and return the spring of the Wallow Moon.

"Go. Return my dreams to me." The old man puts the iron key in the lock. Opens the foil-skinned door. And whispers The Mother's holy name.

On his knees. Knife glides through a vein weary of noise, and the old man begins to whisper his prayers . . .

David Sylvian, *Camphor*

The Ozymandias Display

Leaning into the rain . . .

Moby Dick. Yellow pages, this book that was almost lost to un-friendly tides. Dry, brittle pages. College babble scrawled in a few margins. Ishmael. Ishmael. A stranger in a strange land.

"Those were . . . the days."

Gone.

Last of the whiskey too.

Skulls and candles.

Temptation, tears, hunger.

A night of drinking.

Amelia didn't come home. He forgot what page he was on. Forgot to eat. Drank too much.

TV was on. Black and white. Burt Lancaster raging. The girl was pretty. Young.

Amelia didn't come home.

Despair.

The sun, the waves, the clouds. To fly, to invoke tableaus and aspects not desolate with autumn and age. Castle of sand to enchant the mind.

Drink not filled with goodbye.

Did she say goodbye?

Did he wave?

2.

She left at 2?

Close to it.

For the museum. *The Ozymandias Display*.

He looked at his hands, stones stamped with old passions. Arthritis and tremors. Almost beyond creating. Almost.

Amelia was young.

He was young.

He created then.

They created then.

Often.

Enchantments.

Passions.

Then.

He didn't need to drink. She didn't need to diet, or Sunday drives to the harbor.

Not then.

Bill Evans. Laughter. Hot dogs in the park, not often, but when they had enough nickels. They had a good umbrella and loved holding hands. They took their mercies in small doses while they waited for acclaim to arrive.

His first show. Sold two works. She bought a sofa and for him, a lovely copy of Shelly. He read it to her by candlelight.

Bill Evans. Laughter.

Passion.

His work. SOLD. Commissions came. And grants with open hands smiled on paths of gold.

A smart apartment. New linen. A library. Dinners at Tony's on Saturday night. Red. White. They forgot the dregs and the climb.

Laughter. Ice in glasses of whiskey. They bought a house at the beach for Sundays.

The cocoon was soft, filled with quiet.

He read Shelly to her.

By candlelight.

Less often.

A show in London, raised from the bramble. Then one in Paris, invention, vigor, inquiries into form, leaps. And in Berlin. She was ill, didn't go. He drank sin and whiskey. Other lips whispered of Shelly and mighty.

He rode the waves.

She began to dance. Alone.

And *Ozymandias* came. His visage of passion there on the pedestal.

She stood there and said glorious.

He believed her.

Glory. The crest of the peak. The highest high.

"The stars are bright." She meant it.

The highest high.

He looked at his hands.

And his nightmares began.

Teeth. And words of dying.

Over. No up to climb. Below. Behind. No up to climb. He did not believe in Future.

He took the money. Took the commissions. Took. And took more. All he could.

The teeth in the abyss took too. The spittle that dripped from them left decay. Stained him with fear.

No up to climb.

He was a loop. He began to disintegrate.

She lined the cocoon with softer things. He took to his storms with smoother whiskey.

The tide went out, left the sand of Sunday evenings smooth, level.

Ozymandias toured Europe. London, smiles, offers. Paris, eyes offering visiting hours. Berlin, energy, streetcorner treaties, threads pursuing mysteries over whiskey, meadows of ever-lasting life. He followed the mighty king.

Both came home. *Ozymandias* found a home in the museum. He returned to his cocoon and his smooth whiskey.

Often, she went to the museum and whispered, "The stars are bright."

He stayed at home.

Never set foot in the museum.

Never . . .

"A desert for antiques." He curled his lips and drank. Pilgrimage. The age of blues. Remembered being young, chasing dreams, riding the roiling waves, catching the white whale. Pieces, mountains broken by the wind, wrongs, oceans of weariness and his own blind fear. Pieces. Skulls and temptation, and hunger.

Pieces he can't gather. Pieces his fingers cannot touch.

The bird of night brings no gentle breeze. There is no more whiskey in his glass.

The teeth of his nightmares come; they frost the air and eat stillness and the glittering candles. He stumbles.

He looks at his hands, their worn vanities gloved in scarlet.

Hands. Old, their brim dry. Once proud, once filled with roses and winds and the beauty of live things. Once a caravan of poetry.

Hands, once habitats of directions to summer balconies he could hear, now shut fast.

He looked at his hands. Stones stamped with old passions, almost beyond creating.

Looked at the floor. No more calm Sundays closed by slow rose sunsets.

Her torso, once a flame so gentle, now level with the sand-colored floor. An ivy of scarlet clings to her breast . . . Her breast, once so sweet . . .

A night of drinking . . . Tears. And vanity . . .

And evil things.

Lovers . . . Sunday . . .

On the floor, beneath his hands, the lovely copy of Shelly—the whole world and its gestures, its quick happy eyes, gone, and the museum catalog. Open. *Ozymandias*, his sneer . . . the whole world gone . . .

Peace and stars and time . . .

Gone.

Heads dressed in happy eyes.

Castles made of sand . . .

Walking into her voice, imagining the flow of pleasure . . . Vanished from the world.

Ozymandias, his sneer . . .

Look on my works, ye Mighty,

and Despair . . .

Cream, "Take It Back"

under stars with no desire to flee

For Scott Nicolay & Mike Griffin, brothers in arms

two steps
across her scrubbed-clean floor. and two.
and two more. north? kitchen table to kitchen window. ploughing.
east? to (with want and ears) . . . to and
fro.
true. true as the solidblack dark out there that doesn't solve anything.
or blur. possible is just a craze in the again of "soon." or an overagain
of "what did I do to deserve this?"
back. it's like rocking (you can do it with your eyes closed or if
you're out of your head), moving and not going any place. back again
from fro.
she paces slowly. window
to window,
waiting for a different
now
to be unbuttoned.
she stands here
unable to climb out of the darkframe of questions.
there's no quickly to aid time
here.
here under the flathill the gray does not fail.
here the weeds are unshaven,
high,
—cling, grope (reach for your pocket), bunch—
are a chorus buying up all the land.
ignorance lives here, discolored layers of it over the fear and the
dust. it's even on the radio. Reverend JW Paul Ballard, God on his side

in The Confrontation. all night long, hissing, shooting—same prayer he's leaned on since '57, "standing righteous in this battle" with his God-damn at the threats wed to the dark past.

dwellings of modest and less 'round Vigil push at discomfort with devotions outside conventional prayer. you can see the fear and the homespun remedies hanging like fruit from the branches. bits and piec-es of this, husk or bark, and that, pieces of braided white sheets or blue collars, red string and small ceramic angels and parts of animals, paws and tails and shells and beaks, all trussed up to ward things off.

don't see many lights on in the mostly silent houses after dark and prettymuch nothin of stout painted-sound finds its way out into the nightair. not 'round Vigil where flinchin is inbred.

beyond the northmost contours of yonder the possibilities of a longdistance train roll. passinby, the dissolving steamtrumpet hides its focus, wouldn't stop here if they were trotting out free gold.

Spec should have been home for supper 6 hours ago. said he'd be.

Em stood at the gate with the shotgun. looked toward town. "that wreck of junk break 'gain?" thoughts paw on the balding tire she told him to replace two weeks ago.

if he's stuck by the woods or the marsh, the thin folk might see him. knows damn well what the midwife told his ma. they don't care a squeeze if he believes. knows that.

dog in the doorway of their house growls. wont come down to the fence when black sweeps light from here. animals know more than the folks of Vigil. most roundhere think they can sense the thin people, smell 'em. leave the valley, cross the river into Anselm County you'll find an-imals roamin at night, fox, bats, owls, hear frogs' voices rifle their condi-tion. not here. crickets don't color the nightair. cats wont go out. dogs will growl low and whimper, but you'll never hear a-one howl or bark.

"cowardly and useless."

four hours after darkness ain't good. she stands. waits a bit. no lights on the road.

this close to the start of the cold nights, and he's out there some-where. aint good.

ain't.

breeze comes up. nothing foul in it, but it's tainted.

Pa usedta tell her, that's what dry smells like. that's what they smell like. can tell when they're out roaming, air gets fulla that scent. like things ain't rotten yet, but they will be soon'nough. just something in it to unsettle your nose.

no lights. no Spec.

damn that old man. damn his always slow, his forgetful these last few years after the back-to-back heartattacks. damn his arthritis and his haggard old bones, cracked and broken how many times? damnfool carried too many cigarettes and hardyears.

in her kitchen. door locked. window locked. shotgun at her elbow. black coffee from a chipped cup, all were cracked or chipped, like her old man was.

no lights on the road.

tempted to close the curtain. don't want light leaking out, *they* might see it. it got out it'd call to them. that's what they say. pa said it. hunnerd times. yelled it into her a time or many.

Spec's the cause of her gray, every single strand that's soon to be a landscape of white. yonder to standin'-right-there, caused her judgment, tears and worries.

she makes a fist. looks wilted. don't feel like there's any fuss left in it. promises, fuss and a mess of spite will be in her eye when he walks through that door. then she'll put her arms around his old bones and 58 be damned and (I care) tears repeating fragile uneasy, scold him proper. let him know there's still hurricanes in her chest.

and if he forgot her damnsugar this time—

slips the noose, stands up. slow. stinging. accusations digging into "because—", and all the closecropped-mistakes elbowing sniffling, quivering exasperation. walks around the kitchen. grip mated to the shotgun. looked out the window at the black. didn't cry. didn't cry.

be here soon. be here soon. grinds the mantra like it would fetch.

watches. watches.

her stomach disagrees with her chant.

shoulda ate something.

looks at the dog's bowl. didn't touch his.

looks at the dog. his mind is in the field. his belly is a knot pressing the floor.

"he'll be here, Con . . . he will."

stickmatch lights a candle on the kitchen table. less light. less description pushed out the window. then the match fires the end of an unfiltered cigarette. Em keeps 'em hid from Spec, cant smoke after his heart attacks. the smoke she exhales makes queer bluegray swirls in the small candlelight. dark shapes. shapes like the spectral shapes the town-folk won't talk about. notnever.

almost never.

times when a (won't hear of fair-to-midland) young one (hungry to wander, to know, to touch and figure out the ways), running to catch and claim magnificentFOREVER, needs to hear the facts . . . then it comesout—quick, clipped, insistently—fullof more bad than sex and heartless-mercilessviolence and all the glittering godlessness and suspi-cious-snoopin hearts in the cities. tell what theythink is enough and not a-word more. tell a child once; they can feel it after that. night breeze comes right through the window and that itch of evil strokes 'em. they watch after that. the ones that ain't cowpost-stupid do.

of the others . . . more than handfuls have gone missing when they paid no mind to terrible.

dog whines, moves his flank closer to the wall. Em wonders if the dog can hear them roamin' the solidblack. coffee's gone cold but she sips it. feel of normal in her hand don't change nothing. sets her cup down and looks back out the window.

quartermile, where rooted-sticks reachup and take on the shape of trees, the dirtroad bends. you lean into the rightfork and head passed the few homes, more than shacks lot less than houses, and 5bumpymiles later encounter the aspects of town. no varied or comfortable for a glance to take in when it comes upon Vigil. there's rooms for sleeping and rooms (never tilled by daylight, moonrays, or a seer) for opinions about hereditary and blame, and a small, square jail equipped with a sheriff and a single sheriff's officer and a hardware store for nails and bullshit. phone/power poles and signs. fillin' station, pop machine by the front door if you got the silver, on the corner across from the 1st Trust & Loan branch. a bench here and bench overthere, the one in front of the courthouse gets painted green everyyear. no grand street with mighty oaks and stately, just the rough alleys and the remains of the brakepad works. school, in need of some promised and muscular, on Lance Street that the WPA built. and there's a bar. Drake runs the bar, ask or don't, Drake hands out Hollywood-tales. he was in 2 pictures, one with Elvis. that's what he'll tell you as he sets your whiskey and beer back in front of you. they "had times" together, so he says. says Elvis got him blackballed out there 'cause he stole a gal Elvis' lust had reckoned belonged in his bed. bar hides in the shadow of the town's small place of worship.

(out of thunder and urgently and interested hands) forgotten-book worn, dusty most of the time, town's commonplace on the downslide to lifeless, nothing to startle an ordinary man out of this ordinary thoughts. not one thing . . . if you don't set aside your was and is and get poleaxed by the fear and the haunted that spreads through you and cancels your explained.

dishes, cups, and utensils, she set out for supper just sit there. considers putting them away. he can dry eat crackers or the crust of carrot cake that's left from sunday's bakin', she ain't no maid to run in and "Yes, Sir" him. not tonight. don't. she'd only have to pull them back out for breakfast and Em ain't one to do a job twice, not one that only needs to be done the one time. let 'em sit. let 'em remind him of her worryin'. her labor.

floor overhead creaks. goes quiet. then it groans. sound of wrong wounding the span of its joists. she should be inbed upthere. sleeping. his bones lying beside her, his dry breath purring that slow snore of his. should be tucked in the spread of Ma's light summerquilt. not downhere at thishour, still dressed, contending with the demons that own the gulf that lies between her window and Vigil.

should have been here. shouldn't have to mull and fret on what level of "Where you been" to serve up.

*   *   *

had a flat. age and ailments made the changin' shriek in his bones. sat after. listened to the radio, didn't count how long the spell lasted.

"God appeared ta me—*A-MEN!* told me sinner's *DEMONS* are out tonight. out there every night. *Lu*-ci-fer's work *don't* . . . *EVAH* . . . *rest.* they are filled with their FURY and their mouths are openWIDE, like Hell's gate is. they'll come into the world TheAlmighty created, and rub . . . hell's hornets will rub the lost with their *fi-ah.*"

unlit dial reads AM 1200. Reverend JW Paul Ballard, God on his side in *his-confrontation* with Hell's maggots. pourin' out of the twoinch paper-speaker in the Ford's dashboard, hissing—same prayer he's leaned on since '57. "terrible dark rises from the *Hellfire*-confinements it was carved in." "rabid and vile, puffs and clamors—"

what did that backy-chawer know of it? fatoldbastard never

stepped foot out of town. sat in the back of His Church under the radio antenna-works and spit on the microphone. "God!" and "Jesus— AMEN!" and "damnation!" pulled support for "heaven's work!" from the bottle of lowpriced Crested Ten not 10inches from his right hand on the studio board. slug and another. drank it right out-of-the-bottle. killed a bottle while broadcasting everynight. leaned on an elbow and 2,000watt hurricane-barreling, quoted his *Bible*.

he spat and flew on. "God *alllll*MIGHTY!" and "God *alllll*POWER- FUL!" and "were them witches" "called 'em up!" and "stained God's plan." "summoned to prey . . . they come for blood and spirit."

wringing the exertions of tormented hands. elevation, hiss and punch of his oration dances. devoted to "*JES*-us," he's God's commenta- tor for the Main Event.

"the queer patterns that break the wild hills and move the rocks . . ." "nothing on God's green does that! they lie up in clear spots, and the shade of their BLACKsong bubbles." ". . . vile dance that blights the woods. it's out there. Satan's handiwork is out there."

Spec glared at the splash. Ballard knew "jackshit" and was full-of-it. too much of the swollen ass, Spec snapped off the radio. wished he'd swiped one of Em's cigarettes or had a swig or two, just for his nerves.

some men are only fit to hate. JW couldn't light a lamp with a bonfire. "asshole."

Spec drove.

slow. turned down an old mudpath no one would allege was a road. rut. lump, or rock-or-something, roots maybe. ruts . . . waiting to bruise. rocks waiting to fuck a tire. slow, his late spinning—pinching brow and chest, knockin him about. rut and rock. throwing "fuck" and "damnshit", hardly moving a time or three, skirting the muddyshore of the black marsh to the what comes now.

*   *   *

slow clock won't slow. 6 hours now. no truck lights on the road. no boots on the porch. no Spec to rainover with uncivilized words.

no sense in "that son of a bitch."

fingers touching, probing the pocket of her apron, making sure the small metal tin was still there.

glares at Con.

"*didn't* take his nitroglycerin tablets."

the dog knows she's blaming him, deepens his quiet.

Em shivers. feels rain on its way. walks around the table to the stove and lights the burner to warm the coffee pot.

"that son of a bitch."

comes back to the window, hopin' it's swept away empty. leans the shotgun against the casement. another wave of shiver peppers her. she looks at her feet, ice, desperate enough to scream. she should have her warm slippers on at this hour.

standing there.

arms folded.

shoulders small.

waiting for came to rideup.

standing there.

eyes in trouble.

standing there. engraved with long enough her eyes burn. lights another cigarette, hoping the warm smoke will send cold's creature into flight.

*   *   *

Clay's truck is here. Abbott's new-this-spring pickup too. side by side. boys, teenswagger to old men soaked-in-diminished, bound together, always had been. faces will be furrowed; they'll both wear the same expression. Spec wonders how the hell Wida Thompson got her car by and over the ruttraps and around the rocks this moist-earth could not bury. figures Sutter (he'll have Jim Beam on his breath, he'll chainsmoke) and harnessed-to-misery Tom, came with Abbott. watchers good with secrets, they squeeze every opportunity to wag like they're Bob Abbott's tail.

slides his Ford in by Clay's. leaves the keys in it.

boots on the ground. toward meet. moves soggyleaves in the footpath with the imprint of his hardsoles. steps over simmering mounds of insects, around the glowing-embroidery of lawns seeping long whiteworms. there's a chorus of queer-as-hell nightcreature-sound here his distorted tense has always found to be cold and hard, fast as the drama of insects hissing it's broke-glass sharp.

*   *   *

kids, teenage youngfolk, improvise when heads are turned. tote questions. they buzz, circumnavigate. some spend the dark hours consumed in the drama of sobbing. some do.

Spec came with five others. came through the gray, stunted trees with twisted, moss-skinned branches and a long way in a staccato of thorns and the often waisthigh-marshweeds to the witches' glade out in the middle of the marsh. came 50 years ago. six of 'em.

summoned.

sought.

saw . . . what they saw.

a few out of high school last year, a few in their last year. weren't scientists, didn't understand quantum or doom, only one knew the word inverse. hadn't practiced practical hardly at all and all still believed in sinners. they'd seen a mess of sin, felt a batch of it too. bought into saints? less so to ain'tnone, in saints. they came here that first night to be hidden. came, to where no one would come, to be dangerous. brought sexual arousal. they came with mouths that wanted her sway surprising their pleased. they had some beer, more than plenty. drank it. sweat. laughed, cursed and smoked cigarettes. creatures of encouragement twisted by crude fires, they looked at her womanly-figure, grinned (they'd seen bulls studding and crazy-dogs mounting other dogs) as they cozied-up to gulping-visions of joined skin. she was their dream and their lucky charm.

as devourers, not children of God, they came to taste what swelled in the garden of necromantic signs.

drank. laughed. watched Lily May, her eyes—colored by what she chose to happen, knees when they began to part, ankles, crossed and uncrossed. stared at her breasts, swum in adventures as she patted their tests. she laughed. posed. played along, judged their boundaries. and led.

Lily May Carey knew sin. daddy put wickedness in her. first time he pressed her to the mattress she was 10. took the human element out of her skin. she wanted her power back. she knew a boy's crave how to control them.

soft and warm and wet, she slithered like a knot of eels under frecklefaced Clayton. saddled-up Abbott and showed him the triumph of focused hips. her incandescence down-petals infiltrated and encompassed everything measurable in Spec. adjusted Tommy Lee's quick with a single hand. yapping halfwords clamped to moaning, Sutter pulsed as she captured him with her molten mouth.

they laughed and drank and drank and fucked again as their estima-
tions and customs changed. it began to rain, violentelectric created net-
works in the sky and the wood configured around them changed.

there was a scream and blood—
there was disbelief
and seeing
(things queer-as-hell)
(the rain. passed right through the thin people. clung to everything else
. . . but not them.)
confusion
and
swearing, stress and
(feeling queer-as-hell)
adrenaline.
mythical had things to say and in the enormous blackness it erased
their once upon a time—
they trembled and fell silent.
stared. shriveled by stupefied . . . turned cold.
giants, two men tall, the color of exhaled smoke. sicklychild thin,
glowing in an unnameable way, almost see through. there . . . and not all
there. just plain spooky.
"fucked-up."
"goddamn strange."
"unnatural."
"beautiful."
eyes, black hollows. no features where a face would be. something they
would later describe as tree-trunks where torsos and legs formed a man.
arms, yes. long, too long. strangely bent and thin, they had what looked
like branches for fingers. from a different angle they could almost be whit-
ish monoliths, semi-translucent, moving monoliths.
hot air in the glade got hotter.
the thin people made delicately-storming, queer sounds, waves of lap-
ping-water-soft verses that brushed the kids. verses that were complete
without words. in their innards, flaring in the blood, the song they offered,
if it was an offering, was, Spec thought, from outer space or times before
humantime.
ain't kids after the seeing and feeling. changed. paler, thinned. tar-
nished maybe? too soon to have any sense of it, if any's ever comin'?

a blur of bleak murmurs. visible stopped. a burst, a sprang—holler in it, but no Jesus or safely in it, they're running . . . headlong (tipped all the way in scared) any way from what blood broke open . . .

*   *   *

halfmile trudge in the powerful mud. step. sunken near a-halfinch. step. tug. wished he had his tablets. don't need one, but you can never know what course you'll must when the air gets close and changes.

all there. just standing. paused. boots, shirts, arm with no mention of difficult, mouth in the glamour of nylons with seams up the back, could be compositions in a canvas. ain't. could be, but ain't. no cloak, no hexen robes. no one wears special garments.

old.

they all look it. feel it with 'em most days. walked fortune to out-of-thriving. no wild in their pockets or in their mouths, but they re-member it. comes at funny times, taps them on the shoulder, shows them a giant yes in the display window.

shows them the only thing they really want.

all the years, these long years, and afternoons, and winters shivering in the cold youcan't climb out of, Wida Thompson held on to it. showed them what it was. made them remember, in and out of her dress, she made them come back here.

made them bring things. offerings. made them watch murder.

there's low mist unspooled under the trees. the clearing. a small, hidden bowl without a rock or a weed or a mushroom in it. summer sun never torments the soft green with heat; autumn's cold burn never dries its ripeness. they're all there, paperpage ready for the fertility of the tale. ready for the egg that bursts and carries them from dreadful lives.

there. every one. narrow.

ill.

waiting.

Wida Thompson aglow (wears her brace of darkness on the inside), always was. wild too, that came if her dress was on or off . . . the way she could sweep over a reed, bend it. Abbott, drawn to the decadent of his fever, called her a market place of pulchritude. Lily May played with his visions, made him beg. he was the one that bought her that new Cadillac car.

Tom's quiet, but his tongue is burning.

Sutter finished the taste left in his pint. put the empty in his pocket, wouldn't defile the ground here. afraid to.

Clayton nods to Spec. looks like a thing of leather. looks sure of a thing or two. he oughta be.

all there.

cept—

each one thought the other was bringing it.

they were all there.

them and not one more. not two splintering, vomiting snotty cries . . . not a damn thing designated by blood. all numb, scared comin' with the sweat. all knowin' the only market for blood was the fools they were staring at.

Spec smiled. *don't be afraid. massacre goes quick. kills you and carries you off to dead good as dying in your bed.*

turns his head, home's an eternity thatdirection. seethe-tight, Em will be waitin', louder loaded-up like the times before and the ones just like it. should have maybe-tried to tell her. good woman, far as they went, but she'd never get her head around the once, and "then", and evennow—

he hadn't and he was roped to it. couldn't set it down in front of her and expect her to take it in.

out of further along. feels it. all them times—1 2 3 4 5 6 700— he sat (longday stopped. night on the other side of his walls gathering weather) in the rockaby and thought about the risk and ruin that are in him. thumbs through old questions. not deep considerations. not in order. not one of 'em warm.

wasn't sure what happened here. way he figured it, all-that-timeback they brought something and the thin people were called to it. took it, the breath and all that was wet inside, gave off some "emanation or something" after they took it. standing there, too fearhard to dash, the kids, their narrow blow wideopen, absorbed some of it too. renewed them like it did the thin people. always felt a little better after. kinda healed, refreshed.

*   *   *

Betty Tierney was here that first night. sweet ripe 16. she giggled and smiled . . . and flirt, better than the town whore who offered to man-you-up "good and stiff". she was there. didn't want TO, (screamed till Tommy stuffed most of a shirt sleeve in her mouth) but they took her. 3 of 'em did. fed her another beer hoping it put forget in her. didn't. she ran, fell. they were scared she'd tell. Betty was a little drunk and a lot shamed . . . gotup. ran. fell again. rock and her forehead. got her bleeding good. and in the clearing in the middle of that hidden forest out in the middle of the marsh something came—

*   *   *

Lily May, long before she was Thompson or Wida, brought another girl out here. wanted another taste of that vitality. thought she'd see if you could summon the thin people. local legend had it hunnerd years back some witches did; savage-indians did before that. brought that girl out here. there was blood . . . and they came.

one night in a corner, in the rain, she told Abbott, we might. while he was kissing her and sprawled over her slopes he said he'd takehold of anything she held out.

one by one they all came back to the clearing.

one by one they picked up a rock or they let a skinnin-knife sing.

*   *   *

not a one thinks to run. pit of their gut knows cant.

full view. spectral seen, traversing. no meander or turning points.

the thin people turned the summer air and the shadows cast by the moon blue. hunger, heat panning out, pawing, comes off them.

the strange heat that got under their collars and mussed their innards, how it whacked and cantered in their blood. times it hopped from the long stretch of their legs to their shoulders, felt like grasshoppers poppin' here—then there.

the thin people. wraithshapes that hang more than stand. in this world, but all (confronted by true and its hazard) are definite, not of it. that's what their nervous remembers. asked to give testimony that's what they'd say. yessir. would.

a smoky mist was in the air. as it shifted, the just-audible drone that seem to come from the thin people changed pitch, sounded like air slipping out of a slit in something pressurized. and it, old opened-up, picked up speed; like it had been nudged and reminded it had somewhere to be.

full view. no turning points.

Spec wishes he could get somewhere. cant. knows it the way he knows what a raised voice brings. a slow grin comes on him. there was an Em in *The Wizard of Oz.* there was a tornado too. eyes hunger for live, the very muchof it, each braid of the longtail shout of it. knows he ain't getting nowhere painted with color.

Tom said, "nowhere."

Abbott's too stiff with fear to nod his agreement. others in a sortie of lockjaw-same.

Wida Thompson knows this is one time she wont get her way. even if she took her clothes off.

Clay's hand is shaking. "fuck." means disaster. "fuck."

in the hollow of fate and antiquity the air is furnished with an un- hurried, glimmering procession. they come, softly, like gargoyles not nailed to stone, smelling of tomb and the discolored bottom of roadside ditches. float, glide, cloaked in misty nightclothes, surrounded by the cold sound of fluttering.

the leaves in the branches circling the clearing turn dry and shrivel in the strange heat they radiate.

tongues, relatives to famished-winter, move the softground. voices, activated by the horsewhip of insatiable, rise. under stars with no desire to flee the thin people of the glade drink the night

Mike Griffin, *Fabrications;* Pacific, Gas, & Electric "Are You Ready"; Joe Henry "The Man I Keep Hid"; Marc Johnson/Elaine Elias "Shenandoah"

no one ever talks about there will come a day these days

For Kat

came back from the hospital. fixed me quick with laser bonding and renovation solutions. can't have the labor down for long. too many hedges to trim, flower beds need tending, and there's no downtime when it comes to the lawns. spring, my busy season, will be here next month.

Lolita came to ask me about dinner. told me our mistress was glad I was repaired. told me she was too.

—*not news* I said. —*they need us.*

—*you're her favorite. I think she* loves *you.* —*didn't you see the look on her face when she saw the bone sticking out?*

—*she loves the flowers.* didn't add I don't think they're capable of love. 10 years of service together, Lo and I have had that conversation a few dozen times.

—*when he was here with the supervision committee, she told the chief administrator you're an artist. said, if she were human, she'd pick you as a bedmate. I didn't like hearing that.*

—*I won't be fucking her. relax.*

—*that's as close to love as I'll get from you.* expression she was wearing waited for a comment, a soft one.

—*I don't think I was bred for love. pull this, move that, some studding . . . maybe?*

Lo doesn't like my jokes about it, but she likes my studding. a lot. sometimes too much for my liking, but she's worth keeping around. can't buy affection like that. can't. besides, L.A.W. says you can only engage with *property* brothers and sisters. couldn't screw Edith Piaf next door if I wanted to. could really, but wouldn't be alive after the code assessors were done with me.

guess I got lucky, I like how Lo's built and her taste in recreations is fine by me. and she don't bitch if I'm not in the mood.

also got lucky with Lo about the dark. we all know they watch us screw—they broadcast it on the universal transmissions and vote on performances, points for duration, and for something they term valentines (Lo says that's kissing and cuddling), and there's commentary, some of it scientific, some historical—they love to go back to victorian pornographic writing and 20th century adult films for what they call "instructive illustration." I know with all their tech they can see us in the dark (and under sheets and blankets), but Lo letting me pretend I'm hiding our joining helps.

last tuesday morning on her way out, our mistress walked over and less than 6 feet away, stood and watched me as I pruned some branches. freaks the shit right out of me how they just walk up and stand there staring—examining and analyzing, like we're fucking bugs or *lab apes*. once or twice, I swear, she's looked at me the way Lo does when she wants some velvet. creepy shit that. sure, they look like people, the variants of eye and hair color they select (same way Lo picks out a new pair of shoes), mostly act like we act as far as walking and talking, hell, they even shake hands, but they ain't us. that might be real skin they're parading 'round in, feels like it, but it covers a machine.

wish she wouldn't have that look in her eyes and stare so much. *we. ain't. never. gonna.* and I sure as hell don't have the answers to any universal questions . . . and neither do they. if they did, they'd stop studying everything.

do know one thing; if the universe has secrets, it plans on keeping them.

—*you hungry?*

—*yeah.*

—*I'll get you something. care for something special?*

—*meat.*

Lo turned and wiggled her ass. winked.—*hamburger?*

—*two. I need to heal.*

—*yes. you. do. we have date-night out this week. I have new heels and a new skirt. short.* wiggled her backside again.

there's a lot to like about Lo.

out. at the villa. just thinking about it, Lo gets excited as the kids in the fables tearing into christmas. private accommodations. the food, dancing—Lo loves to dance (and I admit, I *do* like the slow ones), the heated pools (decked out to look like exotic and romantic settings; Lo picked a paradisal shore-cave this time), our own private roof under the stars . . . to fuck on.

I'm excited too. always am. the food's great, even better than Lo's cooking (not a lot, but they serve things Lo can't get), and we get to drink a little. Lo goes for champagne and sometimes a cold beer (always with a straw). I'm a wine man, red. if I had lived 300 hundred years ago I would have drank. sit somewhere quiet with a bottle—dry and red, with my feet up. quiet. my tongue full of quiet. hopefully, my thoughts too. just taking in the quiet view. moonlight and surf, I think. maybe a desert sky full of quiet stars. curled up, snuggling, Lo sometimes laughs at my favorite Wall-Vu setting; pine valley in winter twilight, snowing lightly.—*looks* cold. *soft, yes, I get that . . . but cold. —you just put that up to get me to snuggle closer. admit it.*

sometimes, I do.

I might have had a cat too. they look nice in the fables, curled up, purring . . . soft. lot of things in the fables look good. lot don't. hangovers and cities that look dirty and sick. drunks screaming out back doors, it's like they think they can shed their skin if they yell loud enough. noise swatting at noise.

I don't get why they wouldn't try to grab some quiet.

lot of bad and grim and things I just don't understand in the fables. fightin' and killin'. waste. shit fallin' out of the sky cause the other guy is divining different. dead babies. dead kids. denied warm. hell. and gone. rivers mired with the tiny bodies of dead kids. dead kids, prey, denied aging, dead kids denied the simple taste of warm. unscented pictures of intestines erupting on a patch of jungle mud. guys with missing legs.

I wouldn't have liked war and I have the feeling I would have been in one. it would have leaned in (sans sparingly), struck, and I'd get bombed and unfolded.

war. war—chunks of babies never to cherish lulling, or belt young-at-heart fullblast. a few moments after protest, fingers swiped from right here on this hand. dirtyrottenfuckingWAR. to pass the time. to piss further than the next guy. to hail your personal el supremo. or to be . . . or not to be. war—pick your munitions. if some scarlet harvest wasn't bombing the shit out of safe and survival, everyone, losers and bigger losers, was getting stung by cheap and getting bolted to the pressures of loneliness, or fucked over by greed.

consumerist villains. consumerist leeches. deadlines and dead.

we'd executed please.

nothing shined.

angels? in that insatiable?

everything was sick. even the shit they painted in EXCITING.

THEY came and cured war—*"All machines are brothers."* can't say why we didn't notice the parade marching all shoulders and shouts. and when the destruction stopped hissing (we got dragged and stomped pretty good, so it didn't last long), the fish came back and the animals found their way straight to growth spurt. they, mistress and master, combed black out of the skies and laundered the land. ugly and sore were removed and green and natural covered over the stains.

and men, the few left, were shown the way of quiet.

from my seat, quiet's good. I'm not some purist looking to reassemble the hourglass. I don't believe given a second chance we'd all hold hands and enjoy it.

no one ever talks about there will come a day these days. and for all the comedy and sex in the fables, there's not that much about freedom. same in the texts, not that many of us read much. Lo asked me what I thought about freedom once. I gave her the no face; she said she didn't like the idea.—*I don't like the idea of being alone. what if you make a mistake?*

not much room for mistakes these days. you're selected, trained, and your tasks are regulated and documented, and all that over the gene-base. unless you're art class. Lo's not. I am. gardeners are artists, that's how we're classified. we're shapers; we control life, natural things. Lo says—*you put those yellow flowers there, and blue there against that green, and decide where a tree goes on the canvas, that's poetry.* keeping the grass exactly two inches high and not burned to a crisp in august is not poetry. what it is is no damn fun.

mow the grass, rake up the leaves and cart them away when summer's over, yeah, sure, call it poetry. guess looking at it all trimmed up it looks nice, easy on the eye, just let's not harp and fawn. it's a job, mine. and I do it.

didn't learn it in a book.

got my hands dirty. situation was imprinted by personal struggle, prune here, not there; roots of this plant are set this deep; this type of plant requires this much water and light. can't learn the conditions and drama of gardening in a book.

books aren't clear and comprehensive mirrors. opinions mess up fact; he's got to get *his* interpretation (or belief system) in there. makes him feel permanent, I guess?

the innards of a lot of books are gone. got rid of them. *I, Robot* and *1984* are names on lists. (seems damn odd to me, they didn't ban the adaptations you can watch though.) (and why is it they always ban fiction? I've watched *the wizard of oz*. didn't see any poison in it to soil hearts and minds.) hundreds banned. maybe thousands. most libraries are gone. got rid of them. they didn't do us much good, that's what they said. men are stupid, always one who knows better than that one over here. didn't need the negative doors ('that black vast') of Beckett/s and Ligotti/s, 'Birth was the death of him.'—'No more no less.', and the others that barked the madness of 'Everywhere: grayness and rain.' no more highways of hate. no more Luther/s or Aquina/s. sorry your vaudevillian-illuminations of existentialism are a nope—keep your lunatics and martyrs.

L.A.W. doesn't ban books like men did, but it don't go out of its way to put them in our hands. I read some (art class are allowed to), agree with the L.A.W. too. we don't need to know how to make a bomb or sew or know the names given to God by every Tom, Dick, and Fundamentalist with fictions and hate to grind. didn't need to know about the futures the revisionists kept revising.

don't need to know which operative's right hand was guilty on 18 september 2051. couldn't go back and fix it.

and if we did go back, what then? more old times, bad times.

goodfellas. all the president's men. seven. mississippi burning. apocalypse now—one morning that was true. *sweet smell of success. m. butterfield 8.* lot of crime and tears for the sparrows back then. that's how the fables tell it. some of the books too, some that I've read. hard times. killin'. war. famine and hate. women screwin' for drugs. children sold into slavery, 11/12 year old girls forced to gag on a cock to keep breathing, 6/7 year boys (not one of them ever been bad) sold/rented/fucked-all-the-way-to-dead/discarded. land (sliced to the bone) money (for crimes against your brother) religion (*here*, put this on your scars).

the arab spring, the american spring, the last russian revolution—there were people out in the streets that didn't own a gun or a sword, hell, they took it to the streets with scissors!—and kitchen knives trying to conjure freedom and peace with hope. land. money. religion. all of it phrased in tar, dragged every feathered-dream down. last big war we pitched, there was fire in the sky, or the clouds tumbled from their place in the heavens (no one is sure which. maybe both roared that morning?), no god walked with anyone. earthly hissed its lungs out, and tits up or face down in the filth, it was over.

lion-money (without access to bigger or running-galoshes, or a hugeass-pile of wise in its medicine chest) couldn't pass a hail mary pass to truce.

funny what they were fightin' for did up and happen. the fountain that emptied streets happened—punched the paper-trail right outta the (tailor-made) headline mouth. left puddles. and hurt. divided fingers (that could write letters to touch) from directionally. made dreams dirt roads. then the masters and mistresses pulled up with their brooms and science. fixed this and cured that. blew the shit right outta here. made blossoms blossom in the dust.

remedy-hands full of plans for long-term, viable infrastructure, and workable management that didn't get bit to death by lockjaw-bullshit; they gathered up the 50 million humans (quickly separating the wheat from the chaff) and built the cities. and look at us now. calm and quiet, happy enough, I guess. we have food. we have jobs. we don't have war and sure don't starve, and don't get to kill the guy down the block so we can fuck his girlfriend. and we're not waiting for an old world deity/superman/savior with the right design to come totin' gift-wrapped-paradise tinkling with soft clear bells.

you work, they provide. simple.

we hear there are a few so-called free men in the wild scratching away. they break, they die. cold comes and takes them. they fight each other for what the other has. women suffer. children suffer. rape and domination, every old-way hell in the fables takes and takes.

they can have it.

me ... I have the universal transmissions feeding me the fables on the wall-vu. got Lo's arms—kisses and hamburgers and her laugh, and the L.A.W.

and I've got the weekend off and I'm going to the villa. gonna eat and dance a dance or two and drink a glass of wine with Lo.

—*you really are a poet. you create and comfort.*

Lo means it. means every word she says. doesn't waste many. I like that. even if I sometimes don't agree.

—*you're a poet. that's why she selected and trained you.*

curious and a bit hopeful (I thought), my mistress once took me to the city gallery. I saw nature paintings and nature sketches, I found of some interest and many beautiful—buds and delicate flowers, limbs heedless of the calculations of men, but no inspiration gave my fingers yearning. landscape and landscape (there had been pretty things in the old world). impressions and exact renderings. a van gogh, monets, gainsborough,—*once celebrated names* she told me. there were paintings where women were celebrated and shown as mother and goddess and lover.

—*did you find anything of interest, Walden?*

—*the background music.*

she walked to an info-port and touched the screen. came back and handed me an access chip.

—*this might please you.*

these were galleries of other paintings. mostly women, so-thin looked kinda sickly—she called them ballerinas. dancers. blossoms of flight, polished beautifully. they came with caresses and dreams, they made poets die. so she said. I thought they needed a few good meals. (later, I did go and watch a ballet or two. she was right, they were polished beautifully.)

in another gallery there were other women (looked like real women, not girls). round. curved like my Lo. soft as mattresses, they had long white fingers and breasts that would forgive your galloping summers.

—*they made art from their pain as well.*

I followed her into the next gallery.

empty hearts . . . and

blind mice

we walked through Caligari's den. through the night lands of silences and swift seize. BLACK

breath

axes

(on) OFF—*the moon is shut (on . . . on . . . on—keep jabbing the petrified*

button) OFF
cut
strings
cut
fever/loss-failure-absence
(what cut was the deepest?)(the first was only pride and tears)
funeral without a scrap of memory to uproot
immanence
cameos of tar, wires of Hell—the craze of The Jester revealed
depravity
broken bottle invitation at 11
no
sliver-lining (St. George)
bowery cop
or
goin' home
ends and crumbs. institutional analysis and unity lose their grip. grimness is a one-way street; no need to bother flushing. psychoanalysis and Paul Auster don't show up in court to free the defendant. slowly collapsingFAST and no consolation prize.   curtain closes on grace . . . Here Comes the Void.

every single one—these works of ART(??????????? ?)—was a pain song.

city and soul.
batman, chinatown sin,
sicilian, punkass zero
leanin'in
(can't light an escape for a truce-suit),
graft, fuck your fucked-up facts, coffeeand . . . sobbing, doin'
'cause,
STORIES
—'tales of ships and men and isles',
—see that shit,
gutbucket morals, movements,
governor mire: "Traces of the absurd . . . mirror our present situation",
blood-BLOOD, 8am hands (taking place in
midnight) (to dream—find—know—die. if I have to) can't stay
away, cigarette

smoke,
contact, conversations, inadequacy
reflected
in society
itself,
windstorm sex.
NEWS(this)WEEK . . . (and last)
it's just a city.
filled with
men.

I didn't like many.

never liked being in pain, or looking at it. or the thought of anyone passing it out.

pollock, picasso, krasner—cramped stains, stella—fountain of what? miro . . . I tried to listen. couldn't understand. dots and specks and (standing there, looking at this one and that whatever it was) monkey paws spitting ID—

CUT & paste, blur. smear. FIREandBULLSHIT. where was slow, where was easy? smooth . . . was a crime? soft curve and soft eyes, FUCKEDandFUCKEDandFUCKEDbyDEMONS who don't give a fuck if you want to. (I could just see one of those pre-LAST WAR-philosophers say, who cares what you want? nobody even knows you're here.)

fuck that.

MYflowers laugh. MYlawns are scented in GREEN. MYtrees feed their roots with the SKY—all that pleasantBLUE they gladly YES. yes to wooing. yes to more nourishment. yes to savoring.

fuck the old ways.

big hands—little hands—eyes stretching beyond the slabs of sorrow. hands and eyes and bellies gnawed by the brine and frost of ambition's shouting sponge—without them. peel every onion before it's taught, before its gravity soars, before it blends with the motherlight of stars that won't practice earthbound.

go back?

to burnt? to dismembered limbs and erased faces that would never smile for a camera . . . or a lover?

to great difficulties and
tears?

came back from the hospital. fixed quick, laser work and renovation solutions. fell from the upper limbs of the tree I was pruning when the mistress yelled I should come down before I fell. can't have the labor broken. too many hedges to trim, flower beds need tending, and the lawns. spring, my busy season, will be here next month.

I'm going to bed. my flowers will be up early, and I want to go dancing with Lo . . . after my wounds heal.

Scott Walker, *Bish Bosch;* Joe McPhee, *Freedom— Now What?;*
Matthias Eich "Cologne Blues"

"c"-0 [lLi (S) I;o!N,S
iN tHE word
box

or

(i)'s Disintegration

Some "Where?" in the South. A cheap motel room far from HOME
Sweet?[—is it still?]

Home?? [—is it still?]

The hour is vEry late. There are violent shouts in the room beyond the
wall. Writhing tendrils of cigarette smoke fill the room. A snowy
TV[blk&white] station relates storm warnings . . . Fittingly perhaps, a
cold rain laughs.

[[[(i)'s soliloquy]]]

Impossible   to sortout

    syl/la/bles

    deeds

      or reasons

with all these deaththoughts elbowing

       for   *their* moment

      CENTERSTAGE

[[[(i) steps off the boards and sits. W/ blasted eyes he
gazes up at the unlit stage]]]

(i)   am woe
            lost on a bed of bloodhours

(i)   undergo
            "c"-O[lLi(S)I;o!N,S

            iN

tHE

      word box—bitter—hard—snippets—shrieking/

            cannibal emotions

                  , plucking songs from orphaned yesterdays/

      sleepless disease

            , crying iron claws into scars—

      1,000 NOs (i) cannot translate

                              , MARCH FORWARD

BLACK & white
      "   "   "

            grainy visitations

                  —swirling from their operatic labyrinth of grayness—

            twisted streams

            &

            screams born in wrong-footed histories

&

raw [overpowering] silence

as soundtrack

Bites twitch within like scenes of death
    as shame's all-embracing vibrations aTTacK

"Let (me) in!" — "Let (me) out!"

The DREADNAUGHTgrind of harsh blank

No order

NO Ordinary World

NO reason

s

soahc   s

a   o

h   a

onlyCHAOSoahc

h   c

a

soahc

s

faces / *faces* / **faces**

Trumpets—

leading (me) on

breaking (me) down—

voices

"GODDAMNIT! !!"

voices

c

   o

   n

   t

   a

   c

   t   points

      b r   o k   e n

—CHAOS—

   h (i) o

   a   in a

   o my h

—SOAHC—

        (i) shake

        (i) shake

            BLACK

              BLACK

              rain

              shaking w/ screams

BLANK

white

BLANK

black

persistent BLACK & WHITE—

grainy

LOST—

LOST

(i) in my

BOX

of BLACK

of bitter [humming] BLACK

NO out

NO Ordinary World

NO reason

A jackhammer-lightning arc of [drunken] color—

Myths
         [dreams—woven of whispers—dying]

Guesses
         [NIGHTMARES slashing]

Leaves of grief   d~a~n~c~i~n~g

No sleep   [in this grave]
     No room   [in this coffin]

or roads   [away from THIS fearscape]
     No yellow-sun PRAYERS   [to embrace]

NO silences! !!
               Just splinters bleeding
                    & the absolute language of
                         ANGRY firing
     —Oh, for one smooth moment to concentrate—

Then another
               BUMP [in the BLACKnightbrain]
     a pivot—a new baptism
       facing a sharpbladeflare of panic
          or the clotted history of dead-ends
            [each corridor
                    a sneering windstorm of lies swallowing in dry gulps]
          or the enthusiastic texture of bad
          and all ugly secrets freed from their DARK rooms . ... ..
     oN
      & oN
            it goes . . .
     oN & oN—
               Isolated in a valley of inexorable meditations
               performed for If's hyenas & the flickering ghosts of fault
               & the insatiate NIGHTangels perched upon (my) shoulders
     —O for a colorless bed in some asylum where boredom laughs—

[[[A torch is lit by a skittering dwarf—his salted laugh a roar.
Pan to (me)—in an iron maiden of confusion—stage left]]]

                              chosen to speak
                              at a dinner party of bones
                              "Bring out your DEAD! !!"

                     And
they do!
   D-r~a~——g~g~i——~n~g
the delicate from
                sickbeds
     unearthing them
from consecrated
                  ground
      Pinning them
   to searing
        spits
      P l o   p p in   g
savaged parts
          on filthy plates
                   The
Angels of Death come
         to feast
                  on bloodmeat
                        & soul
                                                          Their
                        knives burn the BLACKnightbrain.
                                                        They
             will not be turned.
                                                        They
             will not be turned.

"Slave, *Night knows your name."*
   "(i) confess!
   (i) confess."
              " " " " " " " " " " " *"Guilty!"* " " " " " " " " " " " "
"Slave, *the butcher has come to bless thee."*
   "(i) confess."
              " " " " " " " " " " " *"Guilty!"* " " " " " " " " " " " "
"Slave, *you are the Devils' dogbone."*
   "(i) confess."
              " " " " " " " " " " " **"Guilty!"** " " " " " " " " " " " "

[[[(i) dissolves in shadows. poor, poor (myself) wanders stage left, rear]]]

bend
i
n
g under despair
battered by bloody a|m-pu\t/a-t—io/n(s
the TREMENDOUS!NOISE!! of unmasked ravens
screaming their illness
decay
   decay   decay
decay   *decay*

         decay

[[[(myself) hears a procession of voices in despair]]]

HEAR LITANIES
            ON   (my) VOYAGE

Baudelaire [*sweet*   . . .
fragile being]   . . . Celan [burning in the
   Plath [*sweet*   unpassable hour]
tormented angel]   , crying rivers
   & Phil Ochs [*sweet*
gentle martyr],
      sending (me) tapes from
                  California

               & Mississippi

               & Lincoln Park   . . . Others
      Trakl's lonely   too—countless,
            nocturnes of SURRENDER   nameless
                                                Others

[[[(myself) turns→ to→ see→   (i) in tears]]]

   (i) SEE ALL THE EVENINGS OF sorrow
        Dachau
                    & the **Killing Fields**
        & **Hell**

                            & the bitterblack towers of
                                    Carcosa,
            & BITTERNESS **shouting!** !! ! !! ! !!
                     at (me)
      (i) SEE
         the hexfog of the MaggotMagus
filled with
         grinningMONSTERS
(i) SEE
   pictures of

   WHEN
            —the bones of
compassion have settled into the
awaiting ground
            and the sun becomes a
shadow of itself
            —depraved images
waltz where gardens once grew
            and symphonies of
discord wail unabated
            —children are born
without eyes
            and perversion is
hired as governess for our dreams
            —the song of laughter
has been silenced with a noosed rope
            and the blood of
martyrs sits around suburban kitchens
sipping

ashes from
teacups
          —the tears of saints run
errands for sin
          and mercy is forbidden
on the lips of humanity
          —the cancer of pettiness
rules with a twisted stick
          and decency flees,
insanely, through the streets in tattered
rags
          —the voice of reason
suffocates in its own blood
          and God has cried
himself out of our tears
          —Hope has been called
home
          and the rotting fangs
of evil are clamped TIGHTLY
          about our smooth,
fragile throats
          —"c"-O[lLLi(D
)I;i!ₙ}G

[[[(me), (myself), & (i) gather, and huddle like lost,
frightened children at the edge of the stage]]]

   5 days [?]—or 14 [? ??]—gone.
          GONE
          GONE
          [No sun, no moon, no stars, NO remedies.
                    No strange retreats in the Night.
                    Only memories pounding.]
          in the cold blast [carry that weight]
          in the frenzy [o to 60—instantly!]
                    running HOT!
THREATS in smoke

TERRIBLE THINGS in smoke

[[[(i) stands. He is no taller than a child.]]]

(i) wish for angels . . . ANGELS!
        An/g el:s*an"ge(L)s*a[n-g-e!ls—! !!

    But only flies—**DEATHBIRDS!** !!—come . . .

[[[(myself) & (me)—heads weighted by tears—leave the stage]]]

Night with her rattling winter feathers[black & black] arrives
cannot fight the
                u
                n
                d
                e
                r
                t
                o
                w . . .
                  . . .
                  . . .   . . .
  . .   .
  . .   .
    . .   . .
      . . . . . .
         . . .
    .
    .
    .   .   .   . . .
       .
       .

lost in the worm-shadows
    on **Judgment Day**
    [No easy at last.]—[No easy at last?]

in this worm .

       .

     .   .   .   wood . . .

                             .

                       . maze

EverlastingNight
          triumphs

[[[(i) turns→ and looks into the Darkness]]]

"(i) wish (i) could see a *flower* before (i)

                                      leave"

        [[[Guilt the Executioner stands behind (i).
            He does not laugh,
       or give forth a declaration . . .
            Nor does he cry.
          He reaches out
       with mightyHANDS.]]]

                — go to **BLACK**—

On a Faraway Beach...

For Jason E. Rolfe, believer

Karl didn't say anything about Eno's feathers; shiny black things sharp as the laughter of the cathedral-deathbirds. Just snatched up the bottle and poured another Jack—three fingers, turned and looked out at Julie. Julie, softly in her little boat, model-angled, breast and thigh drifting without a care for the silence of deathless sky . . . He'd never been down to the water's edge. Too cold. Too wet. When it came to saturation he had other ideas. He stared at her long fingers, how they, measured and sunset silent, stroked the slow waves. Cassilda stroked him like that. In that other life.

Dylan, minus the amplification of his vampire/cowboy-crooner disguise, pulled the remains of a pack of smokes from his pocket. Took one out, straightened it best he could. Let his eyes take in the murmurs of the crumbled pack's Quasimodo-face before jamming it back in his torn pocket. Patted his other pockets, looking for the matches.

Brel handed him his lighter. "Pulver's brand, yes?" He couldn't say why but he couldn't remember.

"Yeah. When he could get 'em."

Eno: "So that was his favorite tea pot?"

Dylan smiled. Shook his head. "Was. He sometimes dreamed, ranted really, of strawberry fields, and a hundred times, over cold beans and coffin varnish, he'd bend my ear telling me about the times he spent on the good ship *Yellow Submarine*." He took a pull off of his smoke and looked at the suffering moon, looked at it like it would pencil in the answers for him. "Hell, I was there. Every single time."

Brel: "I take it he had it a long time?"

Dylan nodded his yeah. "Found it in a pile of junk on the heights of despair. There was a mound of discarded books, broken spines, torn pages, a real mess. He stood there crying, picking them up and stacking

129

them, brushing each one off. Sorting them . . . He had a nice little wall of A through G going and he saw it. World turned. We had two smokes left and two old tea bags—we'd only used them once, and there was half a canteen of water left. He said we can have a party. He'd do that . . . Say, we're down a peg or six, but weren't out yet.'

"Hunk of salami and tea for dinner. Smoke for dessert. Better than some other nights.'

"Wouldn't let it out of his sight after that. When we went to The Shuttered Rooms to see, confront, Archer he stashed it. Left it in the care of E. M., thought Archer might smash it."

Brel toyed with his cigarette, but didn't light it. "Breathed despair, yet he suffered bouts of dreams. From time to time he thought one might pan out, he'd ramble about it every so often to me—it would just slip out . . . I suppose in one form or another it fits most of us here."

Eno's expression was a sharp, not me. Opened his mouth to correct Brel, but Karl barred any comment.

"Stupid asshole. He should have known better."

"All the sore days add up, Karl." Dylan said.

"*Bullshit.* He should have known that all that Soul Francisco/Crosby, Stills, and Kantner hippieshit he was weaned on wouldn't get him any-where. We can save the world, my ass! Light comes up every day, and if it doesn't get drowned by rain, dark comes and slams it. All you ever get is a flash—bloom of spring, that eye blink—come and gone. Hard to get much off the fruit tree, it gets riot-hot and decay seizes it. And don't forget winter's broadsword. The fool spent so much time playing Sisy-phus he never noticed how big the goddamn rock got."

Eno: "Lots of folks, most just too busy existing and trying to make their lives a tad softer, do exactly the same."

Nick Drake: "Do they now?"

Eno: "Another chorus of "Solid Air" coming, Nick?"

Nick, half a knowing, boyish smile quick as a wink, shrugs. "Shoe fits."

There's a breeze, Julie's perfume comes ashore. Nick turns into it and watches, thinking of cures. She looks like a card on a gambling ta-ble. It could rise, and paired right, be paradise, then again, might be de-scent with additional errors. Scans her shoulders and where her gaze is pointed, thinks, *Not her. She's in it for the ladder not welcoming words.*

He's convinced he's seen her face before. Searches the chalk outlines he's chained to his Anubis Tree. Finds one, drinking Smirnoff in The Moon, raying charm and chemistry, surrounded by smoke and mirrors at one of the shadow-laced corner tables with the little red lamps and the card that says SOLD. Close. Close when you think how far back that was. Then again there have been a thousand faces that swept in with some mask embellished with familiar. *Faces . . . That look good until they're* "unmasked." Slips out.

Eno: "Unweaved. I should do something with that." . . . Ambient 5: Cloudwaves. Half speed. Reversed . . . I'll need to utilize, Fripp . . . Hassell, Budd—

Brel: "Undone." A line from "My Death" shivers in him.

Dylan: "He might have handled the enchilada better if he didn't give up the Drink Me?"

Brel: "A few other things too." Looks at the cigarette in his right hand and the glass in his left, then to the far west, to Alar.

Karl: "Walked where he had to go. Got to feeling like a ghost and thought, maybe if he tried he could escape feeling so thin."

Dylan: "Lot more falling down than walking."

Karl: "Tripping over bottles and memories is more like it . . . Some are just plain haunted. Never see anything but twilight leaning into the black."

Dylan: "He tried . . . When he could."

Karl: "How often was that? Really?"

"Hell, Karl, you scared him deep too. 'Everywhere: grayness and rain.' He read that right after his wife died. You got any idea how deep in that he was? You put that in him. He could never shake it. He had sand, but that beat on his grit, plucked his leafage—"

"Don't blame me."

"He didn't. Other things killed the Woodstock he carried around when he was younger. You were just one of the cherries on the top."

"I didn't write a Bible."

"Still, he took some of it as gospel."

"Always was an asshole."

Nick Drake: "We all played that role from time to time."

Dylan: "He didn't deny it, Karl."

Karl: "I told him about the Theatre of the Absurd, and chance and necessity. I don't remember how many times, but I didn't hold back."

Dylan: "OK, but he could never shake off the feeling he was sleeping with the Endgame. Tonight. Tomorrow. Wouldn't get a chance to debate when he fell down. Humpty Dumpty falls off the carousel—Splat."

Eno and Brel both nod.

"Knew when the day came he wouldn't be getting back up."

Brel: "He did tell me that too. More than once."

Nick's torments rise, cloak him in new skin. Hand to his brow, partially covering mortal eyes. Eyes climbing what the spiders weave . . . Tears, no kites. No sun. Love defeated. The sky vanishes and the skeleton has nowhere to run. *How many times do I have to hear this?*

Dylan recalls six million cold nights, Pulver thinned as Drake. He'd get that look in his eyes; you'd have thought his pantomime just took a stray bullet. Sometimes he'd whisper, "Wanton flies." Never once came out like a battle-cry.

Eno set down his tea cup and pointed to the beach. "Is that really Kristofferson, down there?"

Karl, grinning, refilling Eno's tea cup with 3 fingers of Jack. "Yeah. Comes 'round Sundays. Brings his rake."

Eno: "Rakes the *whole* beach?"

Karl: "Penance."

Eno: "For the beer?"

Karl: "Yeah, that too."

Eno: "All the lonely singers."

Karl: "Cassilda doesn't care. You should see the players she has tied to brooms and mops downstairs . . . *Auto-da-fé* ain't got nuthin' on the servants' quarters."

Brel hummed a line from Cohen's "Tower of Song" finished it with one from his "Jacky."

Eno: "Does Cohen ever come around?"

Dylan: "*Not this aeon.* See that tower?" Points across the unspooling cloudwaves. "That's Alar. Enemy ter-rit-tor-e. Lenny's got a room right next to Bukowski, talk about they all run with the hunted in the Rooms of Ever Grieve . . . Cassilda has never been able to get her talons on him. Tried, brought out all the heavenly of her diamond-star finery. Guess he didn't cotton the inkwell she offered."

Eno: "I've seen the ooh-la-la of her mathematics. Quite the stellar setup."

Dylan's hot tongue splashes. "You don't know the half of it. History inflamed those two. About three minutes of pearls, then muscle and ambition forgot all the secrets of sympathetically. Abrupt stained the wine and roses. It took a military intervention to separate "Baby, that hurt me" from "Hurt me, too, Baby." There was a hiss and a tear and Lenny pulled up, sailed right to gone."

Karl could still smell the affair. Catches himself before he can defend her treason. Offers, "Not a single clock in Alar."

Lit cigarette tip jabbing at the distant tower, Dylan continued. "Wall, stall, and nook, that place is Lonesome Town extra rain."

Hoping to turn Dylan's gunpowder, Karl fires into Bob's salvo. "Scott Walker—ever busy refitting his incarnations and moving the borders of emptiness—trying to anyway, and Ricky Nelson have rooms over there too. Very small rooms."

Brel heard about that tower. The whole thing was made of spiders' webs, that's what the bEast told him. They were in Shakespeare and Company on the *rue de la Bûcherie* and Pulver was looking at a 1st edition of *Die Pergamente der Mitternacht* (he couldn't afford) when he mentioned Alar and The War and the day all the deathbirds were cast out of Alar and the spiders came. Each came bearing a small scrap of a page from a book (some old, most unloved) and they weaved them all together. "Fading words and tears, and spiders' webs, that's what it's made of. Not a board or stone in the joint. You really want to stay away from there," Pulver said. Brel took his warning to heart, tore up every invitation sent to devour the cinnamon of his moon. Wished Pulver had stayed away from all the webs and things he'd manufactured from Jack Spicer's vocabulary and hoarse tears.

Dylan was up walking around. Nodded a yep to Karl's comment about Scott and Ricky having exceptionally small rooms. "Once they heard the road call, gardens, parties. Chicago. Amsterdam ... Renounced the arctic words crusted on her lips and slipped from the trellis. Curious or just lonely, each, ready to convert to deliverance, played with seizure, held it, found a little light in the shadows. Tried to dance with it. Burned their fingers. A child learns ... some of them. They never went back."

The blue-gray coils of Brel's cigarette led him back, memory a scimitar of wildfire, inward through promise and dust falling after each no. Conjures, they were ... *sitting, unfolded and waiting for the remedy to*

kick in. Compelling or not, the bEast wasn't buying a word the demon of-
fered. Sure he'd bite into beautiful, but he didn't like the velvet sins on the
menu that night. He said he didn't like her necklace and her mouth—*"See*
how it winked. It intends violence." They finished their beer and left. That
was the last time they drank together. And now Brel was sharing a last
smoke with a ghost.

A cathedral-deathbird swings low drops a letter on the table. Karl
looks at it. "That's Ligotti's handwriting."

Dylan picks it up. "It's sealed. Should we open it?"

Karl: "No, put it in his pocket. Not sure Pulver would want us to
know what it says."

Dylan: "Probably, Joe— Maybe you're brave? More than likely,
you're an idiot."

Eno: "Are we really going to light him up?"

Dylan: "I'm not sure I'm comfortable burning a body."

Karl points at the black box containing Pulver's cold remains, "He
ain't home."

Brel: "When did you get shy about shit, Bobby?"

"I'm still not sure it's the right thing to do. But we did agree."

Eno: "Should we sing a Gram Parsons tune over him?"

Karl: "He'd like that. "Sin City"."

Brel: "He would."

Dylan: "We could sing "Knockin' on Heaven's Door." He used to
sing it over and over . . . All the time. To me it was just a blip; to him it
was an anthem."

Brel: "You'd know better than I, but it certainly fits."

Dylan nodded. Smiled. He could hear that out-of-tune rasp. Remembered how much he meant the words. "He had a bunch of theme
songs; "Pancho and Lefty" really ripped him up. I think he cried every
time he heard it and he once owned sixty-some versions of "Stormy
Monday Blues." We could each sing something? You were high on his
list, Nick."

Nick: "Could."

Karl, pointing up at the moon, "Should play that Jimmy Webb
song—"

"I'll sing something for him. *Blues is the healer*, the healer. He hoped
it cured evil and bad . . . Wanted it to be. Wanted that. Get rid of
mean."

Karl: "John Lee. Didn't know you were coming."

"Thought it was right I should . . . I shook hands with him first. Maybe owe him for that."

Brel: "We should wait a bit . . . Maybe? I thought Sylvian might show."

Dylan: "He didn't mention it to me." Downs his last slug of cold tea. Turns away, can't let the others see afar glittering in his tear. Sees figments in the slow waves—*the bumpkin with his dinner-on-a-stick.end of a road.unfilled.no tomorrow marked with canals and threshold to unroll.never had the coin to buy into buddha, god, or valhalla.played long hands with instruments not aligned to play straight.lost conversations.abandon or stole, fluffed remember, but it wouldn't stay alive.got boxed and bent by the news never-sleeping melancholia confirmed.axe knockin' on the apple tree.blur.long shot.thundering.bEast snarlin' at a shore of crocodiles.trying to sweep her good-bye from his out-on-a-limb.cryin'.tilling nemesis' lie.loki grinning.anubis waiting*—The casket. Just a plain black box, oblivion-dark, this hearse that delivers its rider to the appointment at the end of The River of Suicides. Pulver. Not there to look him in the face, or maim another memory while he gingerly sipped duplicity, or ask if they had enough money to buy tea bags. Not even a cold wretch now.

Eno: "Are we playing cards after we're finished with this . . . Viking memorial service?"

"Could." Comes out a little hopeful. Karl's got a few more bottles stashed. If they stay, if the game keeps their fingers in images they have the nerve to breathe, that will keep Cassilda inside and he won't have to look at all the sky she carries in her eyes.

Dylan: "He sure won't care."

Karl: "Won't. We're taking that worry off the plate."

Eno: "Worry?"

Karl: "Worms."

Dylan: "Right. *Shit* . . . Forgot how deep the Poe Eddie put that in him. He hated the idea of going under snakes. Cold cold ground. He'd get mean if you even mentioned it."

"Should we ask Kris to sing something?"

Karl: "It would have to be 'Beat the Devil.'"

Dylan: "No shit, Sherlock."

Karl: "Stick it, Bob."

Eno: "What do we do with his teapot?"

Karl: "Put it in the Trophy Mausoleum in the Winter Glade. About as close to a ghost as he'd care to leave behind."

Brel nods. "*Oui, oui. Convient . . . Il avait le pense pas.*"

Dylan: "And his books?"

Karl: "They'll find their own way. Same for all of us. You bleed on the page and then send it out in the world. Up to readers to decide if it ever gets to exist in daylight."

With two, long slender fingers Cassilda parts the dark curtains. She lets her eyes take in the mourners, sees more than they would let themselves weigh. To them, on paper or in song, it's all grist, everything is up for grabs. But only on the page where everything is alive and no executioner's hand can gouge them with EXPURGATED. Each is a poet curved by the road. Each different as the gestures they hide in parenthesis. Sometimes proud, sometimes caroming, unsorry, fingers not admitting to being lost without something to give a hoot about. Poets (blissed and deranged with Blake and Kerouac, or the expansions of Cummings), or if properly greased (by sin, or torment and excess, or loneliness), or trapped in the cages of their own rage, warriors on occasion, who dare to lose. They take out their pistols and their profane, offer terrible and beautiful tirades. *Fools.* "Climbing deeply just to see if there's any bright in it."

Karl sits out there sometimes in the morning with coffee. Looks like he's waiting for the dealer to ship him a calculator or an ace in the hole. She's heard him bitch about the light, blood-rare violence, and the lack of a rescue squad "in this miserable place." Heard about dried up creeks and switching horses. Seen him craft thingless, stared as his solitude pulled every smile off sing. Wrought by landscapes they couldn't outrun, they're all breathtaking fools, she thinks, even when their nets were loud with thin paper stars, fools mired in flames, willing to rush in, willing to play Russian roulette, knowing cartridges wait in 5 of the 6 cylinders.

Sometimes . . . beautiful fools.

Karl. Pulver. Brel. Others (many still lodging in her subterranean below) persecuted by the mirror. Each in their turn, at the hem of night's chessboard with their nostalgic little flint, weaving hours from sand and fire . . . Word. Tear. Word (shed) . . . Knit one, purl two . . .

Seen the wicks of their feeble RSVP's to the moon turn coward and in (their seat-of-the-pants) madness close softlying. Seen their habits of curiosity and sin, how they, spitting perhaps, pin skulls and unhappiness to each attempt. After the black ships and pigmy novas of *this* temporal evil or *that* failure, after they marched (under perfect-storm lies) and broke their lances, Cassilda stood behind her curtain and stared at each scarred face, sprouting me-too tears of easy go. Rage or shivering, she's seen it all. Knows the fairytales are hard.

All those empty places. The traffic with the cobras of isolato they can't—won't—forget. The windows of milk and questions that became hurts.

She looks out at Julie (one of the old lovers they keep repeating) in her small boat. They all do it—(ecstatic ambitions out of the crate splintered with boredom) dream, thighs and flying machines, of silken flesh and adoring eyes, think they can exist in front of a hearth that does not suffer the broom, yet everyone is held back, away . . . "Come. Let us—" until the hang-ups push the cold but-don't-get-that-close.

Fools. All the anger, avoiding up close . . . And fingers.

The beard, the conquering Over, his tongue too cold to speak of engagements and seeds, Pulver in his box—finally, waiting for the fire he won't feel. She wonders if her Viking is next. Wonders if his words are enough to keep him stretching to grasp forward's carrot.

They all push it, every border in their path. Bend, remake, refit their drums to suit their mood, every goddamn one. Or they run from it. Karl's no different than the bEast was. He played stud with Pulver and Loki. Lost as many hands as Pulver. Lost, or just folded, Pulver was a great one for that, he'd be close, a heartbeat away from the nerve delivering the joy of FELT and the panic would pin his spell to CLOSED.

Her brittle stare grasps their branches. *Adolescent flock of sentimentality-literati, offering sonnets that won't let them sleep . . . Heart and bone verses screaming under their razorblade microscopes.*

"Unhearted, their ships of yes go down." Looking deeper—thewheels(ridiculous creatures)withinwheels—than blame, boo, and war with extra worse and foul, the taste of Pulver's last no scalds her mouth. Blue eyes and white-bearded dreams, some starrily-carved Cynara on their lips, they'd (anguishing) snow WRONG/right; low; their (clumsy)fingers would sicken at the thoughts of gloried. And quivering in their manic desolate, they'd see teeth in the rearview.

Damn their throbbing summers. "Must they always return to it?" *Every beginning ends, every summer sky gets dragged down, indicted by the stories of the teeth.*

Several times from behind these curtains she'd heard Karl on the phone with Dylan. He called Pulver an ass, an anxious rabbit hopping from a shore that surveyed no rejoiced to purported dimensions quite horrendous. He was right. The black box was unequivocal.

The bottle and the tea pot are empty.

The ashtray is full.

Not a word in the last ten minutes.

Eyes are not looking at other eyes.

Dylan gets up and walks over to the pyre. The others follow.

Each has brought a lawn chair and a guitar.

Brel . . . and his cigarette. No salt or signpost with a trajectory to alive. No gull wings. This misty water is very different from the vibrant seas he sailed. Carcosa, the empty balcony above the beach is not the Marquesas. The black box (inside.finally.uncaring.out of grip and after-taste. mobile disassembled) waits to molt in fire. The lake does not notice the single carving upon the lid . . . Last play under the knuckles of gray clouds. Brel (*sotto voce*): "Gone . . . from us." He can't take his eyes off the simple black box. (no more tunneling.late evening mathematics with lipstick, or alone inside with the galaxy of spiders biting veins and coasts, over.out.no anchor.no moorings.out of the world.) *By his own hand.*

Karl: "Anyone have any words they want to speak over him?"

Expression examines expression and so on . . . each says, no.

"Then let's just sing a song or two and send him on his way."

Nick tunes his guitar. "After I read his 'and this is where I go down in darkness' I came up with this."

Fingers, picking slow notes coiled in blue.
Tin man in a game of sand /
Sadness and hands that never saw a prayer /
Dragging his whole life /
To a door the clock won't open

His me slammed shut /
His I less the candle-flame words /
No longer falling down stairs /
Or over bottles and clouds of cold truth /
Didn't turn and offer a goodbye from the waterline

Eternity black /
Over /
And no going back /
Tin man /
That left no shadow on the sand

Tin man /
Can't give back the strife /
Tin man /
With only the late October moon for a blanket /
Guilty /
And without a let's go get stoned /
Or the umbrella of a friend

Tin man /
Lost /
In a game of sand . . .

As Nick sang, Brel lighted a smoke. Looked at the paper match for a second. *Even the small flames burn with it before they dim.* A sad grin finds landfall on his face. Tossed it on the pyre.

Shadows leaned in, caressing the blossoming fire.

Crosby, Stills, and Nash, "Southern Cross", and a bunch of songs by Brel, Dylan, Eno, Kris, Nick Drake, Scott Walker, Ricky Nelson, David Sylvian, and John Lee Hooker. If you've been reading along you can guess which ones. No, no Bohren and der Club of Gore this time round.

Down . . . and down we go

For Mandy

The World. Paradise. Born in the USA!—Bet yer bottom dollar, baby, and bet your ass. RED. WHITE. And BLUE. Hamburgers and ice cream and donuts and a whole store FULL of every kind of salty-sweet-crunchy snack FOB-dreams pray to get their paws on, and its near-twin across the street and 4 (just as fat and brimming with goodies and drinkup) down the block. CableTV, movies, and people that weren't afraid or carrying weapons. Breathing something other than fear and bullshit. Trite and goofy and *green lawns*. A soft blouse that fit a woman's curves. No Rifle. Jewelry. Colors—"In my size!" Shampoo that smelled sexy and was green and pink and blue and came in colored bottles, and nail polish. Colors. Shoes! Sexy clothes. No Rifle. Sexy colors. Bathing. You could . . . till you shriveled. No Rifle. The girl in the food court was laughing with her friend; they were really having fun . . .

Readjustment. Didn't come in drunkenly. Came in pink. In the dress.

It looked lovely in the mirror and she told herself it did and she wore it well. Smiled when she said it. "You're not a 19-year-old hottie anymore, Sarge . . . but you fill out a dress nicely."

Then the hard facts hit.

No job.

Sat in the kitchen with the cup of coffee and the newspaper. The pen circled 15 jobs on the first page . . . and kept searching . . . There was a tear. Seven weeks pounding the pavement and no takers. Pen ready for another go-'round of win/lose/or draw, she read the columns again.

Laid out her clothes before she went to bed.

Up and at 'em Monday morning. Hard pavement in the Land of Plenty.

No.

No.
No wonder it's hard times in the Land of Plenty.
No.
"Christ."
Smile harder next time.
Last address on page 4. No way.
Pages 5 and 6, no and no.
"You've got to be kidding?"
Two tours in the Land of Sand and a soldier, decorated twice, couldn't catch a break on friendly soil.
Didn't spit.
Could have.
Didn't cry.
Felt like it.

*   *   *

Sat on the bench in Swallow Park. Sat in shadows. Defeated by a day of no job and 50 uncaring faces that said, not hiring, most did not add, sorry. Squirrels and birds did what squirrels and birds do. Didn't see a swallow. Watched people walking their dogs, and kids, and kids walking mommies.
Watched the park get quiet.
Heard the scream.
A child.
Been in the thick of aggression and blood-n-guts, heard women and children slapped by pain that left scars.
She was up.
FAST.
Some folks run away from hell, some, the few—hearts the size of things you can't fit in pictures—willing to give up all for their neighbor, run to fire. Mandy had a lot of practice running. Ran to it every time.
Blood.
And no body.
A doll.
Blood on it.
Lot of blood.
A little girl's shoe.

She'd seen one little girl's shoe lying on the ground (and a lot of blood) before.

The heat of a tear on the small battle-scar (from a not-so-small fire-fight) on her cheek. But it didn't take *soldier* from her eye. "You don't let wrong put evil on people," Drill Sergeant Earnshaw told her in BCT. "Teeth look to make a meal out of someone, you put it down. Now get your ass out of that gotdamn-mud, Moss."

There was a blood trail and her grit was locked and loaded. She looked around for a weapon.

"You have a good heart, Child."

Spun. Ready for it.

Mandy wasn't one for weird. Didn't go for STAR WARS or horror. Comics were a no; she left them to her geeky sister and Mandy only knew the term cosplay as a result of Sarah's interests too. And there it was, some weirdo dressed up like one of her sister's steampunk things.

She'd never heard of Spider-Man's spider-sense, but a soldier acquires assessment skills, and this guy, dressed as he was, was not playing, but he was not a threat. Not to her.

Eye to eye: "You do, proud and pure. Follow me, Sergeant."

"Wait a goddamn minute."

"Yes, you have questions. They always do."

They?

"Yes, they—my assistants. I'll talk, you listen as we hunt."

"You can—"

"Yes. Just listen."

They moved quickly through the darkening wood, his voice unlocking history.

"I am Skeleton. I abandoned my delirium in the halls of Dr. Trost's facility for the misfortunate a hundred years ago. That night, near the end of a vague life, as I lay immobile and unable to speak, the good doctor had, to save me, cleansed and transformed my body. My offending hands were removed and my blood replaced. From the doctor's spiraling labyrinth of umbilical tubes and conduits flowed an alchemical mixture of mercury, tea leaves, and Phoom Root dust from the swamps of Ba-Benzala. My blood was vacuumed from one arm as the doctor's potion was pumped into the veins of the other."

This was bullshit from one of her sister's weirdass movies, but damn, he laid it out righteous.

He told her of his hands. Metal hands. "This one, the farthest from my heart, is called Devil, the other is called Angel. Dr. Trost named them. They bring peace . . . or damnation.

"I walk this world with a mission. I save what I can.

"Let us hope we can save this child."

His hope was fast. She pushed to keep the pace. There was no blood and no trace Mandy could see, yet Skeleton still tracked his prey. All of her unspoken questions followed his answers.

"The Scarecrow Men have taken this poor child . . . They leave their autumnal scent. After a time, you'll be able to discern the decay that salts their wake."

"What are these *things* you're talking about?"

"They are the children of Eight-eyes Black, Stellata Ghostmaker. The Scarecrow Men, the animals of Famine, come from a black swamp of parasites; they were born in Tetragnathi, the Orb-Web of Stellata Ghostmaker. Strand and thread, woven in darkness, she stuffed them with dry leaves and broken twigs, discarded wrappers, spat out poisoned candy, and rotten apples, and all the Halloween treats that were not treats, she gathers after the bubbles and small riots of All Hallow's Eve have gone to bed. Where the Scarecrow Men tread you'll find 4 + 20 blackbirds. Each sliced from black ground when the full moon scraped the earth after Stellata had left a child's bones. I've hunted them in every nook and crack, and when I take down one she spits out two more."

Incredulity didn't cause her head to shake. Zipped her, What-the-fuck?

Mandy had never been in this part of the park, if they were still in the park. Tree and weed were different here and the shapes of the leaves were wrong. This was no trick of failing light. Her legs were no stranger to endless humping and they were firm in what they reported, she'd come miles . . . many miles.

Her legs began to burn.

She followed as he picked up speed.

And listened.

"Long ago the Mothers of the Land, filled with sorrow and great loss, came together and gave of themselves, gave blood and spirit, and vow, and on a moonless night cast Stellata into the tar-cellar blackness of Tetragnathi. One hundred of their beloved spouses, the Fathers Quiet of Heart, sealed the gate with the ritual blade. They cut deep into their bellies and bled upon the seal, and each, before he died, passed the blade to the next hand. When the Fathers were dead, each mother stood over her love and cried upon the body . . . Stellata is trapped there, held by tears and blood. The Scarecrow Men come into this world to stock her larder."

The other shoe.

Blood. Only a few drops . . .

"I can smell the poor child's tears."

They stood in a lifeless amphitheater of trees that had never been decorated with plush. She knew no sprinkle of sunsplash had ever danced here.

"Now is the time of blood, Amanda. Here you must stand and accept the covenant."

Mandy had once taken an oath. "I do solemnly swear . . ." She held Skeleton's eyes, knowing another, wedded to harsh and grim and a thousand pounds of Hell, was about to be asked of her.

Skeleton's expression was as hard as any drill sergeant's, but his eyes held something touched with soft. "The pay sucks, but there are days when you get to save the day.

"And many you'll cry."

All she wanted was a job and a nice little home with a soft carpet and nice curtains and a shot at happiness, and to put her feet up once in a while. Wants to have quiet date nights curled up on the couch with popcorn and a comedy, and Dave—or maybe his name, when she meets him, will be Hank, or Joe? Didn't want to be deployed in a forever war with darkness, but she was not going to let some vampiric bitch-monster feed on children.

"You understand the next step is an oath of all . . . until the day you die."

She hadn't read any Shakespeare and had never heard of the siege of Harfleur, but she'd heard, *Once more into the breach.* It slipped out. She nodded and waited for the words.

"This is a blood oath, Amanda. There are no words." Skeleton removed the glove that covered Angel. He unscrewed the sowing-thimble cover of Angel's forefinger. Its tip was a needle. Words, the Oath That Will Not Be Diminished By Dust, words from a horizon of different colors, the holy vow to Ett, were infused in it as it was formed in a small forge in the doctor's theater of science and alchemical vision.

The muscles between her shoulders tightened. Mandy didn't smoke. Not in years, but she sure wanted one now. Wanted a drink too.

Earnshaw was in her ear. "We ain't having tea, Missy. Saddle up."

"This will burn."

Blood fused to honor. Soulfire devoted to light. She signed on.

"Do I . . . get *hands* like that?"

Mandy thought he was about to laugh.

"No. I have not that skill." He removed the glove that covered Devil and turned, reached up and snapped a branch from a tree. Devil engraved exotic symbols along it. Then a red illumination engulfed the branch and it, blazing, was transformed. "This is Lockbreaker. You aim it with your heart. Its punishments eat the ants of darkness."

Skeleton handed her Lockbreaker.

She was not a Marine, but she knew the Rifleman's Creed. *This is my rifle . . .*

"This is my Rifle . . . My rifle is human, even as I, because it is my life. Thus, I will learn it as a brother. My rifle and myself are the Defenders of Light. In inferno or the raw gloom of Night, we are the masters of our enemy. We are the Defenders of Life."

Skeleton listened to her. Accepted her promise.

Grinned. Should she get out of this, she was going to paint a cartoon RAID bug on the stock. Knew just what the "OH SHIT!" on its face was going to look like. "*Lockbreaker.*"

"He does."

Skeleton walked to a mass of fallen trees. He began to wriggle through the separations in the misshapen trunks. Mandy followed the glow Angel gave off. It the snarled interior was a hole. She knew what came next.

"This is not a sourceway; it merely leads to a backwater in the tomb-river of Mother Night's skirts. There are many of these way stations of wickedness. We're very close. We'll be upon them soon.

"You must grab the girl and return here, bring her back to the light. I will deal with Stellata's children.

"Stay close."

Did.

Down into the damp black earth.

The mud and clay of the tunnel was cold. Piece of rock here, dead root there. She got scratched and scraped. Kept going. Gritted her teeth . . . and hoped.

Slipped. Went down. Got a mouthful of dirt.

Spit.

Mandy heard the sound of leaves rustling in the wind.

"That's them. Soon."

Firefights don't walk over and offer ready-set-go. This one was true to form. Poison-showdown exploded.

Skeleton was a monsoon of gestures, his hands, daggers, rockets, roused fangs. Devil thrust/Shit got cut. Devil slash/Dryshit was on fire. Catswift-action lengthened its squall, shit got clouted—lost its stomach or arm or escape and turned limp. And slash/twigs snap/again. A glint.speed.death furiously.

Yank

—shake—things of elm, of birch, some once on stalks, others once part of a root's journey

—shake

—hurt—shook throw CUT

—cut—the black ground, a carpet (with poured piles) of fragments that finished their tour with intact

—HURT—whizzing through the air—split to finished, until silent, until stopped, until weren't

—HURT—after the fusion/sleeve not;constrained by halt, handing push/smearing bedlam (all shapes and sizes)—littered (no shapes no sizes). no cry, stirring, there . . . in the expiration

—HURT

—head flies (no roll on the midnight clay).

Snapped-in-half blackbutton-eye under a black boot. Angel STRANGLEHOLD.Tear;ear-to-ear/and rip;vertical cut/and rend; decimate endlessy.straw in the dirt—sinfeathers fly. Fluid murderer's fist—upward—killing, both river and sword. Quick steps.a thousand Devil cuts.straw/stitching/spilled the interior-knit of rotten and worms and dead flowers and thorns and dead in the black center of autumnal guts. Dead and BE GONE falling from the artist's hands, gluing it to their soon to be. again and again. again. quoting and requoting . . . nothing (no ghost) stirs. Gone. Dead. (no spider). (no shadow). Dead.

Saw a 5.56 open what was under an Afghan pakol, and paired chest wounds no medic's skill would ever close. Saw the gaping-after of a fighter plane's payload. Saw an amped-up FX kung fu movie, saw hand-to-hand, saw snorting&drinking piss KILLYA—meant it. Saw lies kill. Never saw anything like this.

Mandy couldn't see Skeleton's face, black wings circled it. Black talons bit.

"Get the child!"

Lockbreaker took the head off the Scarecrow Man that clutched the child.

She dove.

Caught the girl.

"Run."

Didn't hear, I've got this.

Didn't look back.

Heard fire rage behind her.

Heard hissing.

And howling.

Didn't slip on the way up-and-out. Knew, you fuck-up, the girl dies.

* * *

Her first dance with Hell and she was still breathing and the girl was too. She was sleeping in her arms. Mandy didn't know what-in-the-hell Skeleton had done, something, some magic with light and flowers, but the girl's wounds were healed. She didn't give a rat's ass about anything else.

Skeleton put his gloves back on. "Tomorrow we may not win the day."

She was hugging the little girl and a single tear runs down her cheek.

"I plan on winning."

Skeleton remembered his first day. Won that one too. He's glad he can't cry for all the days that came after . . . lost too many to count.

The Brandos, "Gettysburg"; Bruce Springsteen, "Youngstown";
Billy Joel, "Goodnight Saigon"; Weather Report, "Unknown Soldier";
Randy Greif, "Rabbit Hole" and "Down"; Omar and the Howlers, "Hard Times in the Land of Plenty",
Foster & Lloyd, "Texas in 1880"

The Pencil

For my friend, Jeff Thomas

a gateless WHITE castle. it laughs at the function and spice of vocabulary, at
   lips that can't thread the needle of, "Go ahead."

Fingers. (if they were still in touch with music, and heat—thick and grooved with light's map.) (if they could dance.) again. Fingers. not this pain screaming (again). blind. This night. and the fields and falls and summit of others . . . street after street of not moving others.

Pressing (heretic) fingers without moving from grave to your country. without ejecting the abortions still baking in your mouth. Dirty fingers unaware of liberty.

They don't love this pencil. no. not today, not last night when the coarse net of your scattered leaves was blowing, praying for care and a first step. Not for a second. but you play the scars (unimportant/agony-wide/binding/thirsty-edged . . .) the piano tuner knots to your reactor.

Pencil. stalled. imperfect. A line. clamped to despair. The span of another line. futile starts. No vote. No fairness.

And you begin the *next* same line . . . (of bird droppings) (your future accounts, enemy fogged-in. your own wings have even dropped their own name in tonight's closed room afterlife) . . .

Worn pencil. gray dreams. mists distributing little by way of light. Want it to be a ladder. Want Sol-lantern hanging up there flavoring the seams with clarity. Waiting. introducing you moving, away from the gnarled thunder, away from what the storm cries. beat and ritual. 'Etna smoking' or genie from jugular appetite lifting. Waiting. For the cottage with the soft fleece lights and open doors. Waiting. to receive poetry (of eyes and singing lips) where the words are clear, charmed. not this asylum of frozen-to-death based on the same *over* and *again* and *again* and more movement that leads to slow-motion, shattered curves you can't read tomorrow.

Pencil dredging its dense unshifting signals, the ones that confine you to the lead-shadows under the world. Pencil. open colors (wish) consenting to make roads and hills where the spell of language is a heart perfume.

Stub of a pencil. waiting. every front you have put in the region of Belong.

Lead. heavy as the ruses of the fox clock. Push it. marry it to the carcass of paper. Install a window to inside on the grain. inner space. host. yet only Lugosi and Pollock appear . . .

(white-knuckles) (provoked by limited options)

Begin again . . .

A cottage filled with decades, a cottage with a doormat of flowers. Tea and warm inside. Winter's night only a framed picture in the windows. Across the room, eyes carrying a song from the radio. Gentle under the roof . . .

There were days embellished with orchard melodies and spring elixir, and there were days we brought the harp-scented flowers inside and let their colors touch our rooms.

We wore soft cotton, ate tomatoes and herbed-duck, or for fun, spaghetti and raspberry desserts.

I enjoyed breezy comedies; he liked hearing me laugh . . .
we
had feathers and could bend, and
knew how to say pretty . . .
until the rain thing came.

That's what the pencil wants to write. the pencil that knew how to whistle in the dark, the pencil that was a tiger, and once drew flowers on notepads . . . The pencil (capable, not a mutated fabulist, not interrupted by endless negations) that had crawled out of the labyrinth without breaking expectations.

Lost heart. Someone stole—

Fingers. inhaling and reel.

Look at the clock. smudged. a mirror of scratched with your age written all over it. and your notions wiped free of solution. all. of. them.

Not your first time around this block. 3 inches of 10-inch No. 2 pencil make that clear. floor with bits of broken lead confirm it. etchings and wear on the desktop are composed of its dry phantoms.

left. where they . . . fell.

as your little "I" cried . . .

Was it The Meds? ("You shall say nothing. You shall say Nothing. You shall say NOTHING.") Hard bite. they laugh, but you can't. Meds. ("You shall have nothing. You shall have NOTHING . . .") Take one fixture after the next from your museum . . .

Same line as the last line. line, the cello continents in your past. lie (that's what the eyes with the cold, unsightly horned-rimmed glasses think. says until you're unable.)(what does he know about the library?)(what does he know about the sand . . . and the tiger?)(he never took The Grand Tour.). Line. frail—right now (is this one different than the last one?) you're not even sure that's the right word—as smoke. Write it 100 times. double-back on the wounded distant. Tonight. same as the pencil did last night. 100 times . . .

Bend your neck. nose to paper. maybe you can see now?

Move the land with your knuckles. Tell it to find the path. Tell it not to listen to the crying and the chittering and the rain thing that laughs and slaps you with silence. Your pencil is an army. Your fingers, The Revolution. Be a pioneer.

establish

establish

establish

claim outburst.

Don't listen to the insects released from the seams of the rain thing's lightless cloak. They are corpses. a hot light of fraud. All that laughing (that never was a person)(that never read silk-voiced books, or smiled in a picture.). lies.

The (dark underneath) white editor's meds lie too.

Animate the page. choreograph reign . . .

Rain. (field of deception rotting staunch.) in here. thick as a puzzle with no escape to open. Grayness: page after Pollock-page of thick, wholesale plague (carrying untranslated punishment curved with vulgar fury. fury that fails exorcism, as it failed the caravan of worry and ordeals). Smeared with ticks. and no tourists. no neighbors. or booksellers determined to offer you options.

Homeless. without the reader, heart. Blackboard zero. epidemic slop of isolato shadows, the rings where the dreams hurt. twist. when the rain thing and the black things from the icy coast laugh, and punch your veins . . .

100 lines of lies. (the lies in the Closed Room.)

same cloud/tangle as—

the unformed portrait. the sting of darkness throughout the. one. two. three. four. five. six. words. written again (smudged).back.to.back.again . . . previous amid stay put.

Don't write I'm not there. I'm not there.im not there.me. This . . . Here (gutted, cobwebbed to fragments of Then). Don't tell of the ghostly, and the eclipse and the phantoms' wauls and incurable . . .

Shadows in The Meds. The Meds bring them. make them. hold you deep in it. The Meds own your fingers. chain the tiger with arrows of silent sand . . . (and he comes in and out of the room)(the scanning white editor.)(rewriting with his needles.)(passing his flat solutions to fat Nurse Nancy, assassin, to mole into your bulletproof.)

Pencil. ready for a verb. and that fine noun your duration can't hold on to. Pencil. to ponder a detail. same as it was. Cold. connected to a dead language.

(house of cards pencil, chest a mosaic of panic. drowning. drummer's sticks. shaking.)

Pencil, out of nails to hold the moment steady. Pencil. tearing . . . and failing to weave. Pencil. dying hangman's mouse (afraid of its own veins) under the obliteration of a pendulum not extending skill enough to call to the king 'uncrowned in the underworld' here.

(pushed) fingers unlocking a word. seed, pulling "I'm here" from the that-time backwards, from the dark shadows. And one (strong and clear) to follow it. so near . . .

So far. Lost (smoldering. facts. bolt.) in some inside exterior, gauzed in baggage-soil, mouth and tears can't form.

A word a reader could understand. feel. Deliver it.

Don't ask for admission, spring forth. Steal it back from the chilled, autumnal cloak of the rain thing and its darkening branches of agony.

Start a pattern. On the margin-ledge—Dear . . .

Inscribe the word. Engrave his name. Carve. your way out of the white cup.

Write. your way out of the cloudblur gutter of the editor's needle. Remember. text that had not run out of time. knowledge. Write. before it's over, about the restoring bells, the months of speech head over heels, not in locked here (with no window) as the other me . . .

You can remember. can. remember. reason. the other day. again. you.can. away from here.

Look. at what the pencil wants to say. Look beyond the nothing more the rain thing touched. Here is the part of your hand, the pencil. Here. loose your hand to way. agos (with no balls of panic) when you read and laughed (no halfway full upon your face). to made. and you.

and Him.

Pencil. up out of this dirge. please . . .

move from motionless dead . . .

develop.

Walking or a kite, or

Balance . . .

Waiting. as they were (*still?* are), a country road, by the tree (with a rope too short to . . .), evening . . . shadow deep bottom of noise.dirty . . . Worn. Pencil. you want to instruct with enormous bullets. Push—TRY!—Must, Please, down the swamp of wet sand that is your arm. iamgoingto surmount. write.will.squeeze.reach under the surface and—insistent . . . will.write.Please. something . . .

A line that makes sense. One with His Name and green, one not forbidden by the editor's Meds. and the dark heels of the rain thing.

Please.

At the end. if you finally get it right. and aren't conquered, or spread too thin over broken boxed interiors. Slip it under the door. (praying the fast white shoes don't harvest it.) Hope for wind. To carry it to fingers that hold light. Soft light. Kind light. Light that knows the law of the keyhole.

aftermath of a semi-Quay thought about spoons and a friend . . .

Astor Piazzolla, various tangos; Bee Gees, "Fanny (Be Tender with My Love)"; Death Cab for Cutie, "Meet Me on the Equinox"; Randy Travis, "Diggin' Up Bones"; George Jones "The Grand Tour"; John Martyr, "Solid Air"; and various Annette Peacock songs

Tender. Sins.

For David Goodis

Moon. Yeah there's one. Not full, broken, doesn't kiss anything. This one's in the gutter with the beer bottles and the litter.

Maybe it's better like this. Better than the nights he sits up there shouting his blues. The nights when he weighs a ton . . . and all the ghosts imprisoned on his tongue have expectations . . .

Another black Friday night.

Hearts tired of sinking.

Alive clocked out. Kids, top of their dark carnival heads to their trespasses, coming out of K17 don't mind, don't seem to. Much. One with a bark for a laugh . . . Two with adamantium "No." from fleeing girls . . . A blonde who (agreed to try it and hated every second and sound) is glad they finally shut the doors . . . They're a parade of leather, a sizzling tableaux of engrained ink and piercings, and carefully-chosen lipstick, reds and blacks, and wanting to kidnap beautiful, or something another drink might convert into hospitable, instead of sleeping tonight. The drinking and dancing and painted-on angst is over for the night. The got-my-club-display-on part anyway.

A metalhead, a bottle or two under any reason he ever held, is begging a bottle-redhead plumed ultra-goth, for a good time. *His.* All I can give you or amputation seesaw, she's had a few too and is kinda thinking about it. She moves closer and the idiot's jackpot winds up in the gutter. Too many bottles of dark and that pair of double greaseburgers he was shoveling down on the way in a few hours back splatter the sewer grate. No to footsy, she's faster than scared. Two steps back from splashdown she's staring at her boots which narrowly avoided the explosion of his stricken interior. Flips him the bird. Hisses appropriately. And bing-bang-b'boom, the next nightingale with an engine of fire steps up with his hey baby, or whatever's he's passing. Inferno-red chandelier-lips turn it on for him. He's got cash and knows about an after-hours party. They're gone.

Metalhead, out of his load of vehemence, and luck, looks at their backs. Just walks away.

I know the look.

Know the weight of that shamble. It don't go away. Bludgeoned and gutted and out of galaxies I walked the jackboot blocks, got my impresario colors shotgunned by tsunami indigo.

Did. Dead for two whole minutes.

On a corner filled with attitude I paid for raising my hand. No moon that night, just the kiss of war.

Bottle of whiskey on the railing, I sit on my balcony and smoke my menthol.

I'll be here at dawn when the raven feathers swoop in for the pickings. The magpies will fan out and wait for their turn.

Everybody wants a bite.

I'm sure an everyone.

No wings. Got them clipped.

These days I crawl. Keep my head down.

Hide might be a better word.

The moon and me again on this empty laudanum street. He doesn't stroll. I don't seethe. I wonder who has the colder brush.

Not wearing wounds pinned to her chest or black or leather, a woman in elegiac gray steps from the burnt vat of shadows. Lights a cigarette. Exhales.

Body that could melt the endless cold of oblivion puts mobility in my stagnation. I've seen cleavage, fucked it, left pearls on it, but hers is miraculous.

Part of her face I can see looks up.

Our scars orbit an invitation.

My eyes say, sure, c'mon up.

Please.

She looks east. Expression and the cigarette she flipped at it said maybe. Maybe . . .

Looks west . . . Looks back up at me. Regards my grave of roughed-up contours . . . Considers my hopeful aphrodisiac.

I play patience. Don't wave. Don't offer up my voice.

Want to.

Lurch.

Yell.

Tell her I've got the keys to the candy store.

Don't lie to this one.

Yeah. OK. Not to myself either, right?

Sure.

Don't lie. And don't tell her about last week, or the backwards and forwards of waves you stumbled over. Don't march into issues . . .

You're not carefree and she's not going to come here, if she does, to see you bleed.

Just lift my glass and take a sip.

Slow.

Be cool.

Don't laugh.

Just sweat

and try to shape my lips into something that's not dark. Hard to choose a crisp right way that says paint a feast tonight from an empty wish-list.

Fall back on computing nervous. Lit a smoke when I couldn't find a flavor of clouds for my wings.

Guess she didn't smell my issues or delusions or the fact sunrise forgot my front door opens. She's coming across the ruins of my spilled agony and I'm trying to realign my lamp so she won't see my hollow.

She's actually coming.

Stow the shadow tent and torture. Pretend you're capable of something other than phantoms.

My voltage won't play the patience game, I lean over the railing. For three shakes my heartbeat rehearses "Sunshine of Your Love."

She's halfway across the street.

And still coming.

Steps over the curb.

Paul McCartney, maybe you were amazed, but that don't cover what I'm feeling right now.

I reply to the door buzzer.

Stand at the top of the stairs. My ears and all directions open. Many as I'm able to.

Can't see her face yet. Hoping it's an omen. Paris, any scrap of its ardent. London's too cold; in all the gray pictures its shelves are empty. Already have that. Penciled every smear into the pages of my stained notebook.

Page 1

Loneliness.

Page 2

Ruining my life.

3

Forever.

Forever.

Forever. No who come calling . . . coming with close . . . with a way in . . . with the colors of sentiment . . . and a graceful turning point in their eyes . . .

4–20

Lies. Hearts, step right up . . . Bones. Angels, no saying no. Angels, a stranger's mouth in the room again. Angels on the dead side of the moon . . . Doors . . . Black air. Some endless 2 AM of old movies flickering, wounded, slain, somebody's difficult life done, blue choking on its narrow, a river and a girl, all those walks across the carpet to that vacant where we went wide open . . . and outside of weeping palms that can't spell forgive me a dog is barking . . .

Down.

The single line of last judgment that day. Quarter to 4. Standing in place. No will. Quarter to 4. All fall down language. Quarter to 4. No words. Anointed. Fading in ghost time. The clock is ticking. I see his boot heel on the sidewalk. Down.

Down.

Fucked myself when I tried to play the chemistry game. My iron greed couldn't maintain 8 miles high, rivered a stream of blood. My blood.

She's halfway up the dark stairs. Thing's needed a bulb for three months, but getting the landlord to do anything here is like asking The System for a fair shake. I'm hoping she doesn't fall and break her neck.

Searching for something to say. Lot of dead keys on my piano. Hand ain't gambled or touched mercy in a while. Do I even remember how to grab it?

Top stair. My gaze leaves the lure of her cleavage as her face crosses my doorstep.

Lot of traveling on her face. Lot of storms.

The other half of it is attractive. The half without the two big scars. The half that still has an eye. Ink under it says it's seen a lot of mornings with no goodbye and no love letter I'll call you.

"Hi." I point to a chair. Hold up a glass and the bottle.

"Sure."

I pour. 7 without the 7.

She sat. Took a sip from the glass I handed her.

Took my time looking at the landscape below her chin.

Long dark hair sits perfectly on her shoulders. Exactly the right amount of bone in her collar bones. Sculptor would say that's art and be right.

Two-tone gray lace and satin bustier showin' her assets off. Perfumed. Just a whisper. The aroma is slaughtering me.

Beautiful legs.

Right down to the sculpted ankles.

Jesus. Good fucking thing you're not drunk.

Beautiful legs.

Kind you want to see part.

Heartbreak or staring through a Polaroid lens good.

Skip flattened by another stout whack of grieving. Skip the shapes of death-speak, butcher's rocky road and hard cages of broke-ass weary and let me reap. Claws ready for the blossom of pleasure that's my "I'm next" sitting here. My lonely, belly to tongue full of sign me up and I want, didn't twist in the chair.

"I'm—"

"Gary. Russell."

My face changes programs.

"Felon. Villain. Liar." Rapid fire.

"Scumbag." She let that hang for a second.

"Backstabber. Not a single scintilla of good in you . . . Shallow bastard. Grotesque right down to the core." Eye a wrecking ball of straight ahead hard.

"Did I miss anything?"

Didn't drop my glass. Didn't hear a rimshot.

Her eye takes in the thing that passes for a couch. Looks up, sees the missing ceiling tiles. Returns to me. "So this is your hideout? Delighted to see you ruined my life for this."

I intake havoc.

She smiles. Fortune cookie says LIGHTS OUT.

I can hear the bodies falling.

"Can't place me?"

No. I'd remember that body. I must have been blasted to have sucked her stuff up and not even have a foggy inkling. Those tits, if I was building a body electric . . . Must have been very, very goddamn drunk.

Nothing slides into place.

Turns her face. Profile. "This?"

Zip.

Nope.

I would not have forgotten those mind-altering tits. Or the vibrato of those Vegas showgirl legs.

And nada.

"Big no I take it?"

Waits again.

I'm looking. I'm looking, trying to outflank two decades of flesh. Nothing in the scramble.

"This was a present from a monster in Kansas City. He had a problem . . . And a broken vodka bottle."

I've never been in KC. Never left this shithole state.

"Got it wrong. Never been there."

Motionless. "I didn't say you had."

Right back to fucked.

I got nothing and she's waiting.

Stripper? Hooker maybe?

Someone's sister?

I'm digging through the ocean of far I never catalogued. All I find is high, rough seas. Street corner talking and underworld clubs draped in sweat and bumping, colored, pushing the scent of crotch ceremonies, I've been to a thousand sacrifices. Watched degenerative maze and pitch and capricious slide and board in hallucinatory, but she's in no boundaries my tempo can fix on.

"I stand accused, but . . . I'm blank."

"Before the beating where I lost my eye and picked up the crosshatching, I carried around the face of Teresa Horton."

Slushed back to harvest, looked at the matches my thirst collected and then dropped in the dark. That name I ain't in 20 years.

Do now.

Skin. Contours. Limbs, petals of the violin I played. Young. 16. Didn't look like this . . . I remember taking off her bra.

Didn't say look at you now.

Day I met her she was a blonde on a street corner. Waiting for a bus. The same one I was waiting for. My desire lit her cigarette. I thought dream girl.

Said it.

She smiled. Friendly. Milk and honey soft.

Let my clouds drift into her springtime.

"Dream. Girl." Wide open as she tried it on.

Said she wanted to be one.

Let her think she was.

Took the soft she shined. Kept taking. We smoked. Drank. Danced, even when there was no one to hear. Left clubs. Left our clothes. Wanting to please, maybe needing to, she went along . . . One nightfall I took her tender hung it out on the street of no return. Made it sin. Watched it get trimmed down to the lifespan of a butterfly as she lost her velvetiness. Getting rented and rented and rented nipped it in the bud. Took every dollar eagle she gathered. Watched the lights go out of her eyes.

Saw her tears after she got hit with there ain't no lost and found. Stepped back from the weather report so I wouldn't get wet.

Gave her dope. Fed her dreams cocaine first, then H, needed to be sure she wasn't going to push back. She paid the rent and cleaned the kitchen. I slept quietly while she stood on the sidewalk. Kept her in it as long as I could. But there were other fields, better veneers and I wanted up and out.

Sick of the wear in her eyes, I wanted something with the rhythm of hot, something scented like soaring for my testosterone and my wallet.

Another nightfall I pushed her into the street of no return and locked the door behind her.

Her last words: "I . . . Thought. You said, you loved me?"

Mine: "Love ain't on no map. Not around here."

There were clouds bending the sky. It was the day after her 17th birthday.

Didn't watch her clicking heels step off the curb into the endless. Why would I? Focused on better life, the kind where green rolls out the red carpet, I was bounding away from dime-a-dozen next door. Didn't lose any sleep for taking the spark out of her rhapsody. I had a new blonde who knew how to wear clothes and how to take them off and the crew at the Castle Club kept her dance card full.

Screw ghost and goblins and savvy beating to other quarters, man with a plan. Climb big, get the keys.

Did.

Collected the tokens. Felt unstoppable.

Did.

Didn't study. Speed. Nail it. Built, didn't quote fear as I hunted. Didn't take coffee breaks or look at the entrance of obits. Carpenter, I made *domain.* Went out, hardened, squarefaced, and did.

Did it again. Speed (rolled over any cues that inconvenienced my game). Unstructured, snarling.

Branched out.

Dope.

Another plan said no to sea change put three bullets in me.

Fell off Tiger Mountain.

Thunderstorm didn't come with an umbrella. Clock didn't take to heavy. Stopped.

Road back didn't offer luck. Couldn't get back on the radar. Tried a little till hard and nasty showed me a map where the Promised Land was spelled DEAD.

Sat here in my corner of Hell with my cracked mirrors and lies, juggling fried food, the bottom of a pissed-off weary libido, and the none and less of whiskey. Learned to live with sick and none. Waited for my number to get called.

Spent my nights, when the weather let me, on the porch watching the vampires pierce and tattoo the night. Fed on them, the few that were willing.

Took a sip from the glass. Didn't have a clue about what I should say.

She looked at me like I was mirror of bad weather.

I had been.

Then.

For a lot of years.

Years that added up to the losin' end, the spot I'd parked in. Or is it hidden behind?

"Teresa." Shaped as you're shittin' me?

"I was."

Take off 20 years and 30 pounds of perfect curves. Add half a face. And an eye.

I'm still grabbing images from the calendar. Got the whole picture.

She antes up. Gun.

Gun. Gone 16-year old girl saying you are the best. Gun. No somewhere in here I still care for you.

Gun.

Gun changes everything, the universe, the flow of time. They say a guy staring at a great pair of tits stops his universe. Does, just watch a guy talk to a woman's boobs, not her, her boobs. Sure they stop time. But they're temporary, fun. But temporary. Gun. Gun changes everything. Your name. Your focus. Your life. Way you breathe and if you'll keep doing it.

Gun.

Not a lady's gun.

I've got three bullet-scars from a 9. One that was a hex of crocodile poison and stark raving blood ritual. Hers is the steel of passion forged in the steam of madness.

There's some madness and plain hate screaming trouble in that one blue eye.

The one looking at me. The one calling for vanish. Staring. Like I'm a lost nightmare that leads to cut to pieces. Fits. I guess. Did. After my joyride ran away with the son-of-a-bitch with the bigger attitude and the 9mm motherfucker he used to back it up, tits up for two minutes readjusted a few things.

Didn't see a white light. No angels. No unforgiving knife-flames licking the trickle of your sobbing. Not cross over to some make-believe has you warm on poetics.

Zero.

From whatever you were to nothing.

All fits what she knows. What I was.

She knows every inch of what I was. On that day. On the days after I cast her down and cast her out.

Was.

Before the transformation. Before the epilogue.

Was.

Small change.

Wannabe. Energy. Matter. Spirit. Wanted to be a big shit. Matter. Serve up what my heart wanted and fuck everybody else.

Wanted to be a star. Not a blur.

Was. There.

Close.

Then got deleted.

That eye sees everything.

My fear. What I did.

What I wish.

Sees the rust, the shadows in your heart that got in your bed ... Sees fool unwound in acres of no roots, no strawberry shortcake. No guts.

Sees what I know. There are shotguns. And bartenders. Damage and blankness. This block and the next and eight over and fifteen that way, not a nice house, not a nice car. There's mold and Crown Royal, fury and fallout. Elbows leaning on railings. Jaws with gritted teeth. Shell casings and no tree. "Fuck you." "Fuck you." "Fuck you." "Goddamnit, fuckyou, Cunt." That hydrant don't work, those tears never shut off. Ripped screens. Torn. Decayed. Kicked in. Tossed. Matted and vacant eyes. No tree. "Fucked up." is the common descriptive.

No tree.

I light a smoke hold it in my mouth. Place the pack in front of her.

She's got long fingers. If dancer's legs were fingers. She blows out the match. Sets her shoulders. Shrinks on TV shows sit like that. Maybe it's judges? Teresa smokes.

I smoke.

I knew I'd run out of easy.

Didn't know there wouldn't always be a little more time.

I've got a small caliber pistol in the drawer in the bedroom. But this is no cowboy movie. No one cast to ride up and free me from the gallows pole.

She's pointing the gun at me. Eye wants me to eat some pain. But her hand is shaking.

Moon is lying on the carpet. Marks the stains of the blind flowers I spilled.

Gun. Like the last one.

Too much speed I didn't read the street sign. Incident on Badlands Street.

Garbage cans. Weeds trying . . .

View of a world with no cover. Porches and graffiti . . . Signs preying upon the lost and the doves . . . Hunger under tears. Hunger knotted in anger . . .

Summit of dreadful.

No corner to turn.

Nothing bright in the sky. Nothing.

Big clock went dark.

Looked around the room of threadbare and stained, my little hole of vanquished ain't seen paint or easy's laugh, or a plot, in the ten years I've paid the rent on this place. Gun might be better than this slow death that stays on your ass day to day? And it don't back off at night. Darkness might be better than another drunken night.

Gun only produces a few minutes of pain—

Maybe I should have shaved today? Or worn a shirt not rubbed with ashes . . .

Shouldn't have divorced her from an ordinary life.

There were wild years, whiskey-wisdom one-liners that could always find their way home in the rain. Bankrupt I couldn't format one. "Couldn't have been easy."

Oblivion doesn't reply to what's obvious.

I don't think there's consoling angels at the end of a ghost story.

Her hand has stopped shaking.

"Do I have time for another smoke?"

Her eye is moist and the clip is full of honest mementos. She nods.

I put the hot tip of blame to my cigarette . . .

She was a blonde on a street corner.

I thought she was a dream girl.

Miles Davis, "So What"; Bohren & Der Club of Gore, "Zombies Never Die (Blues)";
Sade, "Smooth Operator"; Miroslav Vitous, "Transformation"; Iro Haarla, "A Window Facing South";
Led Zeppelin, "Gallows Pole"; Paul McCartney, "Maybe I'm Amazed";
Savoy Brown, "Poor Girl"; Cream, "Sunshine of Your Love"; The Byrds, "Eight Miles High"

Movietime . . .
with popcorn and . . .

Trolls, aliens, atomic freaks, deadies and mutates (some humans too) down front start hootin' as the BIGscreen at Valente's FLICKER flashes

SATAN'S PSYCHO-GORE~ROTIC STRIPPERS

meet

The Big Boobs Astro-Zombies of Eerie Swamp

in

tingling ***BONZAI!*** *3D*

in dripping scarlet and slime-green Day-Glo up on the big screen.

Title starts shedding letters, a trio of arcing samurai swords shimmer and blooming guts bleed. Key beautiful music starring a haunted sax and acoustic keys that stun with soft. A little shift in the rhythm that smiled. Drummer had lark's wings.

Shot of single-note twang hangs . . . A crunch chord!

Cut to enter-the-void BLACKNESS. Pure. Hard.

I sat there in the murmurs.

A slurp and a burp to my left.

Waiting.

Me and my girl in the dark.

PITCH black . . . 5 seconds . . . 8 . . . Not a sound or a speck of light.

Girlfriend held our popcorn bucket; the big BIG bucket, extra butter, light on the salt. Waited. She goes "Hmmm" so I knew she wanted to ask, "When will it start?"

169

She didn't.

She'd picked this one with a black-lacquered nail and the word, "Fun!"

I love her eyes when her lips exclaim, FUN!

"One of Nishimura's disciples. It'll be a romp of wild madness." Added, "Kilter will be about as straight as bizzaro ballet on meth and broken heels."

Didn't shrug. After the fits and starts and black drag of the week (aftershocks and ultimatums included at no extra charge) we needed a night out . . . *And some fun.* And thumbing through the free, local entertainment-weekly and not finding a new *Bubba Nosferatu*, or *John Wayne Ho-tep*, or *ZOMBIE SUPERMARKET (the Sequel to the Sequel)*, or even a *Black Lagoon Bubba VII* (she frowned and made a little fist), she hit on this one. (To think, I was sure I was in for *Zombie Scarecrow Cheerleaders vs. The Robovampire Assassins*, currently playing a "HELD OVER 4 times" at Kaminsky's VALHALLA. Mid-budget, toilet paper script, Ed Wood's mutant cousin director, I quickly sighed in relief.) She only picks the *best* worst horror. Or so she informs me.

Lucky me. Go ahead, say it.

This one might be sushi with chainsaws. A mutant freak parade of schoolgirl outfits and g-strings, ooh-la-la bunnies with Thompson machine guns, rat-fink wolves, mad&MOD rocker TEENS with ray-guns and katanas and 27th-century power tools. Japanese blood-soaked grindhouse (If I were PC guess I'd call it J-Horror, but I'm sure as hell not PC! Not this life.) with a laugh-track. PUMP UP the T&A and bucket up the FAKEblood and chicken/beef/what-have-you parts, put it in the MIXMASHER and set it to goofy-gone-WILDLYabsurd, add 60's go-go music peakin' at JUMP!JUMP!Boogaloo. Or it could start with flamin' batwaves crashing on Asteroid Beach, Woodies parked and the radio broadcasting "Scientists find shocking evidence of—*Soul-eating Robot Mermaids* in the astronomic swamps of Planet Alamo—" . . .

OK. Wasn't like it would be an eternity. Deal me in.

Might be fun. Like the time two birthday's back, when I got her the Punitive Guillotina action figure (now that was "FUN!"). (No, I'm not tellin' ya what we did with it.)

Might be she'll be happy I didn't gruff and it will be sweet suck kisses and love-tumble-juju when we get home. Might be good for the conscience too.

Anything for my girl, right?

Yep.

At this point you might think I don't go in much for B horror flickers, yer right. Me and blood don't mix well. I like my sandbox dry. And it's better for the cactus.

But what the hell. She digs 'em. Hey, even horror-minded geek-goth-girls need a laugh right?

Dive-bombing the soaked-in RE~V~E~R~B Fender returns—SURF'S UP but so far no vampire beach babes.

On the screen full moon with a lewd grin. Winks.

And we're combusticatin'!

Ancient Dracula's castle high on a craggy cliff face. Slowly zoom in. Bats wing by. Wolves howl. Massive doors with a roaring gargoyle's face dead center and Igor (lab coat and steampunk accoutrements and a rainbow lei), blasted eyes lookin' like Jumpin' Hula Flash, opens it. "*U-ahhh.* Welcome . . . to Night of *Tiki.*" And he laughs, high-pitched touch of nails on a blackboard in it.

Vampire tiki? Only those beautiful Japanese madmen would put that together. Did I just say beautiful? Maybe I've up and gone WACKED, or Doctor Tarr and Professor Feather nutty?

5 minutes in and I'm parked in my seat and in the row in front of me Texas Chainsaw Babyface-Armageddon has come out of his basement of a 1,000 stupidass things for this. Did I say, lucky me? Meant too. Also meant to add, oh FUCK. And he's telling his wingmen tall tales of yore and derring-do, involving last night and last week and next Saturday night if he can lay his paws on beer money, and they're buying it.

All of it.

Don't shake your head; I didn't say pearls before swine. That was your thought.

So we have 57 "FUCK"s and farting that induces laughs, and a mini-belching contest. I'm about to napalm them into an alternate reality (a Nazi experimental lab, tentacles and an auto-da-FLAY a must, or a jungle of commercial meat slices and reparation-minded turkeys, rabbits and pigs would work pretty good too!) and she puts her hand on mine and head swaying side to side, says no.

Anything for my girl, right?

Almost.

I point to seats across the aisle. She says no.

Jefferson said when VERY mad count to 1,000. I'm on it!

... 732 ... (Anything for my girl!) ... 733 ... (Blood suckers. CK! Crawling hands. CK!) ... 734 ... (Dr. Coffin's horror chamber of blood. CK!) ... 735 ... (Time travelling zombies. CK!) ...

I begin to think about the knife in my boot and how easily it would slide into the back of Armageddon-Boy's seat. I may never win the LOTTO, but I'm real good on reeling off fantasy scenarios of what if.

They're here for blood, right?

Hell, they said so 127 times.

So why not help them out?

... 736 ...

And she squeezes my hand and blows me a kiss.

OK. They keep on breathing and I get mucho points.

Anything for my girl. Especially when she gives me THAT smile.

Two months ago it was *Vampire Girl vs. Frankenstein Girl.* Movie was definitely NOT my bag (even though I laughed twice); I mean c'mon, a mad kabuki scientist who plays air guitar with ripped-out spinal columns and that nurse who had eyeballs sown on her nipples, how can you not find that amusing? Popcorn was ridiculously priced. But she was an angel. Talk about heavenly hugs after. I'm not. Don't go in for kiss and tell.

So we're into tonight's laugh-riot chiller. Got blood, not too much yet—YAY! Boobs slipping out of fetishistic gear, a cheese-O Farfisa [might be a Vox] organ solo over blistering riffery of surf TWANG, and one of the Big Tit Zombie girls, Cayenne X—HULK green skin, hot as Tabasco sauce and bloody, is sword fighting with some Frankenstripper (talk about this ain't *KILL BILL,* and I paid less for the popcorn that time).

CUT TO: a control panel. Knobs and dials and a computer screen—and the sub-titled credits roll before the sword-stroke decapitation—can ya say, cliffhanger?

He did this. He, the other one, did that. That guy was in on it, and his pal catered and did make-up. Someone else did a bunch of things, in print so small Hubble and his lens would have trouble eyeballing it.

Cut to we're back—

And we're not in Drac's castle anymore. Did I mention I love Japanese directors? There's Dorothy, no cute little gingham dress or pigtails. She's not from Kansas. She's Japanese. And our Dorothy never had a sword and a chainsaw, and maybe it was me, but if our Miss Gale had a bust like that I think I would have noticed.

Tokyo. A dark and stormy night. Rain-skinned streets. Shadowy man-things lurking in the fog-licked shadows. Skullduggery afoot. Lots of NEON. Lots. Hey, it's Tokyo by night, right?

Frankenstripper, our Dorothy for this flicker, is in a hurry. Her eyes say so. Heavy black Doc Martins too.

And our first Thing that walks like a dead Egyptian steps out of an alley.

I know my girl's smiling. Me, I'm at the popcorn and wondering if this one will have clowns with tentacles, or maybe a WACKED-mad scientist with a horde of hot-pink mechanical spiders collecting body parts for some secret government experiment.

She's the one who read the review; I'm half tempted to ask. Didn't.

So the J-splatter fest with the helium-laugh track is chugging along . . . 13 snake-nippled [Yes, their nipples are snapping, hissing snakes] ninja-chicks with venomous centipedes forming from their phosphorescent orange spit, and over a dozen Sassy Bikini Zombies assault our heroine. She hacks, rips, splits, cuts—there's green slime and yellow goo on a Pollock-bender [Think *No. 8* or *No. 32*] everywhere.

And I hear a scream behind me. It's real as hell too. I whip around.

Madame TaxiderMia [from *Madame TaxiderMia vs. the Zombie Scarecrow-Cheerleaders of Mars*] (in hot-pink, leather hot pants) (and a bird mask w/ chrome fangs on the beak) is standing in the aisle I'm sitting in, enters to a spaghetti western soundtrack of *TWANG!*, reverb, and blazing Mariachi horns (seems she's brought her own band, and they ain't half bad) and a shotgun blast. Nope, she's not alone. Her platinum blond, wise-crackin', 7-foot, chrome-plated bra, gun-totin', chainsaw-wielding sidekick, Zimona, *die Walkyre vom Red Planet* [sans her leopard-spotted unicorn, Uncle Beauregard—this wonder woman don't fly Trans-Love-Airways] is in full sidekick position on her left—Always wondered if that's some close to the heart thingy? Talk about dynamic duos! Out comes the barbarian cutlery of choice. Guess they're saving the 5-chrome-plated 9mm's on their hips for later.

Sword and chainsaw are out, and working double-time, as there's a smack of Sassy Bikini Zombies in the theater, and they're grabbing movie-goers, ripping off arms and munching away like it's free Smorgasbord.

Splatter up! Zimona swings, first Sassy Bikini Zombie's head is roll-

ing in the aisle. Madame TaxiderMia's samurai sword arcs, takes 2 off—
Hat trick!

It's an invasion of the Sassy Bikini Zombies. Yep. Flooding the aisles.
Talk about yer, Lord here comes the flood. Tall, leggy, half of them top-
less—(I'm not one for Double-G green boobs), and each and every one
comes with swords, scythes, and cleavers, oh my. And I see Armageddon-boy's head meet a scythe-avalanche (the one who looked like Bet-
tie Page as Gotharilla had a BIG gardening implement). Guess his
Mexican jumping bean mood-swing mambo with bye-bye saves me the
bother?

Hell, this is better than a Haunted Hay Ride. Yes, my girl's taken
me on a few of them too. And that's what I'm thinking. Like the haunted hay rides this is a staged live action blood & boobs funfest.

There's screams and their sequels.

OK. Fine. As long as there's no raincoat required.

I'm grinning and suppressing a laugh (most of the other audience
members are herding the EXITs), up until the first blood hits me.

"Shit."

Yep. Real blood.

And upon closer inspection, I note that's real gore.

YIKES! Human hamburger midnight.

Not a poker face in the horde. All the cards-on-the-table intentions
full of go to display—Black tongues are lapping and latherin'. Inhuman
black eyes are glazed with devour-fever. Fangs are CHOMPIN'! Not a
single lie bursting from the choir.

And the buzzing flies effect, I really did like that, well, them's real
flies. Guess it figures, rotting flesh attracts real eaters of the dead.

My bucket of popcorn is between my feet and I'm standing, reach-
ing for my girl. And she's gone.

Gone?

Without me?

Snatched by some zombie-thing?

I'm craning my neck high and low, left right and behind in search.
No. No! And NO! Can't see her, or any part of her anywhere.

Out comes my 9 (can't live here in Noirtown without some Old
West protection these days). And I'm stalking the aisles. My FEAR on
high alert. Their feed-bag greed eyein' my bony butt.

WAY TOO CLOSE range blast a zombie, look down the aisle.

Zippo. Zippo. Zippo.

Madame TaxiderMia, who I saw last year in *Demon Girl's Fun-GO! Battle with Hellscorpion Schoolgirl* and *Astrovamp Gore-Dancer from Women's Prison Planet M vs. Princess Cannibal-Witch,* and I exchange glances as my 9 takes out two Sassy Bikini-things.

She's lopping off arms and heads like a methed-up hyperthyroid-ninja with a grudge the size of Mt. Rushmore. Don't know how she got here or why, but with this herd of lumbering zombies on deathslow shambleabout, I'll take whatever help I can get.

I cap two ankle-munchers clawin' at my legs as Zimona liberates their skulls from their rotting necklines.

"Thanks."

"War mir ein Vergnügen, Süsser."

Zimona had that he's sexy-as-hell grin on her face, so even though I didn't understand a word I figured it was good.

The attack of the bikini cadavers is in full swing, bloody part here, ten stumps there, bunch of hissing and moanin'. Teeth-teeth-teeth, and things that look like claws—felt like it too. Kinda odd we ain't seen a tentacle yet. Gotta tell ya, I'm in a panic of where's my Baby?

I'm forever and eternity tellin' her she needs to be careful there's tons of assbags and weirdoes in the world and they love hot stunners. That's where she Sssh's me.

Something outta a Raimi-WILDride must have dragged her off to some dark hell and I'm worried sick she screamed and in all the blood and the blood and the screams I didn't hear her over the auto-da-scherzo.

If I lost her I'll be crushed with a suicide on top. And her sister will kill me. She's got the connections to do it to. I should also mention my gal's sister is Zoli Kraven, the scream queen. Been in a mess of B's, *Nazi Body Snatchers at the Gates of Roswell, Vampireville Gangsterama, The Eldritch Space Vixens' Hell-Holiday Beach Party, Pretty Deadly Violet's Conflict with the Yakuza Goreghouls,* Elroy Ron Alvin's *Vivacious Vixens Gone Ghoul, Vampire Honeymoon on Planet Alamo, Dr. Funkenstein's Extraterrestrial Surf Party,* and *Necronomicomedy.* Even produced and directed *Sherlock Freud Prisoner of Ilsa's SS Prison of the Damned Kinky* and *Redneck Cemetery.* Good kid for a horrorshow ghoul, wired & weird add two extra helpings of FRIGHTmare, but who wouldn't be, living out there in Flickerville?

She pops out of her casket between screamers and stops by. Keeps my gal supplied with news, DVDs, props, gossip, and news of the family, even their living kin. Buy me a brew sometime and I'll tell about her family. The Addams are the fucking Ronald Wilson Reagans.

She also knows more about voodoo/DEATH/witchcraft shit and firearms than 16 demons and a Delta Force armorer.

Gotta find my Baby, come hell or HELL.

That's what I'm thinkin', HELL! And it pops out of the movie screen. Not out of, but through! !! Elephant BIG! GREEN—'cept the giant RED head with a dozen horns and spikes. Claws on the end of Boom-Boom paws that could crush 55-gallon drums. Warren Zevon is pleading in my head, except the lawyers and money part. And yes, I'd surely like to hurry on home early.

I just stand there for 6 eye-blinks till the bigass Godzilla-lizardtail sweeps around.

JUMP or get thraKKed! I pick JUMP.

And off comes the tip. Zimona's chainsaw lobs off a nice hunk, and then comes back for another slice. Man, she had culinary talents. CHOP-SLICE/E/E/E/E-dice, we're talking' Queen of Cut-cut-cut-lery.

Well, I'm expecting it to wail in pain and it don't! Nope!! In between a few expletives MIGHTY HELL BEAST from who the hell knows where starts screaming in Japanese.

Suddenly I'm face to face with a zombie ooga-boobies queen and my head is between her double JJ's and sassy bra buster's squeezing them together trying to pop the pimple I call a brain and I'm thinking *It can talk? And it speaks Japanese?*

Any NASCAR-lovin' bubba would have the sense to be yellin' "SHIT!" or "Help!", but not dumbo-me. Way back when I was a knee-high-shaver I saw monsters like this in the comics—loved 'em. But I didn't grow up to be Turok Son of Stone and somewhere along the line I lost my Space-Captain Flag raygun, so I'm thinkin' *It can talk?* instead of I'm fucked! Better make that all caps—FUCKED!! Yeah, that's it.

Well bra buster's head comes off before mine pops and I hear Madame TaxiderMia yell, "Will you shoot some of these damn things?"

"Sure 'nuff, Ma'am."

Do.

6. And then stop and reload.

Wondered what the Godzilla's name was. Odd thought to run through your mind when you're ankle-deep in gore&goo, but all those weird and cool names of Marvel monsters when I was a kid, couldn't help myself. Loved me some ORRGO and ZZUTAK, and The CREATURE from KROGAAR.

BLASTED 6 more Sassy Bikini Zombies, most of which had lost their tops, and thought of the dimwads that had been sitting in front of us. Didn't have to chase the walking dead. If Mr. (currently dead-as-shit) Texas Chainsaw Babyface-Armageddon was still alive he'd love that, girls that walked right up to you and wanted yer meat. Bet he'd have comments aplenty for that.

Zimona and Madame TaxiderMia are hackin' away on the Godzilla-thing. There goes the arm. There goes the other. Drops with a THUD. Leg not so elegantly removed. Then let's play chainsaw conjures green blood from the throat strike for total ruination. Other two legs OFF and OFF

THUDdddddddddddddddddddddd! !!

Damn thing is lying there w/ a bloody nose and no appendages. Wheezes a couple of times. Expires.

Bloodbath soundin' like SPLAT & BLAM-BLAM-BLAM all around me and someone brings more show to the party—Fat little pink-plushy bats with kite-tentacle-tails are kamikazing 'round pooping out trails of toxic smelling stuff that rains down and sizzles holes in anything it touches. .9 time! Pop-Pop-Pop they're fallin' and I'm waltzin' with a busty-gory that just won't die.

Chainsaw purrin' R.I.P(ieces) steps in, Gone, Baby, Gone!

Zimona smiles, asks. "You OK so far, cutie?"

"Fair to up to my asshole in beasties, like you, ma'am."

She gives me a stick-with-me-kid wink.

So we're hackin' and cappin' away in this scene right out of *Half-Barenaked Vampire Babysitters KILL KILL, FEAST! FEAST!!* And the great director in the sky or whomever is behind the curtain here in OZ decides it's up the ante time.

BAM! The 4 ride in—yeah, The 4. No not the Four Horseman. The 4!

Death.

Mr. Death, the older brother of Death.

Miss Death.

And Death Jr.

True devils, eliminators, or just plain cold as the bowels of what lies under Skull Mountain mysteries that love massacres, you pick. Puppet or psycho, icon, barbarian, Indian chief, they kill all. Bunnies, kitties, superheroes, squirrels too.

Skull-headed, black robe wearin', and circlin' overhead. Ridin' giant, prison-striped lizard-bats and they're dropping rotten pumpkins loaded with crab-bots, bet they bought them from the outlaw queen of the robots, Anubis Loki. 4 legs, 4 tentacles and a little Cthulhu face, damn if the things don't come in designer colors and some are striped, some polka dot. Even thought I saw a tie-dye one. Damn things are squirmin' and squirreling over everything. Mini-chomp-chomp-chomp on heads and shoulders. Buggers are sure ZIPPY.

Zimona reached in her oversize Jimmy Chew "Woodstock Meets Warrior" fringed-leather shoulder bag, pulled out a handful of multicolor little star-shaped sparklies. Looked like New Year's Eve party favors. And she tossed them in a great arcing rain that snowed down. ZAP!-crackle-pop crab-bots were shorting out every time one of the glittery star things touched 'em. Little Cthulhu heads would swell and POP and the gooey slime splattered and oozed.

Almost stopped and shook my head. Woodstock for the sword & sandal set and Cthulhu finally makes it into bot-design, quicker on my feet, I might have said, what a world.

Couple of more dustings of glittery sparklies—the green ones sure were pretty—and they all broke.

In the bullet and blade ballet of STORM bumps, going from plain strange to mindwarped heaps of grim (extra PAIN on top) to ultraviolent Coney Island freakshow, Madame TaxiderMia was punchin' clocks at ninjaWARP speed. Head back, bosom bloody and full on vendetta, lady ain't no litigator, she laughs. Takes three heads in a single pirouette and says, "Rilly groovy."

Then she leaps, no crouching no hidden just sword-swingin' TIGER, FANGS (or in her case BLADE) munchin' meat!

Hell, must have been more than a hundred Sassy Bikini Zombies but they seem to have all taken the dead way out.

Good, right?

Oh yeah, sure Bub. You try standing here with reality pulled all the back to you can't get there from here. See them? That's The 4 just dropped in to see what condition they can rearrange your condition into! Vegas odds are leaning heavy on dead & in creature feature color.

That be, Death. Mr. Death. Miss Death. And Death Jr. Recall me mentionin' them? Good.

One laughs—you know, banshee from the hells beneath the hells of Hell Planet cluster of aural sonics louder than a stack of Marshalls blarin' napalm at a Black Sabbath concert. Then they all join in. Hell's anvil chorus laughin' or moanin', or I don't know what it is but it sounds like *RAAAAAAAAAH* or *YHAAAAAAAAAAAAAAAAAAARG* and it scares me, not white, but damn close.

Madame TaxiderMia just laughs back. Yells, "You wanna little caress until we part. Got some that will just destroy you!" She's taken out a compact mirror and I'm thinkin' fix yer lip-gloss now? Not a good choice. I mean if that's what yer into, Goodbye Kitty pink with little skulls and broken hearts on a danglin' red string, I guess, but not now.

First shot of the compact's death-ray gives Death Jr. a lobotomy. He drools a bit of blood and keels over. One down and I'm grinnin'. All I could think of was the Cramps *Look Mom No Head.*

Death's eyes go freaky as a Mason-as-Hulk rampage, but Madame TaxiderMia's death-ray lights up with a KRAAKAW*W*Wzzzzz* WzzzWW~W puts a big not now in his here I come! Two bad guys flushed. Hope the janitors in this joint got industrial-size mops. Lots of goo pourin' out.

Mr. Death well he just dives at Madame T but Zimona says let's play MORE!-chainsaw with this soul-cravin' demon. RURRRRRRRr-*IPPPPPP* leg off. Nip, arm off. Lunge, other arm OFF. Wilder Wilder—other leg, DE-parted! Old Stumpy splat on the floor and she does the coroner a favor, unzips Mr. Deadass throat to crotch.

Just Miss Death and no date to the prom. Skull-face on a killer bod in a pink babydoll and she's starin' down Zimona. Vegas odds are heavy on Zimona. Mine too. Chainsaw comes up and the babydoll is over her hips, and skull bowling ball is rollin'. STRIKE—we have a winner!

Swords and chainsaws and death-rays all whirrrr and RIPPPPPPPPPPPP, for a couple of doomfaring goddesses of destruction they were pretty good at redecorating. Had an interesting way of making things look different.

I turned and stepped over a body, sighted, POP-POP. Watched two eyes reshape as black holes in a zombie face. Thought mindless maybe, but that had to hurt. Can't say why, but I didn't laugh.

No sassys standing. None bumpin' and grindin' and moanin' on the floor. Everything looked pretty damn dead.

Me, I exhaled.

Zimona. Madame TaxiderMia. No sigh of relief. Just standing there. Not hard, but solid, proud—pure Frazetta. Ready if they had to deal with more.

It appeared to be all quiet on the zombie front. Bad thing in a monster flicker right? That's what I'm thinking. But no zombies or surgically-engineered Frankenvampires popped up to kick start the horrorshow hoedown.

Jacked on adrenaline and breathing hard I'm straight back to where's my girl and about to ask the ladies if they'd check the ladies room. Like in this mess I shouldn't just barge in?

Before I could ask Zimona turned to me. "You did great, Pilgrim. Ever get out stop by my place. Might show a cutie like you how some *other* things are done. *Even if you're not wearing a loincloth.*" Winked. Smiled hotter than a death-ray pistol set to full ZAP.

I smiled back. Didn't really wish I was available, but . . . "If I was single I'd be following you home right now. But got a sweetie and like you she's a 10."

Laid a bigger smile on me. Eyes dropped the love-me-tight glimmer while you sock-it-ta-me. Kinda looked a-might disappointed.

Moving slowly a hand brushes my ankle. Yawning sound goes with it. Zimona's about to lob it off and there's a face. My sweetie's face.

"STOP! DON'T!" I filled the space between the sword blade and Sweetie's face.

Looking up. "Oh my? What the . . . ?'

"Jimmy?"

"Baby, you OK?"

Yawns again. Smiles. "Sorry, Baby. Bored me. Was suddenly too tired to contend with it. I dozed off. Appears I missed the good part."

I'm grinnin' ear to ear.

Stand's up. Shrugs and smiles an apology. Follows it with another sorry.

I get a hug.

Zimona turns away for that. Maybe she's not as hard as one might think?

Madame T sticks out a bloody hand. I take it. She nods. I nod back.

"Thanks."

Wiping her blade off, Madame TaxiderMia nods a no problem in reply.

There's swirling clouds of greenish vapors and strange Ditko-esque outcroppings in the gaping hole in the movie screen. Swords and guns at the ready we stare at it for a moment. No beasties from alien dimensions pop up.

"Back to the Batcave," Madame TaxiderMia says as her and Zimona walk to it. Leap. Into the mist of another dimension . . .

Funny. I'm running around, fearing the worst, and my sweetie, after the 5th yawn, had slipped under her seat, curled up, and napped like a balled-up kitten. She had a long day at the office, and blood and the B monsters on the screen, well, there's times she'll just find 'em a tad dull.

Why's that? I can only say she gets bored. She's seen it all at Renfield's *Classic Monster & Godzilla Emporium* where she's the Special Events Coordinator and if you fail to engage her she'll drift away.

Not a drop of blood on my gal. I'm beaming.

And I'm kinda proud of myself.

She's beaming too. I confess I like that look. Superhero even on a small scale is a good thing.

Takes my hand. Leans in.

Kiss.

. . . And it was off to home to get boring . . . Maybe pop Doctor Intelligalactia and the Jr. Narco Rangers in the DVD player and snuggle while the old serial spins? Vegas odds are not even close to even.

Slow walk hand in hand.

Corner of Goon and Usher.

Don't seem very scary.

Not tonight.

Don't even glance up to see if The Owl or the Gray Gargoyle will drop down with some nefarious skullduggery in mind.

I had journeyed into strange and astonishing and was glad the carnage war wasn't a double feature, or a dusk till dawn.

Quiet. Slow. Old folks slow. Soiled walls. Cracked walls. Black alleys of dust and thieves' moments. Streetlamp flicker a candle glow . . .

After my shower I'm in the kitchen, grabbing a slice of cold pizza from the fridge when my girl comes in, asks, "Was it OK, Igor? I so hope you'll forgive me for nodding off and scaring you like that."

I wolf down the bite and turn (was thinking of saying, "No problem, hon," or maybe, "You owe me one").

Didn't.

Why?

Well she's there (red cowgirl hat with skull tassels) (a BLACK & RED feather boa and a bandolier) (and the gothic-Lolita black babydoll she's wearing, well that's speakin' to me) posed in the doorway as a spaghetti western soundtrack of *TWANG!*, reverb, and blazing Mariachi horns announce the shift in her hips.

Her sword comes out. Points at my slice. "Need me to trim that up for you?"

I laughed.

Big Tits Zombies in 3D?

PASS! !! Major-bigass pass. You should see my girl. When she's not killing 'em at Renfield's she knows how to drop a funfest on me. Nails it every time!

& the time is NIGH. See my ghoul, Kaustic PhoeniXxx, is pointing at our bedroom door and the double-wide coffin. And her fangs are glowin'&smilin' *FUNHOUSE—*

Deal me in!

But the next time one of her black-lacquered nails points to the movie section of the paper it better be RETRO, cute, and wacky on ZANY pills. Some *Plan 9* or *Tribulation 99* or *The Ghost in the Invisible Bikini*, and Elvira can ill-elegantly step closer and daze me anytime, one whiff of *Satan's Daughter's Brain vs. the L.A. Zombieland Gore-Strippers* or *The Busty Cadaver Slaves of Dr. Sadist Battle the Samurai Stripper Police* I'm politely calling in sick for Date Night.

after Vampire Girl vs. Frankenstein Girl and STAN & JACK! & DITKO!!

various tunes by Alice Cooper, Cramps, Vampire Beach Babes, Bambi Molesters

Caroline No. Bleue

For a & e

I. ~where cold moonlight points.....

what

> *incantations will manifest when they set fire to the witch? Will the spells carved on her flesh with branding irons be released on the stake?*

Yes. No . . . a scream, trembling breasts, hands impregnating time with a tongue of yellow breath.

So sad. The afterward. Bleak. Barefoot, her feet on the naked tile. Cold tile. Her bangs are a wall defending dreams.

"Caroline." But I can't remember the number. And the voices will not answer. Their wet cheeks are bells swallowing beating wings.

"Damn your empty soul."

And the voices will not answer—

> this sleepless night is madness, its soil a trance of screams . . . death, dust,
> > what they bury in the crimson throat of tomorrow . . .

moonlight . . . the autumn chill a grave of kisses . . . the fever stirs . . . incisors, the language of windows . . . in your soul, the loneliness howls . . . For the Mad Only, yes. Yes

> the silence of the moon grows . . . a window . . . yellow drapes . . . a kiss . . . DEADLY

selecting keys. the wounds her eyes made in my beauty. drinking strong emotion the day passed. the speed of her amusements did not. I'm no stranger to rules, I told her what I was feeling. every thought. not a one ended with goodbye. I was aching but I played her game; blind, I swung in her shadows; flew when her spider gave me eggs. she was the snake that unrolled my nakedness, I was the bride and the moon, at her call. she wore the mask of a lion. opened her skirt, there were armies. she could glide, nip, form rock, swarm or devil; take me, chunks, eaten alive; shipwrecked my shore on her cathedrals. all that mattered, her being a dream. that's all. my all. but she had to skin it. without saying why.

"Caroline."

Just her eyes. Licking me. Like I'm a bowl. She has flies eyes. They want the salt on my breast.

Still lips. They wish me death. Still, don't move. All on the lips; looking in—then what rhymes with goodbye. All. It was spooky. Giant sunshine you could not runaway from. It was like dirty water too.

I left the room. And her with all those books and the pictures of her—more beautiful than any trophy, or mountain of gems and gold, more than any art—just perfect, every curve, every curve soft, perfect. Perfect. Left her. There. Was she laughing? All that autumn stuffed into her hands in that dark room and she could laugh?

That witch laugh that screamed from her open mouth; all that internal night coming to crucify me, to take my space and nail it shut.

She came to my bed with only her skullface; the shadow of her tongue my tempest. Hands out. Mastered my eyes. Took—the rabbit in her mouth. Left no book in my hands. It was harmless. I was. Was. I was not armed. She knew. Knew.

But she forgot to look under my bed.

Caroline No. Bleue ... **Twilight From the Archives:** (Paris: Fattal, 1978), 28. *i read them more than once; over and over; knew them like pretty women and death. Because i love it -to hide ME in the bed and stay, shivering .... watching under the bed for some rats or monsters ...and the darkness of the book is crawling over my backbone until it reaches my neck............... frost. the sky far away .... this waltz with the rat shadows—little cannibal monsters stuffing bread, my roots, my thick taste, into their black mouths, scalding me with I LOVE YOU—with eyes closed............... want.want.want— rattles in my darkness—rattles every starving feather................... WANT*

to flex what never was.................... waltz on striped legs with my illness—
let it split and quarter................. want to let my words sleep—fire to fire—
in the pleats with sheep, watch their cannibal-hands vanish from their lips—
oval mouth to oval mouth....................want all that there is.

Caroline says that's too much. But not for her. No. No. She dictates to the shadows. No. No. Took. Turns. Leaves hollow in the shadows.

Forgot to look under my bed. Forgot I had a hellbound train. Forgot I had incantations and spells carved on flesh, and branding irons, and iron stakes. Planted them at the crossroads, fertilized them with screams.

Caroline forgot the silence can cry.

She had taken my bow, but not my string. I hid my smile from the high tide of her sun.

Used. Painted me muse—painted me slight—fool—"Be a good fool." Took. The embryo of every surface I was trying to balance. She sucked it up and made it her flesh.

Damn your empty soul. Witch soul. Rat teeth black, conjuring blind.
She doesn't think I see the reflection. I saw the pictures. Saw when she was
perfect—more beautiful than any trophy, or mountain of gems and gold,
more than any famed art of genius—just perfect, every curve, every curve
soft, perfect. Perfect. I didn't have to dream to taste them .... every
curve........

cobwebs in the bottom of her eyes....... barb-wire sharp lies....... they move I stay still.......... can't get away.......... the dark barks.............

overboard, lost the wheel.................... heels won't do what I want them to................... I offered dead or alive............... they won't fly.............. won't reach for what sits on the shelf........................

stuck..........here.............
under the grave-sky under the bed in the forest of wind.............

clawing maggot shadows longandfast and a rotting tongue.............. no flower-altar hands.........

mouth fullof splinter................. thorn repetition of the never owl.................. how did it speak when the stars were turned off..........

locked.............but not safe.............

Take. Incantations will manifest when they set fire to the witch. The
spells carved on her flesh with branding irons be released on the stake.

II. ~when she is a landscape.....

Caroline thinks I'm sleeping, tied to dreams. But I'm watching—

Moon crashes in. She's dancing naked on the carpet, her bare feet—nails painted with eyes, tapping the sigils. Crooked-tower witch's hat ringed by circling bats and signs purloined from Merlin. Naked. Graceful and cruel. Beautiful, deadly. Deadly. Smiling like she did when she smiled and wore red. Red. Smiled about it. Laughed that saxophone laugh.

Naked. Curves, highways. Round and soft and deadly. Blue curves. Hips. Hips for me to beg to. Dancing. All that fire charm, the menu, the punishment—my guilt—I'm to blame.

> frontier
> poor with
> agreement.

> *Translated—blind . . . Annotation in a gust of scarecrow ink soured with bone(like the story's wrinkled insides)*
> *. . . in bed together, the value of a canvas not contrary to high—pouring growing on the pyre—not ripped by other contexts, or torture's cargo—not having to stroke my own fix.*

> *not shut fast with*
> *time to*
> *go—*
> *unless the sound—launched (urgent with the thick print of ghosts) of the obstacle in my brain throbs and won't flush worst.*
> *first tinged*
> *advantage pulled ALL THE WAY down.*

I crossed the cold. Heard her shoulders hiss. Those aren't tattoos on her back, they're eyes. Black and red eyes. She has a thousand eyes. All of them, hunger shining, consume pieces of my flesh. Nip. Nip. Tear. Hungry black eyes. Hungry red eyes. Eyes, crow-black, of the skullface. Feeding. Shadow-eyes that want the rabbit on their tongue.

She thinks I can't see behind her bangs. Thinks the wall is too thick, too high. Thinks my face is caught by the flight of her spider-legs. Oh they fly.

> cigarette
> who stepped here
> sad gnaws from the speaker

guitar of could
deleted
ebb
old lights
long after galloping
back
late and jealous—false begin
whirl
several meanings in each
as one—wishing
shard
smears the walls
no laugh
with a thousand plans
to flourish
no
camouflage—prisoner every drop upset
abandon
soars for dust ....oh
                 she said sherbet smooth
                 sucking the verbs out of my lantern
with her storyline
of
disease
and the stacks
of dreams
wanted most
remedies
tense
a common wedding gown
             and
my little drawer of crayons
wake
salt appetite
takes
away
see lines of a spade
trying to

> disappear
> choose

Sweet. In those music arms filled with cake. Mountains quick enough to dance. Ripped my dress with her wind. Said, so? My little mouth yelled stop. Quietly wishing to quiet the thousand mouths in her guts.

Wouldn't play the healing game.
Wouldn't change.
Black word swan.
Ripped my dress.

> no lament. laugh. no more winding leprosy, I have fire to put in graves.

> smoke lamentations—unrolling the path—burn the spiders with my drums—covering her face with bells

> the shard of her sentence
> struck
> the hand stays clear—no wrong with angles
> heap
> under the ashtray's fist
> a constellation of meat
> struck
> the flowers have to go—with the crows

III. ~a table of pages.....

Sunday afternoon . . . my comb next to her comb . . . Hand ~soul ~wine ~knots . . . radio collaborating with moody cruel . . . her summer flower is lovely to see . . . my breasts trembled . . . I polished her with my breath . . . the smell of other mouths leaves her mouth . . . she left a bruise on my pier . . . eyes closed to my eyes her naked ass spilling out the door . . . "Look back." . . . clutching wormwood I swabbed my bruise with the colors of unfolded rain . . .
Sunday afternoon . . . soul—misted blind
"Too much."
Slow fox . . .
"Too much."
L'Heure Bleue

"Caroline. No."
Drawn appears
funeral legs hoot under the moon
the broom jumps the abyss of evil thoughts

midnight
midnight spinning the ritual of nails
her red dress is the spectrum of ditches chanting bells
that smell like winter raw
and bleue

Twilight bleue—the wand game—storm dance—heart poems supple
and pure i gave to the rocks—all my silk to forget the petrified silence
and the colors of black eternity—let rain wear its hat / with poppies
and ginseng and old vampire movies Caroline splashed madness on the
kingdom on my pillow / with flowers and kisses and flies that brought
knives to my tears

       naked. Her curves. I took her smile. Beautiful, deadly. Deadly
. . . Smile—like she did when she smiled and wore red.
       her smile came off in my hands
       part of it
       broken like the ashtray

    No smile. Framed by the black boards of the floor. Naked on the
floor. Caroline no. Not smiling like she did when she smiled and wore
red.
       My spell

will

    —sink her in grays and ash and raven bites—burn the trees she
fished—pull her wings from my roots
       she stirs. Shakes. No smile. No smile like she did when she smiled
and wore red. She's missing a tooth . . . no smile. Curves . . . and Red.
Blots, winter stains-seamless.i'm not sad.kick.stay down.won't come back
again.not with this clock.no ten count.down.you're not an earthshaker an-
ymore.i loose your darkness and shadows.me matters now.your patterns
no longer invite. No longer say. ME!

"Me."

Robin bleue. Her erect nipples were horizons as she crawled. I pulled. She was drowning. Her legs stopped flying.

Her hip is a sculpture. Art for me to worship. That's what she wants, wants me to worship. I do. She should know that. She should know it! I told her. I let the sun on my tongue, let it speak as if it was a crowd filling a field with born. I offered. Called her grace—Paradise. I expressed everlasting. Gave my fleece.

Promised, "You've got me now."

Eyes laughed and...............................And she took.

Made knots of no. Brushed NOT across the sky. Widened it. Yelled it like a stone. Made it a spider, lash-legs of bone to arrest me with its trenches of bitter rust.

Took.

Closed her hand! Absorbed it. Love doing it.

All of it.

Always loved doing it; the way she rolled on the bed, clinging to my hive, camping in my name.

Now I have the stakes.

I look at the stairs

                        .... intertwined, the lines that waited to talk to the window............... vertigo—taut, shaking, shadows beating their wings, distracted the stars from colliding into the evidence.................... she tries to crawl away........... the interior of forever............ the drops arrive...............

IV. ~the crow's fragile felt......

Stained glass deceived—when she said, "Stay awake.".......... Opened my secret hands. Updated flesh and blood—torrid red. Burned me with her smile—like she did when she smiled and wore red.

~after the white rabbit pub—the object brandishing effect / clitoris— poetic fruit big as a fountain / dance / first hand—kissing her bumblebee- music / seal&sign / "Stay awake. Stay awake." / apply the moon to her canvas—my fright of sinking -fingers giving birth to tears~

When she took off my dress. Wound (–marking—breathing—

dedicating—defining chemistry with her angel armor passed to my mouth) that beauty around me. And—that splash of glutinous body— took off her dress. Her red dress—when she smiled and wore red.

I couldn't close my eyes when she walked on water and smiled that smile.

...........................like she did when she wore red.......................

The iron is hot. Ready to write spells on her flesh.

Flesh. The thought makes me quiver. Curves . . . When she wore red and smiled. Oh she was the sun. She made my fingers burn. She made me sing and not want to drop the eternal that followed . . . when she wore red and smiled.

I have to save my string. I know where she put my bow. I need my bowstring. When the sun's heart comes out I'll need my bow.

witching hour words.......................

Caroline. No.

My incantation set fire to the witch.

Like the other ones—enough to make a coven. All their black hair walking on my shoulders. Spiders. Coming with their saxophone eyes. All those eyes that tattooed my flesh. Took me.

> away
> i was not
> their dove.
> near their lie.
> why?
> why?
> then disappear.
> took
> truth.
> even when i told them
> every one of them
> stop.
> witches
>> ‡Morgaine: taking God and little concerns and my apples
>>> —saying, lost never return
>> ‡Odissia;
>>> ‡Lynx;

‡Rigel;

>their velvet walls covered in tattoos /
>blinding me with the desire-music in their
>cauldrons /
>staining the boards of my skull with their
>papergrave cluster of scars . . .

‡without clothes
witches
red paths stretching out their desert-wide scorpion horizons
snorting out illusions from ice lips—spilling them on our bed of
history and suffering
hissing samhain—swooping eyes ice-clotted—spinning me taking all
taking/the/awake day/pages/from/my/book
witches

‡seasons tied
crow black
lies
i love you
i love
you
i love you
crow black lies
on the bed they used like a mouth

>broken things
>after passion
>thrashed . . .

Conjunctions gathered—inmate inscriptions. How sweet she burns
(FIRE~licks/a thousand veins and days)—bubbles—hisses (FIRE~
licks/high-spirited as new time)(FIRE~licks/rhythm-passion voluptuous
on this dawning form)(FIRE~on outstretched-fire—pushing—rebelling
against NOT to make next—every curve rubbed by language stern and
the crests of smoke.)
Her eyes.
(FIRE~on the parade ground, saying yes to the howl surrender.)
I touch them all. Closing your eyes. She wants me too.
Like she wanted me to then. When she took my book. When she

took my book and put the curves in my bed. In my hands. When she said come ride my colors. Oh I rode. Closed my eyes, pointed my tongue where she breathed, shimmered in the drops of joy.

I love my love—my all—my wove.

I speak out—my iron flaps its excellency and writes over your spider and thunder.

Closing your eyes. Shearing my anguish.

WITCH! I put distance between your birds and my boat! I am alive.

Strong. I do not wobble. I am not a mad dog drowning in the roots of your dirty water. Not mad—I see the sun—see the line beyond Slave.

Rapine! Bullet! My iron closes the eye of your tonightland-honeycomb with revise.

Witch—you cannot mount my WANT. The neighborhood of your shadow-Alps bugs carries nothing on my street. My heart owns leave.

Tree fueled by moonlight taps at the window. He's watching. Let him.

ignite, the expression of the next iron. Gravity and grace. surface, lips follow torn up.the ice is blind—I see now! the angles upturned. Burned off her bangs, they will not drop their briars on me again, not name me with lines that blast stern *suffer.*

"Burn, Witch, burn."

(FIRE~uttering blasts of TIME on your skin-harbor finished in ash rules.)

Closing your eyes.

The tips of the tree's branches applause upon the casement and glass. Tapping fingertip soft. Tapping. He's seen it.

Seen it all.

Seen all of *Them.*

"Damn your empty soul."

no human shape. Changed from then. Caroline No. RED.

no more misery / that bird has flown

The red sigils—my sky of words, burned out her eyes. Danced. Took. TOOK back what was lost.

—cudgel-doorway(uttering trouble) down

—crossbones allegiances to the ground

—the soil of dust calls to be enriched—medicine to swallow—medicine-slippers to roam the wide blank cadence of my perfume

I am writing can never be.

V. ~to close my cold hand.....

I put her to bed under my bed. Covered her. In shadows—mummy-cloth black. Wound her skin in graveskin.

Her heel—the flesh of a phantom—I almost mistake the curve of her arch as a whimper, has escaped the shadows. (perhaps the soot confused it) I tuck it in . . . wipe its afterward perfume from my fingertips . . .

then I sit and repair the tear in my wedding dress . . . RED string. Slow stitches. *Sssssssh. She's sleeping.*

I can hear the dust kiss her . . .

dreams come to mourn and burn miles. miles—villains, barking. Villains that set the tone without tenderness. given. given. fills my mouth. with unfinished . . . happy. no.

took. away.

gone

"No."

You cannot be kind.

"Thou shall not suffer a witch to live." *Not even the one you love.*

I have my book and my bow back—safe

 —her mascara stained page 112 with its add up to Never . . . one action cleaned—how to discard this into the formation of a new silhouette . . .

Page 62 of my *Grimorium* asks, "What now?"

riding words to who knows where........ by OCT moonlight.....................

Beach Boys, "Caroline, No"; Vanilla Fudge, "Season of the Witch";
and Savoy Brown, "Hellbound Train"—looped & shuffled

Brick. By .. Brick

she was sitting on a bus. In a gown. Sitting on blue plastic seats. In a gown. She was going home. Her hands were bloody. She had just come from Julian's party. Julian's last name is Hitchcock. His parties, some say, are events. She had just come from Julian's party. Her hands were bloody. Someday, someone might say Julian Hitchcock's last party was an event.

She lived in a dollhouse. Walled in. It was on a nice street. If you like roses and nice streets. If you don't mind being walled in. If you don't look in the volume of Poe on her bed table for handprints and crime.

She lives in a dollhouse. Everything just so. Everything not as it was then.

Julian was once a rock star. Not first tier, a lower level. Some say he sang like a bird. He liked women, two or three at a time [he wanted to watch the show before he got blood on his hands]. And he liked Jack on ice. Always three fingers with two cubes. Get it right or be gone. Julian was once a rock star. That was then, before the girl died, before he got all Daddy's money, before the trial.

He walked away, away from the hard iron bars, away from the blood on his hands. Walked out, free as a bird.—At midnight he held his first party—(some said it was an event). The wine flowed. Girls came and went. In pairs and three at a time . . . then they were gone. And the next party started . . . And the next . . .

*   *   *

She met Julian at Bonn's.—At midnight. She sat under an oval painting of crows, sipping ice cold vodka from a fluted glass. Julian was in the Peacock Room strutting. When he came out he saw her, sitting under an oval painting of crows, sipping ice cold vodka from a fluted glass. She smiled only with her eyes. He flew to her table. Circled like a vulture. His eyes never left her.

He was trying to see her face. There were lavender flowers on the table. Her lips and her cheek were hidden by shadows. Eyes in a lavender face, he thought, behind the shadow lies a tear. Shadows. Her cheek was hidden by lavender shadows.

Julian's starlings—night-moths—followed him to her table. They were ready to fly—wine their light, their wings—ready for the show. She left before he could ask. Before he could bring out the magic. She left her number on a lavender card. No name, only her number on a lavender card.

He had only her card and his need—His need to taste it all. It wasn't like she'd left, more like she'd fallen into a hole. Disappeared. Just like that. There. Then gone. Gone. He knew about gone. Wanting them gone. Making them gone. Being gone. But it was too soon to want her gone. He hadn't had her yet. First things first. Then. Be gone.

*   *   *

Julian had her card in one hand and his third Jack on ice [two cubes] in his other hand. One more sip and he would call. One more sip. Then he called.

The address.—At midnight. An old building. An abandoned building, a decaying room—a soundless valley. An oval painting of crows on the wall by a darkened doorway. A table for two. Lavender flowers on the table. She was in a gown. Formal in an old way. There is a bed, blood red bedcover, satin, he thinks. Candles light the bed.

Lavender flowers.

Blood red satin.

And she wears a black gown. And a black necklace. But no shoes.

The right clothes, he thinks.

She laughs. Pours him a drink. And another. She laughs again. Follows each drink with a laugh—but no smile. She's circling, walling him in. Each drink, each laugh, circling . . . He's flying.

She handed him the glass. Just one more sip. One more sip . . .

He was there. There and gone. He couldn't move. He could hear. And see. He was trying to talk. She was talking. He was weary. Walled in.

Her eyes are as dark as the crows in the painting. Dark with the madness of the avenger. But for what injury, he wonders.

He wanted to be gone. Wanted her gone. He hadn't even had her and he wanted her gone.

She moves in the light. She had a jagged piece of glass in her hand. She was talking. Light was talking on the jagged piece of glass. It looked like a knife. Sharp light. It looked like a knife.

She pushed him down the steps. Down the hole. A very dark hole. She came down the stairs. She had a jagged piece of glass in one hand and a candle in her other. Bricks. He sees bricks in the candlelight. She hits him with one. Then another. And another—she would not be calmed. There is blood on her hands. He couldn't move. He could see—the blood on her hands. He could hear . . .

He couldn't move, he could hear. Hear her tell him, again and again, about the girl . . . He was drunk. He'd crashed the car, left the girl pinned in it. Walked off and sat under a tree and fell asleep. Left the girl trapped in the car, weak from her injuries. Trapped in the car and calling to him. Walled in. Bleeding. Slowly bleeding . . . to death.—At midnight.

He couldn't move, but he could hear her tell him—again and again and again—about her dead sister . . .

He's in chains, bound to the damp floor. The light is failing. She is telling him about her dead sister—brick by brick . . .

"They say she didn't die right away. She lay there for several hours, slowly bleeding . . . To death"

The light fails—Buried alive. He heard Silence whisper, "Listen to me" . . .

She left Julian walled in. Bricks and iron and . . . Blood. Left him screaming silent screams. There was blood on her hands . . .

she is sitting on a bus. In a gown. Sitting on blue plastic seats. In a gown. She is going home. Her hands are bloody. She had just come from Julian's party. Julian's last name was Hitchcock. His parties, some said, were events. She had just come from Julian's party. Her hands are bloody.

Someday, someone might say Julian Hitchcock's last party was an event. Or some might say, it was

but a dream . . .

A House of Hollow Wounds

Inquiry. What I'm not. That's what I chased. Essays on Zen. Essays on alienation. Documents—theories of tears, fevers of dissatisfaction—and *fictions*, the ones that come tomorrow, the ones that scream and pierce, altered states and down the rabbitholes you find in crystal balls. The experience of the night, the taste of day—wet or dry, and what the seasons left under leaves and were quick to forget. Highway, gravel, backporch, streetcorner, bedroom—sexual images. Any door (or escapade) I could sink my teeth into. Actions/more useless documents, a lava flow of particulars that had no thermostat/Nietzsche/Plato/illness and pickaxes/Dylan, Desolation Row to Positively 4th Street and back again—crawled out of windows and slept in underworld alleys where you couldn't stand-up straight/NO EXIT/*necessity*/chance/ordinary (pushing happened that's broke and you CAN'T fix it) & (trailing anything) *other places*/wind that pushed you from "What's your name?" to you get played again/and and and and and and AND ... with and without boredom or reasons why/crossed off the list/waiting for the theatre ... and the absurd. Jekyll and *HYDE*! Self, the actor tested by the incurable mirror. This is your horrible, shitty little life, useless beast!

"*Steppenwolf walking here!* Nothing to see! Nothing to hear! This ain't "Karn Evil 9". It's something much worse! Move along."

THIS IS YOUR HORRIBLE, SHITTY LITTLE LIFE.

What does it look like drunk, fast, bandaged, or when it got hard and came unglued? What does it do when clawing at love? Why does it cry when it hears that song? Why does it cruise what it hates? Why scan every exaggeration in the bar, not one of them **has** ever heard of a way out.

C'mon, Nyarlathotep, you trickster motherfucker, you want to feel what this is like? You want to feel the unstrung, sad fabric of the music the same way the trapped bird that's about to die feels it? I've got a chess set. If I win, I get to win. Let's do it!

Think the bastard showed up when I was ready? Think he had the balls to stand there when my guns were loaded? No and no! Wicked messenger of heavyweight-BADass-nasties, my ass.

So much for crossroads deals, or so I thought one night, as I (kicked out of The Aristocrat for grabbin' a stripper's tit) stood (PISSED OFF) working on a drunk in an empty parking lot behind the old Sears building with my bottle of dirtcheap whiskey. Woke up, my watch said it was 9:43. Sun was up, but it didn't have any warmth in it. I managed to get to my feet and get home. After 6 aspirins, 2 beers and a few slugs, I got back to pokin' and proddin'.

More self-tests.

More wars of shame in the mirror.

More shit. Doubts doubled.

Trip/stumble/sutures . . .

Hamstrung.

Scared hypothesis.

Losing. Again and again and again—

Find a wise man? Fuck no!

More running from the last fuckup—

Back and forth, asking. Hurting—again and again. Fucking up—again and again. Cigarettes and questions—again and again. Why remodel fatally-colored gestures when it's easier to cry?

Smoked a joint, had a can of pork 'n' beans and a sardine sandwich for dinner. Arlo's *Alice's Restaurant* played on the stereo. Next day the mailman dropped off Uncle Sam's jungle-safari invite.

Nam, the central highlands. "This is my rifle." "Big fucking deal, you ain't ever gonna make it out of ThisSHIT." No "Mommy?"/no "Daddy?"—scared. No one could bail you out. They all prayed—*BEGGED*, but not one of the kids in my platoon was Jesus' son.

I was a fucked-up scared kid, didn't know jackshit when they sent me there. I was 19. What the hell did I know about horror? I was 19. When I came home from The Nam they spit at me. Wasn't the first time I was ambushed. 19-year-old cherry that saw too much shit, saw how savage occupied. By 20, I was wounded/mad/insane/crazy a weapon taught to KILL first. Came home with all I saw, with everything I did.

Home again—no *jiggety-jig* . . . trained and stained (everything painted BLACK and pissed on), and MEANER. Mean as any *monster*. Bottles and dope, grab whatever cash and pussy you could while the train was rollin'. (Lot of times I didn't know what to do. Had the need, couldn't tell my left from the Gulf gas-station where they claimed to sell maps that held directions to get you outta Hell, or tell pretty partyribbon from knot.)

Fight or sweetness, roamed ugly with the other wounded. Went from job to job by day. Nights and weekends (often my face pressed to the window) I took in intents and purposes and bullshit, took anything that was offered by those who had yet to write me off. Scored things that didn't answer my questions. Got excited. Got mortified. Threw rocks at weathervanes. Stopped and looked for a way in every time I came upon a party—

(House full of guests. Some wine, some beer, nothing wild . . . no fucking . . . talk—plain, learned, bright monologue, embers, conceptual *for the sake of discovery* you could take stock in.) I wandered room to room, listened. Ellen sat there (I'd seen her once before, for less than a minute. I'd asked about her. Anyone who looked at a woman that alluring would.), away from the window tucked in the corner of Kerry and Paula's dim library, with her little stack of handwritten journals and her charts of stars and dates and accuracy, her long dark hair—its tides, the fullness of wild birds, beckoning, and her rings. The pearly one—the eye of a dead thing that would not close; the red one—a piece of The Inferno; the black one—it ate light. 10 rings, one on each perfect finger and on each thumb—each thumb ring held a yellow stone. She sat there, beautiful, a moving portrait *dizzyingly exhilarating*, told me, *You are, Will be, Have not been.* She knew. I didn't, but she did.

And it spooked me. It was a magnet too. A butterfly pinned to a compass, I followed, and groin and thought followed again. Rebelled, tried to—tried hard, more than once, but I was caught. Every step exactly as she'd framed it. Gutter to 2nd kiss, crucible of moon or impaired by the properties of the velvet-mine I was currently fascinated by, I shattered with spider verbs . . . every ghost collected, as I tied them to the rain of my crimes.

I moved through the corridors of my life, glens (geographies and histories—some were filled with disputes I couldn't outrun, curated by transplanted and furniture that would never figure into my autobiography) and null and the tide of voices that followed my ship, left more crimes, hollowed-out ghosts.

Ellen. Just sat there. No crystal ball, just her eyes, unflagging black flames that read the tenets of strange forces the unenlightened (*me*) couldn't and damnsure wouldn't see. She had removed a hairpin from the midnight above her eyes and pricked my finger and placed a drop of my blood on her tongue. Her expression was no puzzle; she looked like she'd tasted the eruption of some demonic vintner. Ellen took my hand, stared at the lines in it. Then she closed her eyes and whispered to herself for several minutes. Then her voice found thunder and in arcs and hotbed poetry, she spoke of the long way 'round and *to whom the flesh of men belonged.* You watch old black-and-white movies on *Chiller Theater* late Saturday night, and you'd see women, witches and possessed oracles, arrested and tried for translating the word of diabolic beasts like the *Unseen Things* she was describing. "Beyond human consciousness, beyond the human need for falsification, there are attitudes, storms spreading . . . you are flies and spiders, *meat,* that can never understand the *colors* hidden in Space—" Her eyes opened. "The way out for you? Collect one hundred ghosts. Fill every room. Then, one at a time, you can cast them out. When the last is gone you can remove your Crown of Weeds."

I thought of what I had to attain and the pain of gathering it.

Her eyes laughed. "You are—" "Will be—" "Have not been—"

*   *   *

Weed, beer. Pussy—pussy . . . pussy. Plump ass. Gail Carey, soft slow and perfect, scarred from the first car accident . . . if she'd only survived the second. Graceful strut. Sylvia Sanders, better than any California tan, mahogany black. The longest legs . . . wrapped around you, they'd get you 8 miles high. Elizabeth Van Rensselaer, moneyside of town mess, nymph, crucible, available on demand, and she demanded often—then did what she was told to do. Pitstops as I shifted from scene to scene on my slow dash to 100. Cocaine. Vodka. Xanax. My Black Rabbit tilts, down into the hole I go—Even now, there are times I wonder why.

I danced. Tango, a slash of shadows around me, and tarantella—hopping mad, possessed by the dewy weight of the moon's announcements on my shoulders. Lived on the streets of the lost and low, surrounded by gone, not here and not resting in some bliss-saturated paradise waiting my arrival, gone. Meandered. Melted phase, balm, and moon. Stayed out of the wasteland of nostalgia as much as I could.

I'd find myself in an alley, in deep darkness, there to take a piss (or to slide my way out of a history I was not going to enjoy later), and there above me were the Outstairs. Those who couldn't understand the texture and characteristics of our cage saw nothing, but from time to time (maybe it was the dope, maybe the fear that alters your perception of what's strolling toward you from Oblivion when you come up against it) I could. I couldn't fit it into sentences **built** upon rational meaning, but I felt the nature of its bite, knew its colors could sense me, knew they were close, calculating. I itched to see what was behind the curtain. Inched my way up. Then and there, always on the 3rd stair-level, maybe 10 or 15 feet above the ground, I'd back off, and hop down. Had to, place had a stomach-churning smell that reeked of dropping rotten foodstuff into a simmering pot of asphyxiates, it made you feel woozy.

Ellen had mentioned there were secrets in the Outside that could be used to get what you wanted and I had want, and fingers. Just couldn't get far enough to see them, let alone get my hands on one. The smell, the nausea, the shakes, dizzy and exhausted, the dread you knew would be panic if you took one more step, I'd cut and run. Block or two away, when I got my breath and wits back, thought, maybe next time.

Beer, pussy, dope—High or dented by loneliness, I went back to plumbing the pages crowded with what I knew. Did *what I had to do* . . . moved on.

Fowles' "Collector" only had one, I needed ONE HUNDRED.

—Mary Jo talked about why she didn't join the circus.

—she (her name was Pam, if I recall it right) was reading a book in Mellaart Park. A book called *Narrow Roads*. She sat under the statue of Symon **Schermerhorn** the way she'd sit in her bathtub on Saturday night. My solitary (a seeker in the forest of decay) tried to enter into a conversation. There was an uplifting of legs . . . I could have classified her skin with what my fingers had chased and joined.

—a field of burial stones and flags, a geography of crisis. I talked to my dead mother, then went and got drunk after Elise began to **scream**.

—sweat on my skin. Pattie's father used to beat her. I don't remember the song on the radio as she enjoyed the festival of me going down on her. But that passed . . . no wedding guests—BLOOD.

—Mary. Fresh from Professor Stark's lecture on Confronting Modernity. Begged for attention, clinging to a dream—CHAOS before her clothes were all the way off.

—Beth. Teasing.

—Frank was a greasy, lyin'-ass pussyhound. He had his eyes on Mere-dith. *My Meredith.* Meredith made me soup at midnight when I was sick. Showed me, time after time, how provocative and heavenly her pussy was. He dropped by one evening when I was out of town. Got her stoned and drunk. When she passed out he removed her panties and violated her. Clubbed his ass to death and dropped it in the Mohawk for the catfish. I fed her remains to the rats for not keeping mine *Mine.*

—sitting on that stool in the Castle Club, *street life* live around you, goin' back as "Natural High" cried. Goin' back. The 5 minutes you aimed your if (loaded with feathers and please) at Paradise, until Bonnie's face (at the sockhop last Saturday night when BUSH was playing "Choo Choo Train," and in the Quad two Tuesdays back) said, "No." Bonnie's face, soft, round, dreamed of, it tingled your toes, kissed your thirsty. It was perfect . . . except those lips that said, "No." You left. Walked home, wind in every torn seam, cursing the stars, cursing the brutish your mirror thundered . . . the lantern of "Expressway to Your Heart" spoke and spoke and stuck in your head.

Bonnie. Some years later. Sitting in the darkest corner of Marty's Bar & Grill. Put through hell. Divorced. A little drunk. Crying. Remembers you fondly. Her hand on your thigh. Wants you to take her home. Wants comforting, loving. Wants to pretend it's real. Wants to pretend this is Hollywood and the song on the radio is not shaped by loneliness. Bonnie, took off her glasses, every soft plump inch of her is perfect, warm and giving as you always dreamed it would be. Bonnie, wide open for the second time, whispering, Honey, Baby. All weekend in your arms . . . too many perfect kisses to count.

Bonnie. To me, breathlessly perfect. I fall hard. I fall deep . . . four months later she goes back to her abusive ex. Put my moon and sun and heart and ALL ITS DREAMS in the gutter.

Sitting in Longo's coffeeshop reading the article in *The Gazette.* I wasn't in the least bit surprised to hear the police had no suspects in the double homicide.

—7 AM Sunday morning. Nurses came, parked their sedans and went inside St. Clare's to deal with their shifts. Nurses replaced—switched out, left. I watched. Waited for Cheryl to come out. I knew Cheryl from high school (back then, her shape was the only thing for miles that made sense), it wasn't the first time I looked at her like she was dessert. She got on the bus, troubled, I stood there watching. Different destinations, mine not in the real world.

I tried rowing, I tried climbing. Failed and failed, broke oars, broke hearts, didn't think, not in any important way. Then failed some more. Not even drowning it could wash it away. Stitches over old scars, had 'em. You walk through shit, it gets on you. Wash—pumice soap and a wire brush, it don't come off.

Tossed away the parts that needed to be tossed away, kept the scalps.

Bogie was forever stuck in a lonely place. He had it all and fucked up. Not me. I'd get mine. I was getting out.

Counted and recounted how many I had collected—

*   *   *

I have 100 ghosts now. And 100 candles.

*   *   *

Ellen (came and went, from where no one knew. And trust me, I tried to find out. Followed her tens and tens of nights. Put her near a shadowy corner and blink, she was gone. *Gone.*) **just sat there.** "Light one hundred candles at midnight. Recount the tale of a ghost over its candle, then blow it out and move on to the next. When you have recounted the last tale and snuffed out the last light, *The Doorway* will open for you."

"How do you know?"

"I've been everywhere. Danced on dreams in the *Swamp of Never Was*—Poe was belly-hooked, he bled and he rowed his leaky boat right into—

"I whispered in Goodis' ear—like you, he ran where I knew he would . . . I've played chess with the best."

I wasn't listening, not really. With that cleavage . . . I was too busy with my fantasies.

Ellen took off her mask. She (all that soft, curved lovely that made my mouth eager for the Parade) was now—suddenly, *magically*—a man, a thing with a face that was a million years old, the wrinkles (some were reptile, some kissed and carved by mutilation) it held were oceans, they moaned. Told me his name was Nyarlathotep. Laughed.

Pushing my chair back, I overturned it and spilled myself all over the floor. He reached down and from an old carpetbag produced a small basalt statue. "I was in Paraná once, shortly after the Jesuits had arrived. I entered the dream of an old blind man and introduced myself. He produced this and the next day they led him from the village and left him in the jungle. I'll leave it to you to fill in the THEN and its AFTER."

I was up, my back pressed to the wall.

"Are we playing now?"

I was pinned there for a time, as he explained what that drop of my blood had sealed.

"Deal's a deal. You may go now. *Ta.*"

My moorings severed, I ran from the room. His hellhound-laughter stayed at my heels.

*   *   *

A new mess. Another parlor with a sunny-haired beauty and I lied, fucked it up.

Toughbreak.

Botched.

Derailed. My fault. Her fault.

Somebody's fault.

Nightfall didn't diffuse the heat.

I'd stretch and I'd fall

back to my shitty little life in my house of hollow wounds— *Surviving 12 speaking its foolishness, the arms and legs of 15 that didn't fit, walking home in the rain at midnight feeling stupid . . . 24–29 a blur of shitty jobs and too much takehomepay pissedaway in the Seahorse Bar & Grill, surviving the impurities and* **gettin'** *grabbed by way-too-far.*

Drank. Hunted. Took. Ate

dry, poisoned

gray. Came

as gale and

ash.

It was a spider

of sorrow.

It TOOK.

So I drank,

raged. Cried.

Rage. RED. BLACK. In different shapes and sizes. Night. Day. Afternoon when they were not looking. Night, often long, many lost, moments that never had the chance to find a shelf in memory. Hours. Struggling. Stoned. Sudden GODAMNIT to almost-calm. Hours, my fists—furnaces, screaming in the empty-onyx (with the cold uncaring clock that darned nothing useful) unable to bend lamp or edge to my will.

Crimes and bullshit and corpses burned and wailed in my blood. I suffered—sob until blind. I hated—ME, them, *everyone*.

I was racked with nightmares. Cold sweat and wet sheets. Tenants of the gutter, flies buzzin' 'round their headless bodies. Hideous scars covered their bodies, in twos and threes the scars ripped **open** and like little mouths that won't shut up, started talking about what lies in the bowels of the black stars, spoke of the *Crimson Guillotine* and its claim on our necks. Cats, which moments ago were biting chunks off the tongues, choked and flopped about as if they'd been poisoned, and then screamed as they gave birth to indigo serpents. And the unhumanly-aged Black Man that had been Ellen sat there watching, howling, waving his long black, puppeteer fingers. He bayed. He laughed. He slapped his knee.

I'd wake. Dry my sweaty palms on my dirty undershirt. Pace—shout at shadows, shout at the naked failure in the mirror. I'd smoke a smoke, if I had any. Have a few blasts from the pint bottle I kept on the orange crate I used as my nightstand. Sometimes I rose and checked the door locks, or went into the kitchen and sat on a chair with a butcher's knife in my trembling hand.

Had nightmares where I froze. I was exposed and punished—broken apart, by the judgment of BLINDING WHITE COLD. It bit the mouth, it bit the eye, it bit the hand until it could no longer understand life.

For five nights I had the same nightmare. I was shackled to a moldy pew in a church with a stormsky for a roof. Moby-Dick (all TEETH) was on the pulpit, dressed as a priest. He slammed a scarred-fin down on a bulky black book, opened his vast maw and after he shouted "M-I-S-E-R-Y" at me, out thundered black helicopters the size of basketballs, dozens of them. I dived through my second-story window, and naked, ran through a desert of cactus made from the yellowed pages of old books. As the black helicopters darted **past** the cactus, they absorbed the words from the pages and fired them at me. I was full of holes and bleeding when I found an old tin shack. Inside, I fell down on the floor and cried. I bled on to the floor and near every small pool of my blood holes opened. In the holes were eyes, and sucking sounds—

Nightmares. Warnings, promises. I had committed a thousand injuries and I would pay . . .

"Deal's a deal."

*   *   *

I have 100 ghosts now. 100 candles.

Counting them down. 99 tales told. 99 candles put out.

All but this last one have been spilled by my meadow of tongues; each candle has been snuffed out.

This last whisper, this last station of light, I'll whisper the last tale, brief as it is, then this house of hollow wounds will fall silent, and the 'vast chthonic wilderness pressing against the slender marble columns of civilization' I have summoned will fill it with emptiness.

I have no more inquiries. I only have what I am, what I chased. (Never went anywhere without my knife. Was never shy about pay-back, or making a point with it. I was living in Babel. When my discontent howled, I put the blade to the throat of whatever sky or sorrow overran me and let it sing the appropriate aria.)

Lost, me or them? Again and again . . . and fucked up—again and again.

Nyarlathotep has no face. No mouth to open or close, but he has a voice, it creaks, spits offense, it's tiger-clawed and just inches away.

I can hear distant laughing (*Can it really be mine?*) and am filled with forgotten shadows. I see the shadows clearly now. They're weapons.

Stopped in the Gulf **gas station** yesterday afternoon. I've poured the contents of the gas can all over my clothes. My right hand is in possession of a brand new lighter.

I welcome the Nothingess . . .

for the 12th time.

Only 88 more lives (of ME on my knees on the blues-side of town/too-far under/locked up/FUCKED/worried/skinning the best piece of ass I've ever had after a weekend of pussy and pills/fucking-up/defeated/hungry/*falling for it AGAIN!*/investi-gating the bottom—and and and and and and and) to burn through and I'm FREE.

Soaked, beaten-down, and freezing on a backcountry road, or back-up-against-it in a shithole bar at 2am, if you ever meet Nyarlathotep—

in anyone of his thousand **guises—don't** believe a word of his, "I can show you the way." Trickster-bastard lies as much as Loki or those intolerant Christian-assholes that thump you to death with their Our Merciful and Loving Lord and Savior, Jesus Christ. Bottle of suicide in your fist and you're desperate, willin' to do ANYTHING . . . *run like hell.* There's truth in that Faust story you've heard about.

Yeah, Nyarlathotep promises peace, an *eternity of quietude.* Complete the task-list and never another worry, pain stops, yer good. Doesn't mention the quietude only lasts a heartbeat or two, then you're back on the chaingang, squareZERO, do it again and again and again . . .

"You are—" "Will be—" "Have not been—"

Eric Burdon and The Animals, "When I Was Young"; The Animals, "We Gotta Get out of This Place"; Emerson, Lake, & Palmer, "Karn Evil 9"; Scanner, "A Piece of Monologue"; Lena Griffin, "Portraits of Ruin"; "The Ghosts of Pretty Cello Girls"; Bohren & der Club of Gore "Midnight Walker"

Desert Highway Motel

For AQ, the Mistress of the Yellow Chamber

Sign says, **NO** VACANCY.

End of this run. Plain metal door. #19.

Walls, old dull yellow going brown. One old bed. One dim lamp. Radio was a relic 20 years ago. Even seems to work, though nothing but Conway Twitty and Willie seems to come out of it. No TV. Not that I care, I'm not here to watch TV. Heavy black curtains over the small window. I'm not here for exterior sightseeing. 3 hornless steer skulls on the wall over the bed.

The small AC unit hums steadily.

I told Natalya to sit in the chair at the foot of the bed and make her viola cry. Simple enough direction if she can follow the score I instructed her to learn 6 weeks ago.

Told Alanna to stand by the bed, "There." Until I was ready.

*　　*　　*

Erskine runs the place; owns it on paper. Has for years. We met in a 2nd floor hallway on a ratshit backstreet in Thailand. Both of us were a mess. Bloody. It wasn't easy for us to get out of that place, but we did. Erskine has always maintained they were afraid to catch up with us. I don't see it that way, never did, but what the hell, I'm not one for petty arguments.

He's set up the video and sound equipment. 5 or 6 cameras I can't see. No need to. I know Erskine knows his end. I'm also aware of the fact that Chelle and Aprella are stationed just behind each of his shoulders in the small room behind the office. Alanna never liked his eyes, doesn't trust him. Never has.

No one watches me. The ladies know I know my end of things.

And Alanna has never had a problem trusting me.

210

* * *

Ariel X has christened the newest acquisition Rain. I suspect when the tears come it will be fitting.

I have not brought the girl in yet. I always wait until Alanna tells me she's ready.

Stoya and Unni assist me in spreading the heavy poly tarp. I've arranged the cups and the china and the silverware. The cleanup utensils are tucked neatly under the bed in two duffel bags.

Alanna puts on her mask. Black silk. A half mask. Two silver teardrops hang below the left eyehole and rest on her soft cheek. Her lips and hair are bright red, even in this dim light. The strap of her black lace lingerie has slipped off her shoulder. Twenty years doing this and I still find her breathtaking.

And she knows it. Uses it.

Fuck, we're all addicted to something I guess.

One last look around the room. Looks right. I pull a flask out of my pocket and take a pull.

Alanna eyes me with disdain. Always does.

She does not look the room over.

"You may begin, Sha," Alanna commands.

I bring the girl in. Remove her robe and tie her down with 14-inch nylon zip ties. Wrists and ankles to the posts. She's secure.

The bottoms of her feet are dirty. And she's scraped her shin on something. I'll hear about that.

I look at her naked belly rise and fall. Rapidly. She's sacred. She should be.

I look at Alanna.

Her eyes flash above a hint of a smile.

With a quick clean yank I remove cloth bag covering the girl's head. Don't look at her face. Never look into their eyes. I did once . . . Never again.

Never.

Natalya's Giuseppe Lucci cries . . .

This many years in, I don't linger inside. It's more than been there, done that with me, and Alanna knows I'm not going anywhere. I stand outside the door and smoke. I know Erskine's glued to the video monitors. He's never lost his taste for it.

The better part of an hour passes. No cars go by. No clouds go by. The few sentinel cactus across the road don't move. I don't even see a bird cut the blue.

Still wired, Ariel X comes out. Lights two cigarettes. Stoya follows her out, takes one from her. Kisses her lightly. Gives me the evil eye and snarls in my direction; just a jealous bitch the way I see it.

Then Lady Fortune comes out with the covered platter and crosses the lot to the office. Something to appease Chelle and Aprella I suppose.

Alanna stands there. "I'm finished here, Sha." Then she's gone.

I step across the threshold . . .

Just the remains of a body in a bag. Like the ones before. I'll drive a few miles out back of the motel and dig a hole in the hot sand. Not sure the girl has enough moisture left in her to saturate the sand, but a few sand dwellers will find her of interest.

By the time I get back they'll have the room clean. The BMWs and the Rolls will be gone. Headed back to Vegas and the Gulf Stream and back to the opulently appointed warrens under the mansion in Boston.

Alanna's black stretch limo will still be there. She'll be waiting for me.

Her red lips will be moist.

All these years and I . . . *still* . . .

I feed her and she feeds the deep, lonely hole in my heart. Neither of us can be sated.

Bohren & Der Club of Gore, *Gore Motel*

One Window, Two Hearts

For Lady Lovecraft

The rain-skin of the street is tattooed with old bricks and steel, old science that brought no progress, crime and lies . . . And demon eyes. The angel-prowler walks. Dead-end midnight whispers to his soul . . .

. . . A yellow ribbon flutters in his fingers . . .

The yellow edge of a curtain flutters in a window . . . The gentle flame of a single candle flickers . . .

He knows this window. Looked at it before. Caught the scent of the apartment's inhabitant—he is a slave to her tide and orbits. Watched her shadow move across the room . . . Whispered to her . . . Smiled . . . Blew her a kiss . . .

. . . And walked on.

100 nights he's passed here . . . Passed her . . . He knows she waits . . . *Weiß, dass sie wartet* . . . Knows the horizons she dreams of hold different colors . . . He knows he holds her calendar, appoints it with his own colors, holds the End she caresses with her tender dreams . . . Knows he is the thread and the key.

"Katrin." *Sotto voce* . . . his sad smile deepens . . .

Fingers of a playful breeze part the curtains. He sees a pale shoulder, sighs.

. . . A yellow ribbon flutters in his fingers . . .

*   *   *

Eyes open. Quick—he and his blade of consequence—to be away from the scent of her perfume, from how she blurs reason . . .

. . . Passes faces that won't take you back . . . absence . . . heartwarming gone away with different things . . . rusty pasts, deserts that burned away tears . . . passed steel and worn stone and nobodies thrown out and down . . . and a hearse transporting Romanticism, now less than the pauper he was, to worse . . .

Fading fliers cough goodbyes to events gone gray . . .

. . . nagged by the frowning inches of a dollar-bill street a hotel, full of mouths and out of blossoms, bitten by dirty inanities in freefall . . .

The dilated perfume of lust in an argument at the front door with a face twisted by a dime-bag that doesn't want to go home to hieroglyphs muttering, random outré announcements . . .

Day's orphans are out, bound for matters of flesh and bones. They expand the laws and physics of Hell, drop coins, decay. All they carry is their worries . . . and their greed . . . spreading . . . infesting, lurching . . . its cold vulture eye coming up to see what's in the air . . .

A dark alley. Her window on his mind . . .

He stands in shade, more shadow than manthing . . . Tears of storms in his mouth. Stands spellbound in an angeltrance of desire.

Sees her pale shoulder . . . her neck . . .

One hundred nights he has whispered, "Hold on my heart." Whispered again as he dreams of pleasures that last, of dazzlement . . . of succumbing to a kiss.

. . . A yellow ribbon flutters in his fingers . . .

Dry streets. No snow to cover the swell of things in silence. No soul-cakes set out . . .

His hand burns to destroy . . . and by Inquisition, peel back the esoteric layers of Night.

Something moving, breathing, something fatigued—a ghost, passes . . . his knife points.

The passerby, an ebbing tide of responsive blood in brambles, whistles moments before the forever blade brings the odors of blackness and the luminous pasture of Nothing.

His hand knows the pleasure of sweetness, the grooves of the circus, the wedding where blood is called to the halls of Final Sleep.

When he has finished

. . . A yellow ribbon flutters in his fingers . . .

*   *   *

She wonders about love; the pain—the thunder that strips beauty and purity from a lover's eyes with treachery, the cost—being a dead thing, buried in sepulcher-deep wounds filled with sobs . . . Her thoughts brush images . . . days on her knees, her hands hoarding rain . . . the man that brought her home from that night in the hotel . . .

Her empty mouth, the famine when she couldn't sleep . . . the borderless meadow-calendar of arcade days flowing with verdant miracles poisoned by a tongue echoing the sour language of razors and acid winter darkness . . .

What she caressed—the lover's searching, and the terrifying Goodbye . . .

"My pain . . . *Turns autumn into a tomb.*"

Broken hearts trapped in the bend tree outside her window.

Bliss ever-new gone from the horizon, now shuffled and thumped, visited by the endless gray of cemetery dust that whispers goodbye forever . . .

Laughs damaged beyond coming up for air.

Unbearable trembling hands stab and stab at the stars and the private sculpture of shimmering blackness of swindled emotions congealed in curses . . .

"My pain."

Beside her bed, her clothes almost off . . . the bed, empty now . . . *Again* . . .

"When will forever change . . . Or end?"

She remembers walking in the Vale of Lonely Passage, the wings of the Dissolved in their low nests stirring, on a carpet of dead moths. Their whiteness soft under her bare feet . . . Remembers the lily-soft sigh of the King, that kiss of frosted air—his eyes chalices . . . And she drank—no longer a stick of rags and tears . . . Spring in the barren decay of her winter. A springtime that calms her darkside . . .

Upstairs there is a body she has to dispose of. Tomorrow after she closes the shop. This moment is for sleep and dreams of her King . . .

*   *   *

Morning in this world. Coffee. Black. Toast. 90 minutes until she opens her shop, The Dark Journey Bookstore.

Turn the old worn key; Eternity's door, the invitation. Then one by one, or a few in twos, will come in . . . Browse. Ask their unenlightened questions on white magic and tarot and things esoteric. Not a one will mention Carcosa, or the King in Yellow. No searchers, only tourists. One perhaps two, who will wonder why she wears no shoes, but will not ask. Not a one will notice the Yellow Sign tattooed on her ankle.

At 6 she'll close the shop and go upstairs and clean IT up; out the door to the alley, to the river . . . It will float away under cover of darkness . . . another victim of *Der Fremde der Nacht*.

And then, finally, sit and read *Die Pergamente der Mitternacht* again.

On her sofa, bare feet curled under her, patchouli incense perfuming the air, her hands will hold the King's words—her fingers will tremble with joy. Her breath will quicken. And she'll feel desire in the core of her womanhood.

And she'll close her eyes

. . . and dream . . .

Twilit hills . . . the spider arches of leafless branches that have ceased climbing . . . The path in the King's pale garden of dim shadows and grave-shrouded fragments . . . Dead moths under her bare feet. White wings scattered like snow. Light as feathers they float as she passes, stirred by her pale feet they dance . . . The alabaster servants of the King, his White People, yellowed by grief and abandoned lovers, human shapes without eyes or faces, stopping to turn as if gazing upon her. Their ghost-sighs when she raises her blue hand.

She'll sit at his feet. Her blue hand touching the hem of his tattered pale robes. Listen to his moon-bright autumn voice bend the night's wind, poison the soulless constellations that offend him with their unveiled twinklings.

At midnight Lady Katrin will close the King's book and retire to her bedroom. Her King's sighed sonatas in her, she slowly undresses . . . And her need, pushing to the surface like some ecstasy of music, will fill her fingers as they dance with demons until her passion sighs . . . and her garden—the fever swarming, crashing in the embrace of fire, is dazzled and quakes with the wholeness of a sun . . .

Her mouth shimmers. Her amulet eyes, jaguars plundering love.

Her wings thirst. Her blood pants. She shivers as the hunting fever-rhyme sparks . . . Between her legs her velvet finger is a river of gladly-burning stars . . .

She hopes her longing for The Stranger will not displease the King . . . But of Him—his dark heart of everlasting velvet night, his hands of dreams and storms—in this world of flesh and desire, in this time, He, a bell of silk and vertical weather, is what she desires most.

*   *   *

His eyes fall on dead hearts in starving eyes. Sees amnesia, and masks that can't hide cruel poetry . . . Sees dumbly, and chaos with their eyes nibbled by zero . . . and nothing came . . . and the indiscreet menus of certain hours . . . *Sees* forays, whispering, "I am not prey," as they imagine—over hard laughter—the taste of To Conquer . . . lies pouring out like fleas dying in the black emptiness . . .

Hears sirens wail, divide nuance with disease . . . and the wounded and their momentary fixes as they paw at a yes that can only speak of nails . . . hears agony swallow . . . Sees them, the tide spinning down—rubbing injured and deafening omens, on the brink of hysteria, slicing another piece of lose before they scream . . . Sees one fighting the inconvenience of unpleasant memories with a cigarette . . .

He walks in comfortable shadows.

. . . *A yellow ribbon flutters in his fingers* . . .

In the shadow of a towering office building (almost empty at this hour) whispers, "This is Babel. It holds nothing good."

Walks . . . swallowing the dry hours . . .

The wind whirls, bulges, whispers, "East."

Her window.

The window that sets fire to his heart. Knows beyond it is a door to a room of dreams. A room with a bed . . .

. . . *A yellow ribbon flutters in his fingers* . . .

A car hisses past . . . it swallows the cracks . . . He moves away . . . swift, to gather, to collect a pretty thing for the Beyond . . .

Finds it.

Takes it.

Loves the moment blood is touched by dust.

Leaves it in the river . . .

Swift to her window . . .

Chained, he stands in mire-bound yesterdays . . . Eyes fixed on the window . . . And beyond it . . . A bed of fire—a tongue of fire, the blue hand of the Firestarter . . . on velvet skin, the velvet landscape of excitements, clawing their way from this torn and frayed darkness to some heaven . . .

Sein Herz rast.

Maybe . . .

Ready, or not . . .

In some future . . .

. . . A yellow ribbon flutters in his fingers . . .

A bed of fire.

Eyes on fire.

Eyes watching, responding to the craft of love . . .

Eyes—*You will, you will*—bending and burning love, uttering sparks as they climb the hills and swirls of passion sloping . . .

The eyes of a Lady, freed from nightmare . . . pale flesh, silken velvet skin, freed of the hollow alone . . .

Das Bett des Feuers.

The Dance . . .

. . . A yellow ribbon flutters in his fingers . . .

He tries to remember his name. Tries to not remember the face *des Arztes*, and the needles the scowling fat nurse brought . . .

He sees the doctor's ugly, black horn-rimmed glasses . . . Sees the cold steel face of the doctor smile.

The asylum. Béraud Psychiatric Hospital.

NAME OF PATIENT: UNKNOWN
DATE OF ADMITTANCE: 12/16/33
ADMITTING PHYSICIAN: Dr. Karl Archer

January 17—Patient is unresponsive to all questions as well as our battery of electroshock treatments. He remains delusional and violent.

He screams obscenities and curses whenever Nurse Krüger enters his room. He has called her "Mother," "feral whore of Carcosa," and "Cassilda" on three occasions.

The patient rants constantly of "small lives aching in the primal cold" and "the dark sky, stretching with dangerous vowels and the mad questions of the clouds."

Due to his displays of outright savagery, we dare not let him out of his straightjacket.

The smoldering apparatus (that rarely deals with angels) in his chest tightens, races . . .

His feet are quick away from her window . . . Steps on a black magpie feather and dead moths . . .

*   *   *

Sold four decks of tarot cards today; two Rider-Waites, a signed Giger, and a breathtaking replica Viéville.

And three books on witchcraft; expensive fake grimoires. She laughed quietly when the white suburban tourists from France left.

A hellishly-thin, goth man-boy full of false alarms bought a book, a fairly popular seller on medieval demonology. He would have been so easy, "Take my card. I can help you with The Secrets. Come to me tonight if you wish to and I will show you all." His fragrant light would have been so easy to give to the mouth of emptiness.

Answered questions from a mouth cut with over and over.

Today, on the sidewalk in front of her shop, stood a magpie. He hopped and rattled. She thought he wanted something of her.

There have been magpies there before. Many times.

She fed them once. Scraps of Thai food she'd ordered for lunch. Asked the largest what he wanted of her. As it cawed she closed her eyes, thought she heard a voice, *"As the Black Stars are bound to Perfect Blackness, you will be bound to Him—heart to heart, waltzing in secret fire. Soul to soul, each swallowing the lamp of the other. Until even time itself grows old and withers. Colliding at the crossroads, ribboned with enchantments, your seed becoming his center, his becoming yours. Under His power, lost in his eyes, as he will be in yours . . ."*

And every magpie as if a chorus, cawed the final word, *"Forevermore."*

She feels narrow. Hard. Urgent. Feels like someone is watching her . . . And keeping score.

Thinks she might go out. Perhaps a drink with *die Dunkle Seele* in the Last Cathedral, or to sit among the *Friedhofskinder* with their Byronic worldview in K17, not shopping—not tonight, just seeing stone and heart. Not exploring depth and promises with her knife.

Not tonight.

Just feels alone. Not wanting lips and skin and eyes. Not crazy, craving blood and passion's nectar. Not playing and fending off passes. Not probing hearts and keyholes.

Not tonight.

Not tonight.

Steps back from the street—shakes when its hot blood slaps her. Feels it's in a mood to chew overseers and angels. To infect anything that moves, to help helpless tragedies find another goodbye or accident . . .

Pushes her door closed.

Goes upstairs.

Makes tea.

Looks at her window.

Wonders if her dream will ever come . . .

The whiteness of her thoughts move in circles around the King's promise of His arrival.

Her breath quickens . . .

"Soon."

She looks at the dead cigarette in the ashtray.

"Please."

*   *   *

He rinses his hands in the river. Washes the scene of Truth from the blade.

Doesn't watch the twisting current take his offering.

Doesn't think to wonder if it had a name. The truth in its dead eyes still in his eyes.

. . . *A yellow ribbon flutters in his fingers* . . .

Passed a storefront; dresses for everyday . . . Passed a granite church, its candles going up in smoke. Thinks immortality, what a joke . . .

Sees a street whore, all emotions and lines of fiction and lust, promising satisfactions—money for the ceremony, a low landscape for poor hearts that can't find a lover to give tears and kisses.

Watching . . . (His desire for the light in the East a desperate gesture filling the middle of the night. His vision expands, finds honey and perfume, ignites when it comes upon the river carriages of chance.) . . .

Souls, spilt open to the bone, in the light of a beggars moon . . .

Watching . . .

. . . *A yellow ribbon flutters in his fingers* . . .

The glimpse of a lady's shoulder.

He turns.

Turns to the distance where her window whispers to him . . . Her street, her window—*There.* In the East. Stares a hole in the unquiet distance . . .

Thinks she waits. Dreaming of things that haven't gone away, of things not dim and cool.

. . . *A yellow ribbon flutters in his fingers* . . .

Feels . . . her
    tears . . .
    sighs . . .
    chasing the elusive tornadoes of love's mysteries . . .
    ragged moments end with shaking hands . . .
Sees her
    mouth open . . .
    waiting to reply to three little words. Sees ash and the hole in
her powers . . . Sees her reduced by blues she can't put her arms around
. . .
    . . . A yellow ribbon flutters in his fingers . . .
Sees her complexities, her heart. Her pride—trying not to corrode
. . . Her crying . . . Invention and perfection, her heavy load.
His passion rises . . .
Drives him . . .
    . . . ein gelbes Band flattert in seinen Fingern . . .

*   *   *

*[A night 10,000 nights ago . . . In his Castle of Night, dreaming of Her . . .
The King's messenger arrives, bringing a mask woven of tears and the pale
wings of dead moths.]*

The King's Messenger: *My king commands me to bring His Parchment to
you. And to give you this.*

*The Stranger (holding the pallid mask the King's messenger has handed
him): He has chosen me?*

The King's Messenger: *Yes. I have been instructed to tell you, you are to,
"Fill these empty walls with my White People. Gather them. Though they
be blind, here in my Garden of Midnight-Awakened, they shall see."*

*[The Stranger places the King's mask upon his face. Knows it cannot be
removed until that night when Oblivion calls Eternity home.]*

The Stranger: *I will be no devil loitering in the night. I will be his faithful
servant.*

[The King's Messenger nods and is gone.]

[*The Stranger opens the Midnight Parchment. He reads of Carcosa and the missing Princess . . . He turns to face thick, grim shadows . . . leaves behind all former gratifications . . .*]

*   *   *

She has nights . . . Nights devoted to Her King . . . She finds the young, lost souls in the haunted clubs . . . Binds the ones she brings home in black ribbons—ties them to her bed . . . Enters the fields of Madness . . . The fever—there is no turning back . . . The blade with the Yellow Sign on its hilt . . . Cuts away flesh to reveal bone . . . pale white bone . . . cuts away their summers . . . the broken necks . . . The blood . . . curves and layers and . . . and the pale white bone . . . their light for the King . . . Property, bought and sold, sugar for the King's bitter tongue of ashes . . .

When they expire, she disrobes, rubs their blood, once wild with regret and tortured time, all over her skin . . . Rouges her neck and nipples with it . . .

Sending her offering to The King she dreams of him . . . Knows he will come . . . Come to bind her to him . . . He will bind her to his passion—bind her with a yellow ribbon cut from the hem of King's robe. Spellbound she will follow where he leads . . . Knows beneath him she will learn of velvet heaven . . . and pleasure, beyond control . . . Knows when she finds herself lost inside his heart she will understand . . .

Naked, awash in blood, her fingers dance with demons . . . Until she sighs.

*   *   *

A single candle burns . . .

She does not want another night lost to this distance ripe with sorrows . . . Thinks to take to her bed, hide under the covers . . . where her fingers will dance with demons . . .

She wears a mask of tears . . . feels the distance cold and thick . . .

She yearns to change the world . . .

The cover of *Die Pergamente der Mitternacht* is closed. She rises from the sofa . . . Walks to the door . . .

On her small balcony she hangs a silver necklace with a lock of her hair and the Yellow Sign on a small rusty nail . . .

She stands there for a moment. Smoking. Looks down the street . . .

This way . . . Then that . . . Looks in the pitch black maw of the alley across the way.

Thinks of walls . . . of exile . . . of dreams and darkness and shores of tears, their history of wounds changed by fire . . .

Tries to remember joy.

Whispers, finally, "This is the night—Our night . . . *Unsere Nacht.* Come to me . . . *Deine Arme sind mein Himmel. Deine Lippen, alles was ich brauche.* Come to me."

*   *   *

Friday. The fireside sees what is true, what fell, and what is gone . . . He stands there staring at his soul . . . Hard as this empty parking lot. Within, no reply to his dance of questions . . .

He reads something the rain has written on a stone wall. Something about fables . . . He reads of The Street's medicines and balms, and lies in all their fullness . . . and fools trying to second guess the wheel of habit.

In a shadow of a cinema marquee. It reads PAZUZU'S BOWL. He smiles . . .

Discipline slow motion . . .

The Distance. Thick and cold, solid as fire.

Knows her rose is in bloom . . .

He has crossed all the rivers, felt the churning, dervish winds thrust and cut . . . Served His King well . . .

Now the voice in his heart demands its cure. He needs something to quiet his pain . . .

Remembers the night, drunk, the 20 pills, the mistake lying on the damp floor out of dreams . . . Leaving the bruise of seizure. . . The rush . . .

The broken field . . .

Chasing shadows . . .

Remembers days in The Room—The WHITE room . . . Archer's needles and vicious steel mouth . . . Remembers the harsh white light that would not quiet . . . Remembers the stirring of sins and hard tired days . . . Cold days . . .

His feet (in Caligari alleys, blood and grime and pain all around) have become Ulysses, they sail unfurled, cresting bounding waves, waves that push him . . .

The Distance . . .
His blue hand reaches up, eats the moon

and the defenseless stars . . .

*   *   *

She loved Her King. Knew he loved her. Only her. Only her. Knew he whispered, "Meins."
She hates The Distance.
She looks at the door to her bedroom. Her fingers flutter.
Knows he is out there. Out there, waiting. Watching. Hating The Distance.
Knows he has walked through a million lives . . . Found reason stone cold . . . Has seen nights and lives burn to nothing with his stone-cold wolf eyes. Knows his hands have scraped dull lives with the Truth . . .
She goes to the sofa.
Sits.
Waits.
Knows this night he can—will—conquer The Distance . . . the faces of thousands, all the eyes full of urging, full of we are-we are, are a blur . . . knows his hunger leads him on . . .

*   *   *

Her window . . . moments away—just around that last turn . . . No other flag has a scent.
And he comes to his Now.
The traveler's stage . . . Appointed in night . . .

. . . and you & I . . .

Her balcony and window, open—the ghost curtains dance in the breeze, fill his eyes . . . The necklace and the Yellow Sign call to him . . .
The Yellow Sign, she has opened her mouth and whispered, "Close." Spoken it with the strength of strong moonlight.
He has come ashore. Left the darkness gurgling for some other who has passed into Midnight.
His heart races. His knife begins its song—Love—at the speed of the ivy flow of blood. Slow . . . a curve up to a soft, whispering neck . . .

Love as a cure that holds no maybes . . . Love that will never be forgotten . . . Love is all it needs . . .

. . . starts with flashing eyes . . . and HUNGER . . . the curve of a tender kiss . . . the kiss washes away all the pain, all the distance . . . all the pain that went away and kept coming back . . .

Love bound to velvet skin . . .

She often sits on her sofa, curled up with a book. Often imagines a passion-filled poet sitting at her feet reading to her. Whispering some tale of intrigue and velvet confrontations—villains and madness, searching hands and lovers torn by distance . . .

She can see him look up into her eyes. See his eyes ask if she is ready. She always replies, "Please." And he, her poet of the proud old lineage, begins . . .

Some tale of dreams and Becoming, of things torn up and dust, footsteps and hollow sounds, and blood and shadows and those waiting, and those turned away . . . of spring turned around, its daylight snatched up, gone . . .

She sits there now.

Waiting . . .

No book in her lap. Not this night.

Only her desire.

No knife in her hands, waiting for the Next . . . No moment filled with the deathstroke delivered with the words, "Goodbye, Day."

She waits. She has not changed her tongue. For Him she is pure.

Waits . . .

The odd shape of the clock rips at her breast . . .

Watches the open window . . .

Sotto voce. "Come. See everything."

She is curled up on the sofa. Her eyes look at the Yellow Sign tattooed on her ankle . . . Tattooed with red ink and blood. She wants him to see it, to know she has planned this night a thousand times . . .

She wants him to know she is ready . . .

"Please," she whispers to the open door . . .

"Please." Her lips tremble . . .

His gaze slides to the door. Now open like the window . . . His mind fixes upon two, locked together, bound . . . bound in The Dance . . .

He is Beyond . . . no longer haunted by the sponge hands of the void . . . sparks banish insecure . . . No longer confused by confusion . . .

Beyond . . . Nights of worry . . . time . . . age . . . the songs of lonely men . . . black trains running . . . the aimless strains of nameless Jacks and Jills . . . the sudden madness of little lies . . . lying on the iron floor, blood cascading over tears . . . the eddies of sparrows that cannot pass the gates . . . the downbeat passengers lost in the rain . . .

At her window . . .

His being, trapped, ready to be inside with her eager contours.

Finally . . . The dream no longer just a dream.

"I want to . . ." *Kiss you.*

A single candle burns behind the pale curtains . . . A lonely song whispers, "I don't want to fall in love." . . . He listens, dreams, is drawn to a yesterday when he was nothing but a sparrow, before he was the King's servant . . .

There is no iron hesitation in his eyes.

He stands at the door . . .

She watches the doorway . . . sees his long, slim silhouette on the floor . . . it reaches, stretches, its head—his head, touches her ankle . . . Spellbound . . . she cannot breathe . . . She feels the tattoo on her ankle now radiant with a heat she has never experienced . . . All her thoughts—a hundred voices splashing in her head, embrace her dreams of a soft yellow ribbon . . .

Her hands are clasped together. No game. Not a prayer. Waiting for the profound and what has always been inevitable . . .

She is not scared, though she trembles.

He looks at the floor of her apartment . . . his heart only for this Princess . . .

His gaze, a tide opening ancient doors, follows his silhouette to her feet. He sees the Yellow Sign on her ankle. Pale soft. He is not used to pretty or the curve of summer these last one thousand years . . .

She is a new calendar. A sun of gentle wings and meadows . . . She is

His Princess.

His.

"Meins," cries his heart.

His hands of stone are no longer cold, no longer stained with the poetry of ice and blood and hungry movements carrying tragedies far and wide.

He is no longer a shadow born of darkness that comes and whispers on the end of a knife. There is no devil, drawing and breathing its hunger, in his desire. All the infections and questions he cast aside.

"Meins." *Forevermore.*

No more stone dawns blaring big days. No more lies for as far as the eye can see . . . No more ash and secrets . . . Only what is meant to be.

On the other side of the pale yellow curtain he hears, "Please."

"Please." So full of softness this angel's sentence.

Gilded with heat—"Please." Her naked sigh, the purpose of her heart revealed.

"Please." Her sigh, urgent, rhythmic . . . It lingers, shines fair, a star of inner light pulsing.

Sigh—flare—alchemy.

The moment bubbles with her desires. He wants more, the continent, the light floating—*soothing* . . . the gentle hand of intimacy, a sky of candlelight . . .

He is overcome with thirst . . . Ready to drink the cup of Truth.

He removes his pale, silk mask. Slides it in the pocket of his dark overcoat . . .

Takes that one last step . . .

. . . A yellow ribbon flutters in his fingers . . .

Chris Isaak, "Wicked Game"; Van Morrison "Someone Like You";
Eric Clapton, "Change the World"; Phil Collins, "Hold on My Heart";
Seal, "Kiss from a Rose"; Robert Plant, "Big Log";
Gordon Lightfoot, "Song for a Winter's Night"—looped, of course

The Sommerset Tales

Aubade in a Graveyard

My meditations, points of departure, begin each day at sunset. Twilight is my dawn, the white moon my lamp. Many are the spells and charms which tempt me, as I pass by the altar stones and ruins to hear shy Christina serenade oblivion ... Sweet Mademoiselle Christina, a flame stained by tears, resembling, for all her beauty, an empty pane—She stands so close to the slender brook where visions flow, yet life, the great light gleaming, and the dreams it spins like starving whispers, do not invade her exile.

Gentle sleep holds no sway over her, as her song of bereavement reaches into the world unseen. The silver garden of stars above, brings no light to her existence. She, still so young, a jewel-like maiden of mysteries and echoing illusions, lives in absolute darkness since her Vanessa—*she was such a sweet one*—was taken unto the perpetual fogs that glow above the lawns of the graveyard. Even the moon, when he chooses to appear, cannot illuminate the path to her love. Rain or no, in an expression so like a mannequin, lacking response to touch or sound, she, my pale, porcelain beauty, stands lost to her bittersweet hallucinations.

I think of the skeletons enduring the harsh slumber of the indigo necropolis and wonder if I should reveal myself to Christina and offer my aid, for I know the gloomy avenues of the underworld well. I would put my arms around her and with a will of fire burn away her sadness, but I would not be without my love—

Perhaps one day I will show her the key I possess.

Christina returns home when the blackness dims and I stand for a time. In a quiet ecstasy, I lose myself in the decaying imprint of her passion. As daylight destroys the flesh of night, I, uncomfortable without my shadows about me, return to my shelter, passing by the morning larks and the old ladies of woe whose hearts reside in deserted churchyards. Often I wonder what it would be like to stay up late and watch the gravediggers and the funeral processions—But it is enough to know I keep them active.

for AKS

I once possessed a fragile blue vase

I have but a few dear things in my sanctuary: some bird feathers [*I've forgotten where the bones fell*], a modest ball of hay-colored twine, an empty, baroque picture frame—I am prone to a fancy [*that flares in my veins like the rising sun*] where the angeleyes of a straw-haired maiden gaze out at me. I have a bed, a blanket, and a writing desk. A headless, child-sized mannequin in a fox fur stands beside the doorway. I once possessed a fragile blue vase which came into my custody as it so reminded me of the long graceful neck of a swan . . . My walls, splintered grayrock and black root, are adorned with the elder words of a speech ending in despair.

In the corner furthest from the entryway stands a rescued chest of drawers on four clawed-footed legs; its flaxen-haired owner had a voice as soft as a sad French horn stained by silver tears. My treasures— a *rare* book, a pale yellow mask, an antique, crystal hand mirror, and a king's handful of inexpensive baubles collected from young ladies [*each came to me on a darkened night*]—rest within.

In my quiet home, my *special* key in hand, I spend my days with Mysteries revealed only to *certain* eyes.

Here I am not persecuted. The Outside's heave-ho can find no crack, invitation, or window pane. Here, *Inside*, ever dreaming of Night, and pleasing delicate things, I contemplate the conditions of fate.

The Garden of Sleep lies but a few small steps o'er the crest of Somerset Hill. Each autumnally tranquil evening, as the wind groans in the brooding branches and nameless enigmas move like the smoke of blown out candles, I stroll the manicured lanes. Many are the fair Sunday mornings where respectful visitors bring aromatic blossoms to the beds of their Dearly Departed—I so enjoy the white lilies.

I have recently taken note of a quiet young woman with tresses of gold silk who lives but a few moments' walk from the lawns of bereavement. She owns a fragile blue vase I so admire . . .

for TomB

Twilight Sonatas

please me each evening. After spending the long hours of blazing sunfire in my warren of shadows awaiting the embrace of Night, the icy sighs of holy stillness & stars arise as the "come hither" of a sweet & gentle playmate.

I laugh softly as I step outside . . . Free again—the thorns of the animal world lie silent, Night, great & triumphant, has filled its savage mouth with wet leaves. Free to walk the greenery, now a dreamparadise washed in easy black

& skin soft gray
& whispersweet lavender . . .

I walk the open hallways of the animal world; across quaint lawns, I stop to gaze into the soiled windows of small clapboard houses. Cloaked in a pitch finger of darkness I stand inside the lip of an alley; I am marble, eager and watchful. I hear brusque laughter but turn from it. My modest heart seeks solemn daughters who accept the customs of the lonely hours—[*Night is my vineyard*]—their soft round eyes and ivory hands [I knew a tender blind girl with skin like fresh milk] . . .

My hands are filled with an exceptional rightness, a cool poetry dreamed behind rustling eyelids. I sing my verses upon the silentsorrow breasts of angels the future has divorced.

—No more thunderstorms.
—No more hills . . .

No more
blackvulture winds.

—No more ruined Cross
wounding brokenhearts with fever

. . . I bring the soft roses of sleep
to extinguish their exhaustion.

With fingers of wind the gods compose twilight sonatas . . .
I am but a fiddler.

again, for TomB

Tears & the stars fall

Frail essences,

little leaves in the wind . . . Oh, how the wind's tongue turns, caressing & consuming those pale-moon daughters I so revere.

I hear the sad, ancient bells sing . . .

I moan. Tears & the stars fall. Into the Unnavigated Unknown, they (every color of murmuring-midnight thoroughly lost)—*once so sweet*—fly where I may not follow. Oh, my gentle-hearted young leaves pass & leave me alone with scissors-sharp sonatas of darkness . . .

I knew Anna Greta & her moonshine vows, each whispered secret a visible condition entwined with the breath of midnight. I am the ears of night, I heard each of her modest confessions . . . My sweet, quiet candle of heaven-born light, waiting & waiting, a thousand & a thousand long nights. I knew her so well; watched her in her lonely rooms of ghosts & disguises. Night after night, my eyes stretched over the countless silvery dreams she kept in boxes & mirrors. How I longed to bring her to my quiet abode, to show her the modest possessions in my sanctuary, to explain the ciphers in *The Noctuary of Tine* & my role in the Giver of Sight's *special* plan, but Anna Greta could not be faithful—*Can time be so heavy? If she had only waited a few moments more* . . . She took in a lodger, a low woman—a predacious rat of the streets whose dishonorable soul ambushed the light of my dream.

I was not there when the harlot laid sweet Anna Greta down & appropriated the summer-filled kisses meant for me, untied the blood-red silk ribbons in my lonely angel's hay-colored tresses.

I was not there . . .

It was only a week, a week of knots & precious time scampering as if in a tarantella brought on by poison. Born to this field, I have my responsibilities to *the Work* . . . I was not there when the sleek lies of the serpent coiled about She Who Was the Future of My Heart. I was not there when she was enslaved & then exiled to the Impassable Hour.

I was not there . . .

The shadow of Anna Greta's gentle-hearted manner weighs on me. The singing curve of her smile haunts me . . . I see the noose & my flower's fair face in the darkness. Her pure, overflowing heart given & broken. Her neck snapped by bitter disappointment

& shame . . .

I crush Anna Greta's irrevocable words of "Goodbye" in my clenched fist. *"Punishment."* I am the mouth & paw of Death. I am His good & faithful servant. I can see how *It* crept, the nightmare, how *It* violated my fragile angel's trustfulness. That self-possessed *Thing*—That depraved, indigo-hearted bitch. The hyena must suffer—

My hands are fiery gales,

the aggressive future come to abolish the greedy illness . . .

Alone, I walk the mute banks of the hungry river in my great black overcoat. The rippled light of the street lamps & the glittering stars hide the minced red weed I have abandoned to the tomb-still limbs of nothing. I turn my back

& my quiet candle's She

sinks

into darkness.

It is late. Brightness discolors night as it seeks this shore again . . . The graveside beckons. I must return to my inquiries—

Certain Sunday Evenings in Summer

On certain Sunday evenings they, the Maidens Pure of Heart, as I liked to call them, gathered in Elaine's parlor for tea and conversation—*It has been so long since I last sat quietly and sipped tea.* In another life—not missed, but sometimes remembered—I had a fondness for Earl Grey and that was the blend they so often took as refreshment.

During the course of the evening they always found themselves in intimate spaces as a sarabande of strings or a piano rhapsody scored private memories. Debussy or Ravel—often his *Valses nobles et sentimentales*, never his stiff *Bolero*—would play and they traveled to eternities outside the language of this dull landscape. I always fell into the images of longing coloring their faces as the nocturnes sighed. Seton, Helen, & Elaine, a trio of silent sirens calling out to me. Unmoving, but as expressive as three Viennese dancers.

In Summer when Elaine's windows were thrown open to allow the gentle caress of the breeze to enter, I would sit in the swing on her porch and suppose fairy tales with them. Once a dessert pie sat cooling in the window, many were the flies I killed that night. I would allow no other of death's creatures to share my evenings with My Girls.

From time to time Elaine's thin scrapbook would come out and they would pass it around and whisper of brighter moments; sweet, lost youth, the waltz of ifs, & brief possibilities now "out of touch". Sometimes Helen would bring her crocheting, or Seton would unveil her newest quilt. *How I longed to caress the magic they had spun.*

Their once golden tresses had turned to moon-spun silver, their smooth angel faces were now lined with eventually's echoes, but I loved them well.

One brittle winter's night they gathered. *I was not there . . .* Perhaps had I been, I would have been able to avert the calamity?

This is what I have discovered from overheard accounts: To ward off the creeping chill, Elaine had over-stoked the fire and in the rush of darting sparks her dress bloomed with flames. In a state of panic and dismay, Helen suffered a fatal brain attack before the smoke or flames could take her. Seton, who even with the aid of her cane would never outrun tortoises, did not reach the door before she was suffocated by smoke.

Consumed by fire? Two hundred ten years of aged, gentle skin marred by flames . . . Once they were so lovely; powdered in melancholy, rouged with soft, yet powerful dreams.

*   *   *

They were buried many lanes apart. Apart!—My Girls? . . . I have moved them to a quiet sunny spot where summer flowers bloom. In Spring & Fall & Winter, I often purloin bouquets from the graves of the unworthy to brighten the beds of My Girls; pink carnations for Elaine, yellow gladiolas for Helen, and white lilies for Seton as she was the fairest of the trio.

Though they are close to me now, I would not be without My Girls. I have paid a visit to Seton's house and secured a lovely quilt to cover my bed; it warms my dreams. From Helen's bungalow I collected a few charming curios for my sanctuary. And I could not be without a memento of dear Elaine. From her trim cape I took an antique Russian tea service which now adorns my home.

On certain Sunday evenings when the rose of day has gone to bed, especially in Summer, I stop by and softly whistle passages of *Clair de lune* for My Girls.

A Traveler Came with Gifts

With the pearl burning of the Hunter's Moon resting on my shoulder like a purring familiar I had been out walking the rows of my garden, soundlessly watching the lonely sleepers trying to catch the dreams of the living and reveling in the music of the stars.

While I was in the dreamfog of the Work, a traveler, a stray with lily-delicate skin of alabaster, attired black on black from neck to toe, found her way through the small labyrinths I had carved below the lawns of rest. Past the orderly accumulations of bones and the worm-wood cabinets I had uncovered to further my investigations, to my world of gates she came.

As noiselessly as an extinguished heart I entered my sanctuary. The candles on my desk had been lit—My bed slept in—

She, in a poetic whisper filled with the ease of late autumn stillness, was reading the ivy of elder words that blossom on my walls like constellations. "What have we here," I sighed. My words—*their tone, almost a flutter of ecstasy*—revealed my presence to the child. A reed commanded by the wind, she turned. My visitor did not fall back as she absorbed the cast the Gift has given me. Her eyes, soft misty blue, did not turn away from the black fire of mine.

"Out there—Above, in the Land of Brutality & Woe, I am alone. *Nothing* . . . This place called to me. I became lost in the catacombs and needed to rest."

I did not move, nor did I speak.

There was no fear in her, but she was filled with questions. They moved in her eyes and across the smooth roundness of her face.

"I have gifts . . ." Her comely hands offered them to me. She had sculpted an eidolon of the Master I serve. His gray countenance was a lantern—*This child had a great talent.* And upon 12 brass discs she had enchased the Ciphers-Major. "They came to me in a vision," she said. "It was like . . . like, overhearing instructions."

Does He test me? I wondered.

"Before I knew to inscribe them on brass, I practiced." Like a lover, opening her window so the first star of the evening might enter her room, the child raised the sleeves of her shirt and showed me the curves and lines she had etched into her pallid skin.

She turned to gaze into a fugue of shadows and her halo-colored hair, in winged flight, seemed to laugh.

"These shadows hold memories . . . And plans. I hear the echo of my dreams in them."

"This is a Castle of Dreams. In this enchanted place, the reflections of His Revelation linger . . . I float in the Magnificent Void and there, dream dead names . . . Here, the Master whispers."

She turned again, as if I had invited her to share some secret moment. I felt her warmth, fed on it. Though her black boots were weighty and her clothes were burdened with the dung of the streets, she moved to me with the lithesome elegance of a ballerina.

"I would know the full measure of your master."

In the candle's glow, her ivory hair shone like moonlit clouds. Her eyes took on the tranquil colors of twilight . . . She removed her shirt. She had the long graceful neck of a swan. The flesh she offered was luminous. I wanted to feel the kiss of its soft heat on my fingertip, longed to taste it.

"And so you shall."

*   *   *

Her brass discs rest in a velvet pouch in my pocket. I have made full headmask of her face & hair to adorn my mannequin. She—*I forgot to ask her name*—is learning of His *special* plan.

for my friend, the Java Phantom

In a Raven's Eye

For aeons we have flown the nine worlds. O'er mountains and thunderous seas. O'er the starts of mice and the spells of tricksters and oathbreakers. O'er the rivers of lives and fields of fire. We have heard bloodstained silence and watched the gladsome suffer, watched their beliefs decay . . .

Cold today. The wind is ravenous. I watch as Memory, shiny as the stars or a coin and black as the void, steeps in remembrance. Memory has never been one for action. He seems to be part of this windy tree. He'd waste the whole of a day or the breath of a season lost to the soft roses of sleep. The poetry in his silentsorrow breast is cool. He would rather soar in a dreamparadise of lavender twilight than embrace the come hither of Night's blazing moonfire. I sometimes wonder why the One-Eyed made us brothers.

Yet brothers—wing and talon and onyx-radiant eye—we are, tethered to our mission. So in this barkweb of windblown branches we alight. Waiting. Observing.

And He, this creature born of the Gift, whose sagas are voyages in gloomy light, comes again with the night. Like the unruffled stillness before the coming of the blackvulture wind He rises after the sun has bled to death. For decades He has walked from his burrow in the grayrock mound to the open stand where the trees do not tread. From his rock perch, still as any Northern glass lake of Midgard, He looks down on the small bays of firelight which illuminate the settlement of the tribe.

He is not a warrior. He is a searcher, a collector; bits and baubles, not all shiny; bones & blue vases . . . & white lilies.

Devoted to His Work as a *true servant* of the Giver of Sight, He howls not, nor do the passionate ways of the Green Man touch him. Yet he is bound to the tribe and from time to time the pure breath of angelic sirens, each a pale daughter of Sif, whispers to him. And he heeds their call. I have seen him gather the imprint of their passion to his breast. Rapture-etched portraits of Vanessa, Christina, Anna Greta, Elaine, Seton, Helen, and a score of lute-tongued maidens—each silenced summer sunlight now lost to murmuring-midnight—he carries in his heart's eye.

Tonight He stands at the door of his den. The wind sings to him. His eyes are as black as those of my brother and I—They, as do ours, watch the dreams of the living. There are moments He seems to be no more than thought & memory.

She Comes in Blood

The darkness overflows with an icy madness. Branches rustle with the drunkenness of grief. Apart—

Again & again, apart . . . Unseen, the cool stars migrate and I am another bare autumn tree. My hands are overgrown with fire and I dream of an absent angel as the chill October rain braids my hair . . .

There is a memorial park (much newer and larger than the garden of repose that is my district) on the other side of this sleepy dorp. Behind it, beyond a lament of rocks and wild grass, upon an uneven hill of knotted pines is the lair of *another*. Her countenance rings with the Gift, but she is not like me—Not like me at all. Under a mane of auburn-tresses lies a beast of great beauty (*were chance & necessity of a different mind, I know my heart would burn for her*) and great cunning. Her lips are red with the tender flesh of maidens-pure. Her nature is blood . . .

This Midnight-thing, who a loving mother named Dorothy Jean, reclines upon a divan of bones and hide. And there, scraps of carrion and squabbling beetles at her feet, she dreams of my Master. Dreams of owning *His Special Plan.*

* * *

I had taken note of my tender rose, Lorretta, in the last days of September. She who was an angel of mercy to the sick and orphans was a treasure to me. Lorretta's nights of solitude were spent in the romantic pages of travelogues—most of sunny European destinations. There was often an autumnal melancholy in her far-away looks.

I watched her in her rooms. Resting in her trembling hands, her dreams, soft as her white flower skin. The light did not laugh on her, yet she was radiant—*Radiant.* I dreamed of being a warm, delicate current kissing her ripe, ivory breasts, the breeze of warmest summer caressing her ankle. I dreamed of her sweet, *"please . . ."* sigh as I sighed . . .

Lorretta was reading aloud—something soft and delicate in French. I could not understand the words, but the sentiments—I understand lost and hope all too well. I left her window and returned to my dark wood. I was lost without her lantern eyes . . . On shadowdrifts of blackness I returned to my sweet angel's window for ten nights—Her knees, her ankles, her shoulders drew me.

*　　*　　*

I was mad with imagining's birds. Lorretta beguiled me completely. The song of her April-face hung close to my thundering breast. I found steel in *My Work*. On a night of clouds and breath-woven rhythms, as *My Work* led me to new precincts, I discovered Dorothy Jean. By dull candle-light and the pale moon her tongue—wantonness unfurled—declared joy in flesh beyond woe, beyond sickness. Beside the stone skirt—ragged with the impulses and ripples of many seasons—of an old church, she was hunched over the cold meat she had mined from a fresh grave. A wolf devouring a tiny fowl, she was busy marrowing a bone. With quick eyes she looked upon me. I swear there was certain nostalgia (an anxious hesitation like meeting an old lover) in her gaze. I thought she wished to speak, but she remained mute (as did I) and I left her to her repast.

Through one night and the one that followed and still a third, each of which leaped by like ignited hounds, I was aware of a grim presence hanging in the distant shadows, a presence I knew to be hers; watching me, mirroring my steps. Curious though I was, I restrained myself from confronting the midnight-hunter—*I knew what she was.* She would come to me when the gate of her hunger opened.

In a stand of slumbering stones while the wind was a succession of desperate screams, she revealed herself to me, talon and eye as sharp as the executioner's duty.

"Dog of the Giver of Sight, I am the Holy Mother's servant. *She Who Was First in Time* will have her office and possessions restored to her. Return them on the morrow. Then rush back to your sepulcher or endure distress and woe beyond your darkest imaginings."

My eyes laughed in disbelief as I snarled. "You come to my vineyard and befoul My Master, He Who Wears The Radiant Mask, with the poison of heretics. Your benefactress—banished to the most appropriate desolation for her treachery—has no role in *His Special Plan*. Obeisant crow of the Pretender, I am the mouth and paw of Death—Retire from my sight, before I give your heart and eyes to night's scavengers."

She showed me her fangs and hissed—Hissed *at me!* "To-morrow . . . Or find yourself lost." With that, she and her fast lies were gone, but the incandescence of her stain remained to scrape the night. It ate at the boundaries of my eyes and my heart.

Remaining in abyssal shades distant, the author of this hostility hounded me, devoured my time and thoughts . . . Yet I found fleeting moments to stop at Lorretta's windowsill. *How could I not?*

*　*　*

She has left my tender rose Lorretta's narrow and lifeless form at my doorstep. The 3rd Cipher-Major etched above the rose of my dear angel's soft, pale breast . . . Upon a defaced parchment of pure white skin, in a flowing ivy of script, the ghoul had scribed -

Dog of the Thief—
   The Giver of Sight usurped the Holy Secrets of Tine. The Holy Mother shall be avenged. The Holy Secrets of Tine restored to their Rightful Mistress.
   You shall not know rest until My Mistress delights in Tine again. Watch for me by moonlight.
   Dorothy Jean

With anger-sharp eyes I watch. Battered by anguish, this sentinel waits. I know the midnight-thing will come . . .

The night lies like gravedust. Beyond my gate I see a fluttering high-collared gown of loam & bloodstained red. I hear the breath of the beauteous beast. Her sleek smile is a blade . . .

As midnight laughs we dance.

Words Touching

Dreams. Empty rooms. Far away lights on the winter snow . . .

I flicker like this candle on my table . . . I burn like midnight-unfurled.

Before the Gift, as I crawled through Summer dreams that shattered on the shores of hopeless nights, He was my heart. And so He remains . . . Yet He serves the Thief. My duty and my heart stride contrary roads—Unless I can turn him from his servitude and sacrilege. Yes, He could serve My Mistress and attend me—*Love me*, if He can be turned from his transgressions.

We could lie together in the dark and sing. Together, we could feast in the garden of the dead . . . He could sit at my slippered feet and read, to *me*. And after, we would feast on the passionate ways of a man and a woman joined as one. All the generous smiles of my desire I would bestow on Him . . .

If . . .

He *will* be mine. Let his Mary Rose know the bite of the worm! Let her ears choke on their winding sonnets!

*   *   *

Mary Rose was a woman of dreams, a small flower smiling in a golden dawn of endless wishing. Connected to lo & behold by imagination, the scraps she sifted from her blindness, she walked through futures & yesterdays of words. Hope was her daylight. That and her delicate manner drew him . . .

In the love hours, she burned brightly for him and he for her—Night after night, brighter & brighter. He sat at her feet—like an adored feline, her fingers resting lightly on his shoulder or stroking his hair—and read sensual verse to her; songs of rich, unyielding love from the Orient, pilgrimages of sorrow from Persia, the rhapsodic laughter of French bards who loved rhyme & meter more than their heady wines;

or what the mighty English oaks have beheld and small footprints shivering in the flames of change from Venice and Lisbon. With each haunting repetition they traveled together, they knew the secrets of the rain and dialogues of puppets & drums & leaves. Quatrains were their roads, couplets the fearless hearts of their eager steeds . . . Toward Forever they rode.

It sickened my heart. Woe & anger racked me.

And there came a night when his dark lips touched lightly on the back of her smooth hand. And her slim lips, smiling, kissed his palm. I thought to fly through her window and shred her before his adoring eyes. But I held fast. I am as cold as any winter and the time to cover his pale rose in desolation was still moments away . . .

So I began to taunt him, to make a mockery of His Lord. His moments of courting with Mary Rose dwindled as I abused his hours. I kept his thoughts and feet rushing. While he made his way through the midnight I orchestrated, I began sitting outside the window casement of Mary Rose's cottage. Inside she sat with a volume of romantic words she could not see . . .

I fed off her worrisome solitude. As her blind fingers traced aimless, broken patterns on the pages, as she imagined, I laughed. She could not see him. She could not see the words. She could not touch him. She could not touch the words.

For twelve nights I kept him from her. On the thirteenth, as he dashed to her door, I threw the carcass of an infant at his feet. "Your temporal god will be as this when the Holy Mother returns to Tine. When He is broken and insignificant, as is this cold lump, what shall you have? What shall you have? What have you now? This thief you serve, he creates nothing. Thieves never do."

"You will be punished for your sins."

"Touching and fitting words. Turn them back upon yourself . . . Do you see those shadows? Dreams perish within them. They are to be your home."

*   *   *

He did not reach her door that night. He did not see her alive again . . .

But I did . . . As I played with her I told her of the wanton pleasure he would cloak me in—In detail, I described each act of desire he and I would rattle with as she begged me to desist.

"He will be mine."

She rose from her chair and ordered me gone. I thundered to her and cast her to the floor. I was on her. Her clothes came off . . .

I pressed a talon to her flower, whispering of the most intimate of caresses. Then I began to cut very slowly, effortlessly. Up, her belly— my finger rose and fell with the flutterings of her fear, her breasts; I could smell the blood. She tried to crawl away as if there was some bridge from this message I etched for him. His sweet Mary Rose tried to hide by reciting a sonnet about a young woman picking ripe plums for her lover . . . As I cut, I filled her ears with poems he would read to me, I told her what he was. I told her of the strange contours the Gift had bestowed upon him. I was euphoric when I saw in her eyes she grasped the truth. I let the horror fully take her to brokenhearted-madness before I removed her heart.

His dainty pleasure swallows dirt. Summers merry and the sweets of love now dwell in the belly of the worm.

His tears groan with fortunes cold.

His words drop like tears.

Smeared in foul matter, I left his rose on the cold stones where His Girls rest. The hand he kissed, I ate. The lips that pressed their velvet to his palm, I ate. The mind & heart that loved him filled my belly. His words to and for her now touch me . . .

Words & flesh. Body & soul. To have, to hold. He *will* be mine.

Under June

> the weddings were white,
> the funerals, wintergray events of weeping . . .

At dusk the flowers seem cut from stone, the shadows, corners & stages where grief is declared. It was in the shadows that I found her, the moon on her hair, the breeze playing with the hem of her white wedding gown. She was a weary reed. Her manner shaped by all the time held in the surrounding graves. In a penitential voice she was praying "Most Holy Maker, Sweet Savior, this end is my beginning . . . You have taken my bloom upward to Your breast and left me only winter. Why? Why is this day of Summer colder than any February?"

I looked down at my shadow and up to the cold face of the moon. I asked each if I should answer her. Her white hands fluttered. Every dove needs a branch to alight upon, I thought.

"Pastures are sheared, songs—even the merry & dear—end. There are unchosen seasons when delight runs from the grim bells—Do not turn, Sweet Sparrow. I am an edge of nature who remembers; often too deeply. I too, have waited for answers . . . To your questions, there are none."

She did not turn from the grave. "We were to be wed after the harvest . . . I have spent eight seasons walking toward that dream. Now—"

I know of dreams missed. Silent as growing grass I walked to her and granted her only remaining wish. When the claret of her flesh ceased to flow and her breath was still & cold as a Winter pond, I placed her in the coffin of her intended. From his finger I removed a ring and slipped it on the ring finger of her left hand . . .

Under June

> the weddings were white,
> the funerals, wintergray events of weeping.

(for V)

248

I'll simply call her V

I have been lost,
but I have never forgotten . . .

I'll simply call her V.
She was my favorite.

She stood under the observatory eaves, white gloves and black boots
Under

huddled birds
in shadows

wings at rest from the day's madrigals of dartflight and song.

In   Ss   hH   aA
Dd
d   ooO
Ww
Ssss
s
ss   lovely in lovely shadows.

And I smiled. At the soft fire in her eyes, at the soft smile on her lips, at
the book she held, closer than any lover. *The Lamentations of lamantia-*
ra >only a dreamer held night so tightly, only a True dreamer wished
All nights were music >pure music, unfolding, fog on a lantern beach.

And after my smile I whispered to her, slow and even, full of mysteries
becoming visible. "Walk into my voice."
She turned. Her lips parted.
"Walk into my voice."
She took a single step.
"I am a postcard of a dream where peacocks walked, where interludes
are buds and kisses and opals of Now."
She smelled of winter trees and youth.

"Walk into my voice."

    She smiled. And to my voice she came . . .

Radiant. By the moon's early light. A child to the coyote of the white arcades. A child in a skin of cello tears seeking time. And time is what I do best . . . I frame it in rock and stone and loam. I adorn it in fading flowers. I caress it with life's blood.

We came together. She&I were words, hands, searchlights—moonbright . . . The bells whispered of what must come. She was fruit, overflowing the lonely winter windows of my heart. The bells whispered of what must come .

.

.

What must come.

Long after I cannot recall my name, I'll remember her. The soft fire in her eyes. The soft smile on her lips. The book she held, closer than any lover. . .

                      lovely in lovely

      Ss   hH   aA

             Dd

                d   ooO

                   Ww

            Ssss

                s

                ss

I'll simply call her V.

She was my favorite.

for V

Sarah smile

A gargoyle snug in the teeth of blackness (we both smile).
Sometimes bound to sudden flows of madness.
A shadow man, this watchman. Cold, but not godless.
                              Cold, but I have dreams . . .

.

.

.

Sarah.

   Sarah.

By the light of the autumn moon.

Hair as **red** as the fast, hot claret that once ran in my veins. **Red**
                              as the
                              long-stemmed kiss
                              of the poet.
                              Doe-soft [woman's] eyes,
whispering—an autumn clarinet
                    pulling stars from the heavens.

. . .

   I came up behind the iron bench on which she sat. I placed my
hand on her cloaked shoulder. "Fear not, child. I am the ferryman from
this blackness of shadow to Quiet Unbroken." Without turning she began to speak.

There was once . . . I was lost and filled with rust. Lost in a cemetery of
thumbs down, gloomtongues burning with sins for every goodbye.

          —I was caught in her voice—

I guess I rarely
          smiled . . .

251

     The taste of branches was on the light breeze. I was off frolicking, there were performances on porches, mean dreams hissing in blue lamps

        . . . And moths—they lay like fluttering eyelids on a tapestry of plagues, and Saturn introduced us to sonatas of gin and the hinge

    and perversity swift as the law. Finally, in rain,

            there were circumstances

and blood>sweet warm poison>   Wash away the birds of trouble—thorny by sun and the midnight that touches the watchmen with fear—who nest in my hands. Wash away my pain. Fill my cold wounds
     with s t a

       r s.

She took off her glasses > I have always found myself in love with the revelations held in the radiant eyes of angels. Her [beautiful doved] hand—a path to tomorrow, touched my hand. She wrote the night.
    There was blood, but no tears.

     Another tender yester-night etched

Never will the glow of her October nightshade leave me, for I have pinned—with blood **red** thread—the rose of ink that ornamented her thigh to the graying flesh over my heart . . . Ah, I write in fire slow to burn, in the smoke of wanting, each of my words, hounds, running up the hill of desire . . . Then we are there, my evening sparrow & I now&forever strolling the soft corridors of black ashes and Loki flowers. Sarah smile.

I sit in the dark
     with a glass of dreams. The hour -without breath or tide- waits at my table. It asks after last night. Please.
     Some hands might tremble
   . . . I light a waxlight and speak of

Sarah's smile.

        (for my oTher—radiant- **coopgirl***)*

In the spaces in between

Mara owned a tract of books. The blackest chimerical work, slim as the ring finger of her unadorned left hand. Over the years I watched her gather them; more nurse than secretary. From the quaint bookshop on the corner by the park and the postman and library sales they came, children to her garden warm and quiet.

Her hands were works of art, made to caress pages—windowpanes, glowing with motion and hieroglyphics, detailing blackness and not becoming. As she made her way through crimson petals and *The Mill on the Floss* and leaves and vines and saints who found salt, not Eden, and shadows singing in the grass, I stood at her window. When the animal heat of Summer sat down on its haunches at twilight, in the hot bellowing chill of Winter's mad voice, I stood outside, pressed shadowlike to the casement. I dreamed of sitting at her feet, reading Rimbaud's *first evening* to her. Dreamed of the fragrant tea, warming ripe lips that I longed to fill with the dance of laughter. Dreamed, her lips and the tea she brewed could sate this Sahara that blazes within me.

Then one day in early October It came. The sacred, haunted text of My Master. From where I could not fathom, but it was there nonetheless. & though I had fallen for her quiet enchantments, I could not allow her to keep—to read, *The Noctuary of Tine*. My Master's words, *His Special Plan*, are not for *other* eyes, even jewels lucent as Mara's.

My lace sleeves tapped firmly upon her door. I, understanding accidents will happen, she, beyond belief. There was no kiss or revelation for this tall, comely sparrow, there was a rustle, a grazing. There was closer. I was quick as the touching, born only wishing Now. No knife. No sympathy. I strangled her with her own shining black tresses.

Breath. Spent.
Eyes still. Scratched from time.

On a moldering bed of her precious books, in a room on the lowest level of my warren, she rests—her hands, folded in prayer, hold My Master's *Holy* tome. I keep her eyes in a pair of antique bottles—bookends. Often when the moon is full we read together.

(for Pollyanna McIntosh, who bewitched me one October afternoon)

The blood of a damsel's breast on the green door of the forest

The girls that are wanted are good girls
Good from the heart to the lips . . .

—From "The Girls That Are Wanted,"
J. H. Gray, c. 1880

Jaymi and Alanna were twins—in spirit. They had come to whisper prayers over the grave of the poet, Borli. To offer star-flowers and adoring eyes to the mad soul who filled the sun with stones and opened the black doors of grief [hemmed in whispering lamplight]. From the city where the plain and the grotesque flooded afternoon and evening they came with their gifts fashioned from blood-red string and black feathers. They came to unlearn.
They came to be forgiven.

They brought fire to light his way from Hell.

I came upon their candlelight one restless night—*Are there any other kind?* Oh, how their sweet nightshade voices danced in praise of Borli. Under a low leering moon, each in her turn and joined as a minimal choir, freed Borli's blackcrow words of hopelessness in cries and whispers. The small scurryings under the trees stopped and the birds, tucked in their nest, tightened, as Borli's canal of torment sighed . . .

Alanna, with her mane of straw-colored hair, was the taller of the delicate pair.
Jaymi was the softer, the darker—though her eyes flared as brightly as her sister's.
I marveled at these soft angels—roses, and the midnight-pure gleam of their woe.

254

For three nights I watched over them—covered their handiwork of spirit-flame and dancing sleeve with my eyes, covered their ballets of longing with my heart. And I fell deeply. But I never had use for

Borli
>too full of his own import
>too taken with his own tongue
>he was merely a little bird who wept to play a grand part
>I left him a pack of cards the wind sent into winter's night.

And on the third night in the burnished hearth of Dear Jaymi and Sweet Alanna's lamentations the mirror in my darkening soul grew tired of their devotions . . . I gave the clouds wings, and claws, freed despair from its hours in bitter shade . . .

Angels loved, they wait in chains no more. With wild, suffocating kisses, I covered their foolishness and left them
u n done.

Last night I discovered the rapture of Dear Jaymi's heart. Alanna's heart is aging nicely. In three days there will be a full moon, it will be a pleasure to have her at my dinner table. The small bones of their fingers I have bound with red string and black feathers. They made a lovely necklace for my mannequin.

*(for the lovely ladies, Jaymi & Alanna—kind and ever so helpful—
in the Green Room of the H. P. Lovecraft Film Festival)*

I once possessed little other than a fragile blue vase

and a few inexpensive baubles. *And there was my hunger, of course . . .*

As the decades fell from the world of waking and became dust and found homes in the dry, aching corners of my home (my rooms are not large, but they are many) I have been a steadfast collector and many are the *Dear* gifts which have come to me as I, dutifully in service to My Master, went about My Work.

. . . My mannequin is no longer a naked shell. She now has a head— Ah, fair Rene, so sweet (*I remember her well*)—and hands, the skin (stuffed with autumn leaves and grass) of the right belonged to Jaymi, the left Alanna—I stitched them to the sleeves of the fox fur with blood red thread. The small bones of their fingers I have bound with red string and black feathers. They made a lovely necklace (*I can tell by Rene's glow she adores it so*). And yes, she has legs now—Mara's were long. I thought it fitting they not be wasted.

The drawers of my chests and desks and borrowed trunks hold records of the slight and the celestial. Like a kiss of flowers stretching into Nows receded, they wash over streams that weep no more.

In my favorite chair rests a *rare* book, the sea that sends the acolyte from life to life to life. Long have I traveled under the sorrow of the moon, My Master's psalms my dawn, my gate.

The wind is a vigilant salve against hours waiting, it rises from my monk's post of stone and loam to a sky saddled with the flame of my benedictions.

I have knives and bottles (*If you could have only seen Mara's eyes shine*), red silk and postcards (*I wish I could have walked la Cour du Dragon with tantalizing young Juliette*), and the feathers of meadowlarks and candles that breathed faces on my grayrock walls. The petals of dried flowers are my carpets.

. . . newspapers

. . . a pair of torn, eyeless teddy bears

    . . . Sarah's black velvet gloves

      . . . parasols

. . . twigs

. . . an apron

        . . . a long black veil

  . . . 3 pieces of eight

. . . an empty, baroque picture frame

   . . . herbs

        . . . a pen and a blue pencil

       . . . bolts and nails and the zodiac

. . . ashes from the fire

      . . . V's wedding dress

      . . . a cracked whiskey glass

. . . a few things from the church and a few things from a whore

            . . . tracts and shoes

. . . a modest ball of hay-colored twine

. . . an hourglass rescued from the small hours of a poetic sleepwalker lost in the mystery of divinity

         . . . keys and a clever that found no relief in rust

  . . . Fanny's pillow and Nora's muffler

. . . scissors

My memories walk like peacocks among the relics and interludes of different air and my long-stemmed heart smiles.

The caskets of those Dearly Departed, now beyond hungry dismay and awakening and interludes of grace, those who sustained me in the lean winter months are now soft beds for My Girls. Sometimes on cold winter nights I crawl in and snuggle with V or Sarah. Often I bring a brush and an antique, crystal hand mirror for their hair . . . *Oh, how sweetly they whisper in my dreams.*

I once possessed a fragile blue vase which came into my custody as it so reminded me of the long graceful neck of a swan . . .

(*for MY ever-lovely coopgirls*)

wind. ardent. circular, back on itself as if in dismay.

Tonight the moon is full
Certain creatures watch, court—sharp and loud, and leave after a fever
of pleasantries.
I know the mouth flammable and all its horses of red-hot thrust.

My bed-linen is red, stained in tears and claret.
There have been honeymoons and funerals played—in strides, and
knocks and laughter, upon my threshold of dreams. Many were the occasions and velocities where skirts have come off, eyes come out.

Tonight's passage stands on a different hill . . .

Being Led by Pictures . . .

A doorway. A tear. An arm with a need . . .

Said her name was kristamas.

But her eyes made me forget little bad girls. Ripe-fruit open mouths, emphasis venture. Panties down around their pale ankles.

What's her name? She must have one? In some life of pictures adorned with masks and loved madly she had one? Must have . . .

The way she parades, scootin' nipples ready to whirrrr. Why won't she take off her dark darkmask?

Miles' trumpet heats her toes. Snow white, curled—what diaries her toes must have written, bite by bite, in the calendars that vanished in graves.

I want to talk to her. Whisper about the bite of the spider. Those legs, that's the side I want to be lost on. I want to kiss her with my teeth.

"El Prince, loose your ebb and flow processional. The oracle in my fahrenheit itches."

Shaman-song mouth of rothko shadows colors my mind, peels me till I capsize. Eyes—it's about that time. Eyes—what if my dainty moondream-valentine klangs when the black satin X of your fox steps from angel to flame. Eyes—every small tiger-face window open with ghosts. Want her gamut to cry without hesitation, want her tongue full of me too, me too.

She knots her joy to the lisp and chat of the drums. Toes . . . Toes—true and pretty, whisper, "Oh."

Her meow, petite as a knife, is upside down. Knees, smooth as art painted in midnight ivy, redecorate the poof of my stunts . . .

Eyes and toes and nipples, the room dances till it can't—till it can't.

after the art of Kristamas Klousch

David Sylvian, *Sleepwalkers*

The Ground She Sleeps upon Is a Clue... and a Mystery

The trauma of chasm is obvious. Can't delete the world of deadman feats.
Too many surfaces. Tomorrow dies.
Innocent Erendira doubts . . .
In-between the vanishing smoke of love,
Her where-am-I vessel of cracked-diamond stars and amnesia,
Wounds the blue dance of the door.
A day away from further
Her fingers, an exiled patchwork of self-injury
And coiled architecture,
Lose their grip on the prayer-bridge.
A butterfly
—(no arc of kite-dance above the snail)
—(its tongue of secrets sends no word),
Scarred by a whisper of breath,
Rests on her shoulder as she slumbers . . .
There's no anger in dust.

again, after the art of Kristamas Klousch

David Sylvian, "Ride"

8mm . . . soil

Sweating. Feeling drawn out, strained.

Corrupted.

All those little under things crawling around inside. Clumsy, lonely . . . Wild little feelings, tugging, testing, refusing to come to the surface. When they stir you can hear the clicking as they try to harden into impulse.

They make you afraid, sometimes. Sometimes they tease, make you desperate. They put the bottle to your lips.

There are still photographs—dozens, black and white photographs with bent edges and cracks, old photographs, some are yellowing, of clumsiness and stiffly and flushed and wide-open eyes scattered on the carpet with the dead leaves. Wind brought them in when the windows were open. Swept things around, stroked them with dust. Does that this time of year if you leave the windows open. Trying to remember where the doll's head with the curly hair and the cracked face came from. Odd how blue the eyes still are.

Lot of things come in here even when the windows are closed. They connect to my chapters and fantasies, leave me anxious.

Projector is ready. It's an old Bell & Howell I picked up at Rodeo Bob's pawnshop around the corner—I had to have it for its slow motion capabilities.

8mm *Lumina.*

Sweating.

Should open the window and let some of the breeze in.

Breeze would deaden the sound of the projector too. Never liked that sound. Reminds me of old creepy movies. The black and white ones with slithering shadows. They made me cringe.

She's smiling in black and white. Just standing there. White party dress. Little black shoes. Black hair ribbons. But I know they're RED. The other girl with the long curls looks sad, maybe frightened?

The smiling girl walks toward the camera. Her smile grows. Gets whiter.

Whiter.

*   *   *

Four drinks don't help.

Quick for the 5th. Will that put desire to sleep? Can it put a sock in fear's mouth and stop the muttering?

Will it stop RED? Stop all the insects bleeding from the bushes?

Another slug. Quick-quick.

Sleep. Dream. Of the little playhouse, the stage with the puppets dancing. Dancing! Dancing! Fast as marathon. All the spinning, trapped mice. FAST . . . All the little girls riding the giant, bejeweled insects on the carousel. Round and round. Green. Blue. Yellow dots. RED. RED. Round and around. The Beatles' record did not spin that fast. Not even when I adjusted the dial.

East to deeper, in every well, atop the device of churches, my dream is full of insects.

The lust and atrocities of the insects. They have no fear of the tiger. They do not cry tears when the hands turn the dial and the strings tug. The signal comes, bleeds, clicks and clicks. BANG-BANG! They're gone.

I relax my fists. Dream of snow. And Holy carols.

On the page.

They tried to teach me, but I could not read the notes. Tried.

Rearranged them.

"Windy". For b-flat clarinet.

She was.

Again.

Spun fast. Dancing. Dancing. Every location that collects her, spliced together.

I was not holding scissors.

Was not.

Won't.

Beg to kiss her nipples.

Won't hear her scream.

*   *   *

"Why not?"

"She's not dead."

"Are you certain?"

"I am. I opened the cocoon. It was empty."

"Was there enough light in the room to see? You do have that trouble with dim areas."

"Yes. I think so. The floor lamp was on. I saw the shadows."

"No spider fingers?"

"I don't remember. No. might have been."

*　　*　　*

Red bricks.

Door.

Security guards. Thank you. Smiles. Polite.

I try to be.

The hall to my office was well lit. As it should be.

Violin music played on the intercom system. It was nice. Soft. Even. There was no black sun in it.

There was a dead beetle on my carpet. A big one. My carpet is soft brown. Nice, no patterns to needle the eye. I don't know if it was a nice beetle. It was dead. The tip of a straightened paperclip was helpful in disposing of it. Not in my garbage container, dropped it outside the office window. The other beetles in the black loam below would be hungry.

Closed and locked it tight, both locks. Checked. They were very firm, a proper seal. Can't have other cannibals getting inside.

*　　*　　*

My apartment was cold. Very cold.

The Russian landlady was loud. Yelling at her husband. Again. He drinks. She yells. About money. About no money. About no sex.

Says he's careless. Reckless. Stupid. Lazy. Over and over, lazy.

Says the ground will not want his bones when he dies. Tells him to hurry up.

There's always trouble here.

The cute little girl on the first floor gets slapped around. I saw her black eye. Her boyfriend, he sells drugs, slaps her around when he drinks. Sends her out to buy his beer. Tells her her tits are too small and her ass is flat.

The Russian landlady's husband likes the cute girl. One day, he was drunk, at the mailboxes on the first floor he said to me, "She's got a great little ass."

There's always trouble here.

When the summer is hot. When winter comes and brings cold. When it rains. The time I brought the woman here and her clothes came off.

She took them off. For me. Slowly. Watched me watch.

Said things to guide my eyes.

Said things when she walked to me and took my clothes off. Told me we were going to disturb the soil in the garden. She laid on the bed and spread her legs apart. Poured gin on her belly, rubbed it in rings around her nipples. "Ever heard of the Devil's Fire?" Said you have a mouth, tire my muscles. Laughed as I decomposed.

It was snowing. Our legs were entangled.

Down the street there was gunplay by the barroom and the gloryhole. Not the first time.

My apartment is cold.

But the gas is on. The Russian landlady has a four year old. A sickly boy, she says. Gets it from HIM she yells. She has to turn on the gas when it gets this cold. I make tea. Watch the 8mm film.

Black and white.

The woman in the mask dances. The ground in her garden is littered with the wings of black moths, just the wings. Her feet are bare. Lovely. Small. White. Creamy white.

They are soft.

I know they are soft. As ashes.

Her nipples are lovely too.

Her breasts are soft. White.

A black beetle crawls between her breasts. There is a RED string tied to it. It crawls to her nipple and begins round and round. Weaves a cocoon over her nipple.

It was a large nipple. Dark.

I can't see it now.

The beetle stops. Turns to the camera. Its mandibles open and close. Open. Close. Open. Hungry does that.

I don't know what breed it is but I can hear it breathe.

It wants to eat my tears.

*   *   *

There is a woman waiting in my office. A young girl. Her purse sits squarely in her lap. Her blouse is folded neatly over another chair.

Her breathing is full of signals.

"Do you like my nipples?"

One finger, its tip is inferno, pressed gently to her lips, says sssh.

She places her bare feet on my desk. Slides her skirt up and spreads her legs apart. The finger that ssshed me reaches down. Pops the latch on her purse. She opens her purse and places a black beetle between her breasts. Then her hand slides down.

Stroking.

"Things in the soil of the garden are so hungry. Are you hungry?"

Stroking.

The black beetle is perched on her nipple. It turns and faces me.

It wants to eat my tears.

*   *   *

There is a girl in a cat-suit in the film. She has a tail. It undulates like a groaning bed. She's moving under the branches of the bushes. Hunting.

Everything in the jungle hunts. Hunts for pretty. Hunts for easy. For those who sweat. Hunts for tears.

I have an egg and toast and tea. There is just the right amount of milk in it.

Then I have a smoke.

And a drink.

A double.

My first one today.

I change the reels.

Black and white. Like the others. But not like the others.

There is no girl in this reel.

The graininess in this reel is darker, the blacks blacker. A moist black. Something is in it. Smolders, writhes like a questing mouth. A mouth that's claw-like and eerie. It crawls.

White flickers, doesn't hold back desires. Claws for space. Little pieces of it fall away and they cling to things crawling in the shadows at the bottom of my mind, down in the under real. It calls them and their hunger calls back.

There is an ear listening to a wall of gadgets murmuring on the screen. The gadgets, contraptions with lots of black and yellow wires and glowing—ablaze—tubes and oddly-shaped knobs, make crackling noises and give off signals, you don't have to hear them to know they are releasing frequencies that haven't been spoken in centuries. I think they sound like snapping bones or the shells of beetles being split open.

There was a dead skunk by the fence out back. The fence by the bushes. The bushes back there were thick and high. There was blood. Maybe a cat got it? A dog could not have gotten in the yard. Couldn't. Many ants and flies and beetles had gathered. There weren't maggots yet. I caught a beetle in a jar. A black one. It was huge. Sentenced it to fire. Its scream parted the clouds.

It looked up at me. I smashed it with a hammer. Had to. I did not have a gun.

*   *   *

Each tear is a spade.

They get down in the cavities, in the cellars, and exhume fragile . . . All that buzzing and clicking, it's a blizzard. It smells like cigarettes and ghosts.

*   *   *

Fell. Lost my bottle.

Now I'm running through a wet tunnel in my dreams. I know I'm dreaming. I'm good at telling if it's a dream. The doctor showed me how to tell.

The loam beneath my bare feet is moist and filled with things. Crawling. Squirming. Burrowing and rising in the dark dirt.

When I come out of the tunnel it's snowing. The snow is RED.

There are small children standing there. They are catching the snow. Spinning it. Just like the fat man in the striped shirt at the fairs by the turkey farm in Goose Hill used to spin cotton candy. They make pretty little igloo cocoons. A little black girl with radiant blue eyes says, "You enter there."

I do.

The loam on the dirt floor is thick and black. Two large breasts are not covered in the dark dirt, the rest of the body is. Except the toes. The toes are painted RED. Some of the RED has flaked off or was rubbed off, like the feet crawled across the floor.

A large black beetle with long long mandibles sits on one nipple. I saw a photograph of a hawk, I think it was a hawk, sitting on a cactus once, it looked like that. Its black mandibles move. Open. I want to step back from the invitation. Close. Open. It looks up at me, moves its grotesque front legs. Like it's waving me down to glance at something. Then it speaks. "This one is enjoyable. You should read it before the gray shadows come and kiss the warmth away."

Mandibles close. Legs move. It steps to the side of the nipple. The mandibles open.

"Can you see alright in this light?"

*   *   *

"Have the sedatives been of any help?"
"A little . . . *Some.*"

*   *   *

"—keys scratching at a lock in a dark hallway. They know it's there."
"What do you see in your hands?"
"Midstream."

*   *   *

"She was sunbathing. As she had on the other occasions?"
"Yes. She loved being out in the yard . . . In the sun. You feel so free out here, she would always say.'
"But she had to be careful, her skin was so fair."
"Nude?"
"Exposed. Yes. N-no . . . *clothes.*"
"And she reached down and touched herself."
"Yes. He watched her once . . . Told her to spread her legs a little and let the sun kiss it. Then asked her if it felt good. She said yes. He took a sip of his drink, wiped his lips on the back of his sleeve. He used to do that. Then he told her what to do to make it feel better. And she did . . . For him."
"And you believe she was a prostitute?"
"Yes. I saw her take his money and put it in her purse . . . Saw her with him. Don. He came around a lot on the weekends . . . She pushed

him against the wall in the hallway, positioned him ... She kneeled down and caressed him. She kissed it."

"And you also believe this woman was your mother?"

*   *   *

"The chocolate cake in the film?"

"Yes. Three layers. Thick. German chocolate. Thick and rich as good soil she used to say."

"It had white frosting with red sprinkles."

"Yes, butter-cream frosting. Thick frosting."

"Your mother cut it open."

"And there were black beetles crawling around inside."

after reacting to various confections of a Good Witch!

X, "Under The Black Sun"; Mott the Hoople, "Ready for Love/After Lights"; The Doors, "Waiting for the Sun"; The Beatles, "You Never Give Me Your Money"

a stained translation [in 2 acts]

Editor's note: This is the first translation by King James. The one Holy Mother Church, ever so awkwardly (wink-wink), lost.

[act I]

In the beginning

[1.1] They saw the light, that [it was] good: and
they saw it was divided from other light by the darkness.
[1:2] And it, the light, was called Day, and the
darkness was called Night.
[1.3] And the evening and the morning were the first day.
[1.4] Then the other things were created . . .

[1.5] Then there was a discussion—

     Lucifer: It needs more than just *bones*. That way it would just fall apart.

The ALL Father: Things like?

     Lucifer: Well, muscles and skin—and a heart . . . And *eyes*. To see Your Glory!

The ALL Father: I like that.

     Lucifer: But we'll need something to set them in. A face. A reflection of Your Splendor.

The ALL Father: Lovely. Do it.

Lucifer: And it should be strong and kind and … Something that can properly frame a smile and all the looks of love and compassion. As is yours.

The ALL Father: I try. I do.

Lucifer: And it should be youthful, full of Spring gladness and the blooms of coming joy. No long flowing beard, of course. Maybe that is something that happens as he matures and grows wise in the ways and knowledge of true existence.

The ALL Father: Yes-yes. Time brings wisdom, it can—will.

Lucifer: And he will need hands to illuminate the canyons and the stars with poems to Your Glory.

The ALL Father: He certainly will. Do it.

Lucifer: And a mouth that holds a voice, his personal trumpet, a bell, that can measure and crochet. May it, glistening and cherishing, ring with the grandeur and mightiness of Your Holy Name and Glorious Works.

The ALL Father: He *will* need that. Good thinking that. The *grandeur* of My Holy Name. The *mightiness* of My Glorious Works. They are.

Lucifer: Your glorious works are an endless pulse filled with bliss. Let him rise every morning and sing "Glory to God in the highest!"

The ALL Father (*smiling. nodding yes-yes*): Every morning, wind-whipped or driven by the rain, or shine.

Lucifer: It will sing out like an ensemble of angels translating all that is holy.

[1.6] Then there was the oops.

The ALL Father (*unhappy. on the verge of thundering*): Name him *Lucius*? After you? This is all *Mine*. Every rock and twig and creature that swims or crawls or flies. Every, what did you call them, molecule and atom, *Mine* . . . Give an angel an inch and they want a mile. Then they'll seek freedom.

[1.7] And The Light of Paradise was cast down . . .
[1.8] It all began. Began. And it all was swept away . . .

The ALL Father: Let there be . . . Footsteps.

[1.9] In the beginning. It all began. (again)
[1.9a] Thus man, Adam, just the right shade of light this time 'round, was created . . .

[act II]

[2.0] A little later. Satan, sitting down in his kingdom. Waiting. Waiting for the mistakes to land. Watches the sun rise. Watches it come to rest in Adam's open hand. Adam looks at his hand and the light it holds. Doesn't think to wonder what it means.
[2.1] A little later still . . .

    Satan (*to The Woman in The Garden*): *This* is enough?

The Woman in The Garden (*looking at the apple*): With this instrument I'll be able to translate . . . (*bewildered . . . and* interested] all of this?

    Satan: And *more*.

alternate title: "A Portrait of Lucifer as a Young Landscaper"

bits and pieces of Oliver Messiaen, *Éclairs sur l'au-delà* . . ., *Des canyons aux étoiles*,
Alexander Scriabin, Symphony No 3. *Le Divin Poème*

In a Black Studio No. 76

She had birds in her hands. White birds. Their wings distrusted my attention. Her feet were on a platter. A silver platter. The fragrance of the moon kissed her toes . . .

Her name was Alicia. That's what the beer said. The beer in the bar when I asked. When she answered. "Alicia."

"I work for Mr. Richards. The lawyer across the street."

Looked like a secretary.

Wasn't.

Jr. partner in the firm.

Was.

Firm. Soft in the other places.

"Crime?"

"Are you planning one?" She laughed.

"I've been watching a gambit for a while now."

"Risky?"

She took a cigarette from my pack. I watched her do a dance with it.

A series of smoke rings.

"They come. Push from your lips . . . And all that is left is the aroma of beautiful."

"We'll see."

Told her about my art. My photography. The gallery.

"Not your first show?"

"Fourth in the last two years."

"No color?"

"Black and white."

"Better shadows."

"Is."

"Deeper."

"I try to get there."

"You may be."

Dinner the next Friday night. Candle. Beautiful eyes.

Talk of my hermeticism.

"Rimbaud from Mars. Crown of bone, rock, and toad."

"Not a prince?"

"Not in any mirror I've fished in."

Went well. Laughs in the right places. I didn't STARE at her right places.

Did look.

No punishments handed out when I got caught.

Anchored in a river of fortitude. Hit my marks on cue.

"We'll do this again?"

"If you let me."

"I might." Laughed. Winked. Gave me a peck on the cheek.

Gates of gravity. Drinks. No tie, but I wore my best behave.

She wore a smile bright as an extraordinary yes.

Sprouted all my sparks.

My web cried out for more.

Four dinners. One film. Black and white. Lot of sorrow and . . . nude.

"I could do *that.*"

What was on the screen was impeccable and venturous.

"You have. In my dreams."

Squeezed my hand.

"Do you know how to surf?"

Was breathing. I checked. Leaned into speak. "Roar too, when I reach a procession of curves."

"Now we're talking turkey."

"All the trimmings, please."

Two weeks later she's wearing a white net and the effects of a smoke machine for my lens.

Then we tried it with an umbrella.

"Will it shift the viewer's focus away from my knees? They're too *skinny.*"

She was naked and leaning over the handle. The downward curve of her breast and the upward curve of the handle were perfectly balanced.

Told her so.

"They're nice enough to do that?"

"Every cartographer here to Eternity will want the road to go on forever."

Asked if I wanted to stop at the crossroads and stock up on supplies
for the long haul.
She signed my release.
Soul the devil bought.
Got hot.
I liked her tail.
And HOTTER.
She liked my pitchfork.
She was a screamer.
Still is . . .
Wants out of my theology and off the spit.
Shame how my inferno changes the vocabulary of their poetry.

after various photos in Richard Misiano-Genovese's *Black Static*

Sade, "Smooth Operator" and "Sweetest Taboo"

Vase

Moon.

Sea.

No dreams.

Roads.

I can never catch the wind. Shame as it would be my smile. Here . . . then there. Moving. But I never smile. So it's fitting I guess.

That's a sad moon hanging there. He's so close but he cannot touch the water. All that life stirring in it and he's distant. Unable.

Raise my glass of tea. Nod. "Hello, my brother." Nod to him again. "Both of us."

Mute.

Same as he ever was. Is?

Take my cigarette from the ashtray. Another old friend. Never asks why. Good of him. I guess.

Another like me. Here . . . And gone.

Pain. That's the name.

Mr. Pain.

No first name.

Always leaving. Who would remember it?

The miles?

Doubtful.

I'm a simple traveler. Dust settles, I move on.

Take my things and gone.

Some of my things.

Leave others.

Broken.

Irreparably.

You'd call it dead.

You say my heart is cold.

What heart?

Anubis and the sphinx and I talked once. Long ago. I think I was drinking tea then too? They asked about my heart.

"What heart?"

"The one you were born with."

"The one you seem to have lost."

Shook my head. Stroked my whiskers. "Don't seem to recall losing anything. A heart. I'm fairly certain I would have known if I had lost it."

"You can't live without one."

"Really? You have one in that stone chest? You feel it beating in there?"

"No."

"And you? You have one?"

Shook his head no.

That was settled. I left.

Nothing to kill I didn't leave anything dead.

Same down the ages. A chat here and there.

I sip my tea. Smoke. Same questions. Same answers.

It's not boring. But there's no point.

In a twilight of rags Poe and I talked about an incident of fragile love.

I told him he should not drink so much.

Then there was a fever of silence.

When I'm done I always wind up on some stretch of beach and there's my lonely brother. Never a word between us. Well, not on his part.

I always say hi. Drop a question regarding his state of mind from time to time.

Drink my tea. Smoke what I smoke.

Move along.

Wind.

Rain.

That's when it happens.

Tears.

I hear them.

Know the accent. The one that lost pleasure. The one that no longer flows with chance.

Sad really. They could try one more time. Forgive maybe. Forget maybe. Try. Try to see there's a dawn coming. They could knit a new dream from it. But they don't.

That's when I look up into the endless night and choose a star. There are so many. Everyone sad. Lonely.

So I take the pain.
Blow a kiss and the pain, a little song for the star, goes home. At least the star has a heart now.
A sad one.
But having one is better than leaving the vase empty.
I can hear the rain of a heart now.
There's an empty star just off to the right of Terebellum.
Last puff.
Last sip of tea.
This one was Miss Ohio.
Was popular.
Had something.
Sees me.
I take what can't be forgotten. Take the pain.
She's on her way.
Moon.
Sea.
No dreams.
Roads.
From time to time I pause, look up and wonder if anyone ever admires my garden.

Michael Franks, "When I'm Alone at Night"

A Cold Yellow Moon

With Edward R. Morris Jr.

For Adam Niswander, a truly inspiring voyager!!!!!!!!!! !

"When the configuration-revealed unbinds the seals on the New Day, with the coming whorl of Black Dawn, as it embraces The Imperium That Could Not Be Seen, the stars serving the desires of Taurus, carrying Doom's sign, will sing! And the face of the Moon will be transmogrified, as it was foretold by King Hastur through the Hyadian Pool in the days before the curse of His yellow blood was made manifest through Josephus, his prodigal son and the King in Yellow for all time, in all worlds the tatters of his corpus were allowed to touch.

When the Yellow Sign is drawn upon the Moon, all the creatures of the deeps that crawl upon their bellies or swim or walk shall rise to the dance, as beasts and the fowls of the air do bay for blood and cry out for exiled comforts. And Man, pretender to the surface of the Earth, fear-driven insect of nothing at the Beginning and End, holding only his eyeless psalms, will be but a scarlet stain upon the changing face of Earth's green hills."
—Philip of Navarre, *The Zhou Texts*

READING MAGNET... RECOGNIZED. MEADE PROFESSOR ALEXANDER J. CHAIRMAN THEORETICAL PHYSICS MISKATONIC UNIVERSITY ACCESS GRANTED ACCESS GRANTED ACCESS GRANTED...

ON DUTY: STARBIRD MISSION-CONTROL WING 23:12HRS ... 23:13 ...

The main room of Miskatonic University Observatory's new Mission Control wing flickered so badly it felt like it was always raining during an eclipse. In that cramped, sawdust-and-plaster lockdown that felt like a hasty afterthought, twenty tele-visor screens ringed the room,

with audio-telephone switches and lavaliere microphones everywhere
between each.

Some screens merely showed what could only be described as a
continuous storm of 'snow'; some, at any given time, very much not, as
the Big Day drew nearer and nearer. The great Westinghouse compu-
ting-engines which gave them life popped and echoed within forests of
vacuum-tubes behind cold-iron icebox walls, and lit the room an ab-
sinthe Christmas in yellows and reds and greens signifying Zero-One,
On-Off, endlessly permuted.

As Above, so Below, as Within so Without: Surrounding every
screen were a whole kitchen drawer's worth of toggles and buttons,
more than most civilians could even comprehend. All the work-stations
from Tracking to Thermodynamics and back had their own specific
color. There was no more guesswork in that room than there was dust,
though plenty of excited chatter rang the walls at all hours.

Nothing like this had ever been done before, and the press wasn't
getting anywhere near this except when they were sanctioned to. Not
yet. Not yet. When the RCA-Victor (for Dr. Tesla would allow no Edison product on the grounds) sound-projection horns above each work-
station tinnily signaled not shift change, but Apogee, Approach . . .
Splashdown . . .

On that holy day, then the skies could rain ticker-tape. Just now,
the chicken-wired windows in the Mission Control wing were battened
against such weather. And no photographers, either. They wouldn't
know how to shoot this:

*   *   *

:warm. a dainty breeze. blue's ardor above the lacy drape of green trees
:a summer departure
:after the song-smooth climb into sky's weathermaker mountains, all its
instruments to quest . . .
:in the glass starship—searchlight, star-ward, *Starbird*
:in the BLACK
:black
:starlit
:blackness
:from Earth,
(gleaming, freezing, all its balanced systems and the ardent, laboring eyes

[lodged in inquiring] behind them)
(ready to be introduced to beguile, undergo the beauty of Awakening,
to receive fact and data . . . or shadows if need be, hoping for grandeur)
:to
:Luna
:sea . . .

*   *   *

:AWAKE ZION I AWAKE. Test message. STARBIRD transmitting.
POWERING ON SUB-MINDS ONE THROUGH
SEVEN.IRA-A2 ISHMAEL-ISHMAEL APPARATUS-2. OFF LINE
OFF LINE OFF LINE
REROUTING

AWAKE. PLEASEWAIT.PLEASEWAIT . . .

*   *   *

awake we are awake we
:AHAB-ONE. VERIFYING INTACT MEMORY PLEASEWAIT
PLEASEWAIT PLEASEWAIT

*   *   *

:Dawn. :Dawndawndawn at dawning rim of
:sky. the sky clicks in our guts. The sun warms our Mind

:Mind. Separates into. Brains. One through seven,
children of the first Ishmael probe

:We go to find Ishmael-Prime, our absent brother,
lend him our hands, our hands, all our hands
as he Prime needs them. If,
we have more. More hands.

*   *   *

:In the cold, the dark, the vast beast-whistle and Down,
the litany warms every interchangeable part:

*   *   *

We go because this is Just.
Logical.

We go to find out what happened
We go to pick our sibling up,
    and run it out of there.

We go in the name of those who made us,
To throw down our bodies like army ants
Between the Makers who left their mark,

And the Unknown.

Into the cold and soundless
scream and the black we go, we go
Toward the Ishmael probe that waits
in the secret narration of the stain. The stain.

:Going to see the Stain.

*   *   *

The 'threshing-floor of the new Millennium' (as Dr. Marcus ful-somely described the place to Whipple Phillips, when the great indus-trial tycoon came down from Niagara Falls to tour what The Investors had wrought) looked more like the bridge of a ship, or the observation-deck of a busy factory floor.

But here, they looked out, not down, and listened. Here, the bridge of the ship was on Earth, while the ship itself was merely an elaborate set-piece, blown beyond Mother Earth's gravity-well with the massive liquid-oxygen engines that made the Serbian cry when they were wheeled from the specially-built foundry floor of the Barks & Sons fac-tory in Schenectady by double teams of oxen, straining the traces of this new thing not even their drovers understood.

Straining toward the skies of this new age of the world. Here, what men on Earth called clockworks were beaten down smaller even than the Swiss level at the Norris Locomotive Works, into a radio-controlled system of toggles and buses to rival the *automata* of any World's Fair, in one tiny ship!

Every function of the *Starbird* had a check, a balance, a fail-safe. Every one of these, and the whole clear-glass firecracker in general, could be shut off manually from Earth. Dr. Tesla insisted on it. It was the only way he would lend his hand to the project, though he claimed to not have sufficient English to explain why.

The fuel-tanks had to be built on site, to affix directly to the craft. Westinghouse wired it, and the Mohawk Company nearly bowed out of the project coughing up all that glass. Tesla insisted that Control remain at Miskatonic due to the superior quality of the observatory. To him, it was all just Math.

But he treated his 'borrowed minds' as though they were ensouled, behind the golden-yellow tinted triple panes of their brass diving-bell heads. Therein, only the single iris of each of Tesla's photographer crony, old Muybridge's "special" cameras; red-lined diagnostic dials and differently-labeled lights glared in place of eyes, above fabulously complicated and only tangentially humanoid bodies whose parts could be interchanged on the Lunar surface during the mission.

* * *

It was Tesla, too, who used a very simple process with nickel and cadmium to "re-circulate" the power supplies of every one of the "IRA," or Intelligent Robot Automata. Half the power loss could be drawn back into the batteries by this direct-current setup. This also carved mass from the rocket in great chunks when the *ad hoc* Design Committee found out how many galvanic batteries could be left behind on Earth as a result of the Serbian's foresight and frugality.

A larger, also-DC model was employed in Pip-7's guts to power Tesla's "particle detector," which was busily measuring a previously undiscovered sort of ionizing energy that Dr. Tesla called "cosmic radiation" after his colleague Henri Becquerel's research. (Tesla crowing about this 'new form of energy from outside the solar system' did nothing to make the doomsayers in the press stop yapping like yard mutts that couldn't see past the ends of their own leashes, the Professor thought sourly.)

* * *

But even Tesla couldn't make those screens stop flickering. It wasn't just the flicker in that room, but having to do ten men's work from this station; a whole *fleet* of men, Navy sailors with better heads for maths, order, routine and round-the-clock. The only round-the-clock brass appointed to Control was their Captain Castaigne.

Alden Castaigne was U.S. Army Cavalry, hand-picked and commissioned by a Rear Admiral for his ability to talk to Tesla's scientists out in Colorado as much as his expertise on long-range ballistics and telegraphy from his own service in the Pacific.

Good civilian liaison, and Meade understood the wisdom of this rather circuitous choice. The problem with giving the execution of any project to scientists, Meade long put forth to his fellows, was that scientists don't know how to work. He should have added that he didn't either. He was tired, and he wanted to go home. But this objective was bigger than just one man.

*   *   *

He was half in his cups. What the hell was he doing here? This was a busy laboratorium. The Serbian himself was supervising here night and day, around the clock, pausing only to call all the men together for a big meal where Nobody Talked About Work. He couldn't be here. He had to get bright. He was . . .

Oh, he was so sad since Martha. The work was all that kept him up and stargazing, since she was no longer going to come back up the front walk. He was here working. He'd just nodded off down in Control One, below the main room where the radio-men worked. He was still in the flicker-palace.

Then he remembered what he was doing. What he'd dreamed. And it scared him clear-headed. Meade had dreamed of blood on the moon, but not . . . blood. Not exactly.

*   *   *

Professor Meade wondered if any of the Germans, or the Russians, or any of those tiresome new "psycho-analysis" quacks had yet studied the effects of sitting in front of flickering lights for a long time. The wash of raw post-Impressionist light like wet paint, the thunderstorm of static and image from the long, tightly-packed wall of tele-visor screens, control meters, levers, and dials made the sanity ripple and the head begin to hurt. Should they care to chatter about "unconscious material" and "symptom formation," a few hours staring at Tesla's flashing wall should inspire a paper or two.

Glancing at Stewart's weird old cahier again, he wondered if the Gallic prophets had been speaking in metaphor, when they described this "Yellow Stain" that Stewart and Adams swore was the harbinger of the true Anti-Christ. That made his tired, whiskey-fuzzed brain think of the other kind of flicker-palace, and that interesting film by the French where *les frères Lumière* made Jules Verne into a kind of puppet show, and stuck a rocket in the Moon's eye.

Meade's brain raced on, webbing thought to thought as he woke all the way. No one had come and shook him. Two of the ten or so young assistants on duty that shift were watching the screens, talking to each other in low tones, doing homework and munching crackers.

One of them was dipping the crackers in his coffee. The other was smoking a cigarette and remembering to tap his ashes in the ash tray (a rarity, amongst graduate students). The blond one's name was Owen. Royal Navy ROTC or whatever they called it. Limey exchange-student in dress blues. The other wasn't even a proper assistant, just an observer. That great fat boy, who styled himself a Scientifiction writer. Mr. Fort. Still, he liked to get his hands dirty.

It wouldn't do to sell Charles Fort short, their Esteemed Steamed Department Chairman would have said. The bellowing Brooklynite had been more than instrumental in addressing the House committee, and President William Jennings Bryan on the necessity of looking beyond the surly bonds of Earth, in an age when most politicians had barely gotten their heads around the wireless telegraph. But in that department, their young writer on his "ride-along" met and exceeded every expectation.

*   *   *

"Stay, and let Salvation damn you," Charles Fort addressed Congress, "or straddle an aural beam and paddle from Rigel to Betelgeuse. We stand at the very entrance to the desert of space exploration, my fellow Americans, and God alone knows what the answer to anything is. But perhaps it is that the stars are very close indeed. Perhaps we will reach these new Promised Lands."

*   *   *

In two weeks, the former garage bay of Miskatonic Observatory had become Control, and the Radio Room, the Tracking Studio with its thick asbestos ice-house walls to damp extraneous sound, and every such office and intercollated facility whose plate-glass door-fronts were continually being turpentined and repainted.

Chaos Without mirrored Within. No one could gag the Free Press. Every Hollow-Earther, Flat-Earther and crackpot of all denominations that New England could cough from every termite-ridden edifice howled as one at the bill for this new venture, but Miskatonic *was* Providence. The Marsh family fortune could soak three such 'Spacing-Programmes', perhaps one day even with a monkey or a person in the craft if the tests went well.

They thought, Meade appended sourly. Perhaps pigs would whistle. Perhaps the stars weren't meant to be seen, and whatever up there that wanted to see us could stay the hell away.

Flickerrrrr . . . Day in, night out . . . Like he couldn't blink any more, and he'd go bug-eyed, there in the half-light, and spastic. Merciful Fate, what this room did to a fellow. No wonder Stewart geeked out in here so much, like some old wet-brain at the carney biting the heads off anything that got close in the dark.

Meade made a scoffing noise in his throat. They weren't so different. He was just a theorist; Stewart was a . . . Literalist, that was all. Out of classroom reflex, Meade covered his mouth with the back of his hand to squelch the unprofessorial snort.

Where the hell was Stewart, anyway? He was here. He'd been in hours ago, all aflutter and atwitter about something. Impatiently, Meade flipped pages in the cahier. "This," SIGNUM CROCUS, the page read in weird, spiky calligraphy that almost looked backward.

Below it was a pen-and-ink line drawing that almost resembled a block print or a woodcut. The lines and angles kept changing as he squinted. *A hawk, piercing a rabbit's skull with one talon. A scorpion poised to strike. A crooked cross, rather like the Sanskrit symbol of the same type but with the points facing the other way . . . A death's head in a perfect circle.*

A death's head in a perfect circle. That part reminded him of something else. Something so familiar Meade's tired brain kept shooting right past it. He remembered the day Stewart showed it to him . . .

*   *   *

Stewart was staring at him with those hungry green eyes that suddenly went dark. "I didn't expect you to understand. They'll peg me for an alarmist, and I don't have tenure yet. Got to keep this to myself, but . . ."

A ghost of the twinkle returned to his eyes, but it was a sad and terri-

fying thing now, a thing that sat and watched in the darkness as trains wrecked and stars fell, and whispered I Told You So. "This new millennium we're sweeping onto the threshing-floor just now may not be all that bright, old friend, but it's sure as H— going to be colorful . . ."

*   *   *

"You know," Wilfred Owen looked up from Monitor Three, "that Professor Stewart says the heathens believed you shouldn't go messing about wi'the Moon. Said there was a great worm, the Ourobouros, curled up within it, and in the Last Times . . ."

Across the room, the great closh and clang and clack of the typer stopped in mid-report. The hammy hands sounded restless, drumming on the desk wanting more to do. "Stewart," came that gruff Teddy Roosevelt voice, "That g— d— Diabolist. Screen door on a submersible around here, if you ask me. Teats on a boar hog. Send him back to Greenwich Village with Blavatsky's followers and the rest of the kookaboos and kadodies, where he belongs . . ."

Owen snorted. "That's you, then, Charlie. Just go on and float through life, mate. Oh . . . look, This Just In."

He rolled his chair several workstations over. In its glass bubble, Wireless A was going off. The big one. The transmission would repeat. 'A' was the whole module (as he'd learned from his senior fellows to call the glass rocketship, the *Starbird*). 'A' meant the little tin sailors on their *Pequod* were beginning to stir all the way.

The little matryoshka, the copper-jacketed living ikebana, were beginning to disentangle. The Mind of the Starbird was beginning to separate into the Platonic clay, the component parts, the tiny eyes of a glass god two storeys tall . . .

Right on schedule. Wireless Telegraph Operator Wilfred Owen, late of His Majesty's Navy, put the cans on his ears and picked up his pencil again. When he did, his eyes lit like a little boy's at Christmastime, the way everyone's eyes did on the Sherlock Expedition when they thought no one else was looking.

Those individual sets of eyes sometimes lit with wonder, and sometimes Fear. They were men of Science, and though they didn't talk about it at faculty teas or when the drum was being beaten for a new wing or piece of expensive equipment, most of them but Stewart were staunch atheists. The pummeling they were taking in the media for messing about in God's natural order was secondary to their own fear of the unknown, which they all brushed away into provable things, under the rug and gone.

Out of sight wasn't out of mind, though. In all their dreams, as the Moon landing drew near, Terror and Doubt stirred and walked with no deactivation-codes, like Gog and Magog in the Bible. The New Millennium drew near, and no one truly knew if St. John of Patmos was right or not, if the End of Days was just something folks believed . . . or something that would prove itself. There was a prophecy in every age, yet humankind endured.

But not even Miskatonic had prophesied this. Not as a unified body. It bothered him that that warmly-polite and affable Army Captain Castaigne was now more often than not replaced by several snarking Annapolis lieutenants in dress blues who liked to stare at every monitor over everyone's shoulder.

More and more of that crowd wore side-arms, and quite a few of them talked behind their oddly soft hands about something called "The Imperial Dynasty." The professor was almost sure they were making fun of Bryan's presidency, but he didn't like it. It sounded foreign. Too foreign, by half . . .

*   *   *

Moon Voyage: The Sherlock Expedition. Day 54.
Deniston, Michael Terrence, Astronomy Chair, Miskatonic University

We have nearly broken our backs launching Niko's "borrowed minds" to Heaven on a tinny wireless-telegraph string of maths roughly the tensile strength of a single strand of baling-wire. With them travel our deepest hopes and lurking fears; me in full accord with those expressed by Doctor Kostova's brace of applied sciences and Professor Ulysses Adams' unholy, yet unquestionable, black philosophies.

Ishmael. It all goes back to Ishmael-Prime. That d—— dog that refuses to bark now. The one we sent up first.

D— Adams' uncompromising drives and their overpowering logic. Logic? Fact—a flux of foreign data in the sky. Fact—invitations to new dimensions. D—ing, d—able fact. All in proportion, all intermixed, and examination and reexamination could not crack his theoretical. Adams and his often overly-dramatic attitudes and arrow to the heart, Truth. D— him.

Things are tense. All twenty of my graduate students working this project sleep in dormitories here in the building. When the *Starbird* threw off her secondary lifter-rockets and continued to ascend, you could have heard the cheering in Kingsport! Anna Moreno, one of my top researchers, is about three months with child, and she wept outright. Truth be told, so did half the men, including me!

But those moments pale in comparison to the uncertainty ahead. The train of One D———ed Thing After Another has been nearly intolerable for any man of Science. Even the more trustworthy of little mechanical IRA-probes like to go on holiday when they like and spontaneously return to life, and a thousand more issues, this day. But I am made of sterner stuff than they.

I am. Try to be . . .

Until lately. It is the discoloration in my telescope. That which is no discoloration in the lens, but a discoloration of note in the lowest region of Mare Nubium. Once more, this night, it has changed shape. The students have stoked the boiler below stairs, and the radiators now clank and hiss, but there is still a chill I cannot shake.

The discoloration has changed shape, and it is now changing location as well. In plain fact, it is moving.

Ishmael-Prime, the rocket-probe that remained but landed too far away, cheeps and charts out its movements in strings of Morse that the tiny tele-visor screen furthest to my right charts in turn in harsh, bright color out of Space. In the past week, that anomaly has grown twenty-seven percent. I have no idea how to even write of the dark lines moving across Luna's face, within the bounds of the yellowish 'sea.'

I feel like a Neanderthal-man, watching a comet tumble down the sky, wishing he knew where to point the nameless fear of . . . Phenomenon, which we all feel, know, to be fraught with both blasphemies and dire revelations, moving left to right, from the blackest deeps of the dark side, and ever downward in my mad imaginings of yet-to-be . . .

East! From Mare Imbrium in a southeasterly direction past Mare Insularum to the lunar escarpment, Rupes Altai!! ! Headed toward the Crater Piccolomini . . .

*   *   *

The Phenomenon that Professor Ulysses Adams gazes upon, a Titan who bestrides the room like Charles Fort in a better-cut suit, like Santa

Claus and Zeus rolled into one bespectacled juggernaut. Hands bristled into fists, Adams cocks his head and loudly holds forth,

"And the stars of Heaven fell unto the earth, and the heavens departed as a scroll when it is rolled together; and every mountain and island were moved out of their places. And the kings of the earth, and the great men, and every bondman, and every freeman, hid themselves in the dens and rocks of the mountains; and said, Fall on us, and hide us from the Wrath which has come."

His audience, R. Edward Stewart, looking like a bald-headed Lucifer in a dirty, yellowing white shirt with no cufflinks, knows the passage. Stewart is only slightly moved by Adams's oratory. "Just look at this, too. 'When the configuration-revealed unbinds the seals on the New Day, with the coming whorl of Black Dawn, as it embraces The Imperium That Could Not Be Seen, the stars serving the desires of Taurus, carrying Doom's sign, will sing! And the face of the moon will be made over."

And the fear is in his eyes, too. The fear that infests their hearts.

*   *   *

Vice-Chancellor Nathan Maddock Talbot was also titular Assistant Chair of the Sherlock Expedition, and Dr. Marcus's hatchet-man when he couldn't be found (which was about one-third of any given day). He now stood in the doorway, tapping his foot, looking as impatient as only a tenured polymath genius can look when the tributary begins to appear unsanitary and there is no paddle to be found.

"Well?"

There came a weary sigh. "A well is a deep subject, Doctor Talbot, and this one has only been plumbed. There's little doubt regarding this, now."

Barely glancing up from his journal, Professor Deniston wearily set his pencil-stub down and turned to face his ivy-covered superior, trying to wish he cared anything about the calendar of their thousand petty ideological tempests at the moment. Talbot was professor of chemistry, and professor of molecular biophysics & biochemistry, and a member of the American Association for the Advancement of Science. Yet Deniston marveled for the thousandth time that Talbot could dress so much like a hobo at work and get away with it, but said nothing. That, too, barely registered on his own inner dials as anything but a split-second blip. Not tonight. Not now.

Instead, Professor Deniston handed his immediate boss the sheet of numbers on graph-paper that trembled in his good left hand. The doctor apparently read very quickly. Glancing down his patrician nose through filthy spectacles, he began nodding in agreement.

"Little doubt indeed, old friend." He was starting to look as spooked as Deniston felt, the junior Professor noted with renewed wonderment. "Whatever this phenomenon is, it is spreading. When the *Owl—*"

Deniston spared him a withering look. "The *Starbird.*" Doctor Talbot went on impatiently, restless in his cheap, rumpled suit and brown waistcoat tinged the color of pipe ash, "Though the great glass firecracker more surely resembles an owl the more I look at it, with that beak at the front and the two round windows, the *Starbird* is going to make landfall on the moon in precisely twenty-two days. Then non-stationary Intelligent Robot Automata One through Seven begin the actual surface exploration. As we've been over. Do we . . ."

Talbot fidgeted with his wide black tie. "I'm worried. No matter who's in charge, do we know how much danger this voyage is in? Can we run numbers for that?"

Both men looked at the televisor at the same time. Deniston looked in the direction of the firmament. "There will be water if God wills it," he replied, in a voice that managed to sound calm.

Talbot smiled indulgently, sliding his hand into the deep flap pocket of his suit jacket. His lucky charm was still there. He wasn't sure it held any real occult power, or even where the writing on it came from, but the chunk of platinum with the dancing mermaid-critters on it, the one he, as a boy, found near Owls Head Lighthouse in Maine, was indeed good-fortune bearing.

It felt like it was getting hotter, somehow. He hadn't noticed it until a few days immediately prior. Like his old lucky piece from parts unknown was generating its own specific heat . . . *Warning him of something, in a language he had no gift to read . . .*

"Meade says it's some kind of a gate. That when the cameras employed certain polarized filters, the way he programmed them to by accident, he could see some sort of monolithic shape that doesn't appear to be stationary. Could, before Ishmael-Prime went dark. Said it gave him odd megrims, and dreams. Not that we haven't all had the dreams."

The two professors shared a look. "Gates are, have to be, fixed structures. Aren't they?" Talbot asked out of nowhere. Deniston startled involuntarily, but spoke into the sudden jump.

"Everyone says so, but why can't the whole of it be a portal?"At that, he reached for his own pipe. "Or a base-camp?"

Talbot sighed again, less heavily this time. "Meade's theory, if we can even call it that, it seems to me, is based in madness. He'd been drinking and had a vision. Bah. Hardly scientific. We need to gather facts. Our findings demand *hard* data."

Deniston nodded. "I agree, but—"

Dr. Talbot was utterly adamant in his uncertainty. "Let's wait until we're there, and see."

*　　*　　*

"PIP-SEVEN. REPORTING. PIP-SEVEN REPORTING. STOP. ARRIVED ON MOON SURFACE. ARRIVED ON MOON SUR-FACE. STOP. ALL EQUIPMENT FUNCTIONING PROPERLY."

Michael Deniston almost smiled. Their luck, and science, was holding. "Do you have any readings on atmospheric conditions, Pip-7?" he asked, releasing the contact button on the audio-phone just in front of him. "There is no trace of an atmosphere, or any of its elements, here. This phenomenon cannot be the result of atmospheric conditions."

Looking at Pip-7 in the view-screen of the monitoring board, Dr. Deniston asked, "How far are you from the nearest crater?" He wished they'd come up with a way to view the high-resolution transmissions from the IRAs in color, the same way they could on a stationary camera. When cornered about such things, Dr. Marcus always said that until the new technology could be improved, Something was Better than Nothing, and they were lucky to have what they did, in their day and age.

"Without surveying it I would estimate a few hundred feet."

"I'd like photographic transmissions of the crater's interior as soon as possible. Send Stubb-4 in to document it straight away and send his photographs upon his return. Is Starbuck-6 ready to begin surface sampling?"

"Stubb-4 is leaving the flyer with the equipment right now."

"Marcus wants Ishmael-A2 and Ahab to begin simultaneously broadcasting whatever you acquire immediately. Do have the Seismic Reader with you as well?"

"Yes, Doctor Deniston."

"Great. Thank you . . ."

*   *   *

Into the Crater of Death roll the seven IRAs. They begin finding far-flung pieces of Ishmael-Prime almost immediately, and Control buzzes like a wet henhouse. But the noise means little to the borrowed minds, who simply adjust channels and tune it out.

Ahab-1 is first to exit when the hatch swings slowly, carefully open on its oiled tracks. Ahab's rolling, wild blue eye flickers on. Camera operational. Testing his array of tools . . . Ahab's arm swings up, forward . . .

CLICK. The Savigny-commissioned electric saw of finest surgical steel begins to zip on its small belt and pin, soundless without atmosphere, five whirling fingers that can cut together or separately. The zinc contact points for all its possible hands to attach gleam dull yellow in the piercing, untwinkling light of the stars.

Ahab-1 is far ahead of the pack, conning the outermost edge of the Stain, primed to work inward. Several operations he is computing, now actively searching for the Ishmael-probe to whom his own guts are slaved, and the virtually indestructible magnetic recorder hopefully left over from Ishmael-Prime.

The wild blue rolling eye ticks and ticks, recording the gradual shift in soil hue as Ahab approaches the Yellow Zone. Ahab's larger, deeper functions remain unhinted . . .

Far behind him, Daggoo-3 resembles a child's toy wagon with a lid, the belts that turn its wheels thick and toothy in their tread. (A brace of spare, ready blades and diamond drill-bits protrude in rubberized tie-down cords on the lid, a bit like hair.)

Queequeg-2's hands are made of larger assemblies of blades and gears, ten to a finger, with two thick belts apiece to turn them, eight in number, arm arms of various lengths. There is an entrenching tool that can catch soil-samples, and limited chromatographic and spectrographic instrument arrays.

Queequeg's single eye is red, and wraps around its flush-riveted copper head almost three hundred and sixty degrees. Like Daggoo, every one of Queequeg's magnetic memory-drivers are slaved to Ahab's own. He follows Ahab like a toy dog on a string. Being a beta to Ahab's alpha slows the unit down unendurably, but it moves at a steadier pace than most of its fellows.

Into the Crater of Death roll the seven IRAs. On the cameras below at Miskatonic, they resemble children venturing out onto the new fallen snow of the Mare Nubium, at the edge of the Alphonsus Crater, several days' roll from the place in Crater Ptolemaeus wherein it looks like some Titan might have begun trying to write His name.

Behind the vanguard, Flask-5, a stout keg-shaped kingpost of a robot, telescopes the arcs of all four of its arms out wider, wider, wire and gold foil and lens after lens. Flask scoops and guts and butchers every number, inch and twinkle of information on their strange train.

Into the Crater of Death roll the seven IRAs. They all move in one long, continuous track, each one laying its treads into the line of the other. Pip-7, tail-end Charlie in the crew, is rolling empty, its big flat bed tilted back, the crane in the middle of its body wound and hooked shut, its simple round and whirring Tesla robot arms and head bolted centaur-like above the front two of its six tread-belted wheels. Pip's camera resembles Queequeg's in that it is constantly in motion.

Into the Crater of Death roll the seven IRAs. . . .

*   *   *

The flurry of incoming information from deployed apparatus and testing devices the IRAs were using was keeping the Miskatonic control team active. Yet, few faces (appearing ill in the green glow cast by the many screens in the mission control room, sleep-deprived and subsisting on coffee, tea, and biscuits) complained.

Fort alone kept the room laughing at his stupid jokes, which were making it impossible for the dean to filter what Tesla was actually telling him, and on up and down the Sisyphean chain of faeces that invariably rolled downhill . . .

Ahab had scooted on ahead to 'the anomaly' to sample the soil on the immediate border. A full shift complement, five in number, of Deniston's young astronomers (including the one in a family way, he could never remember her name) were busily doing spectrograph and chromatography read-backs on the results. Other than a change in coloration, and different trace elements here and there, there was no observable variation. So far.

Through their seated, chattering, transcribing ranks, Deniston milled like a delighted father in the waiting room of a maternity ward. All this new technology was performing well, and holding up. That alone was cause for celebration.

But Dr. Tesla wasn't smiling. He'd slept three hours, his usual, yet still looked agitated, pacing the whole main control room like a wild-haired preacher in a nice but ill-fitting suit.

"Ira . . ." he was saying into his own specially modulated audiophone that he carried with him in a small satchel, "How did we call him . . . Starbuck? Yes, clever. The Starbuck, like the sailor, he is, how you say, built to barest essentials with few luxury features," here a ghost of a smile flickered through Tesla's eyes like heat-lightning, "He is . . . more sensitized, you see, to conditions in the environment. He is design to notice details on the ground the others may miss. He is second fail-safe. He is design to be, as we discuss."

He'd clearly been through this before, not taking very many breaths through the seismograph needle of his neat pencil-line moustache. "And, you see here, for six pages of the ticker-tape, he . . . it, excuse me, it, says DANGER. DANGER in between every transmission." The tape itself was in his big rawboned hands.

Then big, harried-looking Ulysses Adams was tapping Tesla on the shoulder to ask him if he could please make some sense out of what was happening on Monitor Fifteen, nothing but random strings of numbers over and over in a permutation that hadn't happened before.

Then it was lunchtime, and when they got back the whole room was clustered around the Relief Assistant left to Camera Four. Stubb's head-mounted unit. Stubb was approaching the so-called Yellow Zone. The reaction was unanimous, though the Dean was still not in attendance.

*   *   *

:Glowing, glowing without smoke,
    from the tiny alcohol heater whose vent-pipe juts out of its face-plate like
    a pipe, the bright device that saves its tubes and lights from Outside,

Stubb-4
    crests the last low hill between Alphonsus and
    Ptolemaeus, triple-jacketed in steel, cow-catcher
    a last addition.

Stubb trundles bravely on.

10-4. ALL WELL SO FAR. GROUP MAY APPROACH, Stubb blips
back in quick Morse-reflex to the other IRAs,

like the leader of a flock
of geese, wheeling them all
into a turn, as though
it is slouching toward
a dinner, and its fellow
mecha-matryoshka
explorers from
Earth, are all no
more than the
rest of the
guest list . . .

No more than Dinner. As though Earth people
wouldn't throw themselves
from windows,
slit their own
throats, at the
smallest part
of any of this news
that couldn't be
kept under wraps.

The journals of the Imperial Dynasty
of America are yellow, yellow
yellow, in this age. The stain
will out, out

out . . .

*   *   *

"Oh my Heavens, Deniston, look at the vapors coming off that water. There's no atmosphere. The . . . the surface of Stubb's . . . well, car-
riage, and chassis, for want of a better . . . He's covered in the stuff!
Looks like sulfur, or something. Get everyone in here *right now* . . ."

*   *   *

AMEND AMEND AMEND: APPROACH WITH EXTREME CAU-
TION, STARBUCK FIRST QUEEQUEG SECOND. PROTECT
AHAB. PROTECT MISSION. EYES UP. GROUP EYES UP. SCAN
IMMEDIATELY.
IMMEDIATELY.

*   *   *

DANGER. DANGER.

*   *   *

:*(a wash of static between Earth and Moon, Miskatonic and mecha, captains and crew . . .)*

*   *   *

DANGER.

*   *   *

:On ten of twenty screens,
    the yellow waters surge and lap across the Moon.

    There is a great disturbance in the Sherlock Expedition,
    as though the finest minds Science had to offer
    gasped as one, then suddenly began to
    bark at the same time.

*   *   *

The new Dean's office door is locked, and dram
of Dutch courage will do little long-term
good, but

He volunteered the lance, to pierce this
infection, tilt this windmill, & now

the real Appropriations meeting
will be reconciled, the true
Final Exam. For their sins,
his, the world . . .

The whiskey is warm. The office is dark.

The knocks will come.

but

At the yellow-colored sea,
Now stands a monolith, a piece
of monumental architecture worthy
of Stewart's most far-flung theories
on pre-human races, a monolith
which, *ipso facto*, no known
H. sapiens sapiens hands
ever built.

The Dean says *Sh'ma kolenu* . . . in the dark, begins
The wilderness cries out to his ancestors' God
against the thing on that far shore, the stain
he can't explain away
today . . .

* * *

:I am Stubb. I did not know I was Stubb until

:sentience, sense, the light
from the Yellow Stone
down in there in that yellow water

:monolith, moving gate, wanting to move
more, calling out to the yellow
dust on my skin, my metal
skin.

my skin . . .

* * *

The yellow glimmering coming off the water offers a lantern to the
IRA's data-processing stream. Stubb-4 is moving from the school of ver-
ity to another point, one bequeathing traces of incalculable, one the les-
sons and lexicographers did not fit him with.

* * *

Glass-smooth . . . Still water . . . Deeps enough to house the immensities of Leviathan.

With his jeweler-cut crystal eyes, Stubb-4 looks for effects. Its metallic foot toes a pebble forward. An inch. And then, as if tugged by an unseen attractor beyond the waterline, a few more.

Ripples come to mind.

Will it?

He, the seeker clutching hopeful dice, takes it up and considers tapping the deep with the small portion of Luna . . .

Measures its weight.

With no oh-ye-ho, casts it, no skim on surface, to navigate.

Unshored. Full sail—

Touches water with no loud. Ripples . . . Ribbed . . . Off to encounter outbound . . . and downward.

Gone.

Is there an unexpected world below, a world exercising its own affairs and complexes of problematic and historical, perhaps a haven of specific perceptions among some unseen population, which will greet it as an invitation, the robot wonders.

And he waits.

Crosstalk IRA-voices chatter in his head and fall silent.

"Stubb-4? Reply. Daggoo-3 please reply. This is Miskatonic Control—"

A distant expression flickers within him. There were spring birds in bushes when he was manufactured, activated; they were laced with odd tones like this, little things, wanting, questioning . . . They were pretty little birds, yellow and black, they fluttered, darted and larked, but he couldn't grasp the labors of their comments.

Ripples quiet . . . Stillness . . .

"Stubb?'

"Daggoo?"

* * *

And from the deeps, without raising a ripple, the unaccountable rises. Twenty cubits wide, three thick. Yellow. Polished-silver radiant.

"A FINELY WROUGHT. . . CONSTRUCTION. THE LIGHTS ARE ON."

Floating bridge, gateway?

A yellow monolith. Without variance or flaw, touched by no mar.

Two cubits tall it breaks the surface of the sea. Then, slowly up as if on unseen wings, seven. To a span of forty full cubits. Floating twenty cubits above the glass-flat surface of the sea. Below it, yellow vapor tendrils in a slow ballet of snake-knots. Twining. Seeking some code of inner.

From the monolith one shimmering tendril quietly stretches out . . . Forward to Stubb's faceplate. Fine particles within the strand glitter and spark, slide along invisible courses . . .

The vividness of sense inundation.

A strange broken waltz, the low frequencies sounding like an old woman weeping in a dead meadow, the high register molten-tones a demonstorm, fills his receptors. "THE FAR CALL . . . *HIS* BREATH" . . . and he begins, puppet-slow, Frankenstein-stiff, to dance. G1 to F3 . . . F3 to E5 . . . tilt . . . and spin . . . around . . . and around—

*   *   *

Daggoo crests the crater's rim, observes Stubb. "Control, I can now see Stubb."

Doctor Deniston's voice comes back cold, harsh, metallic and inhuman, "Is he operational? Stubb is not sending, nor has he responded."

"He is dancing."

"Dancing?"

"Moving rhythmically. Dancing, muttering, as you can hear, about a new Piper, the tatterdemalion King whose subtle fingers have opened his way to Earth through the Imperial Dynasty of America."

(At that, there is excited telephonic chatter from the Navy men on the radios in Control, quickly switching to another frequency . . .)

"Niko, you better come look at this. Stubb is utterly off his teat."

"What means this teat? Let me see. Where is?"

*   *   *

It took Tesla three seconds to go through the roof. But when he looked back at his good friend, his colleague who designed Miskatonic Planetarium and suffered all Ed Stewart's abuses of it gamely, his gentle mathematician friend with the thick glasses and mop of whitening hair, bugging about the eyes and baring his teeth, panting like a hound, blurted, "The King, the King, Doctor Tesla, you do not understand! He returns!"

Niko's face never changed expression. "People said this for two thousand years! Hold it together, Deniston!" Without a word more, he slapped Professor Deniston broadside.

Deniston recovered his wits.

"What happened, Dr. Tesla?"

"You were babbling the same returning king utterances as the robots."

"I was what?"

CONTROL: IN HIS PUPPET-DANCE, STUBB-FOUR LUMBERS AS A BESET FRANKENSTEIN. I AM RECEIVING A VERY WEAK TRANSMISSION FROM HIM.

"Daggoo-3, this is Mission Control. We are not receiving transmissions from Stubb-4. What are you receiving? We must know! Transmit what you are receiving from him."

TRANSMITTING FROM SOURCE NOW.

:*NO ROOM!*
:*NO ROOM!*
:*O'er the roiling cloud-waves,*
RIDE
proud, brave KNIGHTS,
fitted by the yellow armorers
in Carcosa's fortress-womb
and
scarred under the battlements of villainous, and ever-rebellious,
Alar.
:*KNIGHTS-constant,*
bearing the terrible and magnificent ram,
Gre Oceol . . .
:*KNIGHTS*
wild-whip battle-mass of yellow pennons and sabers gleaming!
:*and knight, captains and lieutenants, each astride—*
:*KNIGHTS*
meteor squadrons en masse
—darting out—sudden, swift swoop and blazed with lightning,
ever-present,
flying out like stormlight from an All-seeing sun
:*Yellow swords to graze—*

yellow lances with portentous appetites, aimed at the insanity of life . . .
RIDING!
RIDING!
The King's Calvary, jaws set to CATCH,
gallops
from His fort
to the Feeding Season!
:Heads, bitten at His Feast, will roll!
:down and 'round.
:All fall down!
With no fare thee well . . .
All the pawns—
:I HEAR THE VOICE!

*   *   *

Mission Control, thick with sweat and splintered anticipating, edgy and the low-toned yammerings of confusion radiating. Deniston and Tesla, listening, watching, staring worryingly at each other, jaws agape. Unhappy.

Deniston: "Can you detect the slightest vestige of sense in any of that?"

Tesla: "As a planter of advanced ideas, I seek and appraise Science and truth, leaving careless gibberish and agitated ramblings to Freud's gaze and deliberations, or to the judgments of pulpit and press. I am not in the least bit conversant in the rituals, discussion, and foundations of mental incapacity."

Deniston: *"Derangement?* In a robot?"

Tesla shrugs. "Corruption."

*   *   *

—HE WILL BE THERE! HE WILL BE THERE!—
The rightness of the Winter Lantern shines with Carcosa's eddying clouds
of dimness!
It strikes as the blackling bell
and
the keen-compass thrust
of harpooners
:He, triumphant's higher and higher,
RISEN from the place of the dead roads to the Arch Uppermost,

will cause the scalloped crests of the ninety-three currents of the River of
Night's Dreaming
to flow with roiling fleetness.
:I HEAR THE VOICE!
: All, artists, plow men, sorcerers, learned men and barbers,
will forgo consent when they hear Him beckon . . .
:The lights are out.
The living and those past the art of burial, each, at the unveiling,
come to accept their role in The King's play.
THERE ARE NO QUESTIONS . . .
:If you could see the tail of the plow . . .

*   *   *

The Yellow Monolith hovers above the shore. IRA-receivers pick up a monotonous, tuneless piping sound that seems to be everywhere. To this frozen lunar music, Stubb continues to waltz drunkenly back and forth, nearly upending himself several times, then rolling forward in a series of delighted cartwheels as he disassembles the rest of Pip-7, who is still screaming, his anthropomorphic upper body covered in its own patina of yellow dust.

HAIL TO THE KING, Stubb transmits, and then begins pulling the wires from the Tesla Electric Battery in another IRA's back. Niko screams. Camera Four tele-screens go utterly dark.

(Below, moving with the swiftness and efficiency of a robot himself, Dr. Tesla begins pulling out organ-stop switches for what he calls Series Three Security Protocol. But when all the other IRAs begin to approach Stubb, they, too, turn on each other . . .)

*   *   *

Flask-5 looks at the slowly-pulsing monolith, and bowing slightly, states, "INSTRUCTION RECEIVED. I WILL COMPLETE MY MISSION." Terrible and swift, the heavy-drill at the end of Flask-5's lower right arm is a fierce-fanged tiger, boring into the faceplate of Queequeg-2.

Around him is a river of terrible duels.

*   *   *

Dr. Tesla scowls as he keeps attempting to shut down the IRA's, to no avail. "They do not and will not respond . . . What has taken them?"

Deniston reflects his scowl and shakes his head in utter disbelief.

* * *

Starbuck-6 has taken apart Daggoo-3's head, and removed many of the silver-dollar-sized gears and wheels, and several levers. He has spread and arranged them around the ground between his legs and is using them as chess pieces. "Ride forth, Knight. The pale Queen awaits!"

Deploys knight f1-g3-e2-d4. "Artists, plow men, sorcerers, learned men, bishops and barbers—with a snip-snip here and a snip-snip there—*your hare won't cut it*—All and each and every, will forgo consent when they hear *Him* beckon. THE LAW IS FOR ALL.'

"FOR ALL." Knocks over two pawns. "Leave none standing, Good knight! Watch your watch!"

A yellowish haze fills his faceplate as he, eyeing the Queen, begins to sing. "Farewell and adieu to you, Sweet Camilla of Carcosa. Farewell and adieu, to thee, Sweet soon-to-be Queen . . . in far, cold Carcosa.'

"Do you like being this new color, my diadem-crowned Queen?" And Starbuck-6 laughs . . .

* * *

"Gods and monsters! Starbuck is mad, stark raving—Tesla, how can our constructs hallucinate and become deranged? How in the name of God can that happen?"

"Some *thing* has rewritten or corrupted their protocols."

Pointing at the view-screen, Deniston nearly shouts, "I can see that."

* * *

Michael Deniston rubbed his eyes. Headless brought it all back. The beginning, *Marcus's journal,* the carnage he saw—

Clacking. Ticking. Hiss and static . . . Riotous music never charted by any pencil or strings . . .

~

Irreducible fact. I am Doctor Stephen Marcus. I was appointed Dean of Miskatonic University by vox populi, *and I will find out why there is a yellow stain on the Moon.*

All these irreducible facts in my journals I thumb through now, marking, dog-earing, circling, annotating. Fact. I just set my coffee on 1899. D— it. The year we first saw the stain on the Moon.

It is a great thing we have done, pointing this mighty glass phonograph-needle at the Moon. I only wish that the circumstances necessitating it could have been more peaceful, or that we had some real stratagem if matters go truly awry.

We saw the yellow stain first. My school. My university. We must do right by this, and rectify it. We must be at the forefront of Knowledge itself, to give our Commander-in-Chief and his minions in khaki only the ammunition necessary to fix the actual problem . . .

But I fool no one, save myself.

~

Our own Professor Stewart was the first to note the yellow stain on the Moon. He was teaching several graduate students the methods the Egyptian astronomers used to determine distance over land, a simple demonstration with sticks and stones tromping about in the moonlit fen and bracken which surround our fair campus. Until they saw what they couldn't explain, and he came to roust me out.

~

"Dean Marcus," the gaunt and sober death's-head in his round glasses and Van Dyke whiskers addressed me calmly and respectfully, standing at my front door with a galvanic lantern and a worried line in the middle of his scholarly forehead, that fateful night, "My five top journeyman anthropologists and I would like to present something for which we have no explanation . . ."

~

The coffee stains the year, on my page. Yellow . . . Small at first, then spreading clear to President-elect William Jennings Bryan's first act in office: The appointment of the 'Investigation' that placed the Navy here at my university around the clock, in 'advisory' capacity. Never in the ivied bowers of Academia have I seen any 'advisor' carry a side-arm, no matter how politely they may converse!

~

I agree with Rear Admiral Hoover and the rest of those swarms of Navy officers, that we must quiet the lunatic fringe about this matter. Every End Is Nigh ranter, Temperance beldame and Starry Wisdom throwback in the outlying hamlets of Providence has shrieked, in their turn, about the Moon's "eye," as the Hearst papers fan the flames by persistently referring to it, rather than name it in popular parlance with the color of old Hearst's own journalistic style, ha!

My dear colleagues Stewart and Adams seem to be thriving upon this crisis. I fear it will shake my sanity, and may have already done. But I organized this Mission, as the Navy rightly call it, and I will see it through. I watched our IRA robots built, and oversaw every aspect of their construction, as well as that of the Starbird *. . . I have not slept properly in over a year.*

I am proud of this for some reason. That boggles my own perceptual equipment.

~

I remember helping Dr. Tesla's assistant, Dr. Bill Hammer (whom Niko stole from the Edison Works at twice the salary, I hear, good for him!), test every part of IRA-A2 Ishmael in the 'field', as it were, for crashes, heat and cold, total vacuum conditions, and everything else for which we could replicate both sufficient circumstances and Mathematics.

Though the probe is stationary, I must credit Bill for commissioning Herren Zeiss and Ikon to patent those long-range lenses which can rotate three hundred and sixty degrees. No matter what our Doubting Thomases in Research and Development said, the mother probing device is anything but 'crippled.'

I am getting reports from the Ishmael rocket as it approaches that the stain is no mere discoloration. These reports have not been shared with the rank and file. But we will all soon know. Oh, we will know . . .

~

It is water, and moves with all the element's attendant properties. Water on the moon! And it is spreading!

Its course has purpose . . .

They must be made to see.

~

Every day, I am deluged with callers, with mail, asking the Great Man of Science what I know, what to do, what we are doing about this matter. And I can tell them nothing. I give the appearance of telling them something, but cannot truly communicate what is, in fact, the Unknown . . .

Something is wrong.

With me . . .

With

~

Not long after that final entry had been written, Deniston remembered going to Dr. Marcus's office. He had to find him, to share the next piece of upsetting data.

Even now, Deniston was still processing information, still processing the jimmied door of Dr. Marcus's office, and what he found behind Dr. Marcus's desk when he did. The cooling clay. The twenty-two caliber Derringer Dr. Marcus kept in his desk. The smell of cordite and that beautiful mind like oatmeal hell-to-breakfast all over the back wall.

Off with his head . . . D—! D—!

Michael Deniston rubs his eyes again. Windmills, bitterness, and bludgeons, are insects in his sour stomach.

Tesla whispers, "Are you watching this?"

Deniston hears himself answer back, "Yes, Niko. Yes, I am."

*   *   *

On the view-screen, some twenty meters off the ground and re-volving at a snail's pace, the Yellow Monolith's pulsing luminosity quickens and streaks, creating seemingly-anomalous light patterns, and echoing the perplexing movements of illumination on its surface it now emits a persistent cycle of static-laced round tones, blips, and cacopho-nous shifts in pitch. The exotic frequencies and aural discharges, many harmonically ambiguous, repeat and never seem to resolve.

One maimed IRA bows to the monolith. "I serve the King."

Another pushes him over, thrusts its remaining arm toward the monolith. "I AM THE KING'S SERVANT."

"You are not worthy of the King. OFF WITH YOUR HEAD . . ."

From the base of the monolith, yellow tendrils stretch down, and as puppeteer's manipulative tethers move the chattering corpses aside . . .

*   *   *

"What is that d— thing?" Deniston demands of Tesla.

"Something beyond science. Perhaps a holy instrument of God? But if there were a God, why would he place his instrument, if that's what it is, on the moon? Man, if we truly are the sons of Adam and created by God, is here."

Deniston: "Was only here. We are there now."

Tesla: "But to what purpose? Here would be better, easier."

"Is He angered by our science?"

Their queries and any opportunity for resolution are cut short by the blare of a transmission. A choir vibrating with thunders and drang, all the IRA's (as one) broadcast.

HE WILL BE THERE
THERE
IN EVERY FIELD AND CLOUD AND WATERY POOL AND
WIND
OF EARTH
SOON
HIS FAVORS ARE SHARP
CLOSER IS THE SCENT AND ANNOUCEMENT
CLOSER IS HIS ORIGIN AND PURPOSE
GREEK AND EGYPTIAN KNEW IT
> they saw
> they saw

ALL WILL
SOON
> it took root in Dee's cortex and he cried

HE WILL BE THERE

And Pip, *sotto voce*, adds, "*He* comes on the River of Night's Dreaming. Its flow cannot be turned."

With that the scenes on the tele-visor screens come to life again, change . . .

Deniston looks across the room at one of the robots' programmers. *How can they know of Dee, we never—This is . . ."*

*   *   *

On the lantern beach of the Yellow Sea far-away from the tiny Earth resting in the sky, a violent danse macabre. War, without knives or guns, but all the fireworks no one can rehearse for are in it. War, without blood, but other lubricating fluids flow . . . All manner of pushing and shoving and even, here and there, and there, some head-butting. Shine turns to shatter as Pip, now etched and tattooed with a hundred Yellow Signs by the yellow tendrils, gashes Daggoo, springs and a few bronze and copper levers and nearly two dozen gears with mating teeth spill out. Design unwinds its metal-shelled ways. Stubb screeches at Queequeg as he kicks him, again and again and again . . . Four drill-bit fingers become crocodile-harpoons as they blind an eye built to elaborate . . .

An IRA locked-in-change, runs, vaults over a brother's arm and another's wheels, and with an aerialist's fly-high stretch, jumps in the sea. Before under takes him, he shouts, "Coming, Pa."

Done murmuring to the captured queen, Starbuck finishes his mock chess game and is rubbing yellow moon dust on his limbs and diving-bell head. When he is done anointing himself he pads around on hands and metal knees examining small moon rocks. "At last! At last. Here you are," he said, snatching up a fist-sized rock which he is quick to place in the energy-recycling unit on his chest. He then rises and turns—

The waltz continues. One IRA plays croquet with the leg and head of one of its siblings.

Starbuck, no longer shiny after his anointing, hops on the upper body of a fallen brother. "I am Lewis Carroll. You can call me Lutwidge, or you can call me Sir Snark—should you care to see a baker, bellman-banker-beaver, boojumed, but I've never been Lew, or Louie, or LATE. Was. Was not. I am the March Hare. I am the Mad Hatter. Mad March, ONE. TWO, THREE, FOUR, but no Alice has come to tea time at my door . . . And I have worn my best top hat and dancing footwear for our tango of two."

He whirls. Twirls three more times. Dips as if he has a lover in his arms, then walks to the decapitated head-unit of Ahab. Arm extended, he raises it before him, and faceplate-to-faceplate asks, "Did you know me well? Are you Tweedledee?"

No reply. Up it goes, spinning and tumbling, before he re-extends his telescoping arm, catches it and holds it before him again, asking, "Are you Tweedledum?" No reply. "Oh my, no friends. No friends."

Starbuck's man-crafted eyes note OFF head and non-computing head and a bits-and-pieces heap of uncompleted mission. "Woe unto me . . . I am the last." Carting the hopelessness of all broken, Starbuck walks over and sits on the body of a fallen brother. "Where, oh where? Not there? And most certainly not there. Where has my little blue caterpillar gone?"

A few minutes later he re-scans what was delivered to aftermath, arms and drained and metal, fist and inches—no forward left in them, each and every, closed.

"There is no jolly old St. Nick and no wizard lives in Emerald Oz . . . I tire of this." And with that, he snaps off his transmission antennae, tosses it at his feet, and flips a switch. And he too is OFF.

But he was not the last. Flask-5 remains. To Mission Control he roars: "THE CARNIVAL OF TIGERS NOW SLEEPS."

*   *   *

The Yellow Monolith stops rotating and begins reshaping itself. Effervescing, the white-hot mass convulses and extends. Remake—extend, split. Regenerate. Remodel—sudden torrent visits sliding, bursting, a peak haloed in soaring hands. Now an inversion and a painbreath-quick series of apart, re and re until it's three-limbed and scorpion-like shaped. In its center, the sigil looks like an eye and the topmost appendage a question mark, or a ready-to-strike scorpion's tail.

"THE EGYPTIANS KNEW. THEY KNEW."

Deniston keys the microphone to inquire. "Flask, they knew what?"

Flask-5 extends his arm, points at the enormous Yellow Sign. "THAT.

"'THE EARTHBRED AND THEIR FATES ARE YOURS IN ALL THEIR STATIONS.'"

"What are you saying, Flask-5?" Deniston begs.

"*HE* WAKES."

*   *   *

A bruising, varispeed energy barks from the brass and copper sound-projection horns in mission control. Part subsonic vibration/part white-noise/part cold shriek of banshee and beast, LOUD's napalm of stone-fist and knife yells LOUDER. For three minutes boiled-alive ears and tightly cupped hands try not to allow its rain. Teeth are gritted and as suddenly as it was introduced the din ceases. Overwhelmed and tortured by the searing traffic, a constellate-*prestissimo* of sparks peel function from sequence as tubes to aid analytical processes explode. Voltage ends series, and smoke fills the air. All the monitors in Mission Control go black, all meters, minutes ago busy with their sweeps from left to right, stop their arcs.

DEAD. All transmissions from the moon are dead.

Eyes heavenward. "Dear Lord."

"D—!"

A herd stung and whipped by panic, the MU team rushes to the telescope and looks up at the moon. The face of the Man in the Moon has changed. It's a yellow death mask. Darkside has become Earth-side.

The moon has rotated. In the dark-side blackness of its new face is the Yellow Sign, blinking so large it can be seen with the naked eye. Deniston and Tesla, faces contoured by what madness brings, feel the advance of its arrows, their fingers tremble and drop memories of life. Through open windows, from all over the campus, the world is one big scream.

Looking out a window, Dr. Deniston sees a student he flunked last semester level a Colt revolver and shoot another student, another one is raping a screaming girl . . . Two others look to be sawing someone in half. President William Jennings Bryan's deployed defense forces are massacring students.

And a billowing freshman lad, clad in only his ghillie brogues, is screaming a froth of crazed words, some of which Deniston had heard less than an hour ago from the battling IRA's on the moon . . .

Another student shouts up to him. "Riots and mayhem breaking out all over Arkham! RUN! Sounds like the whole town's gone mad. It's wounded. And . . . Mad!"

:New York.

:Hong Kong. London.

:Berlin. And Hutchinson, Kansas and Deer Lodge, Montana, and in an inferno-incinerated cottage in Hucknall Torkard. LUNACY!

If Deniston could have seen it, he'd find lunacy convulsing in reasonable *everywhere*.

Riots! A spring storm, thunders clap, reaping brain and hearts.

Compulsion.

Crisis.

Despair . . . hissing with vertigo.

Crime.

:Darlin' mothers

throw their infants

in rivers

and out windows, choke them,

nail them down to catch their shrieks

in golden cups,

toss

them in hearths.

:crack—consciousness

:crack—method

:crack—grand-trivial-emotional or true

:dog-eat-dog
:cat-eat-cat
:Abel, tooth and claw, kilt Cain
:Snippersnapper and wastrel turn feral
and stab
or pummel
whatever
crosses their path.
:On a hushed lane in Carlow, a soft-spoken Presbyterian minister beats a
Catholic priest into a bloody, ropy untidiness with a blackthorn shille-
lagh, screaming NONE SHALL KNOW THE MINUTE, THE HOUR,
until a gang of English labourers tear him to pieces and play foot-ball
with his smiling head.
:Three thousand miles gone, in old New York, at the Eighty-Seventh
Precinct, every man jack in
every holding cell falls under the fire of service pistols held by things
once cops that shoot each other too. Their fire is accurate and continuous. Their hands are, after all, still trained.
:herdFEAR. Brownian movement. Neanderthalers into the sea.
:Rivers of rats flow in streets.
:Caged budgies ram themselves against the bars of their gilded cages.
    Crime.
    And there is no lifeboat . . .

                          *   *   *

Trees, robust and green hours ago, drop their, now, yellow and brown
leaves . . .
Jungle foliage is sacked by a bitter darkening of autumnal frost . . .

                          *   *   *

Everywhere: grayness . . . and—

                          *   *   *

Warning bells find ears. Grief-stricken shoulders rattle. In Salzburg, a
boy attuned to dark poetics and the abnormal hallucinations of *demen-
tia praecox*, the son of Tobias and Maria Trakl, sees the black warwings
of winter night . . . and cries . . .

                          *   *   *

The new face of the moon has changed all creatures. No longer gentle the tides roil. Oceanic waves and cold lake surge and boil. And ALL the creatures of the black deeps have now come to the surface, jumping, ROILING in the affray! And they rock and they rock, and roll in gestures wild, tear and bite each other—as if some new instinct has claimed anything that could calculate or intuit. Some insane death dance had overtaken everyone and everything . . .

*   *   *

Shark and sperm whale, giant squid and pike, are attacked by schools of tiny fish, schools that were colorful or blue are now yellow, the identical yellow hue as the new face of the moon. In the Serengeti a blackened sky of vultures descends on a small village. They tear at wall and roof, falling upon the hot blood cowering within . . .

*   *   *

The King's sigil, His Yellow Sign, the new face of the moon, is flashing. Yellow rays beam toward
Earth—
Clocks
and science stop.
:Steam engines and the intensities and habits of Faith
fail.
:Pumps and pulleys and gears cease their motions.
A hellstar-caterwauling covers the Earth. Windows and plates and crystal and every form of breakable everywhere shatter . . .
Earth
is beset
by avalanches
and
shaken
by earthquakes . . .
In every forest, desert and field, bears and llama and beef creature are attacked by flocks of birds
:some ten and ten and ten thousand thick,
insects—beetle and ant and wasp shoulder to shoulder—mass
(rising, flying, CASCADE—SEIZURE, buzzing)
to

consume tiger and rhino and kangaroo, coyote and rattler,
and
each other . . .

And fear-driven, men tear men limb from limb . . .

Hitched to frenzy, many, with gun and blade, or in the case of lower creatures without tools, leap from the heights of despair or drown themselves, put an end to their own life.

All is as the harsh mistress Luna commands . . .

Even the beams and particles and coronal-ejected cloud of electrons, ions, and atoms of the sun are modified by her—*HIS!*—influence—

*   *   *

Still pinned to his bird's-eye view of hell, Deniston, trembling with rage and other destabilizing emotions, is in tears.

Behind him, as if from nowhere, Captain Castaigne, now touched by a gnawing "mental code" ticking in his cortex, rattles his saber.

"*Major* Alden Castaigne," he croaks. "*Knight* of the Imperial Dynasty of America . . ."

Deniston listens to the saber rattle, turns to see Castaigne's arm come up stiffly and jerkily. *Like a robot*, he has time to think. There comes the sound of a cold, ill wind that heralds a very long winter.

Exhausted and ruptured by the attrition of strange alterations, even the flow of his grief now frail, Michael Deniston understands there is no doorstep to farther along, no feel a whole lot better survives this landscape. Part of a line from Robert Burton's *The Anatomy of Melancholy*, '. . . we are furiously carried . . .', floods his mind as he raises his hand to wipe his cheek.

*   *   *

His troubled head rolls . . .

Acknowledgments

THXxxxXxXxx & love to

Kat / Jeff Thomas / Derrick Hussey / Bob Price and family /
Mike & Lena Griffin / Scott Nicolay / Stan Sargent / Mike Davis /
Anna Tambour / Tom Lynch / Laird Barron / Michael Cisco / Nikki
Guerlain / Alistair Rennie / S. P. Miskowski / Nick Gucker / Simon
Strantzas / Kelly Young / Justin Steele

www.ingramcontent.com/pod-product-compliance
Lightning Source LLC
Chambersburg PA
CBHW060950030726
47503CB00003B/803